I0574575

FAED TO BLACK

FAED TO BLACK

FRACTURED FAE - BOOK 2

SARAH J. SOVER

Copyright ©2023 by Sarah J. Sover

Cover Design by S. H. Roddey

All rights reserved.

No part of this book may be reproduced in any form or by any electronic or mechanical means, including information storage and retrieval systems, without written permission from the author, except for the use of brief quotations in a book review.

To Colleen and Paul Caron, my parents. One taught me to love books and magic, and the other showed me how to follow my passions. I wouldn't be me without your unwavering support.

1

June 11
9 days until the Summer Solstice

Gwen stared at the wall of the tiny apartment that doubled as C&F Investigations, her feet kicked up on the heavy mahogany desk she'd rescued from the local thrift store and Doc Martens soiling a pile of paper and files. It didn't matter. There was nothing useful here—no new cases and certainly no leads on lucrative work.

Even Gwen's pet shunni, Sorcha, had made herself scarce for the past few weeks, finding better entertainment on the streets of Boston than in haunting this graveyard of a PI firm. Gwen kept Sorcha's bed and dishes at the ready for her inevitable homecoming. Shadow fae creatures lived by their own rhythms.

Rain pelted the window behind her as she waited for Chessa to return from whatever back alley the pixie was casing this week. Even when work dried up, Chessa always found a story to chase, though she rarely ran anything by Gwen. It was no wonder Sorcha gravitated to Chessa—they were two sprites in the breeze. And Gwen was here, boots firmly planted on the ground. She picked up her phone and scrolled mindlessly, trying not to consider the pixie's suggestion that she spend more time consulting at the Academy for Fairy Godparents. Chessa claimed it would give her space to refine her magic skills or some shit, but that place felt more like a prison than a school. Gwen much preferred dark alleys to the phony smiles of perky fairies administering higher education. Maybe she was more like Sorcha than she pretended.

The front door crashed open, interrupting her thoughts. Gwen dropped her phone and bolted upright, the glob of muddy papers from her desk slapping the floor at her feet and toppling Sorcha's water dish. She palmed the wand strapped to her thigh. Chessa wouldn't be back for hours, and the appointment book was painfully blank.

In stark contrast to his loud entrance, the unfamiliar fairy who appeared in the doorway was unassuming. On the gaunt side with a shock of blond hair framing pointed ears and large hazel eyes, he looked like he'd bolt at the faintest noise. He held his hands aloft. "I didn't mean to startle you," he stammered.

Gwen lowered her wand and sunk back into the chair. She tried to disguise her relief. Her defensive magic was coming along now that she better understood her connection to her celestial source, the sun, but it didn't make a difference. So far, her magic was only slightly more targeted than the work she'd done with the Glamour Squadron in the past, not powerful enough to affect real change beyond altering perceptions. She didn't see how appearing as a twelve-foot-tall dragon everyone knew was extinct would help right now, and even if it did, basic glamours didn't work on most fae. For that, she'd need to use real magic, the kind Matron Celeste had tried to teach her.

The thought made her stomach roil. Her mentor might be dead, but even the shadow of her memory made Gwen feel like an insecure apprentice who'd never live up to her potential. Fuck Celeste.

More education wouldn't have helped this situation anyway. As Chessa frequently reminded Gwen, scaring off clientele wasn't a solid business plan.

"Can I help you?" she asked, letting her irritation bleed through. Didn't anyone knock anymore? If she wanted to feel vulnerable, she'd have remained at the Fairy Godparent Academy doing her daily morning duty of helping them reorganize, now that they weren't led by a sadistic serial killer. This was her safe space, and this fool was spoiling it. She looked him up and down and rolled her eyes. Who wore khaki anymore?

The visiting fairy remained near the doorway, twisting his hands around each other. "I was wondering if you could help me. I've found myself in a bit of a situation, and I heard this was the place to come for help."

"Yeah, sure. Normally, we schedule consults with Chessa." Gwen didn't invite the fairy in, but that didn't stop him. He shuffled through the door and closed it behind him. Gwen scowled. "She's more of a people pixie. Who are you?"

"Herbert Dayglow."

Choking back a laugh, Gwen considered taking her natural, small size to put her guest more at ease before opting against it. Something about her five-foot-tall humanoid form gave her a sense of security. "Dayglow? Really?"

Herbert made his way to the worn plaid couch that served as the C&F Investigations reception area. He nodded and glanced around in a way that made Gwen wonder what he was hiding. She leaned in slightly and studied his face for clues.

A shot of energy burst through Gwen, scrambling her cells and forcing her body into its natural fairy size of just over a foot tall. *Not again*, thought Gwen, panic welling in her chest as she realized she'd been hit with a source stick. A weapon of anti-magic, source sticks weren't common outside of law enforcement and security details. How anyone got the jump on her with one was a mystery. Good old Herbie must have an accomplice.

Blackness overtook her vision from the outside in. She heard the thud of a box coming down over her for the second time in her life. Adrenaline surging, Gwen threw her body against the plexiglass wall. Pain burst through her shoulder. She prayed to Danu, patron goddess of the fae, that Chessa wouldn't walk in and become entangled in whatever the fuck this was. Though if she knew Chessa Moon, it would take approximately three seconds from the time the pixie discovered the abduction before she came searching. While that thought should bring comfort, it did nothing but terrify Gwen.

She nearly lost Chessa to the Brain Scraper just last year. She couldn't go through that again. Gwen let her body sink to the bottom of the box as she was carried off into the stormy day, muffled voices outside her makeshift prison revealing nothing.

2

Chessa skulked down a brick street, chai latte in hand, head ducked low to keep the rain from her eyes. She felt guilty keeping Gwen in the dark on this job, but her best friend had begun to morph into a paranoid parental figure ever since the close call with the Brain Scraper last year. It was like Gwen forgot that Chessa had a less-than-squeaky-clean life before she'd come around with her vendetta and emotional baggage.

The errant thoughts only made Chessa feel worse. Of course Gwen had changed. They'd both been through serious trauma, and the need for an adjustment period was the least of the damage. That's why Chessa knew that getting Gwen to sign off on a mission like this would be harder than getting one over on Cross-Eyed Quincy. Her half-ogre informant might seem slow, but he was sharp as a demon claw. And Gwen? She was an even tougher nut to crack.

Nah, it was best if mama hen didn't know she was working for an anonymous entity with deep pockets looking for intel on powerful fae. Even worse, the goon she was tracking was a high-ranking Seelie Court Ambassador. As the estranged daughter of Seelie royalty, Gwen spent years distancing herself from these types. That's why she couldn't know. It was only supposed to be a few photos, and Gwen should be focused on other matters, like developing her magic.

As Chessa approached the harbor, the smell of fried seafood mixed with old beer was oddly comforting. This might not be Gwen's scene, but Chessa felt at home on the streets with grime beneath her feet and a touch of salt in the sticky air. She didn't draw notice of passers-by, partly thanks to the Glamour Squadron, a Kingdom-wide organization tasked with casting cloaking glamours over the magical signatures of fae in human-inhabited public places, and partly because she was accustomed to looking as though she fit in, a feat considering her freshly dyed bright red under shave, tattoos covering her arms and iridescent wings, and love of all things glitter. To humans, she would appear as an alternative-dressing twenty-something, and to fae… well, fae were accustomed to the unusual.

The rain let up as Chessa scanned the front of the Marriott Hotel on her left for signs of her target. She didn't break stride. She'd been tracking this mark for a week now, and she wasn't about to be made. Not seeing his Lincoln Town Car out front, she made her way to the Harbor Cruise ticketing office. The gaudy whale on top was a beacon to tourists visiting the aquarium across the way. The building was owned by entrepreneurs of the fae variety. Sirens had a way with the mortals, but lucky for Chessa, they didn't mind keeping tabs on the occasional Seelie Council envoy. At least, these ones didn't.

"Hey, Chia!" said Maddy, the teenage daughter of the franchise owner.

One look at the girl made Chessa wonder how she must appear to the mortal gaze. Her crystalline blue eyes and seafoam green and turquoise hair weren't the only signs of her fae blood. Gills on her small neck and her diminutive size, albeit nearly double Chessa's, made her look more like the figures on the fountain of a nearby park than remotely human, despite her golden-brown skin.

"How's it going mer-girl?"

Maddy's eyes swirled to a darker shade of blue. "Ugh. I hate it when you call me that."

"But you love me anyway!" chimed Chessa, flitting her wings just enough to reach the countertop and perch on the edge. She dug a kelp bar from her oversized shoulder bag and tossed it to the siren. A smile broke out across the teen's face, and her eyes returned to their normal clear blue as she ducked into the back room to scarf the bar down. While she was gone, a human boy's face popped into the window.

"Maddy, are you there? Oh, hi Chessa. Is Maddy around?"

Dalton worked over at the aquarium, and he stopped in every day to visit with the siren girl. Chessa would think it cute if not for his ignorance of her true nature. To him, she was a teenage girl, an unnaturally gorgeous one in all likelihood, but still just a girl. He couldn't know whatever feelings he had were a response to her pheromones and the alluring lilt to her voice. Poor kid never stood a chance. "Yeah, she's in the back. She'll be out in a minute."

The mortal boy shifted from one foot to the other and shoved a hand through his thick black curls. "So, um, she talks to you, right?"

Oh shit. He was about to ask for relationship advice. If there was one topic Chessa didn't want to touch with a ten-foot pole, it was romance. Her own life was a series of bad dates, and any time she started to fall for someone, she self-sabotaged. Her last girlfriend was intelligent, beautiful, and the kicker, she put up with most of Chessa's shit. Even Gwen had liked her, but after being ignored for a month straight while Chessa ran down leads for a piece about corruption in Korranthia for her blog *Crime Wave*, Aella split. "Not really." Chessa hedged.

Thankfully, Maddy resurfaced just in time to save her. "Oh, hey Dalton! Can you give me a few minutes? Mom will be back in about fifteen, then maybe we can go grab some brunch or something?"

The boy smiled uncertainly. "Yeah, okay. Come get me when you're ready," he replied. He shot Chessa a departing smile and walked toward the aquarium.

"Nice kid," said Chessa.

"Yeah, he's great," said Maddy, her voice breathy. She seemed to catch herself. "I'm sure you're not here to talk about Dalton. Here." She tossed Chessa a manila envelope. Inside was a log of the comings and goings of the target, most in the impeccable handwriting of Maddy's mother Mora, but a few in the girl's more hurried scrawl. According to the most recent entry, the Town Car left in the early morning hours and didn't return until 11am. When the target emerged, his driver, a large, silver-eyed humanoid, followed him into the hotel, carrying a box, while the valet parked the vehicle. A printed image was clipped to the log.

The box was roughly 3'x3' plexiglass, over twice the size of the target and plenty big enough to hold a fairy, pixie, or sprite.

Oh Danu, thought Chessa, *That's the same kind of box the KPD uses to lock up small fae.*

This just got a lot more nefarious. If the Seelie Court was hauling fae off in boxes, maybe she would have to bring Gwen in on the job after all. Her Seelie royal family ties might help unravel the mystery. Chessa handed a stack of bills to Maddy, payment for the overnight stakeouts, and mumbled a hasty goodbye.

She shouldn't get involved in whatever was happening. Her job was to snap photos and hand them over to her employer, no questions asked. That's what a true PI would do, but she wasn't a true PI. Before starting the less-than-lucrative business with Gwen, she'd been an independent sleuth who ran the hottest crime blog on the internet and paid bills with advertisement money from bail bondsmen and local bars. It was *Crime Wave* that brought in cash, not Gwen, and certainly not the PI firm. That's why Chessa had to get these shots, but the mystery of it all was too tempting.

Chessa flew across town. She didn't want the trouble that came with fae public transport, and traveling Leaf Pass wouldn't give her time alone with her thoughts to process her new intel anyhow. But pixies weren't made for long flights, so she took frequent breaks in trees or on light posts to recharge. She was famished, so she snagged a burger from a street vendor by the docks, determined not to waste any time before getting to the root of the suspected kidnapping. She'd heard Gwen's horror stories of being locked up in boxes. While she didn't remember her own stint knocked out in a box waiting to be incinerated by the Brain Scraper, nobody deserved the trauma Gwen described. After a quick stop to pick up some fast food, she arrived at Gwen's old apartment building, their base of operations. C&F Investigations was named for two of the victims of the Brain Scraper, the two closest to Gwen and Chessa, and it was their way of dealing with the hollow feelings of helplessness and grief.

The space was fine for their business purposes, but Chessa never understood why Gwen wouldn't move out of the cramped, smelly apartment. Not only did she seem to like it here, she even tried to convince Chessa to move in with her. Fat chance. Chessa wouldn't trade her spot above the industrial music club for anything. Certainly not for this dump.

She took the elevator to give herself time to scarf down the rest of her cold burger. When she stepped out into the hallway on the eighth floor, it nearly came back up. The door was ajar, the C&F Investigations plaque reflecting light from the window at the end of the hall. Something was wrong. Chessa could feel it in her gut. She dropped her bag of stale fries and darted inside.

Shadows swirled around her feet, coalescing into a vaguely feline shape.

"Sorcha? Where's Gwen?" Chessa's voice broke. The shunni's green eyes flashed, and she let out a low growl before melting back into the darkness, the shadow darting through the apartment and out the window. Chessa stared into an empty room, Gwen's phone on the desk and a pile of wet papers on the floor beneath were the only signs of struggle.

"Gwen!" she called.

Even as she shouted for her friend, she knew the truth. Gwen was gone.

3

Gwen's stomach rumbled so loudly, she wondered how her captors didn't notice. Her phone was back at the office, and she gave herself an internal kick for her stubborn refusal to wear a smartwatch. This wasn't the first time she'd been separated from her tech. For comfort, she reached up to touch the locket hanging around her neck. Inside, the photograph of Frankie, the princess she couldn't save, was a constant reminder of her failure. No matter how hard she tried, she was never enough, and the familiar sense of self-loathing grounded her. At least she knew her worth. A towel had been tossed over the box so she couldn't see anyone or anything, not that the scuffed plexiglass allowed for great visibility in the first place.

Her stomach rumbled again. But at this moment, hunger took a backseat to her bladder threatening to explode. She refused to piss in her plexiglass prison. She let go of the locket and hollered. "Hey, Dayblow!"

The sound of feet on the carpet grew louder, then her little box was bathed in light. She squinted.

"What do you want?" Instead of the timid-looking fairy she was expecting, there was a humanoid male with a wide nose and glowing silver eyes staring down at her. So that's how she'd been hauled around. She briefly wondered if this was the goon who blindsided her back at the office.

"You're not Dayblow."

"It's Dayglow, and he had some business to attend to. You're stuck with me now." The look on the new guy's face was something between fear and determination. Gwen wondered what his deal was, but not enough to ask.

"And what a delight you are. I need to pee."

The man sighed, the breath blowing his straight, dark hair upward from his forehead. "Fine, but make it quick." He lifted the box and jammed a source stick between her ribs, pushing her toward the edge of the table with it. "And don't try anything."

Gwen took a quick survey of what appeared to be a hotel room. A king-sized bed dominated the space. The box was perched on an accent table flanked by a small chair on one side and a desk on the other. The window behind her offered a hint of a harbor view, and she knew the area well enough to figure out she was at Long Wharf. At least she hadn't been taken somewhere unfamiliar. Yet. Gwen flitted off the table, but the man caught her, his thick fingers encircling her waist, and dropped her onto the patterned carpet. "And no flying!"

"Fine. No need to be rough about it." She righted herself and walked toward the door wondering how he'd expected her to get down from the table without flying. It sometimes seemed to Gwen that the larger the fae, the weaker the neuron connections in the brain. The man jabbed her in the back once again with the source stick, killing her fantasy of bypassing the bathroom and hauling ass out the door. She stopped outside the bathroom, just a few feet from freedom, but a few feet in her natural form without the use of her wings might as well be miles. "You going to follow me in?" she asked, dreading the answer.

The man grunted but remained in place as she entered the bathroom and shut the door behind her.

"Seeing as you're stuck on babysitting duty, want to tell me what to call you?" Gwen called through the door.

"D."

Gwen finished up, washed her hands, and looked around for anything she could fashion into a weapon. A bar of soap, a miniature bottle of shampoo, and a toiletry kit. What was she going to do, Q-tip her way to freedom?

"Hurry up in there. And no magic!"

Gwen wondered what magic she could possibly do to help her situation anyway. She could size-shift, but that didn't give her much of an advantage against the brute on the other side of the door. Her basic glamours had a pixie's chance in a blender of working on D. She traced her fingertips over the wand tucked into her thigh holster. A fairy of her rank shouldn't need a wand at all, which is probably why her captors didn't think to search her, but Gwen's magic had been neglected when she'd spent her formative years hunting a killer rather than learning. She'd made a breakthrough that helped her defeat the Scraper and now, every time she tapped into the solar source, it felt like she was back there, turning Matron Celeste's abusive memories into weapons. It made her want to vomit. Now that she was captive once again, Gwen wished she'd listened to Chessa and spent more time honing her magic. Her only real skill was her empathic touch, and she couldn't see any benefit to seeing bits and pieces of whatever had occurred in a hotel bathroom in the recent past.

Instead of trying some futile trick, she picked up the pair of tweezers from the toiletry kit left on the counter. They were at least half the size of her torso, not exactly discrete. She slid them down her back, between her wings, her Metallica shirt pinning them in place. It wasn't comfortable, but an awkward weapon was better than none at all. She was sure that a jolt from the source stick would turn her into a fried fairy worthy of a troll buffet. At the thought of dinner, her stomach rumbled again. "Alrighty, then D, what does a girl have to do to score a cheeseburger around here?"

There was no response.

Gwen opened the door. It appeared that D hadn't so much as blinked. "You'll eat when I feed you," he growled, motioning with his free hand toward the box. "Get back in."

"You're twitchy for hired muscle," said Gwen. "This isn't your typical gig, is it?"

"Just get back in the box."

"Do I make you nervous? You're like ten times my size. What could I possibly do to you?"

D's eyes narrowed and he gestured with the source stick. "Don't try any of your fairy business on me. I'll use it, I swear."

A second jab to the ribs made Gwen move further back into the hotel room.

"We don't have mind control," said Gwen. "What are you anyhow?"

"Ogre on my mother's side, elf blood on my pa's."

Gwen burst into a smile. "See! I knew you weren't just some dumb human doing somebody's dirty work. We can be civilized."

D bit his bottom lip and snatched her up. "Enough of this," he grumbled before marching across the room and stuffing her back into the box. So much for trying to befriend him. That was more of a Chessa tactic, anyhow.

Thirty minutes later, the box lifted again, and a cheeseburger slider and shot glass filled with Coke appeared next to her, the box slamming shut over her again before her eyes could adjust to the sudden light. It was no Jack Daniels, but at least it was something.

4

Chessa stood in an empty hotel room. Housekeeping had come and gone, ensuring that any trace of Gwen was scrubbed away, but she'd known the score before ever stepping foot back on Long Wharf. Her cell had pinged with a message from Maddy a half-hour earlier telling her that the target was on the move. A $20 bill sacrificed to the human working the registration desk provided her with a room number, and another $20 bought her the ability to snoop around. Looking over the sparkly clean room, she cursed the efficiency of Marriott housekeeping.

"What the hell have you gotten yourself into?" she muttered as she squatted to inspect the area beneath the table by the window. Nothing there but fresh vacuum tracks. For a passing moment, Chessa swore she smelled a burger. What she wouldn't give for Gwen's sensory empathic touch right now. Gwen would be able to run a hand along that table and sense fragments of images, smells, or sounds of what happened in this room. Chessa had to be content with good old-fashioned observation. She flitted to the top of the desk, which was just as tidy as the rest of the room. Her inner voice screamed that she shouldn't be wasting time here, but she was used to telling that asshole to put a sock in it. She didn't get to be the best sleuth in

Korranthia by giving in to emotion. Instead, she let her gaze scan every inch of the room.

There, in the crevice between the wall and desk was a little hotel notepad. Chessa had no trouble reaching her hand into the narrow gap to extract it. On the front page, in barely legible handwriting was written *4:45 Crystal Cove.*

Chessa pulled out her phone and searched "Crystal Cove" only to pull up a mortal state park in California. She shook her head at the hypocrisy of humanity. She figured the setting aside of land was just one way they worked through the guilt of destroying the world. Their meager efforts would be adorable if the stakes weren't so high. Little did they know the world would have ended thrice over by now if not for the work of the fae. And the way things were headed, a fourth time was imminent within the next few decades.

Adding "Boston" into the search brought up what Chessa was looking for, a cute little marina about 10 miles away, 5 if she cut across the airport, and it was just past three o'clock. She could cover that distance in two or three bursts. Praying to Danu that the meeting was for today and the humanoid male still had Gwen, Chessa pocketed the paper. She slid the window open, squeezed through the gap, and took to the air.

A FRENZIED FLIGHT LATER, Chessa perched on top of a light post to scan the marina. She was breathing heavily, and the bag strapped to her waist felt like it held a load of bricks, but she'd made it with plenty of time to spare. From the top of the post, she had a clear view of the entire parking lot as well as of all the boat docks. Despite its size, there was plenty of activity, being a warm day in May when the striped bass were plentiful. Boats littered the inlet, and the parking lot was in a state of constant turnover. Chessa checked her phone. 3:55 p.m. There was no sign of her target, the large humanoid who'd been spotted carrying that damn box. Chessa's stomach lurched at the thought of Gwen confined again, and she wondered what nefarious task had driven her captors to leave the hotel if it wasn't to show up early to this meeting.

Stick to the facts, she thought, quelling the despair that threatened to wash over her. She was usually so good at keeping an emotional distance, but this was Gwen. *Her* Gwen. Locked up again, before she'd had a chance to work through the trauma of what they'd already been through.

"I swear to Danu, when this is over, I'm writing the royals to push for a ban on plexiglass," she muttered, stuffing the phone back into her messenger bag. Once she stored up enough energy, Chessa flitted to another perch for a different view. She continued her strategy, moving from one vantage point to another, typing observations into the notebook app on her phone at each stop before continuing to the next until she'd created a list of suspicious vehicles and boats. She'd been at it for a while when she stopped to check the time. 4:43. Gwen had to be here somewhere. But there had been no suspicious activity in the past few minutes. Chessa made another pass, checking on each area she'd listed. Number one, a small yacht that docked just as she arrived still sat, silent and calm. The only thing odd about it was the stillness. Most boats were overtaken by a flurry of activity after docking as those aboard gathered to exit, but other than a lone deck-hand—a human or humanoid male, Chessa couldn't tell which—emerging from below to tie off, the yacht provided no such scene. Once the boat was secure, the man disappeared again, leaving the yacht swaying in the wake of larger boats coming and going in the early evening. Still no changes.

Next on her list was a van with tinted windows that took a parking spot at the very back of the lot. Chessa watched a motor-cycle pull up next to it. The leather-clad rider dismounted to approach the driver's side window of the van, which cracked just enough to slip a small packet of something out in return for the wad of cash the woman proffered. Shady, yes, but nothing to do with Gwen. On down the list she went, checking again on the yacht and making a broad sweep of the area between each of her fifteen suspects. Something in her gut told her to keep checking back on that boat, something more than a hunch. This was part of her pixie gift, and she learned long ago to let that pull guide her. It was what made her a great sleuth. And right now, Gwen needed her to be top-notch.

"Oh Gwennie, where are you?" she muttered.

A movement on the yacht caught her eye. Two figures emerged from below deck, one massive, the other human-sized. Even from this distance, Chessa could tell that the woman was an ogress. That was definitely out of the ordinary. Ogres rarely fraternized with humans or other fae, and when they did, the results were less than ideal. The Great Chicago Fire and the events leading to the Bronze Age Collapse could all be attributed to failures in ogre diplomacy. Sure, there were exceptions like Chessa's informant Cross-Eyed Quincy, but Q was only half-ogre, human blood watering down the ravenous appetite as well as stunting his size to a mere 6'7". The ogress' sheer weight was a threat to the small vessel. Both creatures were clad in black suits, the ogress' hair pulled into a tight bun while the humanoid male's gray ponytail hung at the nape of his neck, and they wore matching stern expressions as they took posts on opposite sides of the entranceway to the cabin stairwell.

Chessa moved in for a better view. If Gwen's abduction didn't lead here, she would throw her camera into the bay. A vacant schooner was docked a hundred feet away from the yacht, its masthead offering the perfect observational perch. Chessa was so fixated on the scene playing out below her that she nearly missed the Town Car pulling into the lot—a move she would never have made if her best friend's life weren't on the line. She cursed her clouded head, her heart hammering against her chest. The same man from the photos carried a box onto the little schooner. She was fast enough to snag Gwen and get out, but not while her pain-in-the-ass best friend was locked up in that damn prison. Chessa photographed every inch of the boat, zooming in on faces.

The humanoid set the box—Gwen—down on the hull of the boat while the guards surveyed the bay. What are they waiting for? Chessa's thoughts raced. She needed a plan.

Just as she was about to go in, plan or not, a woman emerged from the stairwell. She was smaller than Chessa and flighted, hovering at the level of the ogress' head, and she was wearing golden plate armor, an oddity that Chessa caught on camera.

If it weren't for the Faetography lens Gwen gave her for her birthday, she'd never have been able to afford the upgrade that pierced through glamours to capture realities visible only to fae eyes. The wry thought made a lump form in her throat. To humans and stock cameras, the stunning fairy before her would appear as a small, commanding woman. In fairy form, she was far more intimidating.

It's okay, we've got plenty more birthdays to celebrate together, she told herself.

The human guard leaned in and said something to the fairy. Chessa strained for a better view. Suddenly, all four heads turned to stare at her, their collective gaze chilling her blood. A blaze of light erupted from a device in the fairy's outthrust palm. Chessa didn't have time to process what was happening before it hit, sending her careening into the air and downward, toward sail and wood and water. Searing pain, as if her body were cocooned in fire, threatened her consciousness. She freed her pocketknife from her waistband and flipped it open. The sheer speed of her fall would tear her wings to shreds if she attempted to fly, but if she could just reach the sail with her blade, she could use it to slow her descent, perhaps enough to live through this. It was a long shot, but it was the only shot she had.

5

Gwen couldn't see her surroundings—the hotel towel was still in place—but she could feel the movement of the car and hear the opening and closing of the door as D went about his business. At the final stop, her box was hoisted into the air and carried for a short spell. When the motion ceased, she could make out voices. The familiar tones of her captor joined that of another male, a gravelly-voiced female, and yet another woman, the latter sounding both authoritative and formal in the way of upper-echelon fae. These were no humans. Not that Gwen had expected otherwise from what she'd seen of D and Dayglow. Even though her box had been set on something, it wasn't steady. The unpredictable rocking could be the motion of a second vehicle, one far less stable than the car she'd arrived in, but most likely, it was the result of a boat swaying in the harbor.

"We're being watched, ma'am," said the deep-voiced woman.

"From where?" replied boss-lady.

"The top of the schooner mast two docks over." The unknown male's voice sounded familiar, but Gwen couldn't place it.

"Only one?"

"Looks that way, but I can take a stroll around the harbor to make sure."

If they were being watched, that meant someone had discovered Gwen missing. There was only one creature foolish enough to hunt down fae captors with such speed and recklessness. Chessa.

"Chess, what are you doing?" muttered Gwen, having flashbacks of the police precinct when the spitfire pixie attempted a jailbreak on her behalf. She prayed to Danu that Chessa wouldn't pull a stunt like that again. Something told her these people were less likely to let her get away with it than the KPD was.

That's when she felt the crackle in the air. The unmistakable sensation of magic gathering raised the hairs on the back of her neck. Whoever this woman was, she had to be powerful to command that much energy. Someone of that caliber wouldn't be traveling with a band of petty criminals. What in the hell was going on here?

The blast rocked the boat. Gwen screamed. But nobody paid her any mind.

"There. That should take care of our little friend. You brought the package?"

She heard D clear his throat before speaking, his voice coming out rough like he was wishing to be anywhere but here. "Yes ma'am. She's right here." For a tough guy, he seemed uncharacteristically shook by what he just witnessed, yet there was a note of deference in his speech, as if he were a trained soldier addressing a superior.

For her part, Gwen could do nothing but choke back tears at the thought of Chessa being blasted out of the sky. *Please be okay. Please.* The mantra ran through her head on repeat. After everything they'd faced together, she couldn't lose Chessa like this.

Gwen's prison was hoisted into the air, the cover pulled away to let the sunshine stream in, momentarily blinding her. She pushed her grief back to the furthest recess of her mind and took a deep breath as her eyes adjusted. Whatever this was, whoever these people were, she would not tip her hand. She stood, her Docs planted firmly on the plexiglass beneath her, knees bent to keep her balance. These motherfuckers would pay for what they did to Chessa.

"Lady Evenshine. I am in your service," said the commanding woman.

Gwen's jaw dropped. She'd been ready for a fight, but the powerful fairy before her had lowered her elevation in deference and was hovering, head bowed, just below the box. D's hands squished against the sides of the plexiglass prison in a contrast to the formality in a way that would be comical if Gwen weren't fighting to keep her lunch in her stomach. All she could do was gape until the fairy, sensing Gwen wasn't about to release her from her pose, raised her head. Gwen recognized her at once.

"Arabella?"

"Yes, dear cousin. I apologize for the unceremonious way in which you were brought to me, but rest assured your treatment will improve from this point forward."

Her cousin was captain of the Seelie Guard, a force that was more focused on preservation of the status quo than on any actual military action, seeing as the Seelie Court was dedicated to living harmoniously with humanity. Arabella was trained in all manner of combat, but even she couldn't blast pixies out of the sky with impunity. Gwen noticed a device hanging from a loop on Arabella's belt. If anyone would have the latest in deadly fae weaponry, it would be this bitch. It took a moment longer than Gwen would have liked, but finally she got her wits about her. Her cousin might be the head of the Seelie military, but Gwen still outranked her in the royal family, and she had no right to keep her locked up. "Let me out of here at once," she demanded.

Arabella winced, an exaggerated motion designed to appease. "I apologize dear cousin, but my orders come from your mother, and I am not at liberty to disobey."

"You just attacked someone important to me. You will let me out of here so that I can see to her." She let the unspoken threat hang in the air.

This time, the look on Arabella's face didn't seem forced. She paled. Gwen's own magic wasn't nearly as deadly as Arabella's but Gwen could have her demoted, disgraced, and locked away for life. Arabella remained at a lower elevation than Gwen's box, but her fierce green eyes locked onto Gwen's. "The only way I can grant your request is if the order comes from higher than the fairy who issued it. You know that. But since the spy seems to be important to you, I will send Jym to retrieve her so we can provide medical attention. If she survived."

Gwen's head swiveled to look at the man standing on the other side of Arabella. Sure as shit, Jym Hoit, the asshole ex-partner of Gwen's buddy Detective Samson Wayne, was staring at her with a smug expression. His presence brought up questions she wasn't in the headspace to puzzle through. All Gwen cared about right now was Chessa.

Arabella kept talking, likely reveling in her control over Gwen. "She should not have been poking around in official Seelie Council business, and while I do regret any harm done to her, I will not apologize for protecting the Seelie Court from prying eyes, especially now."

"What do you mean by that?" asked Gwen.

Seelie Council business? None of this made any sense, but if there was one thing Gwen knew, it was that Arabella's involvement was a bad sign. She was known for her ruthlessness, and every move she made was calculated.

Arabella ignored the question and motioned to Hoit. He did an about-face and left the boat rocking as he climbed onto the dock and went in search of Chessa.

Gwen switched tactics. "Arabella, what is this all about?"

"Your mother will brief you when we arrive at our destination," her cousin replied. "She knew you wouldn't come of your own free will, and times are desperate. I hope that you will come to forgive me after you understand." Her words rang of sincerity. Since when did Arabella give a shit what Gwen thought? She must be truly afraid of what Gwen would do once free. There was one clue in her answer, though. If they were going to see Gwen's mother, that meant heading to the seat of Seelie power.

"We're going to Avalon?" None of this made any sense. Avalon was more than a short boat ride away, and this little yacht didn't seem like it would handle the open ocean, not to mention the time it would take to sail all the way to Europe. Once again, Gwen's question went unanswered.

A short time later, Jym returned.

"I could not locate the pixie ma'am," he reported. "I see where she tore the sail of the yacht. It appears that she ran some kind of a blade downward, perhaps slowing her fall, though I doubt she was able to recover quickly enough to fly. I could not find a point of impact, however, and the pixie is gone. I did find this." He held out a busted mini-Canon 5000 fitted with a Faetogaphy Lens, Chessa's camera.

Gwen gasped. Chessa would never leave her camera, broken or not. Tears threatened to spill over. But if Chessa was dead, where was her body? If the most resourceful woman she knew was missing, that meant she was alive. Gwen had to get it together for both their sakes. "Arabella, I need to use the ladies' room," she choked out.

"I can't let you out. I've already explained."

"Surely you don't expect me to shit in this box," snapped Gwen. "Even D here let me go pop a squat when I needed to."

Blood rushed to her cousin's cheeks. "No need to be crass. Dirkmund, please escort my cousin below deck. The facilities are to the right. Hit her with the source stick before letting her out, though. She's not to be trusted."

"So much for my treatment improving, huh?" Gwen said with a half-smile, half-snarl.

"Lady Evenshine, please do not take advantage of my patience. Your mother will have you brought to her, if not by me, then by someone more... persuasive. You know the resources she has available."

The threat landed. Unlike Gwen, her mother had the goodwill of the regional royals in addition to the backing of the Seelie Council, even if she was 14th in line for the throne and slipping with every new birth in the extended family. She acted with the decorum expected of a Seelie royal and had all but disowned Gwen when she turned her back on her family to attend Fairy Godparent Academy. The real nail in the coffin was when Gwen walked away from that path as well. Where her family was concerned, Gwen was a failure, and she had no doubt that if her mother wanted her home, she'd drag her back by her wings and hair.

"So, we're going to Avalon?" Gwen asked again as D lifted her box. She needed to be sure she understood the situation. This time, Arabella responded.

"No. It's not safe there."

Arabella turned away and motioned for the ogress to follow. D headed for the stairwell, and Gwen sat to keep from falling over inside the box as he descended below deck. Her mind was reeling, connecting dots and digesting information. Avalon had been the seat of the Seelie Court Council since the treaties ensuring harmonious life with humanity were signed, and short of unsanctioned breaches by two men in history—King Arthur and Bryan Ferry—it remained safely veiled all that time, disguised as ruins atop a hill, the tor of Glastonbury. What threat could possibly move her family from paradise?

When D opened the box just outside the bathroom door, his silver eyes were pleading, but he didn't say a word. He raised the source stick, and Gwen winced, bracing for the searing pain and wondering if the tweezers pressing into her back were about to turn her into a crispy snack for trolls. But he didn't discharge it. He pressed it, more gently than last time, into her side and nodded his head toward the bathroom door.

Gwen climbed to her feet and gave him a nod, feeling more gratitude than she let on. Now that she knew who he worked for, she pitied him, especially since he didn't seem to be as mindless as she first believed. Even so, she'd normally poke at him with a smart-ass remark about escaping out the window, but the thought of Avalon in danger was more sobering than a coffee/cold shower combo. She walked into the room and closed the door behind her.

There was a window, a thick layer of caulk and paint keeping it firmly closed. Gwen freed the stolen tweezers from her back like she was brandishing a sword and got to work chipping away at the paint covering the ridge.

After about five minutes, D began to lose patience. "Oy, what are you doing in there? Hurry it up!"

Gwen gave the window a shove, but it still didn't budge. There was no way she was going to be able to surgically remove all the paint and caulk before D busted down the door.

"I'm almost done," she called. "If you'd given me more breaks, I wouldn't have so much stored up! That burger did a number on my GI tract."

The disgusted grunt told her she might have bought a few extra minutes. Not nearly enough. She focused her efforts on the bottom half of the window and managed to get it open just a crack by alternating wet and dry chiseling. Even in her small form, she couldn't get her head through.

Threatened homeland or not, she had to find a way to get a message to Chessa or the pixie would end up dead, if she wasn't already. Gwen snagged the small, fairy-sized hand towel to dry herself, and that's when she saw her family's crest embroidered into the terrycloth.

They can't resist branding their towels, how the hell did I think my ass stood a chance, she thought as she flattened the material and fed it through the cracked window. It would tell Chessa exactly who was responsible for her abduction—if the pixie found it, of course—and hopefully warn her off the chase. As much as Gwen hated her family, she and Chessa both knew they wouldn't hurt her. At least, she didn't think they would.

D banged on the bathroom door. "That's it. Time's up!" he yelled.

Gwen dropped the tweezers, flitted away from the window, and was splashing water on her face by the time he got the door open.

"I realize you're under orders, but those orders come from people less powerful than I am. By the way you addressed my cousin, I assume you're in the Seelie Guard?"

D nodded and chewed on his bottom lip.

"Arabella may be your captain, but I outrank her. If you want to keep your job... No scratch that, if you want to keep your life, I highly suggest you show me a little respect." Gwen hated to pull rank after the kindness he did her, but this goon worked for her family, and that meant he was in a perilous position. It seemed that he knew it. The anger melted from his wide face, and his silver eyes dropped to the floor.

"Yes, my lady."

"You knew who I was all along," said Gwen as she dried her hands on her jeans, hoping D didn't notice the missing towel, and strode back into her plexiglass prison. It wasn't a question.

"Yes. But I'm not so sure you do."

"Excuse me?" Gwen turned to glare through the scratched, thick plastic.

"Nothing, my lady," D replied, picking the box up more gently than he had before.

Gwen let him get away with it. She had more pressing concerns than impertinent muscle. Like puzzling out her situation. Her family was complicated, sure, but kidnapping her took family drama to an entirely new level. The more information she could gather before they arrived at their destination, the more armed she would be against the greatest adversary of her life—her mother.

6

June 12
8 days until the Summer Solstice

Everything was wet. Convinced she was drowning in her own blood, Chessa thrashed wildly before spewing up half of Boston Harbor. She climbed to her feet to get her bearings and immediately slipped off the side of a buoy into the cold, dark water. Unconsciousness threatened to take her again. She fought it back and paddled furiously back to floating salvation, operating on pure survival instinct. Her tiny size prohibited her from scaling the side, and her wings were too wet for full flight, but she was able to get just enough loft to hoist her body back onto the surface of the buoy.

Gradually, Chessa's vision returned, but she couldn't make out anything beyond the dark water. The clearer her thoughts, the more aware she was of the unbearable pain screaming in her head. It felt like she'd been clobbered with a troll's femur. The last thing she remembered was smashing against the railing of a boat and before that, falling. She'd been blasted by some form of condensed fairy magic while she was looking for Gwen. Oh no! Gwen.

Chessa stood and promptly vomited all over her Chuck Taylors.

She sunk back down, back braced against the bobbing buoy, and decided on a more measured approach. She couldn't go anywhere until her wings dried, and by the look of the sky, the sun wouldn't be up for at least another hour. Positioning herself so she was facing the marina, Chessa opened and closed the soggy things as she took stock of her situation.

She was about a quarter mile from the boat she'd used as an observational perch with no idea how she got out here. Perhaps she fell overboard after slamming into the railing? But how did she get on the buoy?

Screw it, she thought. She could figure out the past later. What mattered now was Gwen. Chessa torqued her body around to attempt to survey the harbor. There were a few lights on the horizon, but she couldn't make out the small yacht and even if she could, she was in no shape to fly over open water. She reached for her messenger bag. It was gone, along with her beloved camera—the camera that held the photos of her latest job in addition to the evidence against Gwen's captors. "Fuck!" Chessa screamed at the top of her lungs. She'd lived through many rough days, but this certainly neared the top of the list.

By the time her wings were dry enough to fly, the sun was cresting over the horizon. She pushed off the buoy, this time with only a retch, and flew over the water, low enough to rinse her shoes as she headed back to the marina to comb over the area where Gwen had been imprisoned mere hours before.

The flight took more out of her than she would have expected. She landed on the stern of the boat she'd been shot off of and stared at the empty dock opposite. The water rose and fell as small watercraft navigated the inlet in the early morning hours. Once she caught her breath, Chessa walked the boat, searching for her camera. She didn't expect to find it in one piece, but she held a small hope that it was salvageable. The sail above her was sliced vertically, an arrow pointing to the ballast that knocked her senseless, but there wasn't a mark on the boat, probably because she didn't weigh enough to damage the wood. She shuddered and made her way to the deck below. There was no sign of her bag or camera.

A seagull perched on the side of the boat, watching her with its head cocked to the side. "What are you looking at?" she snapped. The bird flew off, and she felt bad for a moment before remembering that the bird probably didn't understand her.

Chessa didn't know where to go from here. The boat could have gone anywhere. Perhaps there was a marina office with a log she could peruse. She flew from the boat to the dock and walked back to land. Just before stepping off the dock, she took one last glance back at the area where her best friend had been. That's when she noticed something white bobbing up and down in the water, nearly eclipsed by the wooden deck rail. It wasn't much, probably a washcloth or napkin, but Chessa's gut told her fly down and snatch it up.

Just a deck rag, she thought, setting it on the wooden boards at her feet and wishing it had been her bag instead.

But then there was that nagging again, the pulling of something from deep inside her, telling her that there was something more here. She flipped the towel over. There, in golden embroidery, was the crest of the Seelie Royal family. Chessa felt her world closing in. She knew her target was a high-ranking Seelie Ambassador, but royalty? This was big—bigger than the federal government, bigger, even, than the Korranthian monarchs. This was true power. Chessa didn't know what to do with this information, but she did know one thing—if the Seelie Royal family, Gwen's family, took her, they were both screwed.

7

wen sat, knees drawn up pressing the locket to her chest, back braced against plexiglass, and slept fitfully. When she awoke, she felt like a lifetime had passed since she was bored out of her mind at her desk. She sure as hell wasn't bored now. It couldn't have been as long as it felt. She could tell because her stomach hadn't threatened to digest itself yet. Perhaps the movement of the boat kept her hunger at bay.

She'd hoped for another audience with Arabella, but her cousin seemed content to let her sit with her own thoughts and nothing but the blurry below deck quarters for a view. At least D hadn't covered the box again. A beige couch, a simple table, a flat-screen television mounted on the wall—it was hardly the luxury accommodations her mother would require, so it must belong to Aunt Ember, Arabella's mother and next in line for the throne behind Gwen and her brother Liam. If not for the monogrammed linens, Gwen would have thought it a charter. D had left her box on the floor, wedged between the table post and the couch so her prison wouldn't slide around with the motion of the vessel. Her view was obstructed, and that's why she didn't notice his return.

"I've been instructed to retrieve you," D said, making her jump. "My lady," he tacked on. At least he remembered his manners.

He carried her box up the stairs to the main deck. A whooshing sound drowned out anything that might have been said, and Gwen couldn't make out anything beyond D's muscular, hairy arms. The air was thick and heavy, and the smell of salt permeated everything. The sound was maddening, and everything was dark. Gwen called out, but nobody answered. D kept moving.

The minute Gwen felt D's heavy boots hitting solid ground, her stomach lurched then stilled. She was not made for life at sea. The relentless noise didn't let up, and they made slow progress, the lurching of the box and thudding of her captor's feet synchronizing in a jerky, gut-turning rhythm. Gwen couldn't see out the sides of her prison, but below, she could just make out the rocky, uneven ground. Watching it only heightened her nausea. She focused on her breathing and tried to stay calm. Just when it felt like she was coming to terms with her loosening grip on reality, the motion ceased, and everything went quiet. The sound of D panting heavily was her only connection to the outside world. He set her box down with a thump on a rocky outcropping. Gwen pressed her face against the plexiglass, which was now covered in condensation, trying to catch a glimpse of something other than rock. Soft light filtered in from her right, but it didn't reveal anything beyond shadows and rocky ground. Gwen deduced that she was in some kind of cave. An ogre, silhouetted against the light, was the only recognizable shape. It must be the same ogress from the boat.

Gwen put as much authority into her voice as she could muster. "D, please tell me where I am."

"I'm sorry, my lady, but I've been instructed not to give you any information until you're brought before your mother."

That's what Gwen was afraid of. "Don't give me specifics. Just tell me what's around me so I don't go stark raving mad." There was a long pause, probably for the poor brute to decide how to answer. Gwen knew he was going for silent captor, but ever since she'd reminded him of her importance, he seemed apologetic. Fuck if she wasn't going to use that. "D, I will not be in a box forever. I'm not asking for you to go against your orders, but you could at least offer me some comfort by describing my current situation."

"That's enough of that, Gwendolyn," barked a crystal-clear voice. Arabella. So much for milking D for intel.

"The Graves," blurted the goon.

"I said enough," replied Arabella, her voice low and threatening.

D shuffled off away from the light as Gwen considered the information. A lighthouse rock island in Boston Harbor was an odd place to be conducting a rendezvous with Seelie Court royalty. Just when she thought she was getting a handle on things, they threw something even weirder at her. And who the hell did Arabella think she was, anyway?

"What is your problem?" Gwen growled.

"You, dear cousin. You are everyone's problem. Our family is under attack, and where have you been? Living it up in the city with no responsibilities. You don't care about us, about the Seelie Court, about your family. You only care about yourself. I know you don't like me, but I thought you'd at least come back for Liam's sake."

Gwen opened her mouth to reply, but coherent thought had fled. Was that how her family saw her? Her mother? Her little brother? A pang of guilt stabbed her in the gut thinking about how young Liam was, barely even a teenager, when she left him all alone to their conniving family. But she had to get out, away from the manipulation of her mother, the politics that plagued her family, and the claustrophobia-inducing expectations that followed her since she was born. She had hoped he would find a way out too. But her departure was years ago. Arabella's ire now was perplexing.

"Don't you have anything to say?" Arabella asked, her voice shaky. She'd never dared to speak to Gwen that way before, and she was likely worried about what might happen once they reached Gwen's mother, Indira.

Gwen didn't give her the satisfaction of an answer. Even when the ogress opened the box a while later, Gwen had no words. It was hard to fight when you didn't know the terrain or terms of war. Thankfully, Arabella had gone on ahead, leaving her in the care of the three guards—the ogress, the ex-police officer, and D, who it seemed drew the short straw. He held the source stick in one hand, but it was lowered.

"My lady, we are going to see your mother now. If you please." He motioned toward the back of the cave with his fat hand. Gwen fought the urge to shift into large form, but she knew it would be uncouth here, where few fairies had gained the ability, reserved as it was for fairy godparents. She felt so vulnerable in her natural size. She wasn't like Arabella or her mother. Both women were intimidating in their own rights. She was just Gwen, black sheep of the family, the disappointment who'd turned her back on courtly life to become a fairy godmother before failing at that too.

Gwen's mouth tasted like dirt and sea salt, and her head pounded from the wind battering her prison and from the movement of the boat. She stood as tall as she could, took a deep breath, then began her march into the darkness, her Doc Martens crunching rocks and D at her back. She smirked as she remembered the name of where she was —The Graves. It seemed appropriate.

The inside of the cave was lit with floating orbs set high against granite walls, the same fae lanterns that illuminated half of the remote areas frequented by fae, including Matron Celeste's study back at the Academy. Gwen struggled to keep the panic rising in her chest from hijacking her senses. Her mother might not be criminally insane like the Brain Scraper, but her family had their own brand of viciousness, and the body count was higher. Much higher.

Gwen laughed at the absurdity that an entire family could be worse than a serial killer. Arabella was too far ahead to hear, and D didn't say a word. The human, a wizard if Gwen remembered correctly, and the ogress following them were panting with the exertion of the spelunking adventure. She doubted they'd have the energy or speed to stop her if she turned and flew out of here. That source stick D was holding, however, kept her moving forward. The cave grew increasingly narrow, the larger fae straining to fit. For the first time since she'd been abducted, Gwen was glad for her natural fae stature.

Eventually, the cavern dead-ended at a large wooden door. Arabella waited, her face the portrait of irritation. When Gwen caught up, Arabella flew up to a large knocker, picked it up, and let it drop with a resounding thud against the brass plate. She muttered an incantation. The sound of multiple locks springing preceded the creak of the door swinging open.

On the other side was a large chamber that didn't resemble a cave at all. If not for the lack of natural light and musty smell, Gwen would have sworn it was located inside a palace. A purple carpet runner bisected a gleaming white marble floor, ending at a dais containing four fairy-sized thrones. Gwen gasped. Of all the scenarios spinning through her mind up to this point, she never thought she'd be thrust into a replica of the throne room of Avalon, her home, hidden in rock and dirt. She gaped at Arabella, but her cousin was staring straight ahead as she led the way, her gait stiff and formal.

The thrones all stood empty with the exception of the last, which was occupied by a resplendent fairy gazing coolly in her direction. Ringlets of dark hair topped with a small crown and a golden gown with intricate, sparkling embroidery all paled next to her crystalline eyes the shade of sapphires.

As they approached, everyone in the party dropped into a low bow. Everyone but Gwen.

"Mother?" It was definitely her mother, Indira Evenshine, but she had no business sitting atop a throne. Gwen used to joke that being 14th in line was appropriate for her disaster of a maternal figure. The woman had the warmth of a salamander and the heart of a rock giant. She didn't belong anywhere near leadership. The thrones were reserved for the Seelie Council, the four fairies at the top of succession: Queen Estrella, her son Felippe, and his two sons Faiel and Giddeon, all distant relatives of Indira and Gwen.

"Daughter. Much has changed since I saw you last." Indira's voice was carefully crafted to be smooth and authoritative. Nothing about the woman was natural.

"Yeah. I gathered that. Did you have to kidnap me? Fuck, Mother. What is going on?"

Arabella shook her head, but Indira didn't flinch. "It's all right, Arabella. I'm accustomed to my daughter's uncouth ways. You all may rise."

"Seriously, Mother. Why has the Great Hall been moved from Avalon to this little hell hole? And where are the Council members?"

"It hasn't been moved, it's been replicated to maintain a semblance of order in these uncertain times. The Council has changed much in the past few weeks. That's why you've been brought before me. Should tragedy befall our family more than it already has, you will be seated."

Gwen's mouth dropped open. Her mother's answer was the last thing she expected to hear. Indira was never meant to sit on the council at her place in succession, and if she was, that meant something terrible had happened. Something unthinkable. Gwen struggled to formulate the right questions. "How?"

"Faiel and Giddeon are dead."

Faiel, at only 85, was heir to the throne and still young by fairy standards. The brothers should have lived well into their bicentennials. Even if a freak accident had taken them both, there were still eight other adult fairies in line before Indira, more if the children were counted. "What about everyone else?" she asked.

"Dead. Gwen, they're all dead. You are no longer 15th in line for the throne. You are 5th. That's why I had you brought here. Kidnapped you, as you say."

"Dead." Gwen's voice was a whisper. She struggled to make sense of her mother's cold declaration. The room spun around her. "All of them? How? Why?" She sunk to her knees. Her mother carried on as if addressing the masses rather than informing her daughter that she'd lost uncles, aunts, and cousins.

"Queen Estrella was murdered at the Gathering in Avalon."

"The Gathering? That was on the Equinox, over two months ago! You didn't think to tell me until now?"

Indira continued as if she hadn't heard Gwen's outburst. "A few others died that night. We went into hiding out of an abundance of caution, or so we thought. Over the past month, others have been hunted and killed. Azrah is now Queen of the Seelie Court with Domingo, Eymen, and myself rounding out the Council. We are all in grave danger."

"What about Felippe and Ambrose? Leopold and Lilibet? Gammie?

What about Gammie?" Words poured from Gwen's mouth. She didn't understand. She didn't understand any of it. The marble was cold beneath her knees, her only tether to the world.

"You're not hearing me, Gwendolyn. They're all dead. My mother is dead. Some were assassinated, some abducted before their bodies surfaced days later, mutilated and discarded. Some of the bodies still haven't turned up."

"Gammie was murdered, and you didn't tell me?" Gwen's blood turned to ice, giving her the strength to get to her feet.

Indira stepped down from the dais and moved to stand directly in front of her. Her voice was low. "I'm telling you now."

"Yeah, now that I'm a step away from being put on the Council! All you care about is politics and power."

"Gwendolyn, don't be insolent. I need you to understand the peril we're all in. It's not just my mother and the other adults. The little ones are gone too." Her voice took on an edge. "You must understand the severity of our situation."

"Gone? You're telling me Dahlia and Catellina were—Gracie? Baby Grace is dead?" A sob cut Gwen's thought in half. Her baby cousins were all dead too? It was all too much.

"Yes. We can only hope it was done quickly so they didn't suffer. While they wouldn't have been fit to lead for many years, they are a great loss to the Seelie Court and to the Council."

"Do you hear yourself? Your family has been massacred, babies slaughtered before they even learned to fly, and all you can talk about is the impact to the Council. Who gives a fuck about the Council?"

Indira Evenshine slapped Gwen across the face.

The sound hung in the air like a fog, darkening the room.

Gwen was vaguely aware of gasps from onlookers, but she didn't break eye contact with her mother. The sting on her cheek only served to wake her from her shock. She swallowed the lump in her throat. Her hands warmed as her defensive magic lessons kicked in, but she didn't move against her mother. The contact, as brief as it was, brought images with it, and they were all tarnished with grief. Her mother might not readily show her emotions, but Gwen's empathic touch proved she had them, and they were strong.

Between clenched teeth, Indira spoke as if she knew what Gwen saw. "I do what I have to. I mourn our losses, but I carry on. We are more than just a family. We are the future of the Seelie Court. Without us, the fae of the entire world are lost."

Her hand clenched into a fist, Gwen stared back at her mother. Grief or not, Indira had some seriously screwed up priorities. "I don't give a shit about the Seelie Court. The Council can go fuck itself, present company included."

Indira took a deep breath, and her features settled back into the serene expression that made Gwen sick. It was the look of a woman who believed that her daughter wasn't half as important as her legacy. "Be that as it may, you are a target. We don't know who is killing our family, but you've got responsibilities now. Whether you like it or not, the Seelie Court needs you. It's time to stop playing around in the mortal realm and come home."

Gwen felt like the world was crashing in on her, and here was her mother, so matter-of-fact, so in control. The woman hadn't spoken to her since she left for the Academy. She cut her off and shut her out, and now here she was, callously telling Gwen that half her family was dead as she took control over her life yet again. She'd never hated her mother more. The ringing in her head stopped. She went numb. She stood and stared her mother in the eye, refusing to cry in front of her. She wouldn't cry in front of any of them.

"Where is Liam?"

"Did you hear what I said? You will remain here with me where we can keep you safe so that you can prepare for Seelie leadership. We've got a lot of work to do."

"You don't care about my safety, and you have no say in how I live. Tell me where my little brother is."

"I'm here, Gwen." The words were quiet but self-assured, not at all the voice of the timid kid Gwen left behind years ago when she enrolled in the Academy, but there was no mistaking the timbre. Her sweet little brother Liam was the only thing about her early life she missed. When they were kids, she always put herself between him and the rest of the family, sheltering him from the bickering and politicking that defined the Evenshine dynamic. She absorbed all the pressure to keep him clear of it. Until she couldn't anymore. A pang of guilt pierced through the shock of losing half her family.

"How long have you been standing there?" she asked.

"Long enough."

The last time she saw Liam was at her friend Corrin's funeral. Corrin, Chessa's cousin who had been killed by the Brain Scraper, had been Liam's only childhood friend, and he'd only been a target because of Gwen's obsession with capturing the serial killer who'd murdered her first charge, Princess Francesca Gaviton. Frankie. Despite Chessa's insistence that it wasn't her fault, Gwen knew better. And so did both Laural, Corrin's wife, and Liam. Her heart fell in her stomach as she turned to face him.

Liam stepped forward, Herbert Dayglow following just behind. The latter made his way over to bow before Indira while Liam approached Gwen. He could pass for her twin if she weren't five years his senior, with his black hair and gold-rimmed irises. He was now the age she had been when she lost Frankie. She wondered briefly if he was half as naive. Danu, she hoped not. She met the stranger halfway and threw her arms around his neck, careful not to access her magic and accidentally invade his privacy with her empathetic link. At first he stiffened, but then he returned the hug. Gwen felt hot tears threatening to fall and had to remind herself that her mother was still watching. She released her little brother and stepped back to look him over.

"I hope they haven't ruined you," she whispered. "Why didn't you reach out to me?"

"I could ask you the same," Liam replied. His eyes seemed to hold an accusation, and Gwen winced.

"I'm so sorry I haven't visited. Things are… complicated."

"Complicated, I understand," he said.

"It would seem so. You've been through so much."

"We both have. I'm sorry about Princess Francesca, and I'm glad you were able to capture her killer. I'm sorry I didn't tell you that at Corrin's funeral."

"Me too," was all the reply she could muster. Corrin had been

Liam's best friend long before he was a friend to her, and the funeral had been a blur. She couldn't blame Liam for freezing her out.

"It seems you two have catching up to do," interjected Indira. Gwen hadn't realized her mother had finished speaking with Dayglow and was now standing uncomfortably close while she struggled to connect with her estranged little brother. If she sensed Gwen's discomfort, she didn't seem to care. "Gwendolyn, Liam can show you the room prepared for you. There are no exits beyond the one you came through, and it's enchanted to open only for me, Arabella, and Herbert, so don't try slipping away back to your little Korranthia apartment."

"Herbert? Who is this guy, anyhow?" Gwen glared at Dayglow, but he didn't flinch.

"Herbert is head of my personal guard, and you will treat him with respect. Should you try to go before I give you leave, he will bring you back here where it's safe. Liam can let you in on everything we know about the unpleasantness as well."

"Unpleasantness? That's what you call the murder of my baby cousins? Of your entire family? Of Gammie? Unpleasantness? You're unbelievable."

Liam cleared his throat and motioned for her to follow before Indira could reply. Gwen was only too glad to follow him away from her captors as they awaited their own audience with the woman who had more in common with the mob bosses from Detective Samson's shows than with a maternal figure.

8

As much as it pained her to admit, Chessa was in over her head. She might have gone after a serial killer on her own, but tracking Seelie royals half-cocked was a suicide mission. Snapping photos of an ambassador was one thing, but she didn't even know what this was anymore. She needed backup. Unfortunately, Gwen wasn't the most popular fairy around, and her list of friends was nonexistent. The matrons at the Academy would try to help Gwen if Chessa asked, but ever since their leader, Matron Celeste, was discovered to be the notorious Brain Scraper, they were floundering, not good for much beyond administering a mediocre education to future fairy godparents. Nobody at the Academy wielded the kind of power or resolve she needed for a mission like this. That just left one creature she could turn to—Detective Samson Wayne.

Chessa zipped into the Korranthia Police Precinct, not bothering to check in at the front desk, where Pox, the rookie cop who worshiped Samson, sat on desk duty. Her work on the Scraper case had made her a favorite around here, even if Captain O'Toole was still a bit of a boor. She didn't plan to pay him a visit. He'd probably make her sign yet another non-disclosure form agreeing to keep any intel she learned at the precinct off *Crime Wave*. She landed at the top of the steps leading down into the bullpen to catch her breath, choosing to walk the rest of the way down the empty hall to Detective Samson Wayne's office.

"Chessa! How's it going?" called a witch from a few desks over. Her skin glistened with green undertones, and her wild hair stood in stark contrast to her tailored uniform.

"Hey, Darla! How's the family?" Chessa called as she kept walking.

"No more random explosions, thank Danu," replied the witch.

If she wasn't so worried about Gwen, she would stop to chit-chat about Darla's troubled son who was struggling as his powers came in, but today, she was on a mission.

"Are you okay?" Darla called after her. "You look like you've been through the wringer."

Chessa kept moving. She hadn't thought about how bad she must look, having fallen from a mast, smacked into a deck, and rolled into Boston Harbor. She nodded hello to Kairon, a sprite who served as janitor, in the hallway, and smiled or waved to a half-dozen other familiar faces, all while moving fast enough to avoid a conversation, before she made it to Detective Wayne's door. She knocked three times, and the door swung open.

"Chessa, what brings you in? Our Checkers game isn't scheduled for today, is it?" said the griffin, closing a folder as he rose from the chair behind his desk. It always reminded her of a throne, sized as it was to accommodate his enormous lion haunches. He pushed his round, red spectacles to the top of his beak with one talon and scowled.

Chessa glanced at the folder. It was the Ghost of Korranthia case. Again. For as long as she'd known him, Samson had been bothered by the one that got away, an assassin who took out an Unseelie gnome activist. Samson caught her looking and picked at his wrist feathers, a sure sign of discomfort. She let it go. "Hey, Samson. Something's come up. I need your help if you're not too busy here."

"What's the rumble?" Samson's big yellow eyes narrowed as they moved over Chessa's battered body. Gwen always hated how he talked like those old detective movies, said it was based in insecurity or some shit, but Chessa found it endearing. She wasn't quite sure how to tell him about Gwen, though. He always had a soft spot for her.

"What is it, kid? You're not one to ask for a hand. Snoop through my things, sure. Pay off my landlord for intel, yeah. This doesn't have anything to do with the Seelie royals, does it?"

Chessa was stunned. She wasn't prepared for him to be a step ahead of her. "As a matter of fact, it does. What do you know?"

"Did O'Toole have you sign an NDA?"

"Samson, how many times do I have to assure you that I'd never throw you under the bus?"

"So long as there's a bus, I'm staying off the asphalt," replied the griffin with a low chuckle. "Off the record, we know nothing. There are rumors of trouble in Avalon, missed calls, ghosted appointments, that sort of thing. Our contacts have all gone mum. What does any of that have to do with you?"

Chessa struggled to say the words she knew would throw Samson into a fit. "Gwen's been taken."

The detective stopped in his tracks. He stood, halfway across the cluttered office, balanced on lion legs and one talon with the other held aloft, the perfect picture of a griffin statue.

Chessa fluttered into the air and hovered above his desk to get to his eye-level. "Samson, if you can hear me, blink three times."

He didn't acknowledge Chessa's attempt at a joke. He was used to Gwen, so inappropriate trauma responses were old hat to him. "Taken? How do you know she was snatched and didn't fly the coop of her own accord? It's not like she'd ask permission."

"I know who took her."

"Spill it, kid. Cut the drama."

"I was working a case, trailing a guy, a fairy, an ambassador for the Seelie Council. He took her, met up with a proper fairy, and they bolted on a boat."

Samson seemed to get his senses about him. He walked over to shut the door before returning to his desk and plopping down in the chair. Chessa settled onto the desk, leaning against a mason jar filled with pens.

"Who was your mark?"

"Herbert Dayglow."

Samson made a sound that was more chicken than eagle. "He was one of those contacts. Went off the grid two weeks ago. Who hired you?"

Chessa hesitated. C&F Investigations was still in its infancy, and Gwen's relationship with the KPD was already enough to spook potential clients. She didn't want a rep for doxxing her patrons.

"Quid pro quo, kid. It's off the record, but I need to know what kind of vice you got us in."

"The name she gave was Taylor Swift."

Samson snorted.

"Yeah, terrible, I know. But nobody hires a PI with their real identity. I appreciated that she didn't even try to pull one by on me. She said she needed some photos, that's it. I was supposed to tail the guy, snap some pics, and mail them to a PO Box."

"Knowing you, you already know who the box is registered to."

"Of course, but get this, she rented it out with the same name. I don't know how she swung that, but I sure as shit admire the balls it took. Short of staking out the post office, which could take weeks if it pays off at all, it's a dead end."

"Shit on a pixie stick. Oh, sorry."

"My thoughts exactly," Chessa replied. "This is the only other lead I've got. Gwen left me a message." Chessa pulled the towel out from the tattered bookbag she picked up on her way over. It wasn't her old leather messenger bag, but it wasn't a bad replacement, and the straps were designed to fit around her wings so her movements were unencumbered.

Samson took the scrap of material in his huge talon. He drew in a sharp breath when he saw the monogram. "Oh, Gwen," he muttered. "What are you mixed up in?"

"I wouldn't have come if I didn't need your help," said Chessa.

"My help? You're tootin' the wrong ringer. Danu herself couldn't fix this. Do you know where they took her? Or why?"

"No. All I've got are some physical descriptions and this piece of cloth. I don't even have my camera. They shot me out of the sky, Sammy."

Samson brought his head close enough where she could reach out and pet his beak if she were so inclined, and he pushed his spectacles up again. "Oh, kid, you don't look so good. We need to get you to a healer, then I need to bring this to the captain and get a plan together."

"No! Gwen doesn't trust O'Toole. I came to you first because everything about this situation feels off. I don't know why. We can't bring in O'Toole, at least, not yet."

"Internal Affairs cleared him of all wrongdoing on the Scraper case, Chess. You know that."

Chessa couldn't believe what she was hearing. Internal Affairs had to be on pixie dust. O'Toole was dirty. Nothing Samson said could convince Chessa otherwise. She and Gwen spent the better part of a week in jail because of his involvement in the Scraper case, and Samson just wanted to move on like nothing happened. "He tried to set up Madam Glitz as the Brain Scraper, Sammy. He's had it in for Gwen since he met her."

"He bowed to pressure to make a collar. And yeah, he doesn't like Gwen, but let's be fair here, she gets his goat at every chance. She hasn't exactly bent over backward to tickle his pickle. But he's a good cop, and he would do everything he could to help keep the fae of Korranthia safe. That includes Gwen."

Chessa couldn't even bring herself to smile at his broken turn of phrase or the thought of Gwen tickling anyone's pickle so to speak. The fairy was far too up her own ass to be grabbing anyone else's. "Please, Sammy. Keep him out of this. The more people who know we're going after the Seelie royal family, the less our chances of getting Gwen back."

Samson sighed. "All right kid, you win. I won't tip off O'Toole. But someone at the KPD needs to know what's going on. I'm bringing Pox in."

"Isn't he green?"

"He's been with the KPD for two years now, and better, he's loyal. If things go sideways, he'll know what to do."

Chessa gave a reluctant nod. "Fine. Just make sure he stays quiet until then. We have to find her."

"Agreed. You say you don't know where she was taken?" Samson was gathering up belongings as he spoke. Under normal circumstances, Chessa would tease him about tossing up protests while obviously preparing for battle, but she didn't have the energy for it today.

"No. But we do know where the Seelie Royal family resides. That's where we'll go."

The griffin's beak fell open. "You can't mean—"

"Yep. We're going to Avalon."

Samson groaned as he pulled on a jacket. "You're off your damn rocker, you know that."

"I know. It's for Gwen."

"Fine. But first, we're getting you to a healer so you can die whole."

He was right. Sneaking up on the highest levels of Seelie society would be no easy feat, and Chessa couldn't do it busted up.

For his part, Samson agreed to withhold details from Pox, who, by the look on his face when they pulled him aside in the hall to explain the situation, was already in way over his head.

"You're going where now?" he asked, eyes the size of saucers. Chessa didn't know a humanoid could look so much like a bug.

"Somewhere very dangerous," replied Samson, looking around.

"To kidnap someone that somebody else already kidnapped?"

"Not exactly," Samson began, but Chessa cut him off.

"Look, we just need you to be on standby so that the KPD can mobilize if things go wrong. The less you know about the situation, the safer you'll be," she said. Samson nodded along.

"I don't like this, Sergeant. Can't we bring somebody else in?"

"No!" Samson and Chessa responded in unison, and the warlock flinched in response.

Samson stepped forward. "Pox, you've watched my feathers from the moment you started at the precinct. You're a straight egg. That's why I want you to be my man on the inside."

Chessa was pretty sure Samson was misusing the phrase, but she could see Pox puffing up. He really did idolize Sammy. She took a step back to give them space. Eventually, the rookie nodded and agreed to be a point-of-contact, but only after Samson signed a paper indicating that the information he kept classified from the rest of the bureau was by order of Sergeant Detective Samson Wayne. There was an incident with evidence from the Brain Scraper case that made the kid a bit trigger-shy, and Chessa didn't blame him. They thanked Pox and walked out the front door of the precinct.

"I suppose you have a plan for getting us halfway across the world without the royal guards catching wind of us," Samson said as they headed to the only healer Chessa would agree to see— Laural, the wife of her late cousin Corrin.

Chessa scrunched her nose in thought. Everything up until now had happened so fast, she hadn't had time to consider the how of it all. "We can't book travel through the usual means. We'd need to apply to use fae transport," she replied. In order to cross Kingdoms, fae were required to file with the Seelie Department of Census. It was a tiresome restriction that resulted from the human-fae treaties in which the Seelie Court created a symbiotic system of government with humans. Like all aspects of government, the system was broken.

"And if we use the mortals' transportation systems without filing first, there's a good chance it'll tip our mitts to the Seelie Court too. I know you've got informants, or *Crime Wave* wouldn't hit on so many truths. Do you know any—" Samson's voice dropped despite there being no prying ears about. "Unseelie who could transport us?"

Chessa laughed. Samson didn't realize just how many fae around them were Unseelie or Courtless. Despite all he'd seen at the KPD, his worldview was still very insulated. "I know some Unseelie, but they're not all criminals. They also don't have a centralized transportation system. They operate on an everyone-for-themselves basis, so most just use Leaf Pass for domestic travel and register just like the rest of us to go abroad. I'm sure there are smugglers, but I don't know of anyone trustworthy enough to handle this."

Chessa paused just outside her cousin's house. Every time she visited Laural, the sight of the little blue craftsman cottage felt like a punch to the gut. Corrin had been the final victim of the Brain Scraper. If only she'd pieced the clues together faster, it would be him opening the door, flashing a lopsided smile from under his backward ball cap. She turned away from the house and looked at Samson, a thought tugging at the back of her brain. "You know what, Sammy? I do have a guy who could help get us some fake identification so we could pass for human. Maybe then, we could fly under the Seelie radar."

Samson picked at his wrist feathers. "Of course you do."

Chessa breezed right by his reticence. "Do you think the Glamour Squadron would cover us during international travel?" Gwen's old job during the Brain Scraper's off-season was working for the Glamour Squad, watching the streets and casting glamours to cover magical residue to keep the existence of fae from prying mortal eyes. Every Kingdom had its own systems in place, and not all relied on the Squad. Chessa wasn't sure what would happen when they were in international airspace.

"As long as we book a flight from a United States-based company, they'll have a fairy on board to cast."

That was both convenient and concerning. The Squad normally watched for trends and magical residue, casting general cloaking glamours as needed. "Do you think they'll notice us?"

Sammy shook his head. "The Squadron isn't trained to decipher what they're sensing. I tried to interview them as witnesses to a dozen crimes, but they gave me bupkis. Their job is to cast universal glamours so humans see what they expect rather than what's actually there, and two extra fae on a plane wouldn't be a blip on their radar."

Chessa was glad to hear it. "So it's settled! I'll pay my guy a visit tonight."

Samson nodded, hesitation playing in his big, yellow eyes. "But for now, let's get Laural to fix you up."

Chessa touched her forehead and winced. She could only imagine how she looked. Probably like she'd been through a meat grinder. She certainly felt that way. "Samson?" She said, hoping he didn't notice her voice wavering.

"Yeah, kid?"

"Have you been to see Laural lately? I mean, since Corrin died?"

"No. But I do remember his funeral."

Right. The funeral. Until Laural had been sedated, the demon living inside her took control of the grieving witch and threatened to kill Gwen.

"Yeah. Okay. So you know to brace yourself."

They opened the gate and stepped over a sidewalk that made a perfect circle around the house. Occult markings were painted on it, the work of a KPD officer who happened to also be a witch capable of casting containment spells. While Laural might not be responsible for the actions of the demon inhabiting her body, she couldn't be allowed to roam Korranthia free either. That was the compromise Chessa fought for, one that got Laural out of that dismal institution she'd been confined to after Corrin's funeral.

Laural came to the door. Her long, chestnut hair and white chiffon dress floated behind her. At 5'8" tall, the witch had to stoop low to embrace Chessa. Despite the warmth of her greeting, she seemed distant, but that was just Laural. Always fighting an internal battle nobody else could see.

At the hug, Chessa winced in pain. Her ribs felt like they might snap if the wind blew too strongly.

"I see this is more than a personal visit," said Laural, concern touching her eyes briefly before she stood back to make room for Samson to enter.

Samson pushed his glasses to the top of his beak. Laural always made him fidgety. "Hello, Laural. You look well," he said as he went to the center of the living room and crouched on the floor. There was no furniture here sized to accommodate his mass. Plus, Laural always complained about cat hair on the furniture when he was around.

"Better than my dear cousin, it seems," she answered, whisking out of the room.

Chessa watched her go for supplies, a lump forming in her throat. This was never the life Corrin wanted for his wife. He'd been the only one she could open up to without risking the demon's escape, and now she was alone with nothing but some Xanax to help keep the demon at bay. Her neighbors thought of her as the eccentric lady who always dressed like she was going to a ball, but the fae world knew better. She was alone in the world, and there wasn't a damn thing anybody could do about it. Except bring her Dela's Donuts on occasion, and that's where Chessa came in. She'd visited her cousin-by-marriage every week since Corrin's funeral.

Laural returned with a crate full of tools and props and got to work setting up for her healing ritual. She handed Samson a bottle, which was dwarfed by his large talons, as she ushered him off to stand beside the fireplace.

"Water blessed by a priestess of Danu," she said in response to his puzzled expression. "In case things get out of control."

Chessa wished she could read his mind. Blessed water wouldn't affect fae. This was an emergency precaution should Gailan, the demon possessing Laural, decide to take over. Samson remained stoic.

As they watched, the witch got to work. She dragged a small, round table to the center of the room and set up an altar.

"Chessa, if you please." Laural motioned to the table where a cushion sized perfectly for a pixie was set surrounded by a small bowl of salt, a thimble of water, a lit votive candle, and a sprig of incense that burned sandalwood. Chessa flitted up to it and settled in. This was not the first time she'd been healed with a ritual, and she'd be shocked if it were the last.

Laural stripped naked, exposing her body covered in scars of all shapes and sizes. Chessa's heart broke every time she saw the result of the battles her dear cousin fought. She wished she could do something, anything, to lighten the burden. Samson averted his gaze but appeared otherwise unfazed as Laural cast a protective circle and stood over Chessa, hands outstretched to funnel energy from the cosmos into her tiny, broken body.

The sensation was at once divine and intensely painful. Her fractured ribs knit themselves together and the swelling subsided. It was like a thousand toothed lightning bugs were fluttering and sparking beneath her skin, their tiny jaws gnawing at Chessa's muscle and sinew. Soon, it was over. Chessa felt nothing. Blessed nothing. Laural closed out the ritual, released her circle, and clothed herself before collapsing into the overstuffed armchair by the window. Even a healer without a demon to hold back while channeling would need to rest for a few hours after such exertion, and in Laural's case, it was all the more taxing. Chessa went to the kitchen to snag her cousin a protein bar and put on a kettle for tea.

Once Laural was settled in for the night, Chessa sent Samson home to pack up for the trip and headed down to her favorite watering hole, Pub Nine. If she and a griffin were going to travel across the globe undetected, they'd need papers. And Chessa knew a guy.

As soon as she walked into the small, out-of-the-way establishment, the bartender slid her a beer. Pub Nine was a popular spot for the three nearby fae universities—The Fairy Godparent Academy, Asha'atai, a college for elves to learn all kinds of trades, and Rise, the University of Necromantic Arts. Thankful she wasn't subjected to the chanting drinking games of necromancers-in-training this time. It was a slow Tuesday night. Chessa smiled and took a big swig from her bottle of Flying High IPA.

"How's it going, Fallan?" she asked the bartender, a young elf with purple skin and bright eyes. Fallan was working to pay for that expensive education most elven families saw as chump change. Chessa helped them study for a sympathetic magics final during a slow shift last semester.

"Not much happening tonight," they replied, likely assuming that Chessa was digging for juicy gossip for a *Crime Wave* story.

"I see that. Sorry you're not making any cash."

"That's okay. I've got Ancient Runes homework to get done. You looking for Q? He's in the back throwing cards again."

"Thanks." Chessa left a gold coin on the bar, more than she should spend but enough to help make up for Fallan's slow night, then hopped off the barstool and made her way to the swinging doors leading to the back room. She nodded hello to a handful of regulars and waved across the room to a goblin leaning against the jukebox. It was one of those old-school machines you could only find in antique shops, but the dryad owner, Mel, loved that kind of shit.

Cross-Eyed Quincy held court at a poker table in the back room. To anyone not in the know, Quincy would be terrifying with his intimidating size, green mohawk, tattoos, and scars, but Chessa saw the half-ogre for what he was, a teddy bear in a mohawk.

"Chia," said Q in greeting, using her street name, some silly derivation of Chia pet because she was always growing stories. She wasn't even sure where it originated, but that's how everyone at Pub Nine greeted her. Shelves loaded with boxes and crates lined the walls of the storeroom, but none of the wait staff would be coming in while it was occupied by Quincy and his associates. The game wasn't exactly by-the-books, but everyone gathered around the table knew Chessa. Q's gigantic foot pushed the chair next to him out as an invitation. "I dig the new hair. Did you come to lose some clams?" He chuckled, a deep sound from his enormous chest.

She wasn't here to gamble, not today. "Heya, Q. Thom. Dudlin. Sherrie." She greeted the motley assortment of fae in turn. They grunted or greeted, but nobody looked up from their cards. Everyone hated losing to Quincy. Chessa flitted up to the empty chair, which was about fifteen times too large for her but got her close enough to Q to hold a semi-private conversation. "I'm actually here on business. I need a favor. I would have given you a heads-up if it weren't so important, but it's the sensitive sort." She gave an apologetic look around the table.

"You heard the pixie. Get out, you chuckleheads," boomed Quincy with more bluster than was necessary.

"Damn it, Chia," muttered Dudlin, his chins wobbling from the effort. "I had a royal flush!"

Chessa wasn't sure what manner of fae the pale green Pub Nine regular with long, sagging ears and a bulbous nose was because she was always too polite to ask, but she figured he was one of the millions of unique creatures that fell under the Seelie and Unseelie umbrellas. To her, he was just Dudlin.

"Sure you did," replied Sherrie, giving him a shove from behind. Dudlin shot her a dirty look and let rip some gas. Unfortunately for the brownie, the height differential made it so her face was in the danger zone. "Ugh, males," she griped as she scurried out the door ahead of Thom, a lanky kelpie with twitchy, orange eyes and gills.

"Thanks, guys," Chessa called. "Hopefully I can join the next game."

The door flopped closed, and Chessa flew up to sit on Quincy's shoulder, her usual perch for the sorts of conversations they had.

"What do you need, Chia?" asked Q, his voice a tad softer than it had been. She'd learned long ago that Quincy's hard Boston exterior was mostly defensive. She met with him once a month to talk about life over a few beers, just the two of them, and the guy was a lot more complex than anyone seemed to know. When she visited on business, he'd be giving her tips from the street for articles, not providing life-saving counterfeit ID.

"I need papers. For me and Samson."

"You in some sort of trouble?"

"I'm not, but Gwen is. I don't want to tell you too much because this shit is serious, and the more you know, the more you'll be put in danger. I need some false names for me and Samson, human-sounding, and ID to match."

"For you and the griffin? Ain't he a cop?"

"Q, you know I wouldn't set you up. Yeah, he's a cop. But he loves Gwen, and the KPD can't help with this one."

Quincy's eyes narrowed, his large scar bunching over his nose like mangled train tracks. "He's going to know it was me who done this, and he's going to stick it in a file someplace for when he needs to put the pressure on."

"I won't let that happen. I give you my word."

The truth was, Samson knew that Quincy was Chessa's man, but he didn't ask questions. The good Chessa did with the relationship far outstripped any of the half-ogre's crimes. Samson was a by-the-books detective until it came to the morality of a situation. He only ever needed to see the right of things, and Chessa was a pro at getting people to see the good in the world.

"Okay. I'll bang it out for you. But only because it's you. You need to give me time though. Tomorrow afternoon should cut it."

"Thank you, Q. I owe you." Chessa flitted to Quincy's face and brushed a kiss on his cheek.

"I'll take a well-aged single malt."

"Done." Chessa flashed a smile.

A thought seemed to occur to Quincy. "You need a place to crash tonight? You can stay here. I'll set you up a pillow on the top shelf over there. Nobody will be the wiser."

9

June 13
7 days until the Summer Solstice

All night long, Gwen had done nothing but mourn her family, worry about Chessa, and practice the bits of magic she learned during her adjunct time at the Academy. There was nothing else for her to do—at least not until the Council of Four arrived to take their thrones. Even then, Gwen had no way to assure that they'd let her leave or even let her plead her case. Her mother certainly wouldn't. As a council member and closest in line for the throne, Indira was presently the highest-ranking Seelie on site. Her word was backed by the Seelie Guard, which meant Gwen was locked down. Her time in captivity wasn't lacking in luxury. No room in the sprawling cave system felt like a cavern. Each was decked out in the clean, contemporary look popular with the bluebloods these days— gleaming marble, exposed beams contrasting with rich, luxurious velvets and suedes, and dark bronze grandiose light fixtures, which were mostly for show since the light was provided by fae orbs. Gwen had hoped for five minutes alone with Liam, but her little brother

53

spent precious little time in her company. Her mother, on the other hand, seemed to be everywhere all at once.

"You must begin your preparations to ascend to the Council of Four. Any day now, your time could come," she told Gwen the day after her unceremonious arrival.

If there was one thing Gwen never wanted, it was to climb any closer to the throne, but she would have to figure all that out later. Right now, she was only concerned with busting out of this place.

"Will the others be here soon?" she asked. She hoped that her cousin Eymen, three years her junior, might take pity on her.

"I'm not at liberty to discuss their plans. Gwendolyn. Please do not deflect."

"I'm not deflecting. I'm trying to figure out how to get the hell out of here."

Her mother sighed. "You act like I'm a monster. I'm just trying to keep you safe."

"Safe? Did you care about my safety when I was in the clutches of a serial killer? I'm only important to you now because of my place in the family. My use to you. You don't give a shit about me, so stop pretending like you do."

At that moment, Liam stepped through the door into her quarters. He was dressed in his military uniform, not that there were any visitors or dignitaries here to impress. His white coat with purple embroidery and gold, gleaming buttons looked natural on his stiff form, and his wings pointed upward, a pose far too formal for family. The Evenshines might not be an average fae family, but this seemed like overkill. He pinned Gwen with his cold, golden-ringed eyes. "The way I remember it, you left us. You turned your back on us to become a fairy godmother. Then you botched that up so badly, you got my best friend killed."

"Liam, that's not fair! Corrin was the medical examiner. He knew the risks. And I never wanted to leave you. I just had to leave all this." Gwen motioned widely, but it was truly her mother she was implicating, and all three fairies knew it.

"But leave, you did. Off to help some poor young noble while your family kept the Seelie Court afloat."

Gwen had no defense. Her family was insufferable, and she left little Liam to fend for himself in the sea of sharks. The result was standing before her with accusation written all over his chiseled features. He was a man now, and he resented her. Had she really missed so much?

Indira spoke again. "As you see, you hurt us deeply when you left. But we all need to put our petty differences behind us now so that we stay safe and provide the Seelie Court leadership during a turbulent time. We must present a united front in this unprecedented time of danger. Our brethren need us. Please, Gwendolyn, Liam, find it in your hearts to forgive and move forward. Both of you." With that, she rose from the cream-colored couch, gave a curt nod that Gwen was sure was meant to be encouraging in some way, and left the Evenshine siblings alone together. As soon as she was gone, Liam lowered his wings.

Gwen fought back the lump in her throat. "Liam," she said. "I'm so sorry."

Her brother stood, staring for a long moment as if fighting some internal battle. At last, he walked to Gwen and leaned in close. She braced herself, but instead of more angry words, he simply said "I know a way out."

10

The next morning, Chessa woke to find a bagel and an iced coffee sitting on the shelf beside her. The bar was empty and locked up, so she had the place to herself. She spent the morning writing down everything she knew about the UK and Avalon on a pad of paper she'd dug out of one of the boxes Quincy had stashed in the storeroom. It wasn't much. Laural's healing and a few hours of sleep had done wonders, and sitting here waiting for something to happen was maddening. Still, Quincy wouldn't have her documents for some time, and she technically wasn't supposed to be in the bar after closing, so she had to wait for the eleven o'clock shift to arrive so she could pretend like she just stopped in. Finally, she heard the door open. She stayed hidden until an hour later when Quincy returned. "It's like I'm harboring a fugitive," he grumbled as he handed over the papers.

"I'm sorry to put you in this situation, Q. I didn't have anywhere else to go."

The half-ogre grunted at her. "You got it."

"And you've already done so much, but I've got one more favor I need to ask."

Quincy gave a resigned sigh. "I'm sure you do."

"Could you book me two tickets to Bristol with the new identities? The people I'm dealing with are powerful. I can't go home, and I sure as hell can't use my own laptop."

"That bad, eh? You're not going to bring the heat down on me, are you?"

"Honestly, Q, I can't make that promise. But I don't have a choice."

"I suppose I don't neither." Quincy pulled a laptop out of the backpack he carried, tossed on some reading glasses, and set up shop at the fold-out card table. Twenty minutes later, the printer stashed on a small stand in the corner whirred to life. "The earliest flight out of Logan doesn't leave 'til tomorrow afternoon. Nothing I can do about that," he said as he retrieved the papers and handed them over.

"There's no way to get there sooner?"

"Plenty, but none I recommend. I've got some guys could maybe get you there in the morning, but believe me, you don't want to go that way unless you got no other choice."

Quincy chuckled, and Chessa made a mental note to press him about international travel later. For now, she'd have to be satisfied with a decent night's rest. Chessa thanked Quincy yet again and headed back to Laural's to wait it out and contact Samson.

11

June 14
6 days until the Summer Solstice

Per Liam's instructions, Gwen left her chamber before sunrise and met him in a service hall a few doors over. He was waiting in the shadows, dressed in casual attire and looking like he hadn't slept a wink.

"Why would you help me escape this hell hole?" Gwen asked, bypassing formalities. Liam led her through the storage space at the back of the kitchens. The limited staff was seeing to other duties at this hour, and Indira must not have thought the space vulnerable enough to require guards. At least, not inside.

"Can you tell me precisely what's so hellish about it?" her little brother replied. "Is it your quality linens? The well-stocked bar? Perhaps having your own personal servant is just too much torture for one so accustomed to scraping the mud off her own boots?"

Gwen didn't reply. Liam was probably displacing his grief, or perhaps conflating it with his residual feelings of abandonment. Whatever his issue, it wasn't going to be solved by arguing over the quality of her imprisonment.

"Or maybe it's being around your family that's so unbearable for you," he tacked on with a glint in his eyes. Now that one hurt. Gwen struggled to match pace with her little brother and was barely aware of her surroundings as she followed from room to room, each more luxurious than the next. When they came to a kitchen that could accommodate a staff of fairies working to feed a palace, he slowed. Gwen stopped just short of running into the back of him. He entered a door to the right. It led to a storeroom.

"Liam, I—"

He cut her off. "Here we are."

Before them stood an expansive shelving unit, too tall even for a troll to reach items on the top shelf, which wasn't a problem when most of the staff was winged. Gwen wished she had known this room existed because it was the only place she'd seen in the past few days that could accommodate her in large form. She wasn't accustomed to being trapped in her natural size. Liam muttered something unintelligible and waved his hand. The entire wall swung outward like a door.

Gwen gasped. Liam's magical abilities surpassed her own. When did everyone get so damn powerful? When she stopped to think about it, she realized she should have been able to perform intermediate magical functions without a wand years ago. It was no wonder that Liam and Arabella were so far beyond her. Fairies were limited to perceptive magic, but as the old proverb went, perception is everything. The family members in her generation had been advancing all these years, learning to alter perceptions on scales with tangible outcomes. Gwen, on the other hand, not so much. The Fairy Godparent Academy prioritized diplomacy and exploiting her rarer gift, her empathic touch, over things like linked sympathetic magics and defensive spells, but even they would have ensured she reached at least basic magical proficiency had she stuck it out. When Frankie was murdered, she turned her back on the Academy in favor of seeking vengeance. Who knew what magic she could be performing now had she made other choices?

Briefly, Gwen wondered if the Academy still had eyes and ears all over the fae world. With Matron Celeste gone, she wasn't sure how many of their networks were still in place. It might be worth paying them a visit to see if they had any intel on what was happening with her family.

Gwen instinctively felt for her wand, still strapped to her thigh. She looked at the back of her little brother's head. Soon she would leave him again, and when she did, she'd lose yet another chance to connect. She doubted she'd get many other opportunities. Before she could reel in her errant thoughts, she reached out and touched Liam's arm. Her power sparked to life. A slew of tangled senses flowed into her through the empathic link.

"Stop it!" he barked, pulling away.

With one stupid move, she broke fae convention, along with whatever shard of trust he might still have in her. Silently cussing herself out, Gwen swallowed the lump forming in her throat. They were once so close, but she lost him right along with the rest of her family. He would never open up to her now that she'd broken his trust trying to read him without his consent. She bit her bottom lip and tried to parse out what she sensed from her invasion of his privacy.

The skip of a heartbeat. The perfume of a woman. A dark forest alight with fae orbs.

Little Liam had a girlfriend. Gwen smiled at the most normal discovery she'd made since her abduction. There was no sense in pretending she didn't feel something from the touch. She'd been able to read Liam long before she understood her power, so he knew what it felt like when she picked up senses. That was probably why he kept his distance since she arrived at the island hideout. Perhaps she could get him talking about his life and he'd forgive her.

"Who is she? Is it the girl you brought to Corrin's funeral?" she asked, barely noticing that her surroundings had morphed from the inside of a palace to a dank cavern.

"It's none of your business." So much for breaking through. Liam cleared his throat. "This passageway will take you to a sheer cliff, so proceed carefully. I'd hate to show you the way out just to find you on the rocks below because you didn't think to fly."

Gwen ignored the barb. It was all she could do. "You never told me why you're helping me."

"I don't know. Maybe I don't want to worry that my big sister is going to invade my mind every time I walk the halls. You do want to escape this place, right? I know you're not choosing to be here. If history is any indication, being in close proximity to your kin is the last place you'd go of your own volition."

His words landed. "Liam, I never wanted to leave you with them. I don't know what you've been through over the years, but I never wanted this life for you," said Gwen.

"But you did leave. And now I've lost my cousins, my aunts and uncles. Everyone."

"They were my family too," replied Gwen, her voice quiet.

"Were they?" Liam turned his back but continued to speak as he walked away. "Be careful out there, sis. It's a dangerous world for fae royals. You should know that better than most."

With that, the brother Gwen no longer knew disappeared into the cavern from which they'd come. She could tell when he moved the shelf back in place by the darkness that fell over the stone walls on either side of her. It wasn't until he was gone that she thought of asking if he had a chance to get her phone back from D. Her mother, of course, kept her out of communication with the outside world for the duration of her stay. *Gotta love an Evenshine family reunion,* she thought.

Gwen smelled the sea long before she surfaced on the opposite side of the tiny island from the lighthouse. Whether this was an escape shaft or a service entrance, she couldn't tell, but she was glad when her eyes adjusted to the light and she found herself flying over the harbor back toward the marina. It had been days since her abduction, but she didn't know what had become of Chessa, so she planned to scan the area where she last saw her friend. It was as good a place to start as any. Maybe someone would let her borrow a cell phone.

She was in luck. She found a mortal in an ill-fitting navy suit with a thick gold chain around his neck, hardly marina attire, and commandeered his cell.

The call went right to voicemail. Again.

"Shit, Chessa," muttered Gwen, "pick up!"

From the condition of the pixie's camera, Gwen could only assume that her phone had suffered worse, but there was no way her best friend was willing to go long with no means of connecting to the outside world. Gwen thanked the mortal, who was huffing in annoyance at how long she held his phone captive and handed it back. She was lucky to find anyone willing to help, however reluctantly, at this hour. The fishermen were already out on the water, and the recreational boaters were still in bed.

Boats swayed in the early morning light. In the distance, she could just make out the Graves lighthouse, a beacon to bring ships in from the harbor, and a sentry watching over the temporary seat of the four Seelie Thrones. Gwen shook her head. She never thought she'd see the day the Seelie Court was brought to this. On one hand, it made her sad, but on the other, she had far more pressing worries.

There was no sign of Chessa at the marina. From inside the box, she'd been unable to see much of her surroundings, so she wasn't sure where to start. Her empathic touch was useless because there was nothing to run her hands over to attempt to pick up sensory data. That didn't stop her from trying. She spent the morning hours scouring the marina, touching every surface she could, all to no avail. Once she was satisfied that there was nothing to find here, she ducked around a corner, pulled out her wand, and shrunk once more in a blink of light before darting into the air and flying toward Chessa's apartment in the theater district.

Gwen lost track of time, but the booming sound of The Misfits being blasted over a PA told her it must be Punk Thursday at the club that occupied the lower level of the warehouse. Damn, they started early. Or maybe it was later than she thought. Either way, she could never understand how the pixie got a moment's rest. Chessa always said that silence was far more distracting and that the thumping beats helped her focus. Gwen zipped up to the rafters and ran her hand along the familiar red pipe outside the door. The senses that flooded in were at least a week old. Shit. Gwen used her key to open the place and made a beeline for Chessa's laptop, which was sitting on the tiny roll-away desk under the only window in the living space, its battery depleted. Another bad sign. She rattled off an email to Chessa, but she couldn't risk putting any sensitive information in it, knowing full well her mother would be hunting her down with the entire weight of the

Seelie Court at her back, not to mention whoever was killing off her family.

Chess, Shoot me a message when you can. I need to know you're okay.

Gwen switched over to Messenger to see if Samson was online. He was the only creature she could count on for backup, but it was now the middle of the night, and he was predictably signed out. She sent him a message anyway:

Hey. I need to talk to you. I don't have my phone. I'm heading to your place now.

After locking up, Gwen was halfway to Samson's on the upper west side when stabbing cramps reminded her that a body can't survive on air alone. The sun was already setting, and she couldn't remember the last thing she ate. She would have pressed on, but a Wallow World sign caught her eye. A 24-hour store where she could snag a sandwich and a secure, prepaid phone was too good to pass up, even if it was universally known that the chain was owned and operated by a branch of the Unseelie who thrived on tormenting people with long lines, disorganized shelves, and poor service. The Seelie equivalent was already closed for the night, though shopping at a store with a bullseye logo would fit her current situation in a fucked up, ironic way. Wallow World it was.

Gwen waited in the electronics department for what felt like an eternity. She flagged down two separate employees, who both claimed they didn't work in the department. She convinced the second one to get on the intercom and request an associate to help her before he left her standing in the aisle glaring at the sandwich in her hand. Finally, a teenage brownie reeking of weed slogged up to her. "Oh, hey, I didn't know you were fae or I would have been here ten minutes ago," he drawled. "Oh, right, no I wouldn't have."

Gwen ground her teeth. The brownie only had six inches on her, and she was sure she could take him, but starting a fight in a Wallow World was not the way to avoid detection. Hell, there was an entire social media account dedicated to videos of Wallow World brawls. The clerk's beady, bloodshot eyes seemed to dare her to take the bait. Instead, she paid for the sandwich and the best prepaid phone she could afford, the Moto-something-or-other, and left, thankful her accessories size-shifted with her. The entire ordeal set her back at least an hour, and her new phone told her it was nearly ten when she flew up to Samson's apartment building, wiping mayo from her mouth with the back of her hand. She was sure she swallowed a bug or two, but that was the risk of eating on the fly.

Blue and red lights illuminated the block, bouncing off neighboring buildings. Humans scurried like ants below where a dozen or more emergency vehicles clogged the streets. Firefighters, EMTs, and police officers ran in and out of the building, shouting orders or calling for backup. The ten-story building was in shambles. A crater was blown out of one side. What remained was reduced to a pile of blackened brick rubble. Gwen nearly choked on the thick smoke in the air, but she pressed closer. Screaming from somewhere inside the wreckage melted into the chaos of emergency workers pulling survivors to safety. She landed on a windowsill across the alley and counted windows until she determined where Sammy's place should be. 8th floor, fourth window from the end. The epicenter of the crater.

"No!" Gwen screamed and kicked off the wall. There was no breath in her body as she hurtled toward the chasm that was once her friend's apartment. She wasn't sure what she was hoping to find. No creature could survive whatever happened here. Smoke and soot made her gag as she entered the space. There was no sign of the griffin. Sweat beaded on Gwen's forehead from the radiant heat and her eyes watered. She didn't know if was from the soot or from the heart. Samson had always been there for her, through everything, and now he was gone.

Voices from the next apartment over snapped her out of it. A child was crying. With a last look around Samson's demolished, empty apartment, Gwen pulled out her wand and changed to human-size with a flick and a burst of light. She tucked the wand back into its holster at her thigh, opened the apartment door, and ran up the hall.

Most of the other doors were ajar, likely left that way when the occupants fled, but the one at the end of the hall was still closed. Gwen took the gamble. The smoke got thicker as she approached the threshold, and she had to give the door a solid kick with her Docs to get it open. The influx of oxygen caused flames to explode outward, making Gwen dive back into the hall.

"Where are you?" called Gwen, but there was no answer. She would have to go in blind. She pulled her shirt over her nose and mouth and shrunk back to fairy size to get below the smoke. Sticking to the inner wall where the flames had yet to reach, she moved fast from one room to the next. In the back corner of one of the bedrooms, she found a small boy curled into the fetal position. She zapped herself back into large form, scooped up the child, and fled on foot.

Gwen emerged from the building holding the small form in her arms. He was still breathing. "Thank Danu," she muttered as she handed the child over to an EMT, who gaped at the random woman exiting the inferno.

"Who are you?" he asked, then followed with a "Wait! No! Stop!" when she turned and ran back in. She shrunk back down to her natural size and zipped through the building, searching for survivors. Once she was sure nobody else was inside, she left without waiting around to hear the death toll. The sun was rising, and news trucks were pressing in on the tape. It was time to go.

Exhausted, defeated, and with lungs full of smoke, Gwen stood in the alleyway. She desperately needed a shower and a bottle of water. She couldn't go home, and Samson's place was a no-fly zone now. The sun cresting the horizon, Gwen looked up at what remained of the demolished building. From the damage, it was obvious the fire started at Samson's. The implications sent a chill down her spine. Had she not been delayed so long at Wallow World, Gwen would have been blown to smithereens along with her mentor and friend. She ducked behind a dumpster and threw up. "I'm so sorry, Sammy," she whispered.

Her mother might be awful, but she was right about one thing. Someone was out to get her. They got to Samson because they somehow knew Gwen was going to visit him. They could be watching her at this very moment. She had to stay entirely off the grid.

12

I wish I had my laptop," said Chessa, not for the first time. She spent the night and the better part of the day on Laural's couch, but when she checked her email from her cousin's computer an hour before heading to the airport, there was still nothing from Gwen. She absently thumbed through the papers she'd printed, research on fae life in the UK.

"I know, kid," replied Samson.

Everyone on the plane seemed suspicious to Chessa. She and Samson had the row to themselves. She didn't need much room, even under the glamour that made her appear human, but Samson required two of the three seats and still encroached on Chessa's space. The lack of others in their row didn't take off the edge. At ease in most any situation, she wasn't used to being this jumpy. Everywhere she looked, she swore someone was staring at her. There was the old witch in 22B and the humanoid male in the hideous tie that could only belong to a bogie in 14A. A fairy couple who looked to be on their honeymoon in 10B and C kept glancing back at her. The most suspicious, by far, was the flight attendant, smiling with perfect red lips every time Chessa looked up. But she couldn't be a Seelie Court spy. She was mortal and didn't have the telltale signs of a witch or sorceress—no pentacles, sigils, or sparks. Chessa laughed at herself. The fae would see Chessa and Samson as they were, but humans without magic would see only what they expected thanks to simple minds and the work of the Glamour Squadron.

"Damn kid, you're making me as nervous as a Pop-Tart by the toaster," said Samson. The armrest between his two seats was up to make room for his lion-sized rear end, but the mortals saw him as a large man who was forced to pay double to fly, and they treated him with disgust thinly veiled by put-on politeness. Chessa would never understand human sociology—how a person who looked even a tad bit different could draw such ire—especially one as friendly and kind as Samson. Thankfully, few were as observant as Chessa when it came to matters of the mind and heart. Samson didn't seem to notice.

"Sorry, Sammy. I know I'm being silly," she replied. "It's just—"

"I know. I feel it too." He patted her leg as gently as he could with a talon then went back to scrolling the news on his phone.

"Please shut down your electronic items, stow your carry-on items beneath the seat in front of you, and return your seats to their upright positions," chimed a cheerful voice over the intercom system. "We are preparing for take-off."

Samson tucked his phone in his pocket and gave Chessa a little smile. She buckled the lap belt over her tiny frame, clicking it into place, and tried to put her paranoia to rest. If anyone was keeping tabs on them, she couldn't do much about it now. She covered her lap with the cheap airline blanket and stuffed the pillow they provided behind her. It was going to be a long flight.

Ten hours after arriving at the airport in Boston, Chessa and Samson were on the ground in Bristol. It was already late afternoon on the 15th thanks to the time change, and Chessa couldn't imagine being ready to sleep again in a few hours. It felt like it was all she'd done since Gwen was taken. Samson snored for most of the flight, so they were both rested up enough to take on whatever threats waited in Avalon. The airport was filled with fae, not that the few mortals littering the waiting areas noticed. Chessa smirked at how much they missed.

A troll was devouring a bucket of fried chicken in a dark corner, young sprites zipped around the fluorescent lights, their father yelling "Sit down this instant!" in a futile attempt to control them, and an enormous half-eagle, half-lion wearing red spectacles strolled down the walkway beside her. Whenever she was in populous areas, the humor of all this existing right in front of the mortals' faces struck Chessa. "Hey, Samson, give me your phone," she said. Being out of communication for so long made her twitchy.

Samson handed her a dinosaur of a Blackberry as they walked through baggage claim, but she didn't comment. It wasn't like she had anything better. When it finally started up and Chessa was able to access her email, she was shocked to see a message from Gwen. "Samson, look!"

The griffin stopped, and a human man ran into his backside. The mortal muttered an apology and moved on.

Chessa screwed up her face as she read the message from Gwen aloud. "Do you think it's a trap?" she asked.

"Could be. Keep your cards close. Don't let them get a jump on us."

"My thoughts *almost* exactly." Chessa pulled up her trusty VPN service and shot an anonymous email back to Gwen.

I'm okay. Catch up soon.

"Did she send anything to you?" asked Chessa, knowing full well Samson would be the first person Gwen would go to for help in her absence.

"Not that I know of," he replied. "I was playing Sudoku while you were sawing logs, and now you've got my phone."

"That's not how I remember it," Chessa said, tossing his Blackberry back to him.

Samson's talons clicked the keys more deftly than Chessa would expect. "Holy smoking gun," he muttered. "It appears that I'm homeless and half of Korranthia thinks I'm in the meat locker."

Chessa grabbed Samson's arm and guided him to the side of the thoroughfare so they would catch fewer dirty glares for blocking traffic. "What are you talking about?"

Samson tutted and shook his head. "My inbox is fuller than a ghoul on All Hallows. Someone blew up my apartment."

"They did what?" Chessa snatched the Blackberry back and

gawked at the photo of the pile of rubble that was once a ten-story apartment building. Her mouth fell open. "I hope everyone got out okay."

"Yeah, me too."

If this didn't drive home just how far in over their heads they were, nothing would. "Samson, we've got to get her." Chessa expected Samson to back out or freak out, but he did neither.

His eyes were misty as he snapped the device shut. "I think it's best if the world believes I'm dead. Let's get our girl."

"If this goes south, I don't think we can count on your buddy Pox to bust us all free." Chessa's pace quickened as they stepped out of the terminal into the daylight. "Samson, why would her own family kidnap her? They're not exactly the Brady Bunch, but the guy I was tracking was no joke. Why would Gwen's own family send someone like that after her? And why would they blow up your place?"

"Your guess is as good as mine. There's a lot going on at pay grades much higher than mine, kid, that much I learned early in my career. Usually, I keep my head down, and I don't catch no flies."

Chessa couldn't bring herself to be amused by his expressions. "I'm sorry I dragged you into this."

"You can't drag a bulldozer up a mountain, kid."

She got the gist of his point. No sane pixie would infiltrate the Seelie Court to rescue a kidnapped fairy, but when it came to Gwen, Chessa wasn't sane. And neither was Samson.

"I don't know if they've got a Glamour Squad or what in these parts, so we'd better be careful," said Samson.

"With all these other fae around, I doubt we'll draw much notice. They must have some system for cloaking, or the poor humans would have lost their minds by now. Let me check the travelogue." Chessa reached into her back pocket out of habit. Damn, she missed her phone.

Thankfully, the Seelie Council was big on keeping the existence of fae under wraps. The Travelogue was a database that helped fae blend in by providing information regarding regional customs and procedures, and kiosks were installed in all airports, train stations, and bus terminals all over the world in order to make it accessible. Chessa located one near Baggage Claim. With a few keystrokes, she learned the highlights of fae travel in and around the Kingdom of Avalon, which, according to the database had extended around Avalon proper to include all of the UK. It operated on a similar system to Korranthia. Fairy glamours were utilized to cloak magical essences, but instead of a workforce, they hinged on the talents of a highly specialized cabinet of wizards who amplified a broad cloaking glamour generated by a few fairies working in shifts from an undisclosed location. "Well, that certainly is efficient," Chessa said before explaining the system to Samson.

"What happens if that location is exposed? If there were an attack—"

Chessa concluded, "Then the entire fae community would be exposed." She shuddered. "Let's hope that doesn't happen. In the meantime, it seems we're free to be ourselves. So, Mr. Griffin, can I catch a ride?"

AN HOUR LATER, Samson landed in a field just outside Glastonbury. Cloaking glamour or not, Chessa thought a giant lion-eagle touching down in the center of town might ruffle a few feathers, pun intended. Humans would see them as something that fit their world view—a couple paragliding on holiday or something— but fae would see through the glamour and word would spread about their arrival. She let go of the fistfuls of feathers she clung to and flitted to the ground. She was accustomed to flying in quick, low altitude bursts, and after the plane ride followed by the griffin express, she was ready to have her feet on the solid ground again. "Let's head into town, grab some grub, and figure out how we're going to get an audience with the Seelie royals," she suggested.

"I could eat," agreed Samson.

The town of Glastonbury was brimming with fae, but the vibe was far less friendly than the airport had been. Instead of creatures bustling about their lives, they milled around, casting suspicious glances as Samson and Chessa made their way through the streets.

"It doesn't feel right here," said Chessa.

"You got that right kid. Have you seen one mortal since we got here?"

Come to think of it, she hadn't. The entire town was filled with fae, some even humanoid—ogres, sorcerers, brownies, pixies, witches, fairies, even the occasional griffin or harpy—but not a single mortal. "That is beyond strange," replied Chessa "Even this close to Avalon."

Beyond the behavior and species make-up of the town, there was something else niggling at her. Children. There were no children anywhere. "Samson, I think we should leave," she said as a group of four uniformed fairies appeared a block away. They were moving in tight formation, their attention focused on Chessa and Samson.

"Get on," growled Samson.

Chessa zipped onto Samson's back, and he pushed off with a great heave. One moment they were airborne, the next they were plummeting back down toward the pavement. Chessa opened her wings and flapped furiously, attempting to keep herself aloft, but a hand grabbed her ankle, pulling her downward. The power of a source stick coursed through her body, like electricity sparking between her cells, rendering her body weak.

She'd never been hit with a source stick before. It was a weapon used to subdue fae, and it scrambled their magic. Gwen described it once as a seizing of muscles and a feeling of being cut off from a part of herself. But Gwen was a fairy, a user of magic as well as a magical creature. It was different for pixies, creatures of magic with no control over it. For her, it was like all reasoning dissipated as her body crumpled to the ground. Blackness closed in, and the last thing Chessa saw was Samson's giant form sprawled on the pavement beside her.

13

June 15
5 days until the Summer Solstice

Staying off the grid meant Gwen shouldn't be heading to the KPD, but if there was even a sliver of a chance that Samson escaped the fire, she had to know. The precinct parking lot was empty save for the street cars of the officers out on duty. She snuck by the rookie cop, Pox if she remembered correctly, at the front desk, and made her way to Sammy's office.

The door was closed and the lights were off. Fuck.

A light at the end of the hall told her Captain O'Toole was in. She swallowed the lump in her throat and made her way to his door. She came this far. She might as well get the confirmation she sought. As she brushed the door handle, her empathic magic sparked. She took a deep breath and opened her mind.

The only image she picked up was as clear as flames in the night. Indira's face. Her mother had been here. How much did O'Toole know?

He must have heard her at the door. "Come in," he called.

Gwen closed her eyes for a moment and steeled herself before stepping through the door. "Captain," she greeted, putting on her best manners. Goading O'Toole was a favorite pastime, but now was not the moment for it.

"You," hissed the captain. His blue eyes narrowed, and a small flame ignited in his palm. Why anyone thought a quick-tempered sorcerer would be a good police captain was beyond Gwen's understanding. "You were there. At the fire. What are you doing here?"

"I need to know if..."

"If you got my best detective killed? Is that it?"

Gwen wanted to scream at him. He'd never shown Samson a bit of respect, never once told him he was a good cop. "Is Samson—Sergeant Detective Wayne—is he alive?"

"Your guess is as good as mine. Do you want to tell me why I haven't seen Sergeant Wayne all week? And why his apartment was attacked? And what the fuck you were doing on site? What is going on here, Miss Evenshine?"

Every bit of hope she harbored evaporated, leaving Gwen empty and angry. If Samson wasn't here, he was dead. She didn't bother to respond to O'Toole's attacks. If he already knew she was there, he would be looking to pin it all on her. Again. Instead, she turned and flew down the hall and out the front door.

"Hey, wait!" yelled Officer Pox just before the door slammed. The young cop threatened her in the past out of some misplaced anger and loyalty to his mentor, her friend. She didn't want to stick around and hear his accusations too.

They were all right, even if they didn't know the full story. She got Samson killed just like she got Corrin killed. And that wasn't even the worst of it. If whoever was keeping tabs on her knew about Samson, she'd bet her life they would know about Chessa too. Everyone Gwen cared about was in danger. Thankfully, it was a short list. The pixie was still MIA, and going back to her own place would be suicide. Losing Sammy was too much to process. She wasn't sure she could survive getting blamed for it.

But it was my fault, she thought.

Her stomach flipped over again, but there was nothing left to expel. Showing up to the KPD covered in blood and soot had been a mistake, even if O'Toole had already placed her at the scene. All she did was confirm her involvement. The only place Gwen could think to go now was Laural's. The healer witch hated her almost as much as O'Toole did, but she'd offer a place to get cleaned up and regroup while Gwen figured out her next move, if nothing else, at least as a favor to Chessa. She might even help heal the dehydration and smoke inhalation damage. Gwen had to figure out who was killing her family. More importantly, she had to find the pixie. Maybe Laural would have heard something. Gwen had already faced Indira and Liam, and she would face a thousand Laurals for a single lead at this point.

Laural opened the door before Gwen made it up the sidewalk. "You dare set foot on my property."

It was a statement, not a question. Laural's eyes flashed red, and Gwen stopped in her tracks. She knew a part of Laural blamed her for Corrin's death, and her inner demon agreed, but at this point, who didn't? Corrin was the medical examiner, and he stumbled onto the Brain Scraper's identity through his own investigation, even if he was only on the case because of Gwen's obsession. Chessa tried to remind both of them that it wasn't Gwen's fault time and again, but it did nothing to clear the air. "I'm sorry to bring up old memories by coming here, but I didn't know where else to go," she replied.

Slowly the brilliant gold returned to Laural's eyes. "You're a mess," she said before turning around and walking back into the house. She left the door open behind her, so Gwen followed, wondering if it would be the witch or the demon awaiting her inside.

But Gwen found neither. Laural was back in the kitchen doing Danu knew what, so Gwen shut the door behind her and lurked in the sitting room off to the right. She'd only been in the house a handful of times and not once since Corrin was gone. The space was quieter without his clever, goodhearted banter. A few minutes later, the witch returned with an armful of supplies which she unceremoniously dumped on the couch. Gwen spotted a scrying mirror and wondered what Laural was up to.

"Thanks for letting me in. I didn't know where else to go. I'm being hunted, and I need to find Chessa. I need to make sure she's okay."

Laural didn't make eye contact. Instead, she focused on messing around with the items she brought, picking through and setting some on the small table, an altar of some sort, in the center of the room while casting others aside.

"Chessa was here three days ago. She was banged up pretty badly. I gathered that you had something to do with it, of course." She cast a glare in Gwen's direction, but her eyes remained golden. "Stand still."

Gwen did as she was told. The witch circled her, waving her arms as if wafting smoke away. Gwen collapsed into a coughing fit while Laural stood over her.

"Better?" asked the witch once Gwen regained her composure.

She did feel better. At least, every breath didn't sear any longer. She nodded and righted herself but didn't offer thanks. Instead, she got right back to the point. "She was here? So she's okay. Thank Danu."

"No," snapped Laural. "Thank me. She was hurt more than she let on. It took me two whole days to recover from the healing I gave her."

Gwen bit her lip. How badly had Chessa been hurt to take that much energy out of Laural? At least she was alive. "I'm so sorry." Gwen took a step forward, but Laural moved away.

She sighed and sat back down on the edge of the fireplace. As she did, her fingertips brushed the edge of the white brick, and her vision faltered. She drifted into blackness, but instead of fighting it like she did in her younger days, she embraced it, desperate for a glimpse of Chessa. She let it invade and bring a flood of sensations.

The sensory data materialized in the way it always did, one impression melting into another, all disparate but somehow connected to the place Gwen was touching. The smell of a fire on a cold night, Corrin's cologne, Laural's laughter, the taste of an Irish coffee, Samson's large eyes watching something transpire in the center of the room.

Gwen gasped and the world came back into focus. "Samson was here?" she choked. "When?"

"I told you, three days ago. He was here with Chessa."

"Are you sure?"

Laural's eyes narrowed. "No, I imagined a seven-foot-tall griffin in my living room."

"And he left with her too? He wasn't at his place last night?" Gwen's voice sounded foreign to her own ears, but Laural didn't seem to notice. "He's not dead?"

"He wasn't three days ago. As far as I could tell, he was sticking with Chessa. He's friends with you, so Danu knows what's become of him now," replied the witch. "Do not invade my privacy again," she tacked on.

Gwen hadn't technically broken fae custom since she hadn't read Laural herself, but she shouldn't be using her touch on the house either. It was rude. Knowing that Samson was with Chessa rather than turned into Kentucky Fried Griffin made it all worth it. "I can no more control my empathic touch than you can control the demon inside of you."

As the words left her mouth, Gwen realized her mistake. Laural's eyes flashed red again, and she began to levitate.

"Laural, I'm sorry. You can control him. You do it every day. I know you're in there, Laural," she pleaded.

A voice reverberated through the room. "You will mind your manners in this house or I shall barbecue you and feed you to the witch. She hungers for vengeance." Laural's body floated toward Gwen with an outstretched, red, bony hand. Fire ignited in the palm before it went out and Laural fell to the ground. "Why is it," she gasped, "that you cannot be here for five minutes before incurring his wrath?"

"I have that effect on people," said Gwen. But her voice didn't carry the levity of her words.

A tense moment passed as Gwen tried not to cough from the acrid stench filling the room, then Laural began to laugh. It was the type of laughter that filled a room. Gwen couldn't help but smile tentatively, waiting for the other shoe to drop. It didn't. Laural turned and finished setting up her altar. "What are you doing?" asked Gwen.

"Setting up a scrying spell. You are looking for my cousin, right?

My talents may lie in healing, but that doesn't mean I can't pull off a simple locator spell on a relative."

"Oh." Gwen's mouth went dry. This was more than she'd hoped for. "Thank you, Laural. The people after me are no joke. If they know she exists, she's in grave danger. And that's not even taking my family into consideration."

"What does the Seelie Royal Family have to do with this?" asked Laural, tension gripping her shoulders once again.

"They're the ones who shot her out of the sky. They abducted me. It's a long story."

Laural shook her head. "Why are you always at the center of turbulence? You may not mean to be, but you are dangerous, Gwendolyn Evenshine."

"Tell me about it."

Laural instructed Gwen to stand in front of the scrying mirror as she began her ritual. She cast a circle, called upon the elements to power her magic, and invoked a dual-natured deity before opening a tiny vial and dripping the contents onto the tiny mirror in the center of the altar. She called out an invocation and smeared the red droplets across the smooth surface. Gwen wondered what the substance was but thought better of interrupting the ritual. Instead, she gazed into the mirror as she'd been instructed to do. She saw nothing but smears.

"Gwen, I call on you to use your power on the mirror," said Laural.

Gwen hadn't been expecting this part. She stared at the witch dumbly. Laural returned her gaze. "You cannot lie to me in my circle. You control your touch, so I tell you to use it now."

Gwen pressed her forefinger onto the glass, took a deep breath, and lowered her defenses. The blackness crept in once again, but this time, the sensation of falling was replaced with a magnetism, as if her essence were being drawn into the mirror. Her vision changed from blackness to smeared red, and she suspected she was seeing through the mirror from the other direction. Eventually, the image cleared to show a large hill. No, not a hill. A tor. She was looking at her ancestral homeland. The tor of Glastonbury. Avalon.

Gradually, the image faded back into smeared glass, and Gwen felt her magic snap back into her body. She sat in silence as Laural gave thanks to the energies who'd offered their assistance, dismissed the deity, and dispelled the protective circle.

"I didn't know you were going to have me add my own magic," said Gwen. "What was that?"

"All I did was create a link for you. With my cousin's blood, I might have been able to scry a little, but it would have been as foggy as the senses you pick up. Your gifts made the mirror a portal, and you were able to see whatever was around Chessa at this exact moment. What was it?"

Gwen swallowed, and her mouth went dry. "Avalon."

Laural's head cocked slightly to the side. "She must have figured out that you were with your family and decided to head to the Seelie capital. What's so bad about that?"

Gwen fought back the panic. She didn't want to tell Laural that she'd endangered the only person left in her life connecting her to Corrin. And she hadn't even managed to figure out what the danger was. She opened her mouth to speak, but nothing came out.

Laural's eyes snapped red then gold. "Just say it."

Gwen closed her eyes. When she opened them, the witch was sitting on the couch staring at her. The look on her face told Gwen she was doing everything she could to hold back the demon inside. Maybe being eaten by a demon would be a faster way to locate her best friend. Gwen decided to rip off the band-aid.

"My family in Avalon is dead. Those who escaped are in hiding. Chessa is flying into a trap."

14

Through the window of the truck Chessa was loaded into, she could see the top of the tor of Glastonbury. Mortals would see a ragged hill crowned with the ruins of a tower, but the glamour hid an entire isle, Avalon, a gateway to the land of Faerie if legend was to be believed. Chessa believed it. She could feel the pull of magic from here. She couldn't believe *this* was how she was going to visit the most powerful place in the mortal realm, with her hands zip-tied to her ankles. In this position, she couldn't hope to fly, even once her magic settled from the blow of the source stick. She was pretty sure that was the point. Some kind of divider separated her from the driver, though there were holes drilled into it so she could hear his heavy breathing. Nobody in good spirits breathed that way, fae or human.

Samson had been dragged into the back, and they were now bumping along an uneven road toward the epicenter of Seelie power. Something was wrong—other than being smacked with a source stick and abducted. None of the guards were wearing Seelie purple and gold, or any uniforms at all for that matter, and they didn't speak or act with any sense of authority. Rather, they felt like a ragtag crew who would be more at home slinging cards at Pub Nine than serving a royal family.

Perhaps they're undercover, Chessa thought, but her gut told her otherwise. She knew to trust the inner voice telling her that she and Samson were in way over their heads. She didn't know what to do about it at the moment, but she decided to gather as much intel as possible. Information was power.

The holes in the divider gave Chessa a partial view of a wizard if the beard and hat were any indication. In the old world, magical practitioners, those who would be human without their powers, were considered barely more valuable than mortals, and this man seemed to be treated as such by the fairies—at least the way the fairy barked orders at him made Chessa believe as much. She hadn't seen where the four fairies disappeared to after she got tossed into the vehicle, but she assumed at least some of them must be in the back with Samson.

If Chessa knew anything, it was that every being had a story. If she could discover the wizard's, she might learn something that would tip the scales in her favor. "Hey there," she called. The wizard didn't take his eyes off the road. "Any chance you can tell me where we're headed?"

No response.

She tried again. "My name's Chessa, and if you can't tell by my accent, I'm from Korranthia. I'm here looking for a friend. I'm not sure what I did to land in this situation, whatever it is, but I'm sure it's a misunderstanding."

Still nothing.

"At least tell me what I should call you."

"Name's Norman. I don't think them fairies be fuckin' around when they told me not to consort with you, though, so that's all I'll be saying." He didn't speak with the posh accent Chessa expected from the fae of Avalon. It was rougher, closer to the Cockney dialect she heard in movies.

"I wish we were meeting under better circumstances Norman. You seem a right honorable fellow."

The wizard bowed his head slightly. If he did see himself as lesser, then Chessa held some status over him, even if he was instructed to keep her at a distance. She wasn't ready to give up.

"I understand you not wanting to go against your orders. They didn't seem the type you want to cross," she said, keeping the cheerful note in her voice.

"You got no idea," replied Norman. "I'm sorry they got ya, little miss."

"I won't lie, being abducted isn't the way I envisioned my vacation going. Though I suppose we'll be on our way as soon as things get cleared up, right Norman?"

Chessa knew there was no misunderstanding. This plan of hers was dangerous from the outset, but her gut told her there was more going on than a few angry Seelie royals. She was hoping she could figure out what.

"I wouldn't be expecting so if I was in your position. These ain't your run-of-the-mill fae like you're accustomed to, I'd wager."

"Oh, I run with all sorts. I've got this friend back home named Quincy. He's a bit rough around the edges but with a heart of gold. It's just not in his chest where it should be. You have to know where to look for it. Nobody is all good or all bad."

"Little miss, these back there, they're all bad. You take my word for it, a'right? Here we are."

"Norman, before we go, can I ask you one question? If they're so bad, why do you work for them?"

"Ain't got no choice. Ain't welcome anywhere else on account of my family. It was join this lot or live solitary. I just ain't made to go it alone."

His words hit Chessa hard. Nobody should be held responsible for the actions of others, family or not. "Norman, I know we just met, but I want you to know that you deserve to be happy."

The wizard smiled, confusion touching his eyes. The passenger side door opened, and one of the fairies from the village fluttered to stand on the seat next to Chessa. She struggled against her bonds, suddenly painfully aware of how vulnerable she was.

"Take this spy into the foyer," he said, giving the truck a little kick.

Spy? Who did these people think she was? Who could she possibly be spying for, or on for that matter? All she'd done so far was set foot in the little town of Glastonbury. Who in the name of Danu were these fairies?

"Yes, sir. Don't you need me to help with the other 'un?" asked Norman.

"Your place isn't to ask questions, *human*. Do as I say." The little prick was off without so much as a word to Chessa.

The wizard walked around the truck and hoisted Chessa into his arms. As she was the size of a small mortal child, it didn't take much for him to carry her, but she made a mental note of his gentleness.

The truck was parked on a gravel drive that ended where a wall began. Chessa could sense a glamour in place, stronger than the slight twinge that covered Glastonbury and the airport, shielding all within from the mortal gaze, but to her and all other fae, the tower on top of Avalon was an expansive palace surrounded by a wall with gates aligned with the cardinal directions. Power emanated from each and every stone. She'd seen depictions of Avalon in fae art, but nothing beat the sight in person, even if she was being unceremoniously carried by a wizard. Chessa wondered briefly if Norman could feel Avalon in his blood the way she did or if the mortal side of him robbed him of its beauty.

An ogre and some kind of rock creature emerged from the gate near where they were parked, one carrying two large pairs of shackles, one with a length of rope slung over one shoulder and a source stick in her boulder of a hand. Poor Samson was in for it.

Chessa winced, but there was no way she could help her friend now. The best she could do was focus on chipping away at Norman. The wizard's long, grey beard tickled her cheek as he carried her.

"So this is Avalon," she said, taking in the palace silhouetted by the setting sun.

He grunted in reply.

"I guess you're used to it."

"It's beautiful, I suppose, especially the sacred grove on the west end."

According to the histories, the grove was the most powerful part of the isle, the trees having sprung from the earth with no aid, human or fae. Supposedly, it was the origin point of all fae, the place where the mythical realm of Faerie first opened into this world before the portal sealed forever. If Norman was drawn to it, he must wield enough magic to cut through the glamour. Most magical practitioners did. That made his demeanor even sadder to Chessa, that he could stand before a place like this and still be so wretched. "Norman, your family's actions don't reflect on you. I'm sure if you petitioned the Seelie Court, they would see that as clearly as I do."

"You're very kind, little miss, but at this point, I've done things meself to keep them from ever putting faith in me. I'm in too deep. Don't be sad for me. I don't deserve it. You should be more concerned for yourself."

He gingerly set her on a bench just inside the enormous door, her back leaning against the wall to help keep her upright in her awkward, bound position. As he turned his back to walk away, Chessa sighed. She might be saying these things to break down the wizard's defenses, but she truly believed them. Nobody was ever too far gone to turn their lives around, not really. But it didn't look like she was going to get a chance to convince him. "You take care, Norman," she said quietly.

As the wizard disappeared into the building, the front door swung open again. Samson was shoved through by the goons Chessa saw on her way in. He never looked more a beast than in that moment. His big, yellow eyes rolled. His spectacles had fallen off sometime during the transport. His beak gaped open and closed as if he were gasping for air. Shackles bound his talons and hind legs together, and rope secured his wings to his torso. He thrashed, pure muscle and feathered fury. His two captors struggled to keep him confined. Gone was the mild-mannered detective who fell back on hardboiled slang to try to impress those around him. In his place was a true creature of legend.

Chessa's heart fell into her stomach seeing him this way. "Samson!" she called out, hoping to calm or reach the griffin she knew. At her voice, his beak parted and a guttural roar escaped. A screech, she would have expected, but this was something else. The lion inside him coming alive.

"Samson!" she cried again.

But he was gone, shoved through the same door Norman disappeared through moments before.

Chessa was left alone in the expansive foyer with nothing but stone walls and cold, impassive statuary for company.

15

Laural probably hated Gwen more than ever. After getting Corrin, the husband who served as both her link to the world at large and her buffer from it, killed, she put Chessa, the witch's only surviving family member, in danger. Gwen couldn't worry about that now. She had to figure out who took Avalon. Whoever it was, they were merciless killers, and Chessa had gone in alone, probably half-cocked with the idea that she'd storm the palace and pull Gwen out. She didn't stand a chance. The pixie was so careful in her regular life of hunting down leads and discovering juicy stories, but her history of throwing caution to the wind when her people were in danger scared the shit out of Gwen.

The problem was, Gwen didn't know where to start. Her wings were strong, but not enough to fly halfway around the world, over the ocean, and she doubted she would get within half a mile of Glastonbury by regular means. Not while being hunted by two powerful groups, one of which probably used the town as a stronghold. She wasn't sure which she was more afraid of—the usurpers or usurped. The future of the Seelie Court and Chessa's continued existence hinged on her figuring out who was slaughtering the Seelie royal family. Why the hell were the stakes always so high? All she ever wanted was a movie night, a bottle of Jack, and a damn sandwich. She was nothing but an ex-fairy godmother with stunted magic, but now she was fifth in line for the Seelie throne, and existence as she knew it depended on her next move.

"Fuck!" she screamed.

At least ten heads turned to stare at her.

Way to keep a low profile, she thought as she walked down the dark Korranthia street with iron purpose and no destination. It was late, but she couldn't sleep. She didn't have the first clue where to begin untangling this mess. Chessa would know. Was Chessa even alive? Gwen pushed the thought back in her head as she considered what the pixie would do in her position.

Recon. That's what Chessa would do. When you don't have enough information to move forward, go back and dig up more. It was a hard lesson for Gwen, who was always pressing forward and kicking ass. Chessa was the brains, not her. If it were a local situation, Chessa would hit up her informants over at Pub Nine or one of the back alleys along the harbor, tapping into her cloaked whisper network, but this was beyond the street urchins of Boston. Even that wouldn't stop her, Gwen knew. Chessa was resourceful. She would use what she had, even when that was just a broken fairy without a clue. And ties to an establishment with its fingers in many pies—the Academy.

Gwen was never comfortable at the Academy for Fairy Godparents. At first, she was the black sheep royal running away from her duties. Later she was the underperforming reluctant apprentice, and finally, she was the rogue, on a mission for vengeance. Now that she'd taken down the Brain Scraper, it was worse. Now she was the savior.

She flew to the Academy, fighting the butterflies in her stomach as she approached the gate and announced herself. She knew better than to fly right in. Gwen had been back countless times since her showdown with Celeste, but every time she approached the wall, she felt like she was watching Chessa plummet to the ground all over again.

"Lady Evenshine! Welcome!" The bright voice coming from the call box snapped Gwen back into the present. The buzzer sounded, and the gate swung open.

Different day, same life and death scenario, she thought. She zipped through the gate, down the long drive lined with dead trees, up the stairs, and into the sprawling mansion that served as the heart of the campus.

Matron West, the current Head Matron of the Academy, waited for her. "We've missed you this week! This is a strange hour. To what do we owe the pleasure?" she asked with an uncertain smile. The fairy was doing a fair job considering the difficulties she inherited. It wasn't easy to fill the shoes of the former saint of Korranthia, Matron Celeste Erinyes, philanthropist, activist, and serial killer.

"I know it's after curfew, but I didn't know where else to go," said Gwen, feeling like a novice once again.

"Curfew only applies to students, and the Academy is always at your service. What can we do for you?"

Gwen looked around the empty hall. There were no fairies, students or otherwise, about at night. Gwen remembered how strictly rules like curfew were enforced, and it felt strange walking down the hall at this hour. She doubted she'd ever feel secure in this building, but she could at least limit the chance of eavesdroppers. "Let's go to your office."

When they got to Matron West's office, an unassuming ground-floor chamber unlike the sprawling tower office of her predecessor, Gwen settled onto the small, brown leather couch and waited for the elder fairy to take her place behind the desk before getting straight to the point. "My family is being killed off, and I was hoping you might have heard something about it."

Matron West gasped. "Killed off? We've received reports of turmoil in Avalon, but we were unaware of any killings. The Queen?"

"Dead. Along with many others. I wouldn't risk telling you if I didn't think you'd keep quiet about it, but my relationship with the Academy hasn't always been great, and I don't have time to play games. Please, Matron West, tell me if you know anything."

The Matron sat with her head in her hands. "The Queen is dead. How can that be? Who will lead us?"

"They were ambushed at the Gathering. But that's not what's

important right now. I'm trying to figure out who is responsible so we can stop this."

"I'm sorry, my dear. I'm so sorry for your loss. I'm sorry for all our losses. Queen Estrella was a great woman. Is Felippe now king?"

The Matron was now openly crying. Great. Just great. It wasn't time to mourn, it was time to act. Gwen was wasting her time here. She wasn't about to let on that Felippe and half the rest of the line of succession had followed Estrella into the afterlife. "Nothing has been formalized. I need to know if your network has picked up any whispers of what might be happening."

Matron West sniffled and ran one of her long, flowing sleeves across her face. "Our most recent report out of Avalon was nearly incomprehensible. First, there were notes about a flurry of activity, a wave of fae descending upon Glastonbury around the Equinox. We thought it was pomp around the Gathering. But then our contacts went silent."

Gwen scowled. "That was months ago. You didn't think to mention that weird shit was going down at my home in the dozens of times I've been here since?"

Matron West blanched. "As you said, discretion is best in such matters. I didn't want to alarm anyone."

"This is my family!"

"Yes, dear, but it's also our leadership. And after things with Celeste, I just, I didn't know—"

"Unbelievable," said Gwen. "Is that it?"

Matron West looked like she'd rather be catching wisps in a mosquito-infested forest than having this conversation. "No. There were reports that surges of magic had been detected emanating from the grove."

Well, that was something new. "What do you make of that?" Gwen grew up playing in the grove when she could escape her duties. It was a place of power, the heart of Avalon, but harnessing that power was impossible. It wasn't celestial or elemental magic. It was wild magic. Nature itself.

"We don't know. Some of our old texts imply that the portal to the realm of Faerie lies in the grove of Avalon."

"Faerie is a children's story."

"Perhaps not. There are still magics beyond our comprehension. Surely Matron Celeste taught you that much."

Gwen sighed. "Ok, say Faerie truly is a realm that was once layered over this one. Say the stories are true and it was a brutal, kill-or-be-killed place where mortals would disappear and never be seen again. The portal has been sealed for as long as any of us have been alive. Are you suggesting someone wants to open it?"

"I'm only reporting rumors. We hear a lot of things through our channels, and most of them come to nothing." Matron West was backpedaling, but Gwen wasn't going to allow it.

"No, you implied these things, and I need to get to the bottom of this."

"Matron Celeste would have sent an emissary to investigate, but I didn't feel it prudent considering the current state of the Academy."

"So you did nothing?" Gwen stood.

"Wait, Gwendolyn, there's one more thing," sputtered Matron West. She reached into her desk and pulled out a sealed envelope. "This arrived last week. It was hand-delivered by a Seelie guard, and the seal was unbroken. He claimed to come on behalf of Lady Azrah and would give it to nobody but the head matron of the Academy. He told me to give it to you and you alone. I haven't told a soul about it and I wonder if it might have something to do with what's going on."

Gwen took the envelope and inspected it. The royal seal was still intact, and she could sense some lingering magic as if there were a protection glamour placed upon the paper itself. She cast a quizzical look at Matron West.

"Yes, I felt it too. I believe it's enchanted to alert the sender when the seal is broken. It must be very important."

"Yeah, sure," replied Gwen, stuffing the envelope into her back pocket. "Is there a place I can rest for a few hours undisturbed?"

Matron West clambered out of her seat and flitted to the doorway just ahead of Gwen. "Of course." She pulled a large key ring from the shelf by the wall and removed one tiny key. "Here. First room on the second floor is vacant. You can stay as long as you like."

Gwen took the key and walked away without another word.

The dorm room, identical to the one she'd lived in when she was a student, was furnished in outdated but rich purples, reds, and golds. It wasn't her style, but it was quiet enough. She pulled the envelope from her pocket and plopped down on the bed. On the front of the envelope in perfect calligraphy, was her name. She broke the seal and felt a jolt of electricity, like the shock of dragging your feet across carpeting on a dry day, on her fingertips. Inside was a single folded piece of paper reading:

Gwendolyn,

If things go the way I suspect, someone will need this information. You must keep it to yourself, telling no one, not even the Council, and destroy this letter immediately after reading. You are the only one I trust. Baby Grace is alive. She's under the protection of her mother, being held in a location beyond the reach of our enemies. Should the time come when she is heir, she will need to be raised in secret, and her throne protected. I hope this duty doesn't fall to you or to me. It's a burden neither of us are prepared for. Please stay safe for the sake of the Seelie Court. If any of us has a chance, it's you.

With hope,

Your Cousin, Azrah Tupaou

With hope. Azrah always was an insufferable optimist. When things were darkest, she saw the light. Strange that she wasn't the one with the solar magic. Tears welled in Gwen's eyes. Sweet little Gracie was alive, and so was Audrey, her mother. It was as if the spark of good news allowed space for the pain, for the overwhelming sense of loss she'd been stuffing deep into the recesses of her being. She gasped for air. Or was it a sob? Gwen had to get it together and make sense of everything. A million fragments of a picture had been shattered and left in all the most painful places of her past, and she had to retrieve them one at a time, cutting herself open in the process. All she could do was focus on what she knew. Her family in exile, assassins hunting them down. Avalon in turmoil. And this.

She closed her eyes and ran her fingers over the parchment. The pinpoint of light, the spot of sunshine that was Gracie's life, warmed her and she fell into blackness.

The senses that flooded in were more disjointed than usual. The sounds were too chaotic to parse out, the smells and tastes were too muddled. Voices whispered in the dark. Gwen only caught a few words. "Head Matron. Nobody. Right away." A pair of murky green eyes formed and vanished as Gwen was thrust back to the present more confused than ever. Her reading yielded nothing useful, so she read the note again. Despite the signature, nothing about it sounded hopeful. Why wouldn't Azrah trust the Seelie Council? What else did she know?

"What the fuck is going on?" said Gwen, her voice lost in the empty room.

WHEN SHE AWOKE before sunrise the next day, Gwen knew exactly where she should go for more information. It was dangerous. It was stupid. It was the last place in the world she wanted to go, but fuck it. She faced the Academy, Laural, and her mother over the past few days. How much worse could the palace of Korranthia, the home of her lost princess, be? The Korranthian monarchy consisted of the most powerful fae in the Kingdom. Well, second most powerful now that Gwen's family had taken up residence. Hopefully, they didn't want to lock her up. The last time she was there, she hardly faced a warm reception. Gwen steeled her resolve, snagged a quick breakfast in the mess hall, and found a secluded doorway to duck into for a quick size-shift before she headed off to the last place on earth she wanted to go.

Security at the Palace of Korranthia was on high alert. A patrol of sprites stopped Gwen at the gatehouse. They surrounded her, their sharp teeth bared, and malice gleaming in their oversized dark eyes, stark contrasts to their colorless hair and ghost-white skin. Gwen wondered how many perched in the trees, ready to pounce should she give them cause. The sprite inside the gatehouse spoke as the others stood in a circle around her. "Can we help you?" The sprite flashed a smile that didn't touch her black eyes.

"Yes, I'm Gwendolyn Evenshine, and I'd like an audience with Queen Charis."

"She isn't accepting visitors, particularly unannounced ones."

"Announce me." Gwen held her ground. Having hunted down the serial killer who slaughtered the crown princess should earn her some respect here, if not a warm welcome. She remembered the first time she saw this gatehouse. She'd flown right over it in her eagerness to report in for her first fairy godmother assignment. There was no sprite army charged with security back then, only one sorcerer with some meager protective spells. She shuddered to think what would have happened to her if she made such a misstep today. Of course, she'd been expected back then. Matron Celeste, the beloved head-mistress of the Academy sent word of her imminent arrival.

The sprite closed her eyes for a moment, presumably to commune with someone inside the palace. Sprite telepathy always freaked Gwen out. "Lord Grimore permits you to enter the reception room, but you are to have an escort." She kept her eyes pinned on Gwen but nodded her head to signal to the sprite at Gwen's elbow. "Snike, please escort Miss Evenshine to the reception room."

As Gwen followed the silent sprite up the path to the palace, a feeling of dread began to pulse in her stomach. She kept her eyes forward through the garden where Frankie's fountain, the first and final place she'd seen her young friend, stood in silent remembrance of the princess, and dismissed the feeling as grief. But when Grimore, the Courtless fairy with the ear of the Queen, emerged and stood on the dais, it thrummed all the way up into her brain. She shouldn't be here.

"Miss Evenshine, to what do we owe the pleasure?"

In large form, Gwen dwarfed the fairy, which was probably why he took visitors from on high, but it didn't matter. His demeanor of detached confidence made his presence fill the room. He was larger than life. A suspicion Gwen had been harboring since last crossing paths with the black and silver-haired, green-eyed enigma of a fairy suddenly snapped into place. Grimore wasn't the advisor to the Queen. He was the monarchy. He was Korranthia.

She knew the answer before she asked the question. "Hello, Master

Grimore. Thank you for receiving me. I hope you are well. I wish to have a word with Queen Charis. It's a matter of some importance."

"I'm pleased your manners have improved since we last met, but I'm afraid that isn't possible. Is there something I can do to help?"

Asshole. Gwen considered appealing to him, begging for his help in discovering who was hunting her family. He certainly had the resources. But that sense of dread was now a hammer in her chest. Chessa always talked about listening to her gut. Gwen wasn't a pixie with a gift of intuition, but she was a fairy with over-developed empathy. She didn't trust Grimore. She never had. Wishing she could get a hand on him to pick up some helpful senses, Gwen forced a polite smile. "No, I don't think you could. Please give my best regards to the king and queen. By your leave?"

Some emotion flicked across Grimore's flawless face. Gwen wondered for a moment if she was going to be allowed to leave, and every muscle in her body tensed. She battled the panic and folded her hands together to keep from clenching her fists as the moment stretched into many. Finally, Grimore lowered his head in acquiescence.

Gwen's mind whirled at the possibility of the Korranthian royals being a part of what was happening to her family. If they weren't, Grimore certainly knew something. And she had to find out what. There was a killer hunting her family, and her best friend was heading into a trap. She might not trust him, but she didn't have anywhere else to turn.

Halfway to the door, she stopped. Panic swirling in her chest like a sack full of squirrels, she turned around. Grimore was still perched on the dais, cool emerald eyes fixed on her. "Master Grimore, perhaps you can help after all. Have you noticed any unusual stirrings?"

"Excuse me?"

"You serve the Korranthian monarchs as ambassador to the Seelie Court Council, to my family. You must know that we're facing troubles unlike anything we've ever known. I was wondering what you heard. Any bit of information could be helpful."

Grimore stiffened, if such a thing were possible. He gave a barely perceptible tilt of the head, and the silent sprite moved in, grabbing her wrists before Gwen's brain processed the change.

Oh, hell no. This was not happening.

Gwen brought her knee up into the sprite's stomach, took a step back, and kicked. Her Doc Marten shattered the creature's nose. Blood sputtered out, covering his powder-white skin and splashing his hair like a Jackson Pollock painting. In the brief moment she made contact, a slew of sensory data pummeled her consciousness. She didn't have time to make heads or tails of the faces she saw or scents that flirted with memory in her brain. She paused only long enough to remove her mental barriers and let it soak in. A wave of vertigo threatened to introduce her head to the marble floor.

Gwen didn't hear Grimore call out, but she felt the heavy wooden door behind her open. Sprite soldiers filtered in, some with spears aimed at her head. They began to encircle her. Gwen only had one shot at getting out of here alive, and it hinged on the vast majority of fae being unable to size-shift. She snapped her wand out of her thigh holster. Before the sprites had a chance to process what was happening, she shrunk to her natural size in a flash of light.

In the confusion resulting from her sudden apparent disappearance, Gwen flew through the door, through the entrance hall, and out into the fresh air of the garden. She didn't stop by Frankie's fountain or even to take inventory of any possible threats. She shot through the air, over the trees, and as far from the Palace of Korranthia as her wings could take her.

16

June 16
4 days until the Summer Solstice

Chessa didn't know if her captors forgot her before turning in for the night or if they were simply preoccupied with her much larger friend, but she wasn't going to wait around to find out. The only objects in the room were enormous statues of Seelie fae champions. She recognized David Bowie, Rolf the Muppet, and a few of the others, but it was Joan of Arc who caught her attention. Perched atop a horse, the statue's face was stern as she held Chessa's salvation, a sword, aloft. The weapon was far too large for a pixie to wield. Joan had been a dame blanche disguised as a human woman and had great physical strength that Chessa did not, but that edge still looked sharp enough to sever a couple of measly zip ties. She pushed off the wall behind her and flapped her wings. With her hands and feet bound together, the action sent her careening into the air like a tiny cannonball. She spun wildly, missing Joan by a good fifteen feet before slamming into the foot of Homer.

"Ha ha, real funny," she muttered at the smiling face of the bard, pain radiating up her spine. The sword was above her head and to the left. Chessa rolled to right herself and imagined she was one of those fat fuzzy bees that defied the laws of aerodynamics. She took a deep breath, engaged her abs, and flapped her wings. This time, her attempt was more controlled, but she still missed the sword and fluttered down to perch over the hoof of Joan's horse. Pixies were sprinters, not marathoners.

By her fifth try, Chessa was a ball of panting, sweaty, cussing rage. But to her surprise, her aim was true. She hung for a moment from the sword, like a ring at a carnival game, and caught her breath before she began to swing her body back and forth, creating enough tension to break through.

Two snaps later, and she was free. Just in time too. The internal door swung open just as Chessa took refuge atop David Bowie's head. Thankful the statues were oversized, she pressed her body against a stone spike of the notorious fae shifter's hair. Now that she was unbound, Chessa was in her element, hiding in the shadows and gathering intel. Her sleuth senses sharpened, and she took in every detail of her current situation.

"If you bring two captives in, I expect to see two captives in cages!" boomed a voice she didn't recognize. It was high and sharp, certainly not human.

"Yes, madam. I understand. The fool wizard brought her in. I assumed he'd followed protocol." This voice was familiar. It was the fairy who zip-tied her back in Norman's truck. Without a visual, Chessa could still feel rage sparking through the space, like electricity in the air before a thunderstorm.

The first voice responded in dark, quiet tones that shook Chessa to her core. "You assumed? You are responsible for the wizard. You will pay for his actions."

The fairy gasped. "Yes, madam. The fool said he left her here, bound on the bench."

"Do you see her there? Bound on the bench?"

"No, Your Grace. She couldn't have gotten far. She's probably on the grounds still, though likely getting farther away with every moment."

Your Grace? Only royalty was addressed that way. Chessa desperately wanted to get a look at the woman, but she knew it would be her death, so she stayed put.

The guard mumbled, "He knew better. He knew protocol."

So the wizard had helped her after all. Chessa grinned. *Norman, you sly bastard.*

"I will give you one chance. Find the pixie by sundown, or you shall see protocol up close and personal."

The sound of the door slamming shut accentuated the threat. Chessa could sense the fairy remaining in the room. She didn't dare breathe. A moment later, the huge, wooden door opened, and she heard him call for his underlings. They were organizing a search for her, expecting that she'd fled. Perhaps she should have. But that didn't rattle Chessa, mostly because she planned on doing the opposite. If Samson and Gwen were both imprisoned here, she wasn't about to run. She was going in deeper.

17

Gwen went to the only safe place she knew—a neglected warehouse down by the docks. When she was hunting the Brain Scraper, the space served as her command center for over four years. Now that she was in the PI business with Chessa, it was nothing but a museum of painful memories. Still, she paid the rent every month. Moving on never had been one of Gwen's strengths.

Outside of Samson, Chessa, and some goons on the KPD force, few knew the warehouse was her secret lair, not that her family wasn't capable of hacking into the KPD. And who knew what those hunting her were capable of? Still, her old equipment was there, and she needed to download the sensory data she picked up from the sprite. It was the only lead she had.

Gwen tried not to consider what Chessa might be going through right now as she flew over the quiet storage space until she spotted her green building below. Her wings ached, and she was beginning to feel confined by her tiny body. She wasn't used to being in fae form for so long, and she certainly wasn't used to being without her little blue Subaru.

She landed by the door, the familiar sound of her Docs crunching gravel sending endorphins to her brain, took a furtive glance around to ensure there were no prying eyes in sight, and switched to large size in a flash of light. She could open the door while small, but since the key was hanging alongside Frankie's locket from a chain around her neck, it needed to size-shift with her in order to fit the keyhole. The mechanism clicked into place, and Gwen opened the door into the dark, hollow space beyond.

The warehouse was just as she'd left it. An enormous, empty space with an office tucked into the back right corner and a cot in the back left, the two areas separated by a freestanding board that Gwen used to organize all her Brain Scraper data. The board gleamed new and empty, having been replaced following a ransacking last year as Gwen closed in on the killer. Well, mostly empty. She'd tacked the black and white, laser jet printed photo of her and Frankie back up on the back side, facing the cot. The bottle of Jack was just where she'd left it too, top drawer on the right. Gwen pulled it out and took a swig.

Chessa had righted the office space following the break-in. That was Chess's MO—fix all the broken bits of Gwen's life. Too bad she couldn't fix Gwen. A lump formed in her throat as she sat at the swivel chair and fired up the computer. If she didn't pick up any leads from the sprite's sensory data, her friend, the only person on this planet who didn't think she was a total waste of magic, might be lost to her completely. She attached the sensors to her head and powered on the little black box that read her brain waves. The contraption had proven invaluable to the Brain Scraper case as Gwen struggled to understand her own empathic touch and make sense of the data she gathered. Sometimes she could decipher bits and pieces on the fly, but most of the time, she needed the tech to analyze it. The download would take hours, even when her contact had been as brief as the touch she shared with the sprite guard. She'd been accustomed to playing Crime Boss during the wait time, but Boss Glitter wouldn't be on, so what was the point? Instead, she shut her eyes and listened to the thrumming of the machine.

SHE MUST HAVE DRIFTED off because the *ding* of the computer registering the completed download startled her. The program she used to play her sensory data allowed her to isolate by sense, but she always began by letting it all wash over her at once, the way she experienced it in the moment. In this case, she had to slow the feed down by 75% to account for the adrenaline of battle which made the senses flick by at an incomprehensible speed.

Images flashed across her screen, visual representations of each smell, sight, and sensation that she picked up from the sprite. Her speakers played the soundtrack with captions flashing at the bottom of the screen. Physical pain in the stomach—that would have been from the impact of her boot. The musty smell of woods, a voice cracking out commands, a face speckled with red, the aroma of fried food, laughter... a full five and a half seconds with sensations flitting by ceased abruptly.

Gwen opened a notebook, typed in the command to make her computer isolate sound at a tenth of normal speed, and wrote down every clue. She followed with the other senses. When she played the visuals, one face flashing by caught her attention. She paused and rewound, stopping the feed at the exact time signature of the face. Liam was looking back at her, specks of red dotting his perfect complexion, smeared across the top of his forehead, and a look of horror haunting his bright golden-ringed eyes. Was that blood? Gwen gasped, feeling like she was the one who had taken a combat boot to the gut. By the vividness of the image, this data couldn't have been more than a few hours old when she gathered it. Had the sprite captured Liam? Whose blood was all over him? Was he even alive anymore? She scoured the photo, searching for indications of location. There, just over Liam's left shoulder, was a window with curtains the emerald shade of Korranthian royalty. Panic rose in Gwen's chest. Fuck staying off the radar. Samson was dead, Chessa was in enemy territory, and now her baby brother was in trouble. Gwen's entire life was spiraling out of control.

She was about to slam the laptop shut when a notification popped up on the screen. It was her email. She had a message from her mother. Gwen clicked the icon to open it.

Gwendolyn, I tried to make you understand the gravity of the situation, but you've left the shelter of my protection. I know you don't believe me, but I care for your safety. You are too important to the Seelie Court to be selfishly putting yourself in harm's way. I beseech you to return. Arabella is dead.

There was no signature, just the symbol of the Seelie Court Council.

Gwen put her hands in her face and screamed in frustration.

She held no love for her cousin, but she didn't want the fairy killed. Arabella would have been seventh in line for the throne, following just behind Liam and Aunt Ember. But her mother hadn't mentioned Liam. She had to know he was in danger, or missing at least. Was Indira unaware of the trouble he was in, or did she want to keep it from Gwen? It was always games upon games with her family, even when the stakes couldn't be any higher. It was why Gwen walked away, but Liam hadn't been old enough to walk away back then. He grew up with this shit, and Gwen left him to it.

Gwen picked up her prepaid phone and dialed the last number she had for her mother. The phone rang without end. Fuck. She didn't want to reply from this IP address and give up the location of her last safe place, but she didn't have Chessa's technical know-how to cover her tracks. She needed to make sure Liam was safe.

Mother. I think the Korranthian royals are mixed up in all this. I picked up traces of Liam at the palace. Please tell me he's safe with you. -Gwen

Gwen sat back down and stared at her screen for what seemed like an eternity, waiting for an answer. Her answer burst down the door.

Fairies flooded through the opening, some on foot and others winged, all wearing Seelie Court uniforms and armed with silver-tipped wands. The wands were for show. The Seelie Guard was trained in magic from a young age and didn't require tools to command advanced combat magic. Still, all those wands on her pinned Gwen to her seat without a hint of magic involved.

Once the warehouse was lined with fae guards, Indira Evenshine appeared in the doorway.

Gwen had known it wouldn't take her family long to locate her, but this was ridiculous. She certainly didn't expect a personal appearance, not in the—she glanced down at her screen—six and a half minutes since she'd sent her reply.

"Mother." It was more of a statement than a greeting.

"I told you this wasn't a game." Indira had traded her silks and velvets for a hunter-green long-sleeved tee and black, formfitting pants.

Is she wearing yoga pants? Gwen knew she was displacing, focusing on something mundane when the world was on fire around her, but she'd never seen her mother wearing anything so common. Yet, Indira shone with grace and power that would probably be evident had she chosen a burlap sack. Her iridescent wings, positioned in their usual formal pose, somehow reflected light that didn't seem to exist in the cold warehouse, and Gwen felt a rush of rage seeing her mother corrupt her dark sanctuary. This was not the place for sparkle.

"Being kidnapped and held as a prisoner made that apparent," quipped Gwen. But then she remembered Liam, eyes full of horror, face speckled with blood, and she changed course. "Is Liam safe? Please tell me he's safe."

"Your brother left shortly after you did. He always looked up to you, you know. If he's in any kind of danger, it's danger you drove him to."

Gwen saw red, but for the first time in her life, she didn't have a barb to throw at her mother. Indira was right. Through all the abusive expectations, the cold relationships, the demands piled on their shoulders, all Gwen and Liam ever had were each other. Until she left to find more. And he had nothing. "Please, Mother. We have to find him." Gwen didn't recognize her own, quiet voice.

Indira's full lips pulled into a tight smile. "For once, Gwendolyn, I agree with you."

"If I come with you," asked Gwen, "will you work with me or will you keep me in the dark on some rock in the middle of the harbor?"

"I believe I have need of your skills, such as they are. We shall not be returning to our island refuge. You will come of your own accord?"

Gwen's nod was barely perceptible but seemed enough to satisfy her mother, who raised a hand signaling the guards to lower their wands.

18

Navigating the palace proved challenging. The inside was a labyrinth of great halls and doorways. Long corridors lined with stained glass led to locked quarters and more halls and doors. Chessa couldn't believe this was where Gwen grew up. She couldn't picture her surly best friend sulking in such a luxurious place, decked out in all black while everything around her practically shimmered with light and magic. No wonder she was the outcast of the family.

Once the foyer was clear, Chessa ducked through the door they'd dragged Samson through into a huge chamber, far larger than the building should have been able to accommodate. At the far end of the room was a dais set on a platform with four vacant thrones sitting higher than the rest of the Great Hall. The walls were lined with purple and gold tapestries depicting Seelie life, lineages, battles, and the like. Rows upon rows of ivory seats with purple silk cushions all faced the front of the room. It resembled the human churches Chessa visited on occasion back in Korranthia, but it dwarfed them all. There were eight separate doors, three on each side of the room, and one on each end. All were closed except the closest one on the right. In the distance, she heard voices and footsteps, but she couldn't tell where the sounds originated.

Chessa flitted to the top of the molding and peered down the long corridor. It was lined with fairies, all in military gear. They wore red and silver as opposed to the Seelie purple and gold. A chill crept along Chessa's spine as the implication dawned on her.

"Oh, fuck me," she whispered. These were Unseelie guards. Unseelie forces hadn't been active in nearly three hundred years. The Unseelie she knew were all regular people going about regular lives, but this was something else entirely.

A voice behind her sent a shiver up her spine. "I would, luv, but somefin tells me it wouldn't work out."

Chessa turned around slowly. Standing behind her was the largest troll she'd ever seen. He had to be at least nine feet tall as his bulbous nose was level with her perch above the buttress. His eyes very nearly crossed as they locked onto her, and his thinning black hair was pulled back into a greasy ponytail.

Chessa pushed off the door frame, locked her knee, and flew straight into the troll's right eye, foot first. Her pixie speed gave her an advantage, and she made contact. The troll bellowed, his rancid breath nearly knocking her out as she struggled against goo and tears to free herself. A giant hand swatted at her. Just as she was about to become pixie puree, it stopped in midair.

"Go, little miss!" Norman's command wasn't one Chessa had to consider. She pulled her black-and-white Chuck Taylor free of the troll's eye and flitted into the air. She was halfway across the chamber when she glanced back.

The wizard was standing, hands aloft, streams of energy emanating from his fingertips and morphing into webs of light which the wizard used to bind the troll's arms to his side. The troll thrashed wildly, thick arms tearing through the webs, feet stomping, and water streaming from his injured eye. The wizard's tricks wouldn't last long, and then what? Norman would be defenseless against a very angry troll.

"Shit," muttered Chessa, doing an about-face in the air. She couldn't leave him to die. She briefly thought about smashing a window to let the sun stream in, turning the troll to stone, but she wasn't sure what, or who, might be on the other side.

With no weapon but her wits, Chessa dove at the troll's face. If she could keep him distracted, maybe she could buy Norman enough time to properly tie him up. The troll swatted at her, but she reversed direction, and his hand whizzed by. She landed on the back of his head, braced her Chucks against his skull, and gave his hair a mighty tug.

"Get his legs," she shouted. She had no way of knowing if Norman heard her. She had to keep moving or she was toast.

Chessa pressed her tongue against the roof of her mouth and made the most annoying buzzing sound she could muster as she did figure eights around the troll's sagging ears. He bellowed in frustration and began to sway. His cries turned to alarm.

Chessa heard Norman's husky voice. "Timber, little miss! Get out of there!"

She bolted away from the troll just in time. From the waist down, he was a cocoon, wrapped so tightly in the magical threads he couldn't separate his thunderous thighs. In the distance, the thudding of boots running down a corridor jolted Chessa back into action. "We've got to get out of here," she said.

"That way," yelled Norman, pointing to a door to the left of the raised dais.

She threw open the door, darted through it, and came to a stop on the other side to catch her breath. Chessa heard a huge crash and shouts from the great hall. Norman caught up a few moments later.

"Better move fast, little miss," he panted. "These wankers don't play."

19

Gwen kept her small stature, as was customary when in the presence of members of the Seelie Council. If there was anything that could get her to utilize her etiquette training, it was her little brother in danger. She sat in the back of another Lincoln Town Car, this one retrofitted for small fae, with a raised, leather bench seat spanning the back. At least she wasn't in a box this time. Herbert Dayglow was on her left, a perma-smirk plastered on his face, and two Seelie guards sat to her right, each keeping one hand on the source stick strapped to their side. Gwen might have come of her own free will, but it appeared that her mother wasn't taking any chances of her escaping at a red light. Typical. Her family's words and actions rarely aligned.

She brushed the seat with her fingertips, attempting to pick up sensory data that might give her more information about her situation, but the few flashes she got were mundane. It seemed this car hadn't seen much action besides transport missions of high-ranking Seelie officials.

"Gwendolyn, I take it your defensive magic is still as feeble as it was when you left?" Indira spoke from the throne-like front seat installed on top of the Town Car's stock leather upholstery. A male humanoid chauffeur remained as silent as the guards, and her mother spoke as if they weren't surrounded by an audience.

"I did well enough against the Brain Scraper," replied Gwen.

"Come now, we both know it was your pixie friend who handled that unpleasant business."

"Unpleasant business? Are we really doing this again? We were almost butchered by the most notorious serial killer of our time."

Indira sighed. "Don't be overdramatic, Gwendolyn. I'm merely trying to determine how many guards to put on you over the next few months. We must protect the entire family, after all, not just you."

Gwen couldn't believe what she was hearing. First, her mother kidnapped her, then she lay on a guilt trip over the resources needed to keep her alive. Resources Gwen never asked for. "I don't need guards. I'm fine on my own. I'm only here to help find Liam."

"Your brother was with Arabella when she was attacked. He was injured, but the Korranthian Royal Guard saved him. They took him to the palace, cleaned him up, then notified me. He's meeting us in an hour."

Gwen stood on the leather seat, blood rushing to her face. She knew she shouldn't be surprised by her mother's manipulation, but using Liam as bait was too far. "You lied to me."

"I did no such thing. I merely told you that any danger he might be in is on your shoulders. And it is. He never would have been with Arabella if it hadn't been for you."

Gwen wanted to scream. She wanted to launch into the front seat and pummel Indira's smug expression off her face. Instead, she stammered. "You said you wanted me to help find him."

"No, I said I had need of your skills and I agreed that we need to speak with Liam. And we do. Perhaps he learned something that can help us hunt those who would hunt us."

"Let me out. Now." Gwen's voice was a growl.

The chauffeur looked at her mother, who gave a barely perceptible shake of the head. The car kept moving. "I need you safe. One day, perhaps you'll be a mother. Then you'll understand."

Gwen considered fighting, but she didn't want to make the mistake of underestimating Dayglow again, and if the door was unlocked, she'd change her name to Twinkleheart. The two guards were staring at her, waiting for her to make a move. The golden-ringed green eyes of the one nearest to her seemed to plead, and the one to the right of him removed her source stick and held it in her palm. Gwen did the only thing she could. She kicked the seat back and screamed in frustration.

A divider rose to cut the back seat off from the front.

"I believe your mother has had enough of your tantrums," said Dayglow.

Gwen merely glared. Who was this asshole, anyway? Even Arabella respected her station enough to refrain from openly mocking her. She was about to ask when the car stopped in front of a brownstone in the Leather District. The Seelie Guards exited first to survey the area and secure any threats. Indira remained in the car but didn't lower the divider. Gwen considered bolting. She would have if two thoughts hadn't stopped her. First, the appearance of freedom didn't guarantee it. Indira always had a plan, and if that plan involved keeping Gwen here, she likely wouldn't get far. And second, she had nowhere else to go. She had nothing but her mother's word that Liam was safe, and getting halfway around the world to face whatever was happening in Avalon would be next to impossible if Indira used her resources to stop her.

Gwen remained in the backseat of the Town Car until the guards returned and ushered her inside ahead of her mother, who walked with Herbert at her side. The entourage traveled through a parlor, into an elevator that felt out-of-place in the old brownstone, up to the top floor, and down a long hallway in silence. Indira peeled off, accompanied by a single guard, while the rest took Gwen to makeshift living quarters. The building was obviously used for office work, but the room they led her to had been converted into a studio apartment, complete with a kitchenette, bed, and bathroom. The window was boarded shut.

"So, I'm a prisoner again," she muttered.

The guard nearest her replied. "No ma'am. The queen instructed me to inform you that you may leave at any time, but for your own security, you must petition for guards to accompany you wherever you wish to go."

"That sounds like imprisonment to me."

"Be that as it may, I've given you the message and will now leave you to get settled." A dark-haired fairy stepped forward and gave a curt bow. "This is Germaine, and he is under orders to care for your needs. Should you need personal effects—clothing, toiletries, and the like — he will be happy to assist you."

"Anything I need?" Gwen asked, receiving another bow. "Cool. I'll have a Jack and Coke, please Jeeves."

The chauffeur/lead guard fairy left her to torment Germaine, which soon lost its appeal as the guard was less forthcoming than even D had been. After her requests for a laptop, phone, and bottle of liquor were denied, she sent him away and headed to the kitchenette to make a sandwich. At least her mother had the fridge stocked.

Hours later, Gwen walked the hallway, which was empty save for Germaine, who was fast asleep in the hall propped against the wall next to her door, and a second guard stationed down the hall by the elevator. She carefully side-stepped her sleeping guard, made her way to the elevator, and pressed the down button.

The guard she didn't recognize straightened himself before speaking. "I'm afraid I must insist on you using the correct protocol to exit the building," he said.

Gwen glanced back down the hall, but Germaine didn't stir. Back home in Avalon, sleeping on the job would have been grounds for immediate dismissal, but the guards in the brownstone all seemed exhausted. Keeping the remaining Seelie royals alive must be taking a toll. Gwen would use that weakness.

She looked the new guard up and down. His eyes were a dark shade of green, familiar somehow, though she was sure she'd never seen him before. Unlike the other guards, his uniform was pristine. He didn't seem the type to go against a direct order from his superior. Gwen decided to pull rank.

"I am Seelie royalty. Are you planning to detain me?" she asked, keeping her voice low but firm.

The guard hesitated. His eyes cut down the hall as if he were considering calling out to Germaine, but instead, he brought his attention back to Gwen. "My lady, this building is under strict lockdown. For your own safety, of course."

"Funny how everything my mother does is for my own safety," she replied.

The elevator dinged, but the doors remained closed. Typical. They were using fae magic to keep her from leaving. Gwen laughed quietly, earning a skeptical look from the guard. He might be skilled in magic, but fairy magic involved perception. She was willing to roll the dice. She flashed a smile and walked right through the closed door into the elevator. She pressed the button for the ground floor, the guard on her heels sputtering and pink.

"You can't leave without approval. Please, my lady, they'll have my head."

"Look, I don't know you. I understand that you have your orders, but I'm walking out of this building, and there isn't shit you can do about it." She saw the guard's fingers move to his side, but he hesitated. "And don't even think of hitting me with a source stick. I've had my fill of them, thank you very much, and you won't like me when I'm pissed off."

His hand moved away from the source stick "Please go back to your room. You don't understand. It really is dangerous out there, and I don't want your blood on my hands." The guard's eyes were big and pleading.

That was it. Those eyes were the same ones Gwen saw when she read Azrah's letter for sensory data. This very well could be the same guard who brought the message to the Academy. If that was the case, he might be more reliable than the others. Gwen decided to test him.

"You need to get yourself a better job. I'm just going to find a liquor store. The way I see it, you have a choice. You can attempt to restrain me, which will not go well for you. You can go alert my family and face whatever they decide to do to you as punishment for letting me escape. Or you can come keep me safe for the ten minutes it takes to pick up a bottle of Jack and get back to my cell."

The guard opened his mouth to respond but shut it just as quickly. He sighed. Gwen knew she had him. Maybe there was hope for these

Seelie guards yet. He didn't speak, and when the elevator doors opened into the downstairs hall, he followed her out the door. When they were on the street, he stopped. "Fine. But please let me do my job and scout ahead, my lady." By the way his voice broke, Gwen thought the guy might burst into tears if she denied him.

"I agree to your terms. And, please call me Gwen."

The guard nodded. "I'm Curtis. There's a liquor store a block east. Now please stay here, out of sight, and wait for my signal."

Gwen smiled and ducked back into the entranceway while Curtis scouted ahead. He returned three minutes later, looking calmer, and they proceeded down the dark Boston street together.

20

Norman led Chessa down a long hall. They passed doors, some closed, but some hanging open with fae gathered inside, deep in discussions or casually lounging in chairs. At one, he slowed to a leisurely pace and cracked a grin.

"Lola! How are you this fine day?" he asked as Chessa hung back from view.

A cheerful voice replied something she couldn't make out. Norman gave a nod of the head, and Chessa flitted past both the wizard and the doorway, letting him overtake her again once she was in the clear. He walked confidently through a door in the middle of the hall, headed down a set of stairs, and disappeared around a corner. Chessa thought of taking off and going it alone, but her gut told her she could trust Norman. And having an insider in her corner could help her slim chances of surviving the overrun seat of Seelie power long enough to find Samson and get the hell out of Dodge.

The room Norman stopped in was about half the size of the throne room, lined with shelf after shelf of books. A curved track allowed for a ladder to be moved from one wall to the next. To the right were large, glass-paneled doors, through which sunlight poured. Could this be a way out? Chessa started toward them.

"No, not that way," muttered Norman.

"Where does it lead?" asked Chessa.

Norman shuffled to the far wall and rolled the ladder to the center of the bookcase. He paused, staring at an expansive mural on the ceiling with his arm extended, index finger and thumb forming an L shape.

"Outside. But there will be sentries on the balcony, and the guards are scouring the grounds searching for you. There!"

Norman moved the ladder another half foot to the right and scaled it, still focused on the spot on the ceiling. Chessa craned her neck to see what had caught his focus, but the mural was far too busy for any one element to stick out. Scenes merged into each other, battles and elements, nature and industry. It was as if the evolution of existence was laid out in abstract images, and somehow it connected to whatever Norman was doing. He pulled a book from the top shelf, and a section of shelving fifteen feet off the ground creaked open right where the top of the ladder ended.

"Come, little miss. You'll be safe through 'ere."

Norman climbed through. The pounding of footsteps didn't give Chessa time to consider an alternative. She flew through the opening, and the wall closed behind her with a grinding of gears. Norman waved his hand. From the other side of the wall, she heard the screeching of the ladder wheels and a thump as the ladder returned to its original place.

Chessa looked around. If she didn't know better, she'd think she was on the ground level. She was standing in another library, albeit much smaller than the one she just fled. At the far end of the room was a desk covered in papers and Mountain Dew cans. A laptop sat open on top, and trash overflowed from a receptacle beneath. One small stained-glass window let in a little light, but the space was mostly lit with orbs floating above the bookshelves. There was only one door on the wall behind the desk. "This is awesome."

Norman didn't smile, but Chessa could swear she saw a little sparkle in his eyes. It died as quickly as it formed. "This is where I was hiding when the Seelie were here." He turned away quickly before pointing at the door, "There's a bathroom and a kitchen through there. Make yourself comfortable."

Chessa could tell by his demeanor that Norman didn't want to talk about the bomb he just dropped—the revelation that he was here before Avalon was overtaken. She filed it away in her brain to poke at later. She wasn't the best sleuth in Korranthia for nothing. Besides, if she ever wanted to get back to Korranthia, she had more pressing matters. Like her bladder. She gave Norman some breathing room and went for a pit stop. On the way back, she raided the kitchen. She didn't know what the next play was, but she was sure she'd need the energy.

When she returned, Norman seemed calmer. There was nary a Mountain Dew can in sight, and he sat at his laptop, staring intently. "You really stirred them up, little miss," he mumbled when he noticed Chessa looking over his shoulder from a perch on a shelf behind him.

His screen was filled with windows that appeared to show live recordings taken from various points around Avalon. One displayed the grove, one the fields, and the rest showed various rooms of the palace.

"Thank you, Norman."

He looked back at her. "For what? I'm the one who brought you into this mess."

"No. You're not. I brought myself here, and you did everything in your power to help me. You're a good man."

Norman's cheeks flushed, and Chessa swore she saw water welling up in his eyes. "Begging your pardon, little miss, but I am no such thing. The things I have done. Well, I won't be having you thinking I'm something I'm not."

"We all make choices every day. Today, you chose kindness. I don't know what you chose in the past, but I know that I'm only alive because of you. So, begging your pardon, mister, but I'll make my own choices too, and I choose to believe in you."

Norman opened his mouth to speak, but no words emerged. He turned and stared at the screen even more intently. Chessa did the same. In the frame on the second window to the right, she noticed bars, like those on a cell. "Norm! Is that where my friend is? You've got a camera in there?"

"Hold up, little miss. There ain't no way you're getting to him. You saw how seriously they take security around here. If they want him locked up, that's how he's staying."

"They wanted me locked up, and look at me now!" Chessa grinned.

Norm didn't seem to see the humor in the situation. "And you nearly got us both killed. I ain't bustin' no griffin out of here, you understand?"

Chessa flew down from the shelf and landed on the desk. She put her small hand on the back of the wizard's larger one. "You've done enough. You lay low, and I'll find a way to get to Samson."

"You're not hearing me. There is no way." Norm pulled his hand away and pushed the chair out so he could get to his feet. "You go back out there, you're dead. And you can't say I didn't tell you so."

Chessa watched the wizard disappear through the door, muttering to himself. She walked across the desk to the open laptop and got to work.

21

June 17
3 days until the Summer Solstice

Gwen returned sometime after midnight with Curtis by her side and a bottle of Jack tucked under her arm. The brownstone was just as they'd left it, down to the sleeping guard, Germaine, propped against the wall outside the door to her quarters. Gwen bid a quick farewell to Curtis, who was distracted with scanning the corridor for any activity, likely convinced he'd be fired or worse if anyone discovered them missing, but he was in luck. There was nobody around at this time of night.

It wasn't until three hours later when a knock on the door woke Gwen up. She'd fallen asleep in the recliner by the sealed window but jumped to her feet at the sound.

"Yeah, come in," she called.

The door swung open and Germaine stepped through.

"You've been summoned by the Seelie Fae Council. You are to report immediately."

Gwen rubbed the sleep from her eyes. "You know you're talking about my mother, right? You don't need to be so formal."

Germaine stood as if frozen in place. He didn't even crack a smile.

Gwen yawned. "Fine. Give me five minutes."

Still, he stood, staring ahead.

Gwen leveled a firm stare in his direction. He might be tasked with keeping tabs on her, but in this building, she was his superior. Pretenses or not, she was here of her own free will. "Get. Out."

At that, the guard gave a salute and walked back out the door to wait in the hall.

Fifteen minutes later, Gwen clutched a cup of coffee as she followed Germaine down the hall. She glanced toward the elevator to check for Curtis, but he'd been replaced by a woman with dark hair and an expression as stern as Germaine's. So much for a friendly face.

The meeting room was on the third floor at the far end of the hall, opposite the elevator. The doors were shut, but Germaine knocked twice and then let her in. Liam stood at one end of a long, rectangular table. Azrah sat at the other end in an executive rolling chair, her brown ringlets framing her face and topped with a delicate golden chain headpiece. It was the first time Gwen had seen the acting Seelie Queen since her arrival, and if she didn't have such pressing business, she would have laughed at the show of pomp clashing with the dated meeting room nestled in a brownstone. Liam abruptly stopped speaking at Gwen's entrance. She tried to catch Azrah's eye, but her cousin didn't so much as glance in her direction.

Indira rose from her seat to Azrah's left. "Gwendolyn. Good of you to join us," she said.

Gwen glanced at the clock on the wall before she replied. "Well, it is five o'clock in the morning, and as you said, I am here of my own free will. I required a moment to prepare myself."

Indira looked Gwen up and down, and her mouth twisted into a frown. She opened it to reply, but Azrah cut her off, finally seeming to register Gwen's presence.

"Thank you for coming, Gwendolyn. I only wish we were seeing you under more pleasant circumstances. We've all lost a great deal, and we could use your help."

Gwen nearly choked on her coffee at her cousin's formality. Was this the same woman who'd sent her the letter about Gracie? *A little bit of power, and she's the bloody Queen of England.*

No. She was more. She was the Seelie Queen.

Gwen bit her tongue. Nobody expected Azrah to be in charge in this lifetime, and Danu knew Gwen didn't want that kind of responsibility. She dropped her head. "Whatever you need, Your Grace." Gwen could feel waves of smugness radiating off Indira. She couldn't make eye contact.

Liam stood. "What they want is for you to read me," he said.

Gwen detected an edge to her brother's voice, and for once, she didn't think she was the one drawing his ire. She kept her focus on Azrah, who shifted in her chair.

"Of course not. Such a request would be illegal not to mention immoral," Azrah objected.

That told Gwen that Azrah was still a decent fairy, or at least trying to be, despite the influence of their ruthless family. Her demeanor here must be an act, but for whom? As far as Gwen knew, the Seelie royal family was all in this together. Between the cryptic message Azrah sent her about baby Grace and how guarded she was here, Gwen deduced that her cousin didn't trust those closest to her.

This was getting more and more interesting.

But Azrah was right about one thing. Compulsory reading was an unforgivable violation. It was bad enough to sneak a read in on family, but reading someone against their expressed wishes was considered assault under Seelie law. Gwen would do it anyway if it had a shot in hell at keeping Liam safe or bringing Chessa home, but it would do neither. Reading objects was difficult enough. Getting anything useful from a living being was unpredictable if not downright dangerous. She didn't need wild wisp chases on top of everything else.

"So why am I here?" Gwen asked.

"We want you to read his armor. He was present when Arabella was murdered. The Korranthian Royal guard intervened in time to save Liam, praise Danu, but he wasn't able to identify the attackers. Our hope is that you will pick up some vital clue as to who is slaughtering our family."

"I would never hold anything back. I loved Arabella!" Liam was red in the face.

Indira interjected. "Liam, nobody thinks you would. But perhaps Gwendolyn will be able to sense something you missed in the moment. Don't be insolent." Indira's eyes cut to Gwen as if to say 'like your sister,' but she closed her mouth.

It might be juvenile, but Gwen enjoyed the feeling of being the valuable one for once. Normally, Indira reserved that tone of voice for her alone. Guilt drove the spike of joy away. "I'll do anything I can. Can I do it in private?"

Liam scowled, but Azrah flashed a weak, relieved smile. "Yes, of course."

"Oh, and I'll need to return to my warehouse to analyze the data," Gwen tacked on. She didn't believe it would fly, but it was worth a shot.

Azrah's smile deepened. "There's no need. We've had your equipment moved here."

"What?"

"The equipment from your warehouse. We moved your entire setup to the terrace level here. You should have everything you need. I know it's not ideal, but it's the best we could do."

The world went out of focus. Just when Gwen thought she knew the extent of her family's overreach, they did something to gut her once again. "You moved my warehouse?"

"Not the entire warehouse, of course. Just your things. You should be well-outfitted downstairs. Germaine will show you the way, and we'll have Liam's armor brought down to you." Azrah looked positively proud of herself as if she wasn't talking about uprooting Gwen's entire life without consent.

Gwen stole a glance at her mother, but Indira was looking out the window. Even Liam avoided eye contact.

AN HOUR LATER, Gwen sat in the windowless terrace-level bedroom outfitted with the contents of her warehouse. The desk alone took up three-quarters of the space, and her precious board covered one wall entirely. Her equipment was sized for humans since fae didn't tend to rely on such specialized tech, so Gwen had to take large form to use any of it, which meant turning sideways and climbing over things to navigate the space. It was a far cry from her wide-open warehouse.

Liam's armor was carefully positioned on her desk beside her laptop, and it was nearly pristine save for the splattering of blood across the front of the breastplate and helm.

Gwen swallowed the lump in her throat that formed as she saw what her sanctuary had been reduced to. She pulled the bottle of Jack from the inside pocket of her leather jacket—the other reason she preferred large form. Anything on her body when she was 5'1 would shrink with her, and transforming the fifth into an airline bottle would be criminal, not to mention the molecular changes turning the whiskey to swill. Besides, her size made her tower over her guards, giving her the illusion of control.

"Do you need anything else?" asked Germaine.

Another male voice answered, "If she does, I'll see she gets it."

Liam.

Her brother strode through the door.

"Yes, my lord. I'll be right outside," replied the guard as he backed out and closed the door.

"Did you come to oversee my reading?" asked Gwen. "You know I don't need moral support."

"No. I came to apologize."

Of all the surprises from the past week, this one hit Gwen the hardest. She couldn't find the words to respond, so she let him continue.

"I know how much all this means to you. I know how hard it must be to lose our cousins after everything you've gone through. And I know how hard it is for you to be here with us."

"Not you, little brother. *Her.*"

Liam nodded, and Gwen suddenly felt awkward in large form. Even sitting at the desk chair, she was big enough to flick Liam across the room like a bug, and here he was, finally opening up to her. She pulled the bottle of Jack out of her pocket and set it on the desk before extracting her wand and shrinking in a flash of light. Liam didn't flinch as she took her place standing on the desk next to him.

"Mother means well. She has so much on her shoulders, especially now. She has to look out for all fae, not just us," he said.

"When has she ever looked out for us?" The expression on her brother's face made Gwen instantly regret her tone. "I'm sorry."

"No, you're right. You were the one who looked out for me. Did anyone ever do the same for you?"

"Well, there was this serial killer," she quipped.

Liam turned and pretended to study her board. She didn't mean to make him uncomfortable. She'd simply had her fill of dwelling in the past. She stooped to pick up his helm and turned it in her hands. "What were you and Arabella doing? Mother said you came after me, but you're the one who helped me escape. It doesn't make sense."

"When Mother discovered you missing, she was…angered. She sent Arabella after you. Arie wanted to go alone, said she would draw less attention. Mother made her agree to take an escort."

"You were guarding Arabellla? Do you realize how insane that sounds? You're closer to the throne than she is, and she's the head of the Seelie Guard for fuck's sake!"

"It's been a long time since you were home," snipped Liam. "I have training too."

Gwen sighed. She hadn't meant to offend him. "I know. I just didn't think Mother would be willing to risk your life, not with you being important to the Court and all."

Liam didn't flinch at Gwen's implication that his station was more important to Indira than his value as her beloved son. "She didn't know I was the escort."

That explained it. Liam snuck off to follow Arabella into mortal danger. What an idiot. Gwen figured he'd already been read the riot act, so she let it pass. "What happened?"

"We were cornered in the woods just outside of the Korranthia Palace grounds." Liam's voice was thick, and his eyes cut to the armor on the desk.

Gwen didn't need her empathy link to feel his grief. As the eldest child of Aunt Ember and Uncle Monty, Arabella grew up in Avalon alongside him. When Gwen left, Arabella was the closest family member in age to him. Gwen had no way of knowing how close they might have grown in her absence. She hated to push him when he was so clearly pained, but she had to learn as much as possible if she hoped to discover who was responsible for the deaths of half her family. "What were you doing there?"

"We were heading to the palace. Arabella thought you might be stupid enough to try to hunt down the killers yourself." Liam raised an eyebrow, and Gwen blushed. He had her there.

"Then what?"

"We were ambushed. Someone hit me in the head. Hard. I'm a fair fighter, but I was blindsided." Liam gave a shudder, and Gwen could sense that pushing him might make him close up again. Instead, she put a hand on his shoulder.

"Don't do that!" he snapped.

She took a step back. "I wasn't. I just want to protect you. That's all."

He pushed a hand through his dark hair and looked at his feet. "I'm sorry Gwen. With your talents, I never know if you're going to pry into parts of me I'm not ready to share. I already feel like everyone here is against me."

Gwen nodded, and turned her face away so he didn't see the hurt in her eyes. "I know what that's like. Do you remember anything else?"

"I blacked out. When I came to, Arie was dead. The Korranthian guards had run off the attackers. Her blood was everywhere…"

The haunted look in her baby brother's eyes made Gwen's stomach roil. She wasn't much for affection, but she felt the compulsion to hug him. She couldn't do that, not when he didn't trust her to touch him. He did have his reasons.

"I'm so sorry Liam."

"What's done is done," he replied. His hands moved over his arms like he was trying to dust off the past.

Gwen flitted over to her chair. "Want to get this over with?"

"You mean, I can stay while you read my armor?"

"Sure. Why not? It's hard to open myself up for a reading when I'm surrounded by so many people who want to see me fail. You're different. You're my little brother, even if you aren't so little anymore."

Liam gave a sheepish smile, and Gwen felt a rush of joy seeing those dimples for the first time in years. She set the helm on the desk with the rest of his armor and dropped to her knees over it. She closed her eyes and envisioned the walls in her mind crumbling away. Reaching out with her right hand, she traced her fingertips over the cold steel. A feeling began in the center of her being and radiated outward, a sensation of falling, and darkness. She gave in to it, and the last of her barriers melted away.

She'd expected flashes of the forest since her empathic link, when used without direction or focus, connected to times and places of strong sensory pull. That usually coincided with violence, emotional turmoil, or disgusting situations. From Liam's description of events, she assumed the armor would take her to when his adrenaline peaked. But that wasn't the case.

Flashes of stone walls, marble statuary, and purple tapestries indicated she was picking up glimpses of the inside of the Korranthia Palace. Arabella's face flashed in front of her and disappeared. Blood splatters. The smell of tin. A screamed word. Laughter. Indira's tearful eyes.

The senses calmed, sounds muffled, visions blurred. In the past, Gwen's connection was broken by the intrusion of her own memories, but ever since she avenged Frankie, she could hold it as long as she desired. Only the strongest senses broke through, or those she connected with most. When she was sure she'd picked up everything from the attack, she let go.

The room grew brighter, and Liam was on the edge of the desk, staring at her with a concerned expression. "Gwen, what did you see?"

The room spun.

"Gwen? Did you get anything?" Liam's voice made her head throb. She was still sitting in the desk chair, her hand resting on the armor. She should have warned him that she'd need time to adjust to being back in the present. He sounded worried. She hated to make him worry about her.

"I'm ok, Liam. Give me a minute."

Once the world stopped spinning and her head didn't feel like someone cracked it open, she got to her feet. Liam reached out as if he wanted to help her but then pulled away suddenly, likely remembering how invasive her touch could be. "What did you sense?" he asked again.

"I won't know for sure until I get it processed. Some images, some sounds. You said you were attacked in the woods, right?"

"Yes. And then brought back to the palace."

That was weird. She thought she'd seen Arabella standing inside the palace. Maybe it would make more sense once she uploaded the data.

"I'm going to have to analyze it with my equipment," she said. "This part isn't very interesting. You don't need to stick around."

"How long does it take?" Liam asked.

"Extraction only takes a few minutes, but the program takes a few hours to isolate the senses and convert them into files that I can use. Until then, it's hard to make sense of anything. It's overload."

Liam seemed to struggle for a moment, his jaw clenching and unclenching, as if he were fighting with himself.

"Gwen," he said. "All this has made me realize that we might not have forever. I mean, life is short, even for us. Especially for us. And I —well, I missed you."

Gwen looked at her little brother. She knew she'd hurt him, and all she ever wanted was a normal life for them both. "I missed you too, Liam," she replied.

"Do you want to go grab some coffee? I mean, after you're done here, of course. I don't want to die with things like they are between us."

Gwen was afraid to reply in case she said the wrong thing and somehow made him retreat back behind those emotional walls he'd erected to keep her out. She simply nodded. And that's when Liam did the most amazing thing. He hugged her.

It was stiff, sudden, and more than a little awkward. She was careful not to read him this time. She didn't want to do anything to push him away. When he let go, there were tears in his eyes.

"Let me get the download started, and we can go while it processes," she said. Liam abruptly turned and flitted out the door. He must have cleared the outing with the guards because when Gwen stepped into the hallway thirty minutes later, he was alone, scrolling through his phone as he leaned against the wall.

When he saw her, he pocketed the device. "Everything go ok?" he asked. He'd dropped all formalities and was now just her brother, and Gwen hoped it would last.

"Yeah," she replied, shutting the door behind her. "That's the easy part. Where to?"

"There's a little place nearby. They serve the best bread pudding you've ever tasted. You still like bread pudding, right?"

Gwen grinned. As a kid, they'd shared a love for warm bread pudding with sweet rum sauce and a scoop of vanilla ice cream. She was touched he remembered. "Won't the council have a fit if we hit the streets?" she asked.

"I'm having it delivered," he replied. "You still take your coffee black, right?"

Gwen's heart dropped. She'd hoped she'd get some time alone with Liam, but she should have known better. With family dropping like flies, coffee and dessert out didn't exactly rank as mission-critical. Oh well, at least he was willing to talk to her.

They took the elevator to the ground floor. "Since when do brownstones come equipped with elevators?" she asked. It had been bugging her since she arrived, but it wasn't the kind of thing that she cared to pester the guards about. She preferred to harass them about booze and HBO.

"Since the Seelie Royals took over the entire block and collapsed all stairwells to limit points of entry," he replied. Naturally.

Two guards stood in the entranceway, one on each side of the front door, and another pair perched on the molding above it. Gwen was sure there were more stationed around the outside perimeter. Liam led her to the back of the house into what had once been a dining room. Now it was filled with fairy-sized tables. One wall was overtaken by a long bar, on top of which stood pastry trays, an espresso machine, and an assortment of other café items. Behind the bar stood a bored-looking fairy with dark hair and even darker eyes.

Something about her mannerisms reminded Gwen of Chessa. Members of the royal family milled around the tables and soaked in the sunlight pouring through a large window overlooking a private, walled-off garden. As she suspected, Gwen noticed guards standing at regular intervals atop the wall. Two of her younger cousins ran through the garden, and their squeals were the first natural thing she'd experienced since arriving at this makeshift safe house.

Liam walked to the counter, and the bored fairy produced a bag and two insulated Styrofoam cups from behind the bar. Unlike the provisions in the room, the takeout was sized for humans, so it was bulky for the fairy, even if she did have fae strength. Liam snapped his fingers, and the bag levitated to a nearby table.

"I didn't know we could do that!" exclaimed Gwen.

"Most can't. But you probably could if you bothered to learn," quipped Liam.

"But our magic is limited to altering perceptions, right?" Gwen felt like a clumsy foal wobbling through an unfamiliar forest. Matron Celeste had done things that nobody could explain, but Gwen had the impression that the other matrons didn't believe her when she asked about it. Or maybe they were too frightened by the possibility. Either way, Gwen wasn't ready to open up to her estranged brother about the second worst night of her life.

His gaze was intense as he answered both the question she asked and the one she hadn't. "Perception is reality. You do know that there's more to the fae than your precious Academy, right?"

"Obviously." Gwen could feel her own defenses snapping into place. Since when did she feel the need to defend the Academy? She declined the job as their leader because she never jibed with their view of the world. Her life there had been miserable. Yet something about Liam's words hit a nerve.

He must have realized it too. "Fairy Godparents have a specialized set of skills, I'll give you that. But there is nothing like the old fae bloodlines. *Your* bloodline."

"I didn't peg you for a purist," replied Gwen. This was taking a dark turn.

Liam sighed. "And I didn't peg you for a humanophile."

Gwen's jaw dropped. They were both members of the Seelie Royal Court, dedicated to living in peace with humanity, even if most mortals were ignorant of fae society. She didn't understand Liam's hostility. "Just because I can size-shift doesn't mean I'm a traitor to my kind," she said.

"I'm sorry, Gwen. But you have to understand that fae will judge you based on the company you keep."

"The company I keep? What can you possibly mean by that? I run a PI firm catering to fae. With a pixie. My only other friend is a griffin."

Liam took a sip of his coffee. "I don't want to have this conversation. Here, try the bread pudding."

Gwen wanted to shake him and ask him what the hell his problem was, but she was afraid. If she said anything wrong, he might block her out of his life completely. It was so unfair. He could casually drop bombs on her, and she had to take it if she wanted any kind of chance at a relationship with her little brother. What a load of shit. She stuffed a spoonful of bread pudding in her mouth. He was right on one account, though. It was delicious.

Once they finished eating, Liam insisted they take a walk in the garden. Gwen had hoped for personal conversation, updates on his life and things like that, but all her brother did was give her a rundown of what the meetings were about. Mostly, there were very few clues regarding who was targeting their family.

"What happened in Avalon?" Gwen asked, seeing this as her opportunity to glean intel. If she wasn't going to bond with Liam, she might as well get something out of this.

"That was the first strike. They blindsided us at Gathering."

Gwen remembered the yearly feast known as Gathering well. It was the one part of Seelie Royal Court she didn't hate. The entire family would congregate in the great hall to feast. In the courtyard, there would be a drum circle around a fire, and they would dance into the night. Twirling and flipping above the flames was the solitary moment of happiness in her miserable childhood.

Liam continued, his face ashen. "They assassinated Queen Estrella right there at the dining table. The gnome assassin was dressed as a royal guard, so it took a while for everyone to figure out what was happening. In the resulting chaos, we lost Felippe, Faiel, and Lilibet. The guards rallied at first, then seemed to turn on each other. It was mass hysteria. We had no recourse but to flee with the handful of guards we could trust. We scattered. I don't know where everyone else went at first, but we took refuge at The Graves. Mother wanted to get close to you. When we finally located the others, Leopold, Saladin, Ambrose, and Catellina had been hunted down and killed. Gammie was holed up with Giddeon and the girls—"

Liam's voice trailed to a stop, and Gwen laid a hand on his arm. Grief washed through the empathic link, even as she tried to block her magic. "I know, Liam," she said.

The grief flickered to something else, something menacing, before he pulled away and broke the link. "You don't know."

There was nothing she could say. They'd all been slaughtered. She might not know what he was feeling, but she was old friends with grief.

Liam left her there, standing alone in the garden. She watched him disappear back into the brownstone. She considered taking to the air and flying over the garden wall, leaving this place and her family forever. But something kept her feet planted on the ground. She told herself it was the possibility of finding answers, but that was only because she didn't want to face the truth that she couldn't bear to leave things like this with Liam. She paced the perimeter of the garden for a while, thinking about their conversation, then decided she needed a drink. She returned to the terrace office to check on the data and retrieve her bottle of Jack. The room was just as it had been with Gwen's desk, chair, and board dominating the room, but there was one notable exception—The armor was missing. And so was all of her equipment.

22

Norman's battered laptop was somehow faster than Chessa's MacBook Pro back at home. It was beaten to all hell, and Chessa didn't recognize the brand, but she couldn't argue with the results. Norman seemed like a decrepit old wizard, but his tech was next level. The windows she had open displayed video from all over the palace, and Chessa used the footage to draw out a rough schematic of the structure on some free software she found online.

Samson was being kept in the west wing in a space that, as far as Chessa could tell, had recently been converted into some kind of prison. The camera in the room didn't show the insides of the cells, but Chessa could make out a row of bars with cinderblock partitions. It didn't match the rest of the palace architecture. "Norman, did you set up these cameras or are you tapping into an established security system?" she asked.

"No way I could have installed them myself in this time. They'd be too hard to hide. Nah, I just hacked them. Not hard to do, really, since I'm onsite. The Seelie had them in place to protect from outsiders."

Chessa shook her head in amazement. This guy was something else. "And that one," she said, pointing to the screen showing the hallway outside the miniature jail. "That door at the end. It looks like it leads outside."

"Aye. But I know what you're thinking, and it's a bad plan. You can see them guards along the hall for yourself. You ain't getting by them with a griffin, even if you could get to him in the first place."

Norman claimed he wanted nothing to do with helping Chessa, but every time she asked a question about the layout of the palace, he was quick with an answer. She could tell that he wanted her to succeed, even if he was terrified to have any part in it himself. He filled her stomach from the rations he had stashed in the small kitchen, answered her every question, and even pointed out a few hidden passages—hidden to the Unseelie occupiers, at least—though none of them came close enough to the west wing to be of much use, all the while pretending to read a musty old book from one of the shelves or tooling around by the tiny window.

"I'm going to get my friend out, Norm. You can either help me come up with a plan, or you can sit by and watch me die on your screen. As far as I can tell, you don't seem like the type to let the world move on without you."

The wizard grunted and flipped a page of his book.

She decided to switch to other tactics. "What were you doing here?"

Norman set the book on a side table with a thump. "What do you mean?"

"You said you were hiding out here back when Avalon still belonged to the Seelie," said Chessa. "So you've been keeping watch a long time. Do you know anything about Gwendolyn Evenshine?"

Norman nodded slowly. "I was made to learn her face in case she showed up. But she weren't here the day these ones took over."

"Has she been here since?"

"Not that I've seen."

By the amount of surveillance he'd done, Chessa doubted he would have missed them bringing Gwen in. That meant her family probably still had her. That was something, at least. It would have been a whole lot harder to get both Samson and Gwen out of here alive.

"You also said you did bad things, I assume you meant for the

Unseelie. Other than being their lackey, what was your plan before I showed up?"

"I completed my mission, little miss. When you came, I was content serving those above me."

"Your mission included leaving a Seelie prisoner unattended so she could escape? Of fighting a troll to save her life? It doesn't seem like you were content at all."

Norman stammered. "No, my-my mission for them. I just—what I mean to say is—I'm Unseelie. I'm one of them, and I'm here to do a job, which I did, well—I…um…did my part, anyhow."

"Being Unseelie doesn't mean supporting whatever is happening here," replied Chessa. "I know plenty of Unseelie back home making lives for themselves on their own terms. I understand that the people you work for are powerful, but you did whatever job they brought you here for while hiding in a secret location that they can't find. You're still hiding. It doesn't seem to me that you're one of them at all, Unseelie or not."

"How do you mean?"

"These Unseelie overthrew Avalon, Norman. That's not something that happens peaceably. I don't know what part you had in it all, but that's in the past, and you have the chance to make things right."

Norman's head fell.

Chessa continued, "I'm going to get my friend. I'm going to sneak down to the west wing, find a way to open his cell, and leave through that door right there. You can try to stop me, or you can do what's right. But sitting here in this little room isn't an option."

The vein in Norman's temple throbbed. He stared, unblinking, at the screen for a long moment. Finally, he sighed. "I won't try to stop you, little miss, and I'll help as much as I can from here. Your plan is shite. You will die. So, here's what we're going to do. You're going to get some rest, and I'll help you come up with a better plan in the morning. After that, you're on your own."

Chessa smiled at her new friend. "Deal."

23

Gwen pushed her Docs against the floor and took to the air in a great heave. She flew down the hall, into the elevator, and seethed all the way to the top floor.

Who the fuck do they think they are, bringing me here, pushing me to invade my brother's privacy, then stealing my shit?

Blood pounded in her ears. She burst out of the elevator so violently that the guard squeaked. Gwen rolled her eyes but kept going, all the way down the hall to the meeting room. The guard outside the door moved to stop her, but she was too fast. She flung open the door, and someone let loose a startled cry. The four council members crowded around a table, their eyes wide. Even Indira looked startled at her sudden entrance.

"Where is it?" Gwen barked, receiving only terrified or empty gazes.

Indira's face hardened once again. "Gwendolyn. I taught you better manners. What is this about?" she asked. Gwen thought she caught a tremble in her mother's polished voice.

That's when she noticed how terrible everyone looked. Azrah was the worst of them, her ringlets frizzed, her complexion washed out, and her eyes underscored by dark circles. Domingo looked like he

133

might throw up at any moment, and Eymen was no better. Even Indira lacked her usual calm composure. All the steam fizzled out of Gwen.

"My equipment. It's been stolen."

Nobody seemed to register her words. They all stared at her.

"What's going on?"

A scream cut through the tension, raw and filled with pure anguish. None of the council moved. A fairy wailed in the hallway. Three guards were attempting to hold her back, but she flailed, pushing and pummeling them with her fists.

"Let her in," said Indira quietly.

The guards moved aside, and Aunt Ember appeared, her face a mess of tears, her face twisted in rage. "Get him back!" she screamed. "You're the council. You're the fucking Seelie Queen, Azrah! You're supposed to be the most powerful entity on earth! Get my Augustus back!"

Azrah covered her face with her hands.

Indira stood and walked to her sister. "Ember, I know your pain. My child is gone too."

Wait, what? Gwen's mind spun, and darkness closed in around her. "What do you mean Liam's gone? I was just with him! And Augustus was playing out in the garden half an hour ago!"

Nobody paid her any attention.

"Your *child* is a grown man, and it's not his blood staining the garden path! Liam can protect himself. Augustus is a boy. Just a boy. My boy." A sob cut Ember's words short.

"You're right. Augustus is probably dead. That's why it would be foolish to make rash decisions and put more of us at risk. The Seelie Court must keep calm and make hard decisions in this trying time."

Ember launched at Indira, but the guard by the door was faster. He caught her around the waist and held her back. "Azrah, quit letting my sister speak for you and tell me what you're doing to get my baby back!" She screamed.

All Azrah did was cover her face and cry.

Some queen, thought Gwen. She realized that for all their meetings and appearances, the Council had no more of a handle on what was happening than she did. And they were far too busy chasing their tails to do shit about her or Liam. It was clearer now more than ever that she needed to go to Avalon. It was where the insurrection occurred, where Chessa and Samson lost contact, and, if the abductors planned on keeping Liam alive, it's where they would take him. If they didn't—well, she was already too late to do anything about it. The thought made a lump form in her throat. No. She couldn't dwell on uncertainties. She needed to act. The first step was to get the hell out of here before she ended up as helpless as poor Ember. She walked around the guards restraining her distraught aunt.

Nobody made a move to stop her.

AFTER A QUICK VISIT to her room to load up a few provisions, she was back out in the hall. She could still hear Ember's screams from the floor above, and a door near the elevator hung open. She peeked her head in. Uncle Monterey was sitting on the couch, holding a stuffed toy in his hands and crying. As much as she didn't want to deal with this right now, Gwen needed his help. "Hey Uncle Monty," she said, more to let him know she was approaching than to actually greet him.

"They said they could protect us," he said in a far-away voice. "First Ari, and now Augustus."

"They say a lot of things." Gwen sat next to the man and put her arm around his shoulders. He wasn't a blood relation, so she didn't have to shield her empathic touch to keep from reading him, and she doubted there was much to read anyhow. He was a father in mourning. "I'm going back to Avalon," she said.

Monty nodded.

"Can I take your phone?"

He turned his head to look at her, and his face contorted as if he were about to say something. He reached in his pocket and took out his cell. He palmed it for a moment. "They told us to steer clear of you, you know. Ever since you left for the Academy. They told us you were dangerous." After a long pause, he continued. "Unlike Ember, I don't hold any delusions that my boy is alive. Can you promise me one thing?"

Gwen nodded.

"When you find the sons-of-bitches who did this, you kill them. All of them. Can you promise me that?"

Gwen swallowed hard as she recognized the feral look in sweet Uncle Monty's eyes. She'd seen it in the mirror after Frankie was murdered. "I'll try."

He handed her the phone, and Gwen left. As she breezed by Curtis in the hall, she muttered "I'm going on a suicide mission. You coming?"

A KPD vehicle whizzed to a stop in front of the brownstone as Gwen and Curtis walked out the front door of the not-so-safe house, lights and sirens in full effect. Before she was five steps away, Captain O'Toole scrambled out, Detective Pox at his side. When the captain saw Gwen, he froze. To Gwen's horror, he dropped into a bow.

"You're too late," said Gwen.

"My apologies, my lady, I wasn't apprised of the full situation until five minutes ago. What in the name of Danu is going on here?"

There wasn't a note of sarcasm or barb in his words. If Gwen weren't so worried about her brother, she would give him shit, but as it was, she had bigger fish to fry. She wasn't about to blow precious moments laying it all out for him. The KDP wasn't remotely prepared for a fae civil war, and that's exactly where this was headed. "The Queen is inside," she replied as she strode by him. "I'm sure she'll be happy to brief Korranthia's finest."

As Curtis scouted ahead, Gwen turned just in time to see the captain climbing the steps to the brownstone. "O'Toole," she called. "Keep my family alive until I get back."

24

Norman insisted that if Chessa was going to make a rescue attempt, she needed to wait until the Unseelie gave up the hunt for her. He spent the morning helping her come up with a plan to get into the holding cell through the air ducts.

"Aren't they protected?" asked Chessa. "The fairy guards are small enough to patrol the ductwork."

"They've only held the palace for a couple of months, and in that time, I ain't never seen them go near the vents. I'm sure they will after you've had your way, though."

"It certainly beats marching right up to the door and demanding they free my friend," she replied. If the Seelie ever took Avalon back, Chessa would have to ask Gwen about security going forward. She couldn't imagine the Council would leave any avenue of navigating the halls of the palace of Avalon unprotected. Not that anyone, fae or otherwise, had ever dared to make a move on Avalon before now. It wasn't like fae magic was something you could steal away in the night. Spies and assassins, on the other hand, could make great use of such lapses in security. And those looking to make a jailbreak. Too bad Samson wouldn't fit through an air vent. The idea of his feathers puffed up in indignation at the thought of being stuffed into one made her grin for a moment before she stood and paced the floor. Again.

Sitting around a hidden library all day long while Samson was locked up made her stir-crazy, even if Norman was wise in advising a cautious, planned approach. Chessa made good use of her time. She charted the comings and goings of the Seelie guards for much of the night and all through the day as they scoured the palace in search of the runaway pixie. They were mostly stationed at entryways with high traffic, guards coming and going as they conducted their search. There was no audio, but she could tell that the leader, a blond fairy with a regal bearing, was convinced the prisoner had fled. She kept sending groups of guards out various exits to search the grounds. It was a solid tactical decision. If Chessa had an ounce of sense, she would have been long gone.

Something that caught Chessa's attention was the large number of guards stationed near the south exit night and day. She never saw anyone enter or exit through the door, but there were always ten guards in the hall. It was nowhere near the holding cells.

"Hey, Norman, where does that door lead?" she asked.

"To the grove," he answered, buttoning up his coat.

That only raised more questions as far as Chessa was concerned. "Is there something important about the grove?"

"Can't say as I know, little miss. Maybe they're keeping something out there. We'd best avoid the area."

Chessa nodded. "It's probably for the best. We don't need any unexpected surprises. Where are you going?"

"I need to report in."

Chessa looked up from the screen. "You can't. The troll will have told them what happened!"

"He didn't."

"How can you know?"

"Because I killed him."

Chessa bit her bottom lip at the shadow that passed over Norman's face when he said it. "What if they saw you on camera? I'm sure they've already combed through every one of the recordings to find me."

"Look here," replied Norman taking his seat at the desk and opening the laptop. "There are two cameras in the great hall, one pointed at the entranceway and one at the thrones. Like I told you, the Seelie weren't protecting from inside. As far as anyone knows, I'm an incompetent oaf who didn't secure a prisoner, not a traitor. If I don't report in, they'll figure it out."

There was nothing Chessa could do to stop him. Norman was already opening the secret exit. "Be careful," she said.

"Don't worry. I'll see you tonight, little miss. Don't do anything until I come back, got it?"

Chessa gave a reluctant nod and flew across the room to sit at the computer once again. There was no more light shining through the tiny stained-glass window when Norman returned, and the laptop clock said it was after eleven at night. Chessa was still sitting at the computer when the wall slid open and the wizard appeared. He had a black eye.

"Norman, what happened?" she asked, rushing over to him.

"Ain't nothing but a small punishment, little miss. It's like I said, they just think I made a mistake. The good news is they think you're long gone."

"How could you work for these monsters?" Chessa asked.

"Monsters aren't born, they're made. That's what me da always said. And believe me, when you get to the higher-ups, there are monsters all around."

"Your da had a point. But Norman, you deserve better."

"Begging your pardon, little miss, you don't know what I deserve."

Chessa didn't care. As far as she knew, this man was tortured by the path he was on, and when it came down to it, he acted to help her. She wanted to hug the wizard, but she wasn't sure he'd appreciate it. Instead, she flitted up so she could look into his eyes. "Perhaps not, but I know it's not this."

Norman gave up the fight, flashed a half-smile that didn't touch his eyes, and turned away. "Do you need something to eat?" he asked as he headed to the kitchen.

"No, I stole a Pop-Tart from the cabinet an hour ago. But thanks."

When he returned, he plopped down in the red velvet high-back chair by the window, a bowl of warm canned pasta in his hand. The noodles were shaped like Mario characters. It gave Chessa an idea.

She flew over to the computer, pulled up the website for the RPG she played with Gwen, and logged in. The Seelie Court might be tracking her email, but there was no way they would think to hack Gwen's game of *Death Mob*. She opened the chat window and rattled off a message.

> *Doc,*
>
> *I'm sending this message to warn you that the base has been overtaken by the red and silver forces of the hidden enemy. They've imprisoned Eagle-Eye. I had help in eluding capture, and I'm going after the copper. If you get this message, please reply with your status.*
>
> *-Boss Glitter*

The code wasn't hard to break, but any layers of obfuscation could mean more time before it was cracked. Gwen would get it right away —of that much, Chessa was sure. If Gwen was still with her family, she might have figured out more of the situation, or more likely, knowing the royals, she was locked up somewhere alone. Chessa hoped that Gwen's mother had decided to act like one for once and had everything under control, but even she had trouble believing in the best of Indira Evenshine. Chessa's insides twisted. If Avalon was compromised, there was no place on earth where Gwen would be safe. She didn't understand what was happening with the Seelie and Unseelie, but she'd always been a pragmatist. She swallowed and stuffed her feelings back in their metaphorical box. She couldn't be distracted by uncertainty when there wasn't a damn thing she could do about it. Right now, the first order of business was rescuing Samson. "Norman, the guards will be changing shifts at 8 a.m. so long as they keep with their schedule. I plan to make my move then," she said.

Norman set his Mario noodles on the table, the spoon clattering against the edge of the bowl. "You're going to get yourself killed."

"You've helped me this much, and if you want to stay out of the action, I understand. But there's one more thing I need. You seem to want to make up for what you've done. If I'm going to get killed, you might as well tell me what that is before I go. I want to understand what's holding you back."

She didn't mean to be so harsh, but all her softer attempts to get the wizard to talk had stalled out. He would seem to warm to her, then shut down entirely. If he wasn't going to help her rescue Sammy, the least he could do was tell her everything he knew, and arm her with information that she might be able to use to survive the escape attempt.

Norman looked pained. He paced back and forth in the middle of the room while Chessa was perched on the desk, flitting across the keyboard to navigate the internet. "Please don't do this. Stay here for a few more days, then fly off in the night. Go home, little miss. I'd feel better knowing you're out there safe somewhere in the world."

"I can't do that. I'm going for my friend with or without your help. If you would tell me what your deal is, I might be able to help you before I go. I promise I won't judge you. Hell, one of my best friends practically lives at the bar, and I'm fairly certain he deals pixie dust out of the back room."

Norman stopped dead in his tracks. "You don't use, do you?"

"Do you see me casting spells and levitating objects? Though a little active magic might be helpful in my current situation." She laughed. For years, pixies used pixie dust to become magical practitioners, but the cost was too great. Some used occasionally, for specific reasons, but they were few and far between. Most used in secret. The combination of the power and the chemical dependency was too much. Chessa made light of it, but the true reason she'd never tried it herself was because she'd lost a childhood friend to dust addiction. A taste was enough to hook even the most straight-edged pixie, and the dependency only grew with time, turning their minds to mush. Kimmie hadn't been herself for months before the KPD found her dead in a ditch at the ripe age of fifteen. Chessa didn't see what good it would do to discuss it now.

"Good. My family is mixed up in the business of it all. It's why I could never break into the Seelie Court."

"Oh, Norman. Fuck those squares who would judge you for what your family does."

"Yeah, well, fuck me, too, then. I've done so much worse."

"Please, Norm, I won't judge you. Whatever you've done in the past won't change anything, but it is holding you back. If you get it off your chest, you might be able to move on with your life."

Blood rushed to the old man's face. He marched over to the desk so quickly, Chessa thought he was going to squash her, but he stopped short. He looked down at her, anger or anguish blazing in his eyes, she couldn't tell which.

"Fine. You want to know what I did? I killed the Seelie queen. As good as, anyhow. I let them in, opened the door. They brought *her* in." Norman shuddered.

"Who did they bring?"

"The Ghost. It was her that killed the queen."

Chessa couldn't help but feel a surge of excitement. The Ghost of Korranthia was a notorious fae assassin from her neck of the woods. More than one *Crime Wave* blog post was dedicated to speculating about her motives and whereabouts. And she was also the only criminal on Detective Samson Wayne's most wanted list. He was going to flip his feathers when he found out she was here. "Delilah Johnson was here in Avalon?"

"Long gone, now I reckon. That's her way. Do the job then disappear. Ain't seen nothing like her though. One minute she was a gnome, the next, a monster. Her eyes as black as night, her hand quick. There was nothing natural about the way she worked."

The thought of Samson sitting in a cell while Delilah Johnson might be around chilled Chessa's excitement. This wasn't research for *Crime Wave*. Her friend was in real danger. Norman must have sensed the change in her mood.

"I stood by and watched the Ghost slit the queen's throat wide open. Might as well have done it meself. Still want to be best friends?"

Chessa stood on the desk, her stomach churning with a wash of emotions. Whatever role Norman played in all this was peanuts. He'd been holed up for weeks living with this on his conscience, but he was nothing but a pawn in a game he'd never understood, having been sidelined by society for things beyond his control and taken in by the only fae who would have him. And it was eating him alive. Now, here he was, angry, confused, and defined by the worst thing he'd ever done, admittedly a crime against life itself. Chessa had known men like him before.

"Oh, Norman," she said, trying to keep emotion from her voice. "Yes, I do. What you did was horrible, you know that. But since then, you've regretted it. You saved my life."

"All this. I'm to blame." He motioned around the empty room, but Chessa knew he was referring to the occupation of Avalon. She had to help him.

"This was happening with or without you. The fae occupying Avalon right now didn't wake up one day and say 'there's this wizard, wouldn't it be cool to have him help us kill the queen?' This was in the works long before you were sent here. And if it wasn't you, it would have been someone else. You were used, but you don't have to be their tool anymore. Are you going to sit around and pity yourself for the role you played, or are you going to do something about it? Are you going to make it right?"

The color drained out of Norman's face. His shoulders sagged. Tears welled up in his eyes. Chessa knew she had him, but she also knew this was what he needed. If he sat back and watched her die today, there would be no redemption for the wizard. He would waste away. "Fight back, Norman. The Seelie were wrong for shunning you. The Unseelie were wrong for using you. Show them all that you're worth more than they ever gave you credit for. You have a chance to make things right, and it all comes down to the choice you make today. Right now."

25

Gwen and Curtis walked side by side through the Leather District. The latter kept his head swiveling, searching for any potential threats, but Gwen stared straight ahead. She was done being a pawn in someone else's game. She didn't know the first thing about getting across the ocean, and she didn't know what she would do once she got there, but one thing was certain—she needed weapons. And she knew a half-ogre who could get them for her. She headed to Pub Nine.

It was already eleven at night, and Cross-Eyed Quincy was sitting at the bar shooting the shit with the regulars. The buzzed faux-hawk horse mane belonged to Thom, but Gwen couldn't place the other guy. Wait. It couldn't be.

"Jeff Jarvis?" she gasped as she approached. The necromancer flashed her a guilty grin.

"In the flesh, so to speak," he replied. The kid was a victim of the Brain Scraper, and last she saw him, dead twice over.

"I take it your frat brothers succeeded in resurrecting you."

"Yeah, I was their class project." As he spoke, he scratched at his ear. It became dislodged, and he blushed as he scrambled to reattach it. Gwen shook her head. She had worse things to worry about than a sheepish undead barback.

Quincy wasn't nearly so friendly. "What do you want?" he barked.

"Glad to see you too, Q."

"Don't call me that." His face was twisted into a snarl worse than his usual resting ogre face, and the scar over his eye was white with the tightening of facial muscles.

Thom's orange gills moved the air. He vacated a barstool on the other side of Quincy, gave a mock bow, and pulled Jarvis away, the latter walking stiffly as if he were afraid of dropping more body parts. The necromantic arts still had a long way to go.

Gwen didn't sit. "Is there somewhere private we can talk?"

"No."

"It's important. It's about Chessa."

He sighed. "Of course it is."

"I'm going after her, and I need some supplies."

"Of course you do. What is it this time? Some other serial killer got her locked in a box?"

"Worse."

Quincy shook his head, drained his oversized beer, and got to his feet. "Come on then."

Gwen followed him to the back. On the surface, it was a supply room with shelves holding napkins, condiments, dishes, and more, but Gwen could tell from the folding table and chairs in the center of the room that the space was used for other things. What exactly, she could only imagine.

"How are you getting to Avalon?" asked Quincy once the door swung closed behind Curtis, who had the good sense to keep quiet.

Gwen narrowed her eyes. "How do you know where she went? You're not in league with *them*, are you?"

"I don't know nothing. I just know what the papers I got her said. She was trying to stay below the radar if you know what I mean. She was going after you. So how come you're here and she's there?"

"It's a long story, and I've already wasted enough time." Gwen didn't want to tell Quincy that the Seelie Court was faltering and that she doubted anyone cared enough to stop her from traveling the good old-fashioned way. If word got out, there would be chaos amongst the fae. Besides, she didn't trust Q as far as she could throw him, and even in her large form, that would be like moving a mountain.

"Sure, old Quincy is a waste of time. I get it. Have you ever thought that maybe Chia would be safer if she didn't pal around with you?"

He might as well have flattened her on the spot. It was all Gwen had thought since her best friend had been shot out of the sky while casing the Academy.

Curtis cut in. "Um, hello. I beg your pardon, Mr. Cross-Eyed Quincy, but none of that matters at the moment. Presently, we're in need of equipment that Lady Gwendolyn seems to believe you can help procure. Two fairies don't stand much of a chance breaking into Avalon and rescuing a pixie and a griffin with our magic alone."

Q squinted and pointed at Curtis with a fat thumb. "Who's the narc?"

"Don't worry, he's with me," replied Gwen.

"That's exactly why I'm worried. Here."

Quincy rummaged through a box tucked on the top shelf behind some barware. He tossed Gwen a tiny vest, which she caught in one hand, then went back to rummaging, talking as he did. "That'll absorb your standard offensive spells, source sticks, and the like. And I got one for Mr. Sprite Scout too. Oh, and you could probably use this seeing as how your magic ain't so hot." He extracted an amulet from the box and handed it down to Gwen. "It's like that little twig you carry, only it amplifies *and* directs your magic."

Curtis' mouth hung open, but he seemed smart enough to say nothing about the contraband.

"And from what you say, you'll be needing the last resort." He pulled a Glock out of the same box. "The body is plastic, but the rounds are iron-tipped. You need to be real careful not to breathe in when you fire or you'll end up burning up from the inside out. Don't bother asking about extra rounds. You got 15, that's it. Put it in your wand holster, and it should shift size with you if I understand all that fairy godmother twinkly shit correctly."

Gwen paled but nodded. There was no wounding with iron-tipped bullets. One scratch, and poof, no more Gwen. "Is there a safety or anything I need to know about firing?" she asked. All her gun knowledge came from Samson's detective shows.

"Not like you're thinking. Just point, and firmly pull the trigger."

Gwen nodded and holstered the gun next to her wand.

Curtis cleared his throat. "I don't mean to be a 'Sprite Scout' as you say, but how are we going to get on an airplane with all this? The mortals may not care about our wands, but I don't think they'll be thrilled with *that*."

"You ain't going by plane, Scout. If you don't care who knows your whereabouts, I've got a much faster way to get you over the sea. There's just the matter of payment."

Gwen winced. Her family had money, but they weren't in the business of funding their delinquent daughter. "What're you thinking?"

"Between the equipment and passage, it'll run you around five big ones. And I'm cutting you a break."

The breath left Gwen's body in a gust. "Can we work something out, Q?"

"I said don't call me that."

Curtis straightened up and puffed out his chest. "I can cover it. Give me thirty minutes, and I'll be back with five hundred dollars."

Quincy burst out laughing, and even Gwen felt a tug at the corners of her mouth. "Where did you get this guy?" huffed the half-ogre.

Gwen turned to Curtis. "We couldn't book a place on a barge for five hundred. You don't happen to have a few *grand* sitting around, do you?"

The smaller fairy blanched, which made Quincy laugh harder. Gwen took the opportunity to press him. "Quincy, I know you care about Chessa. I don't know what kind of trouble she's in, and I need to get to her. What can you do for me?"

His booming laugh stopped abruptly, but the comic relief seemed to have thawed him. He grabbed one of the folding chairs, flipped it around, and sat backward on it with his elbows on the table. "You and Chia," he said, his expression serious. "You got this thing going. Seems like a good thing. I'm looking to go straight. I want in."

"What thing?" Gwen couldn't imagine what Quincy was getting at.

"That business of yours. Where people pay you to snoop. Chia told me all about it, about how it gives you purpose or some shit. I could use that. Purpose."

Gwen was caught entirely off guard. "The PI firm?"

"Yeah. C&F Investigations. That's the name of it, right?"

She nodded dubiously. She'd never known Quincy to have an interest in anything but gambling and drinking. "No offense, Q-Quincy, but the reason you're a valuable informant is that you're connected. Do you know what I mean? If you're working cases with us, nobody is going to want to give you information."

"That's just it, I've been helping Chia here and there, and nobody gives a shit because they know nothing's going to blow back on them. But you. Everyone knows you're in tight with the KPD. You're already hurting my reputation showing up here like you own the place. The way I see it, if I own a piece of the PI action, I can assure everyone that their names will stay off the KPD paper pusher desks. I can do what I do here, and nothing will change, except I'll get a say in what happens on your end."

"Let me get this straight," said Gwen scowling. "You want to be a sanctioned double-agent?"

"Sure, whatever you want to call it."

"And you want a piece of C&F Investigations for doing exactly what you're already doing?"

"I want an equal part in it."

Gwen shook her head. "No way."

"Look, Twinkletoes, you need what I've got. This is my offer. Take it or get the hell out."

"I can't make a deal like that. Chessa and I are equal partners, and I can't give what isn't mine."

Quincy's eyes narrowed, and he scratched his chin. "Then I'll take half of what you can give. Chia can keep her half, and you and me split the rest. It's only fair, anyhow. She's the one who runs things."

Gwen knew Quincy wouldn't leave Chessa in a bind, but she didn't have time for this. She needed to get to Avalon, and she needed Q's help. "Fine," she said. "You've got a deal."

Gwen and Curtis left Quincy to arrange details. They sat at the bar, Gwen in large size sitting on a barstool, and Curtis perched atop the main bar in front of her at the tables set for smaller fae. Gwen didn't recognize the bartender, but that didn't bother her. The Pub Nine staff was constantly changing with the semester shifts at the three local universities, and this young elf was obviously an Asha'atai coed. It didn't matter to Gwen, so long as they could pour a stiff Jack and Coke.

She pulled out Uncle Monty's phone and signed into her email. Her inbox was filled with junk with the exception of two emails, one related to a case that had been on the backburner, and the other a notification from her *Death Mob* game indicating she had an incoming message from Boss Glitter. "What the fuck?" she muttered. Was Chessa really working on her virtual crime empire from Avalon? Then it hit her. "You little genius!"

The message was cryptic but simple. The Unseelie had taken Avalon, Samson was captured, and Chessa was going after him, possibly with help from someone.

This was bad. Very bad.

Gwen jumped to her feet, making Curtis knock over his lime and seltzer. "What is it?" he blurted, reaching for napkins.

"Can't talk here," she murmured, then she turned on her heels and strode back through the swinging doors, leaving Curtis to settle the tab.

Quincy was still sitting at the poker table, this time with a laptop in front of him and with a pair of glasses she'd never seen him wear sitting on his wide, scar-cleaved nose. He pulled them off and glared at her. "Ever heard of knocking?" he griped.

"Are you finished yet? I've got to get to Chessa."

"Uh, yeah, I know that already. What crawled down your pants?"

Gwen wasn't sure how much she wanted to share. She was certain there were Unseelie in Quincy's circles, though most of the fae underground was Seelie or Courtless. The Unseelie didn't generally mingle in cities, and even the ones who'd taken up residence in Boston stayed to themselves, tormenting humans on the down low. She had no idea what could possibly organize them into taking over Avalon and killing her family. Whatever this was, it was bigger than she ever imagined.

"I just got some new intel. Well, sort of. And she needs to get the fuck out of Avalon."

"Wait up. Doesn't your *family* hold Avalon? That's why Chia went there in the first place."

Gwen bit her lip. "Q, if I let you in on something, you can't tell anyone, do you understand? It would cause panic. If the leak got traced back to me, it would get me excommunicated from Seelie society. And it would get Chessa killed."

Quincy smacked his fat hands on the table as he rose, rage playing in his eyes. For a moment, Gwen thought he meant to make a fairy kabob of her. "Look, you royal fairy bitch. I'm sick of you acting like you're the only one who gives a shit about Chia. I've known her for longer than you've been around. There's more to her than you give her credit for, and there's more to me too."

Gwen was shocked. She'd never taken Quincy for more than a goon, but he had a point. Chessa had a life before she entered it, and she had friends, which is more than Gwen could ever say for herself. Maybe she had Quincy all wrong. "I'm sorry. I'm scared, and frankly, I don't know who to trust. It's not like we've ever been on the best of terms. But you're right. We do have one thing in common. And if you want to help Chessa, I suppose I should tell you what she's up against."

After a tense moment, Quincy sat back down and motioned to the chair beside him. As Gwen sat, the door swung open again, and Curtis flew in, breathing as if he'd flown across the entire bar in thirty seconds flat. Both Gwen and Quincy ignored him, and he settled on the table.

Gwen paused for a beat. "My family is under attack, and half of us have been killed already. The enemy took Avalon, and the rest of my family is in hiding. I knew this much when I came in today. But I just received word from Chessa that the Unseelie Court is responsible."

Curtis gasped. "What would the Unseelie want with Avalon? Why would they turn on their own kind? It's humans they hate, right?" He looked over at Q. "Right?"

"I don't understand it either," replied Gwen. "Joining the Unseelie Court has always been an option for fae who didn't want to coexist with humanity. They're free to make their own way, and I've even heard that they have their own communities in the more remote parts of the earth. As far as I know, they've issued no demands. Attacking the seat of the Seelie Throne makes no sense."

"Actually," interrupted Quincy, "it makes perfect sense."

Both Gwen and Curtis gaped at the half-ogre.

"You fairies, you live in a world away from the rest of us. And the royals are the worst. You have no idea what goes on in the streets. That's the real reason nobody here trusts you."

Anger burned in Gwen's gut. Quincy knew nothing of her life. She'd always been an outcast, emotionally abused as a child, always viewed as other by the Matrons at the Academy. She gritted her teeth. Going off on Quincy now would break everything she'd been trying to build. "What do you mean?" she asked, her voice level and low.

"I mean that nobody gives a shit about us regular fae, especially those who can't pass for human. Even the Seelie. The Seelie Council is a figurehead and ain't done nothing but divide fae power and hand it over to the rich leaders of the kingdoms. I don't know how it is everywhere, but the Korranthian royals are human-loving trash."

"Frankie was not trash." Gwen was seething now.

Curtis cut in. "We're Seelie. We get along with humans. It's what the Accords were about, and it defines us."

"Well, sure, that's the official line. But we don't all buy into it. Seelie live in the shadows just as much as Unseelie, all in the name of serving *them*."

Gwen stifled her anger. She couldn't afford to piss off Quincy, not now, but she didn't understand where this was coming from. "I don't get this anti-human rhetoric. Frankly, it's concerning."

"Concerning? What's concerning is that any of this is surprising to you. Goes to show what our leaders are good for. The Accords were hundreds of years ago. They protect mortals, not us. Who protects us? Cuz it sure as shit ain't the Seelie Council."

"You sound like one of them. Are you Unseelie, Quincy?" Gwen backed away from the ogre. He was a criminal, but she didn't peg him for Unseelie. If he was one of them, he might be gunning for her too.

"You see, there's the rub," said Q, rolling his eyes. "There ain't no room for civilized talk with your type. My mama was Seelie. She believed in the lie of peaceful coexistence. And I'm Seelie too, or I wouldn't be here, mingling with humanity in the pubs of Korranthia. But I gots plenty of Unseelie friends, and guess what? They're fae like the rest of us."

Curtis nodded as if this all made sense to him, but Gwen's brain was still struggling to get around it. This was the most Quincy had ever said to her. She figured she owed him a listen.

"Look, I get along fine with mortals. Their money is as good as anyone's. I'm just tryin' to tell you that everyone don't see it the same, and those Korranthian royals, they's barely fae themselves. Some pointed ears don't make you a part of the fae realm. Only a few years ago, there wasn't a non-humanoid fae in the palace besides Grimore. And he can only do so much."

Gwen had the same thought when she first arrived at the palace of Korranthia to meet her first charge, the beautiful Princess Francesca. The non-humanoid fae were relegated to one tiny table in the lavish ballroom. Come to think of it, she hadn't seen many others at all until the Royal Trials, when Frankie proved herself worthy of becoming the Crown Princess, just before she was murdered.

"Quincy, do you know anything about the death of Princess Francesca?" asked Gwen. Her mouth was dry, and her heart was pounding.

"Well, ain't that a change in conversation?" he replied. "What would I know that you don't? Ain't you the one who figured out who the Brain Scraper was? Chia killed that matron of yours. There was many who said it was a shame. Matron Celeste did a lot of good helping to promote non-humanoid fae interests. Nobody pegged her for a serial killer."

"That's just it. The Brain Scraper—Matron Celeste—she had her own issues. But she did speak up for downtrodden fae. What if, just hear me out, what if somebody used her? Think about it. After Frankie was killed, King Marco turned into a recluse. The Queen let Grimore take charge. A change in power that served Grimore's interests."

Quincy rubbed his scraggly beard and nodded. "Does seem suspicious when you say it that way. But Grimore's Courtless. Everybody knows that."

"Exactly. He's only out for himself," she replied.

"So you think he's done this? Mucking about in Korranthian politics is one thing, but you're talking about a full-on rebellion. You think Grimore did all that from here?"

"I don't know," admitted Gwen.

The world spun around her, pieces clicking into place like a giant three-dimensional puzzle. King Marco's humanoid staff, Grimore's reverence for Matron Celeste, Queen Charis' cold demeanor. She didn't have the full picture, but something inside told her she stumbled onto the truth. The princess might have been murdered by a serial killer, but Matron Celeste had merely been the weapon. Someone else wielded it.

"They killed her," murmured Gwen.

Curtis rushed to her side as she involuntarily flashed small. If she could have poofed out of existence altogether, in that moment, she would have. The realization that Frankie's own mother had a hand in her death was too much. Before the tears had a chance to fall, her anguish turned to anger. Still in small form, she flew to the center of the table, rage bubbling in the center of her being like magma beneath the earth's crust. "Whatever your politics, whatever your thoughts, you have to understand that what is happening right now is bigger than any of us. And Chessa's in the center of it. I will not let those motherfuckers sacrifice her the way they did Frankie. Either you're going to help me, or you're in my way."

Quincy sat in the folding chair, his mouth agape and computer pushed off to the side. He pulled the laptop back in front of him. "I was already helping you before you busted in here and turned this into the fucking resistance," he mumbled. "I've been hearing the people sing. No need to flay me."

He said it like a joke, but Gwen didn't detect even the faintest note of sarcasm. A few keystrokes later, Quincy stood abruptly. "It's done." He scribbled a note on a Post-It and handed it to Gwen. "If you don't bring Chia home, I don't want to see your face in here again. Got that straight, *partner?*"

26

June 18
2 days until the Summer Solstice

Norman was a badass. Chessa knew he had goodness deep down. Why else would he have risked his life to save a pixie he just met? But her initial assessment barely scratched the surface. Once he seemed at ease with his decision to side with Chessa, he seemed a different man. At the break of dawn, he emerged from the bedroom, startling Chessa awake from her makeshift bed on the chair. As she stretched, he walked over to the bookcase directly behind the desk, reached up and grabbed a copy of *Histories of the Twenty-Four Runes* from the second shelf from the top, and opened it. With the press of a button, the bookcase groaned as the entire shelf moved forward and swung outward. Chessa was on her feet in a moment, standing behind the open bookcase staring at a vault filled with magical weaponry.

"Good morning to me," she murmured, eliciting a grunt from Norman.

The vault was divided into three columns with shelves from floor to ceiling on either side holding source sticks, shields, enchanted amulets, imbued wrist cuffs, arrows tipped in who-knew-what, and much, much more. The center space was filled with staffs, swords, and bows mounted to the wood paneling behind. Chessa had never seen anything like it.

"Norm, you're a one-wizard cavalry!"

He scratched his beard, and Chessa swore she noticed a slight reddening of his cheeks beneath the white whiskers. "They didn't send me here for no reason, did they?"

"The Unseelie know about this room?"

Norman shook his head. "They just know I'm a guy who can get 'em things. I'm sure there are Seelie who knows about this place, but in all the time I've been here pretending to serve them, only one ever came in here. And she 'ain't around no more."

"Who was she?"

"A housekeeper, the one who showed me the space. She was kind to me. Like you. She either scattered in the takeover or was killed. I don't rightly know."

Chessa nodded, noting the edge to his tone. She guessed this housekeeper fairy was another in a list of wrongs plaguing Norman's conscience. She decided to alter course. "You've managed to stockpile all *this* over the course of a few months and keep it secret from everyone?"

"Nah, I just moved it here from my family's property. They have a full inventory, I'm sure, but they don't know where I've stashed it all."

Chessa shook her head in wonder. "I'm glad you're on my side!"

For the first time since they met, Norman smiled a true smile that touched every part of his face. The tension melted from his hard eyes, the lines of his forehead disappeared, and he looked at peace. "I suppose I am. Though I'm not sure how much this stuff will help seeing as we don't have bodies to wield it."

"Maybe not, but this drastically improves our shot of surviving the day." Chessa smiled, and Norman blushed again. It was like the wizard had never heard a compliment in his life.

An hour later, Chessa was decked out with a source stick strapped to her side, a chain that would project a clear shield around her if she said the word, wrist cuffs that flung balls of energy, and more information than she ever wanted to know about dangerous ancient artifacts. Norman turned out to be somewhat of a historian in that regard. She tried to get him to take the cuffs for his own protection, but he insisted they'd serve her better. She was about to walk away from the stash when a small leather satchel caught her eye. She picked it up, untied the cord keeping it closed, and carefully removed the contents. Inside was some kind of talisman or charm, but it wasn't a coin or rabbit's foot. It was a metal disk with delicate runes inscribed around the rim, an opal inlay ringed the inside, and at its center, the deepest purple amethyst Chessa had ever seen forming the eye of a raven.

"Norman, what does this do?" she asked as she stared into the stone.

"Nothing at this point. It's said to have belonged to the first Unseelie Queen, but whatever magic it held is long gone," he said.

That didn't jive with what Chessa felt. She was drawn to the artifact in a way that made her believe it held great power. At least, that's what her gut was telling her. Chessa never ignored her instincts. "It belonged to Morgan le Fay? No way," she said as she held the disc in her palm. She couldn't believe that the Unseelie Queen of legend, the famed sorceress who'd brought about the downfall of Camelot, had held this very trinket in her own hand. She ran her thumb over the Amethyst. Suddenly, the medallion seemed to warm. "Norman," Chessa said uncertainly, "why is it getting hot?"

Her excitement turned from wonder to terror.

The wizard rushed to her side, but before he could pull the talisman from her hand, Chessa screamed and dropped it. Seared into the flesh of her left palm was a perfect replica of the disc—a ring of runes encircling the mark of the infamous enchantress herself, a raven with a crescent halo. Her hand throbbed, and her entire body trembled.

"Are you okay, little miss?" asked Norman, touching her shoulder. On her tiny frame, his hand was huge, but his touch was comforting.

"I need ice!" blurted Chessa. The pain was unlike anything she'd ever felt. It was as if acid etched the image into her flesh. Norman scurried through the door as she was left cradling her injured hand.

He returned a beat later with a cup of ice, which did nothing to alleviate the pain.

"I thought you said that thing was inert," gasped Chessa.

"I thought it was. It ain't never done nothing like that before, not as long as my family has had it. Hey, now, where did it go?"

Chessa looked to the spot on the ground where the trinket had clattered, but it was gone. "I don't know. It was just there. Did you pick it up?"

"I may be an old fool, but I'm not about to pick up something that just did that to you."

Chessa opened and closed her fingers, breathing deeply. As suddenly as the pain had begun, it abated. She looked down at the brand, which now looked like it had been there for years. It was the same charcoal color of the tattoos on Chessa's wings, the skin around it perfectly smooth. "Whoa," she said. "This cannot be good."

"I'm sorry, little miss. I didn't think anything here could hurt you. You see? You don't want me on your side."

"Bullshit. I don't know what this means, but it's not your fault. Besides, I was looking into getting some more ink." For emphasis, she flitted her wings, showing off the intricate designs.

Norman's expression flashed through a hundred emotions at once and ended at perplexed.

"Relax, Norm. We'll figure out what this all means later. I feel fine now. We've got a griffin to free. I don't want Delilah Johnson to get wind of him before we can bust him out. There's history there."

Her words did the trick. Norman gave a resolute nod and then armed himself with a few trinkets while Chessa tried to pretend she wasn't deeply unsettled by the brand on her palm. It did no good making Norman feel worse. She needed him. She set the cup of ice on the side table and turned her attention to the wristlets. She raised her right arm and aimed it toward the wall. A ball of energy burst forth with a crackle, hit the stone, and left a scorch mark.

"This is awesome! No wonder pixies get hooked on dust if it gives them power like this!"

Norman shook his head. "It's not worth the cost, believe me. You never seen what dust does to a pixie, have you?"

It sounded like he was holding back laughter, despite the serious topic, maybe because he'd been repressing so much. Or maybe because Chessa was striking superhero poses as she shot energy balls at the stone walls, leaving all manner of blackened stains behind.

"I'm never giving these back, you know that right?"

"Get caught with 'em, and you'll be kicked out of the Seelie Court faster than they stamped my own file," he replied. "And those got limits. Each item in here has its own rules and abilities based on the type of magic it taps into. We got no way of knowing when it'll dry up, so you should probably save it for when you're fighting something more dangerous than a library wall."

"Oh. Right." Chessa sobered and flitted to the laptop to watch the cameras. They would make their move during the guard change at 8 p.m. It was now 6:30. This was going to be the longest hour and a half of her life. She retrieved the book she'd been reading from the shelf and settled into the soft chair in the corner to study the history of Seelie-Unseelie relations. It was a dry, boring read about the Great Divergence obviously written by the Seelie since there was very little about the workings of the Unseelie Council. The gist was that they were a self-governing entity preferring to stay away from humanity altogether, but every fae knew that much. Nothing in the pages gave Chessa a clue as to what they wanted or why they would choose now to step into the light.

When the time came, Chessa went to the kitchen and retrieved two beers, one at a time since the bottles were half as tall as she, and toasted Norman. The wizard grinned, a light in his hazel eyes where before there had been none, and said, "To your mate, who doesn't know I exist. If we die, at least we went out fighting."

Chessa beamed back at him. "Hear, hear!" She chugged the lager, not her first choice, but all Norman had in the fridge, and took her place next to the air vent. She was to get to Samson through the duct-work, and Norman would meet her at the door to bust them out. It wasn't an infallible plan, but it was all they had.

Norman touched the buckle of his belt, and he transformed before her eyes into the spitting image of an Unseelie guard, but with

Norman's large, crooked nose and long, scraggly beard. Chessa gasped. "No wonder this stuff is illegal!"

"Little miss, it is not only illegal, each piece in this collection is unique. My family spent decades gathering magical artifacts and paraphernalia from some of the most powerful Unseelie practitioners in existence."

Chessa looked down at her wrist cuffs and felt the weight of the vest on her shoulders. She wondered how much magic had been confined to these objects, and at what price.

"And, boy, am I glad you did," she replied in a rare, serious tone. "See you on the other side."

With that, she popped the pre-loosened grate off the duct and climbed in.

27

Gwen's back ached from the fitful few hours of sleep she snagged in the wooded area of Boston Commons. She and Curtis took turns keeping watch while the other slept since Quincy's contact couldn't meet them until early in the morning. She had no idea what to expect as she trudged through a back alley in the harbor district, stretching out her sore muscles. The smell of rotting trash, fish, and human waste crept into her nostrils and pressed against her gag reflex, but she kept walking.

"I still don't see why we can't fly," griped Curtis, who was always a step ahead.

"You heard Quincy," replied Gwen in a low voice just above a whisper. "We're not dealing with travel agents. If they see us coming, they'll bolt, especially with you in your ridiculous regalia."

"What's so ridiculous about my uniform? I'm proud to serve the Seelie Royals."

"Curtis, you're a walking billboard."

A soft whistle sounded from somewhere overhead, a warning. It was exactly as Q had said. Gwen had to act now or miss their chance for passage to Avalon.

She fluttered into the air so she could project her voice loud and strong. "Sludge sister's dance party."

At first, nothing happened. Had Quincy given her the wrong code phrase? Curtis remained on the ground in a squat, ready to push off into the air at the first sign of danger, his head turned upward, scanning the walls and balconies of the surrounding buildings. Movement came from the ground level. A brick pushed outward, and a bulbous creature emerged. He wasn't much taller than Curtis but resembled a slug with two short eye-stalks protruding above a blob of a body. He did have arms, but Gwen couldn't tell if there were legs beneath the piles of gray flesh. A mouth cracked open across the upper middle section of the blob, slime dripping from the top lip like honey off a hive. Gwen had never seen a hobgoblin before, and after today, she hoped to make that the norm.

"Papers?" it rasped.

Gwen thrust out the paperwork Quincy printed up for them, and the creature enveloped it in a slime-coated arm that split off from his left side. Instead of holding it up to its eyes like she expected, he absorbed the documents into his body with a slurp, then belched.

"Mmm. Q knows what I like," it said in a tone that sounded vaguely sexual. Gwen's stomach lurched. "Head to the end of the alley then go straight up. All the way up. Talbot will be waiting."

The creature's mouth hole made a perfect *O*, and a long, sweet-sounding whistle followed by two short ones echoed down the alley. "Have a good trip," he wheezed before slurping back into the space behind the brick. Gwen and Curtis exchanged perplexed looks as the brick slid back into place.

28

After using a wrist cuff to blast the vent cover off her exit, Chessa found Samson collapsed in the corner of a small stone cell, his body taking up a good half of the floor space. The sound of her entrance startled him, and he thrashed against shackles that were chained to the floor. His glasses were nowhere to be seen, and his feathers were a mess.

"Sammy, it's ok! It's me," Chessa said in a loud whisper. She didn't see any evidence of an intercom, but she didn't want to risk alerting the guards to her presence. This was her one shot.

Samson jumped up, his big yellow eyes unfocused. "Chessa? Is that you?"

Chessa flitted over to sit on the feathers of his shoulder. "Yeah, big guy. I'm here to bust you out."

The walls were stone on one side and cinderblock between cells, there were no windows, and bars looked out into a narrow passage. It smelled like a zoo. Samson's head cocked to one side then the other. Shit. He was as good as blind.

"What happened to your glasses?" asked Chessa.

"Gone. Smashed, most likely."

"Fuck."

"You got that right, doll. And these bracelets aren't going anywhere anytime soon. How did you get in here?"

There was the Samson Chessa knew. "Through the air vents, though by the smell of this place, there isn't much air circulation happening."

Samson blinked. "How long have I been in here? I lost track. Why didn't you come sooner?"

"Four days. I've been hiding out with a friend, and it took us a while to map out the ducts. Plus, I kind of needed to win him over. Stick out your talons as far as you can and turn your face away."

She aimed her right wrist cuff at the chains binding Samson's restraints to the floor, careful to sidestep a fitting that looked suspiciously like iron, closed her eyes, and let loose the energy ball. A loud crack and a blaze of light later, he was free to move around the room, bits of chain dangling from each of his talons.

"What in Danu was that?" gasped Samson. "Are you on pixie dust?"

Chessa struck a superhero pose with her wrists crossed in front of her. Samson squinted in her direction and shook his head.

"Really, Sammy? You're going to throw shade about a little illegal trinket when I'm in the midst of busting you out of a cell?"

"I am an agent of the Seelie KPD."

"And I'm one fucking pixie against an Unseelie insurrection. Get your priorities straight!"

A voice, deeper than any Chessa had ever heard, reverberated off the walls. "Damn, I thought you were going to bring me a little recreation."

Chessa paused, her heart in her throat.

At the look on her face, Samson broke into a grin. "He's just pulling your talon," he said.

"I don't have talons, and just who are you talking about?"

"The prisoner down in the last cell. He's been filling me in on these brunos who've got us locked up. They're not the same ones as nabbed him."

"What's he in for?" asked Chessa.

A voice, dark with a purr that sent shivers up Chessa's spine, answered. "Murder, mayhem, drawing attention, you name it, love.

While you're in the busting out mood, think you can give a poor sinner a second chance at life?"

Chessa looked dubiously at Samson, who shook his head. "I'll see what I can do," she replied, her voice louder than it needed to be.

The only response she received was the swishing sound of a large creature shifting position. Another voice, this one from a cell in the center of the room, answered. "They ain't going to help you."

A feminine voice replied, "Shut up, Wyle. Nobody asked you."

Chessa waited to see if Samson was going to elaborate on his new companions, but the griffin had questions of his own. "I take it you've got a plan to blow this joint? What are we waiting for?"

"My friend."

"Chessa, how did you make a friend that was willing to risk their life to help you bust a griffin out of Avalon in four days?"

"You think you're the only one capable of forging friendships under duress? I'm a charismatic bitch!" Chessa zipped up to replace the vent cover. She didn't want the Unseelie thinking to use the ventilation system to map out the secret passages of the palace.

Samson shook his head. "Ok, who is this joe?"

"He's an Unseelie spy and a smuggler of ancient artifacts who helped to overthrow the Seelie Royals in the first place. But he's on our side now. He should be opening that door any moment now."

"I regret asking."

They were silent for a long moment, staring at the still, closed door.

"How do you know he didn't give you the old double-cross?" asked Samson.

"I suppose it's possible," replied Chessa. "It would be easier for him to side with the enemy and turn us in. But I'm not wired to assume the worst. If you show people you see the good in them, you give them the chance to make the right calls. He'll come through for us."

"And if he doesn't?"

"Then I guess pulled pixie and roasted griffin are on the mess hall menu tonight."

Just then, the door in the hall let out a loud creak, and Samson's feathers puffed at the sound. An Unseelie guard peered in.

"Whoa there, I'm here to help," murmured the crackly voice of Norman, who still wore the visage of an average Unseelie humanoid. Most of the guards were fairies, but there were a few humanoids prowling the grounds. Chessa breathed a sigh of relief that he hadn't been caught.

"The prisoners giving you a hard time, Mike?" Another guard called down to Norman.

"All good," he barked back. He closed the door behind him. "It's now or never, little miss."

He touched the ring on his right thumb. The illusion faded, leaving the familiar, crackly old face Chessa had grown to love. As Norman fought with the keys to Samson's cell, she darted between the bars and covered his back. The door creaked open. Without hesitation, she blasted a pulse at the guard who entered before the poor sap had time to raise an alarm. He slumped in the doorway. Chessa heard footsteps echoing down the hall beyond. "We're out of time, boys."

The trio burst from the room and took a sharp right, heading for the door of the west wing as fae flooded in from the great hall to their left. "What about the other prisoners?" gasped Chessa.

"I'm a cop. I'm not about to free a murderer," replied Samson, his great paws padding the stone behind Norman. She had to admit, he did have a point. Besides, they had their hands full at the moment.

The hall was too narrow for Samson to spread his wings, and his bulk made for a big target, so she hung back, zipping through the air to distract any guards coming from behind. Norman brought up the rear. She could hear him muttering spells but didn't turn to see the effects. She heard someone yell a command just before the earsplitting sound of multiple guns firing. The chain around her neck sprung to life, spreading a warmth across her chest. Bullets, energy blasts, arrows, and Danu knows what else bounced off the invisible field surrounding her. "Holy shit!" she gasped brushing the hot metal with her fingertips as she flew. "A girl could get used to a life of crime!"

"Just keep going," Samson screeched over his shoulder. Chessa slammed into his haunches as the griffin came to a grinding halt. "Door's blocked," squawked Samson.

Norman screamed from somewhere down the hall behind them.

Chessa righted herself and looked back. He was splayed out on the floor, fairies swarming his body while others vaulted it to come after her and Samson. "Get out of here, little miss!" the wizard yelled.

Hovering in the air just above him was a tiny, but familiar form.

The Korranthian royal advisor. Grimore.

Chessa climbed onto Samson's back and snagged a handful of feathers to hold on. "Keep going," she panted.

"You're going to have to clear the way."

Four guards stood between them and the exit. But more were advancing from behind, and they didn't have time to hesitate.

"Go!" screamed Norman from down the hall.

Samson's paws lurched into a run as Chessa scrambled over him. An arrow whizzed by her head, and her ears rang from the gunfire. She pushed off Samson's shoulder and fired off an energy ball that sent the four fairy guards slamming into the walls just before she and Samson were upon them.

Chessa heard the crunching of bones as Samson's lion paw crushed a fairy, but she couldn't dwell on it. They crashed through the door into daylight beyond.

29

Hobgoblins didn't make the best travel guides. Some were nearly gelatinous like the scout while others were knobby and lanky, but they all smelled of stale ale and excrement. It was no wonder they didn't mix with the rest of fae society. The hobgoblin atop the building called himself Captain Talbot, and he was of the lanky variety. His long, bumpy nose eclipsed the rest of his gaunt face, and two beady orange eyes regarded Gwen and Curtis with suspicion. "Quincy sent you, eh? Said we'd take you overseas, eh?"

Gwen nodded, wondering how he learned all that from a few short whistles. He pulled the papers from inside his patched leather vest. Somehow the hobgoblin in the alley had transported them. This was getting weird. "You are Glitter and Castor Sparkle, eh? A bit on the nose, eh?"

Gwen tore her gaze away from Captain Talbot. She hoped he'd think it was because she was hiding her true identity, and not because of a juvenile urge to laugh at his choice of expression.

Curtis cleared his throat. "Yes, that's us. We're newlyweds who can't afford a honeymoon by any other means. Mr. Quincy owed us a favor."

Talbot burst out laughing. "Her, maybe, but you? If you know Quincy, I'm a fucking princess. You *newlyweds* ready to leave in an hour, eh? I gotta clear my gullet before we go."

"We're ready to leave as soon as you can," replied Gwen.

"There's a shop down the corner. They serve mortals out the front, fae behind. You might want to consider getting this guy some new duds for the trip, eh? I don't mind a good fight, but if a Seelie Royal and her guard are traveling with the likes of me, I'm guessing you'll want to go unnoticed, eh?"

Curtis stepped in front of Gwen, but Talbot had already melted into the roof below them. Gwen shuddered. "How do they do that?"

"Hobgoblins are disgusting creatures," said Curtis, looking all around. "We learned about them in basic training. Their bodies are gelatinous and can mold into their surroundings. We suspect they possess some space-altering magic, but they steer clear of the Guard and the KPD alike."

"Are they Unseelie?"

"Some may be, but here in Korranthia they're mostly Courtless. None are registered with the Seelie, but they get along just fine living in relative peace with humanity and forming alliances with whatever lucrative fae crime rings they can."

"They teach you all this in basic?" It occurred to Gwen that she'd been surrounded by Seelie Guards her entire childhood but had no idea what they went through to become protectors of the royal family. Quincy was right. She was out of touch.

"Yes, my lady. It's our job to keep your family safe, and that involves documenting all potential threats. The hobgoblins wouldn't move against you of their own volition, but they could be used by someone who would, especially if that someone obscured their purpose. Are you sure you want to do this?"

"It's the fastest way to get to Avalon," said Gwen. "We're doing this."

Curtis sighed, and Gwen looked at him, really *looked* at him for the first time. He was rather attractive, she supposed, with dark hair, a square jaw, and intense green eyes. But his stance was more knightly than street, and he stood out like moss on marble in these parts. "Talbot's right," she said. "We need to get you some new clothes stat."

An hour later, they were back on the roof. Curtis looked awkward in his jeans, hoodie, and tennis shoes. Gwen made him pack his wand and source stick in his new backpack, alongside the food and water provisions he insisted they pick up. In fairness, she was feeling much stronger after devouring a ham and cheese hoagie from a convenience store. She didn't remember the last time she'd eaten. Probably with Liam the day before. That seemed like a lifetime ago.

Liam.

The thought of her brother being killed by the Unseelie cut through her like a butcher knife. She hadn't seen his body, but she couldn't conceive of any scenario in which he'd been able to escape a second time. It wasn't like they were in the business of taking prisoners. Still, she couldn't help but hope. The best thing she could do was to go to the place overtaken by Unseelie usurpers, her former home, and figure out what this was all about. On the slim chance he was still alive, someone in Avalon would know where.

Just when she was thinking that Captain Talbot had taken off with whatever Quincy had paid, he appeared out of the shingles in front of her. Somehow, he looked even skinnier and more sickly than before. "Ready?"

Gwen ignored the uneasy look Curtis was shooting at her. "Let's go."

Captain Talbot whistled long and low. He drew himself upright, only he didn't stop once he was full height. Instead, he kept growing, stretching until he was a full head taller than the fairies. His entire body began to stretch outward until he resembled a great pancake with a long-nosed head on top, his legs doing a full split in either direction. Curtis' face was stoic, but Gwen couldn't help but gape. She'd never seen anything like this.

With three short whistles, a slit formed in the center of the hobgoblin's chest, the flesh parting like meat curtains from neck to ground, slime dripping down the opening and pooling on the shingles below. "All aboard!" said the Captain's tiny head.

Gwen stood, staring into the cavern formed by Talbot's dripping putty body.

"In there?" gasped Curtis from beside her. "You expect us to walk inside you?"

"If you want to reach Avalon," replied the hobgoblin. "Fare's been paid either way, so I don't give a boggart's ass what you do."

"No way! You're going to digest us! You're going to suffocate us! You're going to *slime* us!" Curtis's voice got more high-pitched with each of his protestations, but Gwen was already walking forward. "My la—honey, you can't!" He was nearly whimpering now.

Gwen stepped inside Talbot. It was hot, humid, and smelled vaguely of carrion. Her stomach lurched, but her resolve was steadfast.

"Please keep your wings tucked safely at your back, orifices closed, and limbs at your sides for the duration of the trip. Do not attempt any magic during travel. It gives me gas." The voice seemed to be everywhere at once.

She heard Curtis curse a moment before he stepped in beside her. The opening sealed shut behind them, and the hobgoblin's body collapsed around them.

Flesh pressed against every part of Gwen. The wind left her lungs. Her joints creaked and popped with the pressure of the hobgoblin's mass squeezing her body. Panic rose in her chest. She couldn't breathe. She couldn't scream. She couldn't move. She couldn't see. There was nothing but pulsating blackness and complete paralysis.

Gwen didn't know how long she'd been in that state when she was expelled in a gush of slime into the blinding brightness of the outdoors. She hit the ground hard. Curtis landed next to her, gasping, coughing, and purple in the face.

A hobgoblin stood beside them. This one wasn't lanky like Talbot, but thick and blubbery like the first hobgoblin they encountered, perhaps more so. Had it not been for the long, bumpy nose, Gwen would have sworn it was another creature entirely.

He belched, and it smelled of rotten fish.

"Welcome to Glastonbury. You'll find Avalon at the top of the hill. Be sure to leave a good review," gurgled the blubbery mass that was

Captain Talbot before melting into the asphalt, leaving Gwen and Curtis plastered to the ground in goo.

Curtis climbed to his feet and offered Gwen his hand. "My lady, are you hurt?"

"I'm fine," replied Gwen, ignoring his hand and prying herself off the ground. Her wings were glued to the back of her shirt with slime, and her hair and clothes were slathered in it. She wiped a sleeve across her face, but it did no good. "What the hell was that?"

Curtis looked off into the distance, towards a stone wall. Rising above it, Gwen could see the palace atop Glastonbury Tor. She was home. "I believe he ate the space between Korranthia and Avalon. We should probably vacate the street before a car comes along."

As if punctuating his point, the sound of an approaching vehicle cut through the fog. They walked to the side of the road and stepped onto the curb just in time to watch a truck pass.

"First things first, I need a fucking shower," growled Gwen.

30

Samson tore through the door with Chessa zipping out behind him. It was an ambush. Guards of every fae species gathered in the sunlight, weapons raised. Pixies and sprites hovered overhead while fairies, ogres, and mortal magic practitioners blocked the way on foot. There was no way to ascertain what kind of magic would be coming at them at any moment.

"I knew that was too easy," said Samson, panting to catch his breath.

"Tell that to Norman," replied Chessa as she braced for whatever was about to come.

Instead of an organized assault, the guards outside descended upon them all at once, fairies breaking ranks to take to the air while others attacked on foot. There were too many guards for anyone to use ranged weapons without wounding their own. They swung source sticks and blades in a mob of chaos. Chessa zipped around the griffin, using her own source stick to intercept anyone who got close, her amulet protecting them both from the magic-muddled onslaught.

"Samson, use your wings!" she cried, tucking herself safely between his shoulder blades. "Now!"

He did as she commanded. When he flapped, the smaller fae were caught in a hurricane, the sheer force sending them flying through the air and slamming into the wall surrounding the palace. Humanoids ducked and covered. Ogres roared and thrashed against the wind. The bubble of space gave Chessa room to take stock of the chaos. Above them, swarms of pixies, fairies, and other flighted fae littered the skies. They would have to run for it before the ground fae resumed their attack.

"Through the gate!" Chessa cried, but Samson was already on the move, angling his wings to create a path forward as the palace door behind them swung open. Grimore stepped through and lifted his hand, but Chessa was faster. She shot an energy ball at the keystone above the arched doorway. It exploded above Grimore's head, raining stone and mortar down on him, and causing him to stagger backward. "We've got to go! Now!" Chessa shrieked at Samson.

Samson barreled toward the gate. The Unseelie forces clambered after them. Chessa couldn't tear her eyes away from the figure in the doorway, malice rolling off him in waves. Grimore's intense eyes stared back.

31

"A bout that shower?" asked Curtis as he and Gwen walked through downtown Glastonbury. Other fae passed them on the street, casting disgusted looks their way. Gwen spent her childhood on these streets and was accustomed to the occasional critical glance, being the black sheep of the Seelie royal family, but she never visited town covered in hobgoblin goo.

"I'm taking care of it."

She strode past a row of shops along a normally well-traveled road, which now was eerily quiet save for an occasional car or pedestrian passing by. She and Curtis were more exposed than she liked, but there was nothing to be done about it. They couldn't break into her childhood home with their wings gunked to their backs. At least the humans wouldn't see her in this current state, not with the UK glamour in place.

The thought gave her pause. Normally, Glastonbury was teeming with humans, King Arthur buffs here to snap photos of the Glastonbury Tor and tourists flooding the giftshops for Excalibur replicas and other Camelot paraphernalia. But she hadn't seen a mortal since she emerged from a hobgoblin gut in the middle of the street. The

Unseelie takeover must have sent ripples through the town. Even the fae passersby seemed more guarded than usual.

Gwen breathed a sigh of relief when she turned into the novelty shop on High Street. The shopkeeper took one look at her and blanched. "Lady Evenshine, you shouldn't be here," gasped the rotund gnome standing on a stool behind the counter. She appeared to be in her seventies, but Mrs. Walsh had been around for centuries. There was a time when Gwen called her friend. Her and that spitfire daughter of hers too.

"I need your help, Mrs. Walsh."

The gnome stared nervously at the door, then glanced at the patrons in the store, a pair of elves who were picking through vintage vinyl records and compact discs. Mrs. Walsh's place was always a hodgepodge of items, both new and outdated. "Bloody hell, what happened to you? Never mind that. Quickly now, dear. You're likely to get us all killed." The gnome spoke low enough to avoid drawing attention and waved them to a door at the back of the store. She remained in place behind the register.

Curtis followed Gwen. The room beyond was just as Gwen remembered it, filled with shelves that spanned floor to ceiling, each containing more oddities than were for sale out front. During her teen years, she spent many days here, escaping the pressures of Avalon with a book on the windowsill or asking Mrs. Walsh about some mummified finger or hunk of rock she found on one of the dark, dusty shelves. She even brought the gnome a few of the treasures herself. She didn't have time to marvel at the new trinkets now. She made a beeline for the stairs leading to the apartment above. It was a happy space, painted light blue and white. She didn't have time for the warm shower she craved, but she managed a fair job of de-gooing herself in the bathroom sink before returning to the sitting room to offer Curtis a turn.

Mrs. Walsh emerged from the stairwell as Gwen was toweling off. "Gwendolyn, dear, what are you doing here? You must know it's not safe."

"Yes, Mrs. Walsh. I'm so sorry to have involved you, but I didn't know where else to go. We needed to get our bearings before I go take care of some business."

"Take care of business? Oh no. You can't mean—"

"Yes. I'm going home."

Something in Gwen's gaze must have given Mrs. Walsh the correct impression that arguing would be futile because she shook her head with tears in her eyes. "You always were a willful child."

"Tell me what's going on in Avalon."

"I can't." The gnome's face was red, and tears were falling. "It's too risky."

"I need to know what I'm facing. The Unseelie are picking my family off one by one, and now they've got the pixie who means more to me than anything in this whole damn world."

"Gwendolyn, you don't understand."

"Mrs. Walsh, please!" Gwen was nearly begging now. "What am I about to fly into?" She stared at the gnome. Mrs. Walsh was so much smaller than Gwen remembered, and she looked as if she might be sick.

Finally, Mrs. Walsh met her eyes. "Death."

All hell broke loose on the street below. The shouting and banging were so loud that it reverberated through the building. Gwen flew to the bay window overlooking the tourist street. Fae ran this way and that as a large force of Unseelie soldiers swept up and down the thoroughfare, busting through doors, flying to second-story windows, and bullying anyone in the way. A fairy in full red and silver armor pressed his face to the glass, and Gwen ducked just in time. Mrs. Walsh gave him an awkward wave, which sent him on his way. A moment later, the shop below erupted in banging and smashing, and the gnome ran for the stairs.

"What in the name of Danu!" she yelled as she hurried down to protect her shop.

Gwen rose from her crouch and flitted back to the window to risk a peek. She wasn't prepared for the sight that met her. A griffin and a pixie hauling ass down High Street as chaos erupted around them. For a split second, Gwen swore time slowed. Samson, with Chessa clinging to his neck feathers, ran on his lion paws and talons like the reaper himself were on his heels.

"Get down!" Curtis yelled to Gwen, but the fae forces on the street were no longer peering through windows. They had spotted their prey, and they were on the move. The commotion downstairs faded as every Unseelie in the area poured back onto the street in pursuit. A moment later, Mrs. Walsh reappeared, red-faced and panting.

"They ain't after you, love. But you need to get out of here while they're occupied."

Her words were lost. The window was already open, and Gwen was airborne.

32

Chessa wanted to take to the skies, but the entire airspace above Glastonbury was filled with winged scouts, and there were no clouds for cover. Instead, they hoped to get lost in the town. But Glastonbury was no Boston, and there was no network of backstreets in which to hide a griffin. It was only a matter of minutes before they were spotted by the legion of Unseelie that swarmed out of Avalon in their wake.

"Samson, go right!" she shouted. The griffin tore around a corner. Chessa cursed herself for not doing more reconnaissance around town before breaking him out. The street was a dead end, far narrower than Samson's wingspan. By Chessa's calculations, they only had a few seconds to move or be caught. Samson must have thought the same. He gave a mighty heave with his lion legs and launched at the three-story building ahead of them. Chessa took to the air as he caught the roofline with his talons, pulled clear of the buildings, and spread his wings. A dozen fairies flew at them from the south, another group of four pixies came from the east, and a single fairy dressed in all black flew at them full speed from the southeast. Gwen?

"Samson, it's Gwen! Come on!" yelled Chessa.

Gwen altered course and headed due-north. Chessa followed.

Samson was the slowest of the group, but every flap of his wings sent the smaller pursuers spiraling away from him. Pixies weren't made for sustained speed, and Chessa's energy reserve plummeted. Thankfully, she was able to fall back and drop onto Samson's back from above as he followed Gwen to the outskirts of the little town. They flew low, taking advantage of the lead they had on the Unseelie soldiers, and dipped below the tree line once they were clear of Glastonbury. Gwen dropped to the ground in a wooded area behind a little cemetery, and Samson followed with Chessa on his back.

Chessa tackled Gwen. "I thought you were dead."

"No time for that," growled Gwen, gently wriggling free of Chessa's grasp. "This way."

"Am I glad to see you, kid!" rasped Samson. "Even if you are blurry around the edges."

A small mausoleum was hidden just behind the beech trees of the cemetery, and that was where Gwen led them. "Come on. We've got to get out of sight before they realize where we went down. In here."

A rustling in the leaves behind them nearly sent Chessa airborne, but the panting fairy who appeared wasn't dressed as an Unseelie guard. He had on baggy jeans and a hoodie.

Chessa raised her wrist cuff. "State your business!" she barked.

"Whoa, there. I'm with her," he said, motioning to Gwen, who was straining to push the stone slab blocking the entrance to the mausoleum out of the way.

He was cute, with dark hair and murky green eyes. He had the build and gait of a soldier, but he made no threatening motions. Chessa wondered who this gorgeous fairy was to Gwen. She smiled and lowered her arm. "You are, are you? Hey Gwennie, who's the hunk?"

"Chess, focus! Samson, a little help?"

Samson walked in the direction of Gwen's voice and easily slid the stone aside. "Sorry, kid. This dick's got a bum noodle."

"What?"

"With my glasses gone and all that's happened, I'm a busted flush."

Gwen sighed. "For fuck's sake, Sammy, speak like a griffin, not a Sam Spade stunt double."

When everyone was inside the tiny building, Samson jostled the slab back in place.

"Cut him a break, Gwen. He's been through a lot. We all have. He's been in a cell for most of the week, and he can barely see his own talons without his glasses." She turned to Samson, who was little more than a silhouette in the dark mausoleum. "But you do need to cut out the pity party, Samson. You were amazing back there, and we're alive!"

"For now," said Gwen. "What were you thinking coming to Avalon?"

"We were thinking that we needed to save your ass. *Again.*" Chessa knew that Gwen was scared, but she was too exhausted to put up with her bullshit. And she'd be damned if she let Gwen talk to her or Samson like that after everything they'd been through on her account. Still, she was relieved to have her best friend back, even if she was a cantankerous pain-in-the-ass.

Gwen must have picked up on her mood because she backed down. "I'm just glad to see you both alive," she said.

Chessa smiled, but she didn't know if anyone could tell. The darkness in the mausoleum was oppressive, the only light filtering in from the narrow slits in a ventilation port over the doorway. As far back into the trees as the structure was, even that wasn't much. Gwen perched on the molding, looking through the slats into the forest beyond. As thankful as Chessa was for the refuge, she was anxious to figure out their next steps. Her stomach rumbled. Loud.

"I don't suppose anybody has a Twinkie?' she said. Her last meal was before busting Samson out, and that felt like a lifetime ago. The new guy rummaged in his backpack and pulled out a handful of protein bars.

"When did you restock?" asked Gwen.

"Back at Mrs. Walsh's shop. I figured we could use some nourishment," he replied. He flew up to hand Gwen one of the packages.

"You're such a Sprite Scout," mumbled Gwen, but she took his offering.

Chessa, for one, was glad someone was prepared. Normally she was the one thrusting food into a grumpy Gwen's hands. "What is this place, anyway?" she asked, stuffing her mouth.

"This is the resting place of Morgan le Fay," replied Gwen.

Curtis gasped and Samson choked.

"No fucking way! Are you kidding me?" blurted Chessa, glancing down at her palm. She didn't want to worry Gwen by mentioning the brand until she figured out what it meant and they were far away from Avalon.

"Nope. As a fae structure, it's hidden from mortal eyes, but it's been neglected for hundreds of years. When the Seelie Court took over Avalon, they didn't care to preserve the tomb of the first Unseelie Queen. Eventually, the forest took the land back."

"Who owns the land?" asked Samson.

"I'm not sure. My family approves any development within twenty-five miles of Avalon, human or fae, so I don't suppose it matters."

Chessa traced her finger around the walls as she made her way to the back of the structure. There she found a pedestal, upon which sat a stone box. She flitted her wings and rose in the air, alighting on the top. "She's still here, isn't she?" She bent to place her palm on the cool, stone surface.

Warmth spread through her fingers, into her hand, and down her arm, the same way it had when she first held the talisman. The mark on her flesh began to burn, but she couldn't pull away. Magic crackled in the air around her.

"Chess, get away from there!" called Gwen, but the pixie was transfixed. Power coursed through her, the brand getting hotter and hotter. Chessa screamed in pain.

Gwen was at her side in a second flat. "What happened? Chessa? Answer me!"

The pain began to dull, and Chessa pulled her hand away from the stone. "I'm okay, I'm okay. Sorry."

"What the fuck was that?" Gwen asked. "I felt something."

"It's really nothing," Chessa replied. She wasn't finished with Avalon yet, and if Gwen knew what was going on with her, she'd make what was to come more difficult. "I got spooked by something, I guess."

Gwen scowled, not looking convinced. "We don't know what residual magics might linger here."

"Maybe not, but I can't wield magic, Gwen," she replied, sounding as cavalier as she could. She stepped off the box and fluttered to the ground.

"I used to come here all the time as a girl. I swear, sometimes I could feel her presence. I thought it was my imagination, but just now, I felt something powerful here. I've known you for a long time, and you don't spook that easily."

"I've been through a lot." Chessa hated to close herself off to Gwen, but it was what she needed to do. She tried not to think about the hurt that flashed across her best friend's face.

Thankfully, Samson saved her from further interrogation. "I might be as blind as a New Metta molent in daylight, but it seemed to me you wielded magic like a pro back in Avalon," he said. "Care to spill the beans?"

"She did what?" said Gwen.

Chessa recounted the whole story, minus some of the sensitive details about Norman—she loved Gwen, but she didn't want to see what would happen if she found out about the role he played in the deaths of her family. She told them about the escape and about Grimore. Gwen didn't seem surprised by that last bit at all. When she got to the part about the Ghost of Korranthia being the assassin who murdered the queen, Samson perked up.

"Delilah Johnson is in Avalon?" he said, his voice wavering. "There was always more to that Simcoe Jones case than I could make heads or tailfeathers of."

"According to Norman, she's in the wind," replied Chessa.

"Good," said Gwen. "We don't need any extra complications."

Samson scowled at her.

Once they finished their information exchange and pieced together as much of the situation as they could, Chessa was antsy to figure out their next move. She wasn't about to leave Norman in the hands of the enemy, not after he'd found himself, and Gwen seemed convinced she needed to search out Liam.

"How long do you think we need to hole up here?" she asked.

Samson cleared his throat. "I don't know about the rest of you, but I'm in no hurry to get bumped off by a bunch of pissed-off fairies."

"We'll give it overnight, then we'll scout a way out. Samson, Curtis will get you and Chessa home where you belong."

"Wait just a second," interjected Chessa. "Do you really think you're going to send us away? So you can do what? Charge into hostile territory alone? You don't know what it's like in there. They'll have your head on a pike in half an hour!"

Gwen flew back up to her post by the vent, looking out at the forest and cemetery beyond. "Chess, I've been worried sick ever since you were shot out of the sky. I almost lost you to the Scraper, then to my own fucked up family. I can't risk your life again. If there's even the smallest chance that Liam is still alive, I have to find him. Who knows? Maybe I can find a way to end all this."

"Why do you always do this?"

"Do what?"

"Make everything your battle. If you haven't noticed, whatever is going on here is bigger than you and Liam. It's bigger than your family. You can't fight it alone, and you sure as shit don't have to."

Samson cleared his throat. "If I may? I suggest we call for backup."

"Backup from who?" asked Gwen. "My family is hunkered down in a safe house with a handful of guards at best. The Korranthia royals are in league with the Unseelie, and we don't even know what they want. The KPD is an ocean away, and Avalon has already been overthrown. There is nobody to call. We are the resistance."

Chessa seized the opening. "There's Norman."

"You said he was captured," replied Gwen. "What did you call him? An Unseelie spy smuggler who helped overthrow my home? What good could he possibly be to us?"

Chessa closed her eyes for a moment, glad she left out the accessory to murder part. "You write people off too easily, Gwen. Norman is good. Real good. If we can bust him out and retreat back into the hidden library, I know he'll be able to help get us to Liam."

To Chessa's surprise, it was the new guy who spoke next. In a stammering, unsure tone, he blurted out, "I'll help. I mean, if you'll have me. I mean, I would like to."

By now, her eyes were adjusted, and Chessa could just make out the shape of the fairy standing closest to the door. His voice was soft, but his shoulders were rigid and his jaw set. He was downright hot.

"Who *is* this guy?" she asked.

"Curtis Steele. I was a corporal when I left my post with instructions to aid Lady Evenshine."

"Instructions? Whose instructions?" asked Gwen, landing on the floor of the mausoleum next to him. Chessa could feel waves of anger emanating from her friend. This was about to get ugly.

"Queen Azrah Tupaou. I begged her to give me a mission to redeem myself. I served as personal guard to the Seelie Queen Estrella Tupaou before she was assassinated."

"You didn't tell me that," said Gwen. Her voice sounded a little softer than before.

"You never asked," replied the guard. This time, his voice didn't falter. "Besides, would you have let me serve you if you knew that I was operating on orders from your family? Or that the queen died on my watch? I could have saved her. I could have prevented all of this, and I failed."

The fairy was obviously pained over the past, but Gwen offered him no mercy. Sometimes, Chessa wished her best friend could see more to the heart of others. She flitted over to Curtis and put a hand on his arm.

"I don't know about her, but I would be glad to have your help, Corporal. I need you to understand that the person we're trying to save is a good man who has made some terrible mistakes. He was a pawn in the hands of the powerful. Their weapon. Without him, they could not have pulled off the assassination that you blame yourself for."

Gwen cussed and flew back up to the vent. Chessa ignored her. Right now, she needed to focus on Curtis. He and Norman weren't so different. They both blamed themselves for the schemes of the powerful. They both deserved a chance to make things right.

"If it weren't for Norman, Samson and I would both be dead or rotting in cells. For that, I owe him. I understand if you can't bring yourself to forgive him for his part in all this, and there is no dishonor in returning to Korranthia to protect the remaining Seelie royals. But if you help us, you both will have your chance for redemption."

Curtis didn't speak. He looked up to where Gwen was still motionless on the ledge above.

"Shut up Chessa," said Gwen. "We're all going in."

33

This was suicide, and not just for Gwen. She sat by the ventilation shaft of the mausoleum looking out into the patch of trees that bordered Glastonbury Cemetery as the others tried to sleep. Remaining holed up for the night would give them time to rest before striking at dawn. The Unseelie would think they'd fled, a course of action any sane fae would have taken, and be blindsided by the attack. It was the only advantage Gwen figured they had.

She looked down into the darkness of the tomb and tried not to think about how appropriate the hideout was. From here, she could just make out Chessa's tiny form curled up with her back to the pedestal of Morgan le Fay. There had been times in her youth when Gwen sat in that exact spot, pouring her heart out to the long-dead Unseelie queen, back when she thought the Unseelie of old were merely shadow-lurkers. She wasn't sure what to think now, with Unseelie forces occupying Avalon. After Chessa's outburst, she was beyond disconcerted. Chessa was a lot of things, but she wasn't one to scream like that without cause, and Gwen knew what the flow of powerful magic felt like. The pixie was peaceful enough now, with her head resting on the end of Samson's tail while the griffin gently snored.

"Lady Evenshine, you should rest too." Curtis' voice was gentle and low. She hadn't noticed that he'd awakened. He stood up from the front corner of the space where he nodded off slumped against the mausoleum wall a couple of hours earlier.

"I've told you a million times to call me Gwen."

"Yes, well, you need sleep too, Gwen." Her name sounded awkward from his lips. "I'll keep a lookout."

Her head was a bit heavy, now that he mentioned it. She glanced back out at the forest. "I doubt the Unseelie will come this way if they haven't already."

"I'm sure you're right, but I'll keep watch just the same. I'm plenty rested."

It was a good call. Gwen awoke two hours later stiff but with heightened senses and an idea. She grew up in Avalon, flying the halls, playing on the statuary, and swimming in the courtyard. Chessa might have discovered a hidden library, but Gwen knew the kitchens, the lavatories, and the other places necessary for life in the tower and beyond. She gathered her friends around her.

"Chessa, Samson, you two have seen how the Unseelie are using my home. I need to know everything about their day-to-day movements. When do they eat? When do they exercise? When do they take bathroom breaks? When do they sleep?"

"There are cameras set up throughout the tower and surrounding grounds," replied Chessa, "and I watched them for four days. Patrols operate in shifts with breaks at regular intervals. The guards are using a room off the frontmost western hall as command central. It's close to the cells where they were keeping Samson."

Gwen nodded. She could always rely on Chessa for intel. The pixie was unable to exist in new circumstances for any length of time without absorbing details others would overlook. "That makes sense. It's where our guards were quartered. If they're meeting there, where are they sleeping?"

"I'm not sure. Wherever it is, there are no cameras."

"You flew through the ductwork to get to Samson, right? Do you think they were able to figure that out and backtrack to Norman's hidden library?"

"I replaced the vent cover, but there's a chance they've addressed that little gap in security by now. I can't believe it hadn't occurred to them earlier, to be honest."

Gwen nodded. "My family had guards conduct regular sweeps of the vents. There are too many small fae in the world to grow complacent. I'm guessing the Unseelie aren't used to maintaining defensive positioning with the way they live in the shadows."

"They don't all lurk around dark forests and alleyways, you know. Many Unseelie live just as we do," said Chessa. She was giving Gwen that look again, the one that said 'your worldview is the size of a banquet hall'. She hated it.

"I guess you would know," she replied.

"Retract the claws, Gwen. We're on the same side."

Despite Chessa seeing the best in everyone, she was always there for Gwen. Gwen supposed she should act like she knew it. "Sorry, babe. I'm just so tired."

"That, I can relate to. I do wish we could get to the library. Norman's got provisions we could make good use of."

"With him captured, we have to consider it compromised. It would have been nice to have a secure room on the inside."

"There are secrets within secrets in there. He has a whole cabinet overflowing with magical artifacts I'd kill to get my hands on at this point. If the enemy found it…" Chessa trailed off, leaving everyone to draw the obvious conclusion. If the enemy found it, they were screwed.

There were nods all around. The music of crickets filtered in from the trees beyond. It was still dark outside, but dawn was rapidly approaching, and that's when Gwen wanted to make her move.

They were going in through the kitchens, which were located at the southeasternmost end of the palace. They would come from the south, using the trees of the grove to cover their approach. The chimneys would be in use during the breakfast hour but should be safe to enter as soon as they cooled. Once they had Liam and Norman, they needed an exit strategy. The Unseelie wouldn't let them get far, that was sure, so they needed a safe place to retreat to, somewhere nearby in Glastonbury.

The other problem was Samson. There was no way a griffin could fit through a chimney, at least, not without a fairy powerful enough to alter the perception, and thus reality, of space. For what had to be the billionth time, Gwen kicked herself for letting her magic lessons lapse. "Samson, you need to stay back. There's no way to get you in without drawing attention."

The griffin started to protest, but Gwen held up her hand. "This isn't up for debate. One wrong move and none of us make it back to Korranthia."

Samson's beak snapped shut, but his feathers remained puffed up. Gwen couldn't be concerned with his feelings at the moment. Each decision she made could tank the whole mission, and if that happened, she would lose everyone she cared about.

She had to work with what they had. It wasn't much. Gwen flitted back up to the opening and looked out. By her estimation, they had about four hours give or take a pancake to iron out the details. After they took turns sneaking into the woods for a necessary commune with nature, Gwen had Curtis procure a stick and cast a basic enchantment to allow the tip to draw on the stone floor. It was simple perceptive fairy magic, but even that was too advanced for her. She had no time for shame. Instead, she got to work drawing out a rough blueprint of the palace on the Tor.

34

June 19
Morning before the Summer Solstice

While Gwen and Samson planned, Chessa and Curtis stole away to Glastonbury to search for a safe house and supplies. Chessa's bursts of speed and sleuthing abilities meant she could disappear in any town, especially without a griffin in tow, and Curtis knew this one well enough to guide them.

"What's the plan?" asked Chessa as they darted through the cemetery, keeping low to the ground.

"Scouts will be looking for a griffin and a pixie," replied the strait-laced Seelie guard. "They'll assume you'll travel by air, and they won't suspect stealth. We should be all right if we keep our heads low and move with purpose. Gwen has a friend who knows we're here. Her shop is as close to the tower as we could hope, but I don't know if she'll be willing to help. If nothing else, we can go there, grab some provisions, and decide on our next move."

"Sounds good, Ace. Lead the way."

Getting back to the gift shop was a breeze. They didn't spot a single Unseelie patrol on the streets or in the air. "Something doesn't feel right," Chessa said as they ducked inside the store.

"I agree. This was too easy," said Curtis.

The shop was empty, so he led her to the back door and up the stairs to a small apartment. Chessa could hear muffled voices, but nobody answered the door when Curtis knocked. Instead, everything fell silent. He knocked again. "Mrs. Walsh, it's me, Curtis. I was here with a *friend* earlier."

The door opened and a gnome with a face that looked like she was facing death appeared. She hurried them in, slamming the door behind them before throwing the deadbolt. The room was filled with an assortment of fae. They crowded on the couch, stood in corners, or sat on the floor with their backs to the walls. The blinds were drawn.

Curtis's mouth dropped open. "What is going on here?"

The gnome answered, "If Gwendolyn Evenshine is here, that can only mean we're taking back Avalon. We here have all pledged our lives to the Seelie Court, and it seems our pledge is being called upon."

"But you said death was waiting in Avalon," said Curtis, looking bemused.

"Aye, that I did. Gwendolyn is like a daughter to me. My own doesn't speak to me anymore, and I'll not be losing both. Avalon belongs to the Seelie."

There were determined expressions and nods all around. At first, Chessa felt a flutter of hope. These were regular citizens, ready to fly into battle to defend their lives and homeland. But then she realized the implication. "You're talking about a full-on war," she said.

"If that's what it takes," replied the gnome. "Danu knows, I owe it to Avalon. I owe it to my people."

Mrs. Walsh's expression softened. She began to cry. Chessa looked to Curtis for an explanation, but he shook his head and gave a small shrug.

Chessa put a hand on the gnome's shoulder. "Gwen has been my best friend for five years. She told me all about you and how she spent so much time in your shop. You've always been loyal to the Seelie throne. She said that you were one of the only reasons her years in

Avalon were tolerable. You and your daughter, Delia, were friends to her when she had none."

Mrs. Walsh sniffed and wiped at her eyes. "I always thought of her as one of my own. But the truth is, she's better than us both. My sweet Delilah was never the person I hoped she would be. She stopped being Delia many years ago."

The gnome's words felt like a brick to the face. It couldn't be. "Delilah?"

Mrs. Walsh nodded.

"Delilah Johnson, the Ghost of Korranthia, is your daughter?" said Chessa, a pit forming in her stomach.

Mrs. Walsh nodded. "Her part in all this was the only thing keeping me from standing up to the invaders. I'm not proud of it, but I am a mother before all things. But now that Gwendolyn is here and Delilah is gone, I can't sit on the sidelines any longer."

"How do you know she's gone?" asked Curtis, his hand resting on the hilt of his wand as if the assassin might burst through the door at any moment. His face was eerily calm, his expression steely, and in the moment, Chessa could see why he was chosen for the elite forces of the Seelie guard.

"Because she came to see me the day before the Equinox, for the first time in years. She told me she had a job to do then she'd be gone for a long time. When Avalon was taken over, I was scared. I knew she had something to do with all this."

Chessa gave a low whistle. She didn't want to twist the knife by telling Mrs. Walsh that it was Delilah who killed Queen Estrella. "Does Gwen know?"

Mrs. Walsh shook her head. "I don't think so. And I'd like for it to stay that way. They were friends, once. And Gwendolyn doesn't have many of those."

Chessa didn't know how long she could keep the secret from Gwen, but Mrs. Walsh had a point. Gwen already mistrusted the world. Now wasn't the time to pile on, not if the threat was neutralized for the time being. "I may have to tell her someday if Delilah resurfaces, but for now, I'll leave her memory intact."

The gnome gave a weak smile and looked around the room at the gathered fae. "Delilah made her own choices, and now it's time for me to make mine. I need to make amends for what I unleashed on the world, and it starts today."

This was bad. Chessa had hoped for a stealth mission. Get in, save Norman, search for Liam, get out, and never look back. Gwen wasn't planning to take back Avalon. That was suicide. And a group of twenty fae on a quest for redemption or revenge wasn't going to tip the scale. Everyone in this room would die. Chessa had to stop it. "This can't happen. Not like this. Gwen is my best friend, and I intend to keep her alive, not use her to start a war that's sure to fail."

"Then I suggest you help ensure it doesn't," replied the gnome. "The war is happening. It's been brewing for long before any of us were involved, but we're the ones who will end it."

While Chessa struggled for an argument, Curtis spoke up. "Tell me your plan."

There wasn't much of one, truth be told, but the civilian army was armed better than Chessa could have ever imagined. It wasn't quite Norman's cabinet, but the trinkets in Mrs. Walsh's collection were far from the novelties they appeared. A set of six communications devices was only the tip of the iceberg. There wasn't a single fae in the room without some kind of armament, though most were merely defensive—protection from fire attacks, untouchable barriers, source-stick absorbers—that kind of thing. Still, it wasn't nothing.

It didn't completely alleviate Chessa's misgivings, but it was clear Mrs. Walsh would not be deterred. Once a few of the other fae spoke up about their dedication to the cause, she gave up. Spending precious time trying to discourage fae who were fighting for their very way of life would be a waste. It was either work with them or watch them die waging their doomed war.

"We were just about to clear out. The Unseelie know I'm Delilah's ma, and I expect they'll be sniffing around here looking for her. She's a valuable asset."

Curtis stepped forward. "Where are you headed, and how can we help keep you safe until you get there?"

Chuckles resounded around the room.

Mrs. Walsh gave a wink. "Don't you worry about keeping us safe. We've been preparing. This way."

As she spoke, a pair of pixies, siblings with dirty blond hair and a smattering of freckles over rosy cheeks, left out the back door of the shop to scout ahead. The rest of the fae split into small groups and waited for the all-clear. Then they followed quietly but at a leisurely pace.

Smart, thought Chessa.

If an Unseelie battalion happened by, only a few fae would be spotted, and it would seem like nothing more than neighbors on a stroll. Curtis and Chessa brought up the rear with Mrs. Walsh. They walked out the back door, and across the street. As they were about to cut behind a row of shops, a humanoid Unseelie guard, likely a wizard or sorcerer, rounded the corner.

"Oy there, you Walsh?" he called.

Curtis stiffened. "Down, boy," whispered Mrs. Walsh. She shot Chessa a reassuring smile before turning to address the guard. When she spoke, her voice cracked with age and she sounded almost feeble. Damn, she was good. "Yes? How can I help you?"

By now, the guard was a mere ten feet away. There were no others in sight, and for a brief moment, Chessa wondered if there was going to be a fight.

"You're the mother of Delilah Johnson?"

"Yes, but I haven't seen her in fifteen years. Is everything okay with my Delia?"

The way her voice softened when she used Delilah's childhood nickname broke Chessa's heart. Before the Ghost of Korranthia became an assassin with a death count in the triple digits, she'd been little Delia, loved by her mama. The pain Mrs. Walsh suffered must be unbearable.

"I'm afraid not, ma'am. You need to come with me."

"I'll do no such thing. If you want Delia, you'll have to find her yourself."

The guard reached out, but before he could lay a hand on the gnome, Curtis tackled him to the ground. "Go, get out of here," he hissed at Chessa and Mrs. Walsh.

The gnome grabbed Chessa's hand and dragged her away behind a building. A moment later, Curtis joined them.

"Is he alive?" asked Chessa, thinking about the troll in Avalon.

"Of course. I just hit him with a sleeper jolt," he replied.

"I've got such magic-envy," said Chessa. She knew Seelie guards underwent years of training to master glamours that would work on other fae, but it was just so *cool*. She didn't understand how Gwen could just let all that potential waste away.

"Haroo, haroo," came the call of a pixie pretending to be a bird from the nearby trees.

"This way," said Mrs. Walsh, leading them through a vacant parking lot to where a lone garage stood. Spiderwebs covered boarded windows and the paint was chipped off the walls. By the looks of it, the garage had been abandoned for years, yet the door was raised just high enough for a pixie, a fairy, and a gnome to duck inside.

"You took longer than expected," said a siren who was waiting next to the door. Chessa recognized her from Mrs. Walsh's living room. "Everything okay?"

"We had a little dalliance with a soldier," replied Mrs. Walsh, raising her eyebrows as if the run-in were illicit.

The siren giggled.

The inside of the garage, dimly lit with fairy orbs, was larger than it appeared from the outside. Even Samson would be able to spread his wings without a problem, and it made for a perfect training ground, so long as the Unseelie remained unaware of its use. When Chessa's gaze drifted to the back of the space, she nearly fell on her ass. Curled up in the corner was a dragon.

It wasn't a big dragon, but it dwarfed any fae Chessa knew. Black scales caught the light as the creature rose, and deep violet eyes blinked, taking in the sight of the newcomers. The dragon made a low clicking sound in its throat. Mrs. Walsh stepped forward and reached her hand upward to offer up a pat, and the clicking turned into a high-pitched whine.

"Shh, Henrietta, it's just Mama," cooed the gnome.

Once the dragon settled back into her corner, Mrs. Walsh waved them all further inside. The pixie pair, Hobbes and Marni, darted inside last, each taking a rope hanging from opposite corners of the door and using them to pull the door back into place.

It took a moment for Chessa to get her wits about her. Dragons were of the realm of unicorns and pegasi—magical creatures that had been gone for so long that nobody knew if the tales were legends or history. She thought they were extinct if they ever lived at all. Now here she was, closed in a garage just outside Avalon with one. And she was beautiful.

Chessa looked at Curtis and saw her own awe reflected back. Curtis was from Avalon, yet even he seemed blown away by Henrietta. So their existence wasn't just a UK thing. Mrs. Walsh must have read their expressions because she chuckled.

"One of the items that came into my possession three years ago was an egg. It came from a collector who thought it a relic of the age of legends. It lay dormant in his storeroom for many years. Turns out, she just needed a mother's touch." The gnome gave the dragon a scratch under the chin and Henrietta purred. Chessa laughed. She had no idea that dragons could purr.

"You've had a dragon hidden in a garage twenty feet from Avalon for three years?" Curtis asked.

"You Seelie guards aren't as observant as you think," quipped Mrs. Walsh. "But no. That would be cruel. I've got some property out in the country. Henrietta has a good life with me. She's still just a baby, you know."

Any other time, Chessa would have wanted to spend the week asking questions and marveling over the creature, but they didn't have that kind of time. She left Curtis to begin training the assortment of gnomes, fairies, and sprites gathered. When she ducked out of the garage, he was addressing them but still staring at Henrietta with trepidation. She needed to head back to the graveyard to gather Gwen and Samson.

She kept to the shadows, flying in short bursts from one hiding spot to the next, but as she neared her destination, something felt off. She couldn't pinpoint the feeling, but her intuition was never wrong. She flew into the dense brush of a tree at the edge of the graveyard. To one side was the sleepy cemetery, empty and quiet save for the occasional car whirring by on the road beyond. To the other side, she could just make out the top of Morgan's mausoleum through swaying branches. A curl of smoke rose above the tree line. There was no way Samson and Gwen were roasting marshmallows, so that could only mean one thing. Intruders.

Chessa flitted down to a lower branch a few feet into the trees and watched. The smoke was thicker here, and she could hear voices and laughter. She had to get closer, but she didn't want to risk being seen. Chessa scoured the area for a good hiding place. A large chestnut tree had a knot in its trunk near its lowest branch. She would be able to see the entire mausoleum from up there. She zipped over and tucked her body into the tiny alcove.

She was positioned just above a gathering of Unseelie guards, mostly fairies. She prayed to Danu they wouldn't look up. They were relaxing in the shade, despite the smoke-thick air, talking and telling jokes. Chessa pulled her shirt up over her nose and mouth as she stepped out onto the branch to see what was burning. Soot stained the stone walls of the sacred site, and the plume of smoke was coming from the vent in the side of the mausoleum. From the look of things, it had been burning for a while. Tears welled in Chessa's eyes, but then she realized the stone slab door was open. More smoke poured out the top of the doorway. Samson and Gwen were gone.

Chessa was trying to figure out what to do when her foot slipped. She flitted her wings to steady herself, but a chestnut was knocked loose. It fell downward and landed in the center of the Unseelie guards. When they looked up, she was already gone.

35

Shortly after Chessa and Curtis left in search of supplies, smoke wafted in through the mausoleum vent.

"I think our welcome has worn out," said Samson with a snort. "Time to shake a tail feather, kid."

"You want to dance?"

"Jokes? At a time like this? No, you pain in the ass. I want to split."

Muffled voices yelled orders from the other side of the heavy door. Gwen used her boot to smudge the plans as much as she could while covering her nose and mouth with her sleeve. "They must not have any large fae with them, or they wouldn't need to resort to smoking us out," she said. "So here's what we're going to do. I'll cast a glamour on you, make you look bigger. You push the stone slab as hard as you can to make yourself an exit and fly north. When you're clear, turn east and drop below the tree line. I'll go through the vent and cover you."

Samson looked unconvinced. "Can you do that?"

"Do what?"

"The glamour. These aren't a pack of regular old joes."

Gwen sighed. The truth of it was that she had no idea what she was capable of. She hadn't tried any substantial magic since putting on the amulet Quincy gave her. "I don't know, Sammy. But we can't just sit here and suffocate."

The griffin nodded and raised a talon as if to push his glasses up on his beak before lowering it again. "All right, then. Let's make a show of it," he said, his voice resolute.

Gwen hoped like hell he would make it through this alive. "I'll find you. If I don't come to you by tomorrow, go home for the love of Danu."

"What about the others? The plan to move on Avalon?"

"None of it matters if we get barbecued here," replied Gwen. "Now go."

Gwen raised her wand. The amulet around her neck began to glow, and it felt like her very essence was being sucked out of her soul and focused through her palm and into her wand. She cast the glamour just as Samson gave the stone door a great shove. The Unseelie screamed and scattered at the sight of a monstrously large griffin bursting out of a mausoleum two times too small to contain it. Gwen screamed in delight. "Thank you, Quincy!"

Samson flapped his wings, the force of the air pinning fairies and pixies to the ground as he took to the skies. Gwen didn't stick around to watch them regroup. She kicked off the stone wall and followed, taking care to keep clear of the draft.

She heard shouts from below. A trio of pixies had gathered their wits fast enough to dart after her. Fuck. Pixies were faster than fairies for short bursts. She'd never shake them in time. Gwen reached down to her thigh holster where the gun Quincy armed her with was strapped against her leg. She slid her wand into the strap, pulled out the gun, held her breath, aimed behind, and pulled the trigger.

A boom split the air. She was knocked off course by the recoil. She righted herself and looked down just in time to witness the last of the trio dissolve from the iron particles in the air. It was surreal. First, he was flying, his face contorted in anger, then he simply wasn't there. With a shudder, Gwen tucked the handgun back into its holster and disappeared into the cover of the clouds.

Ten minutes later, she caught up with Samson in the sky, as he was cutting east. They dipped below the tree line together and settled on the ground to figure out their next move. Gwen grew up a stone's throw from Glastonbury, so she knew all the best hiding places. For a fairy. A griffin, on the other hand, made things a little more complicated. Samson didn't exactly blend in with his surroundings. She used to have friends out here in the countryside, but she didn't know who to trust. This old campsite was the safest place she could think of. But it was only a matter of time before they were spotted and turned in to the Unseelie.

"How did they find us?" panted Samson.

Gwen shrugged. "We have no idea how they're getting intel. I suspect they have spies everywhere. Even here. We need to move quick."

"What about Chessa and Curtis?"

"Honestly, it's better this way. I want Chessa clear of this. You too. I need you to fly to London. You'll find friends there to help you get home."

"Do I look like a breezy boob to you?"

"What?"

"A breezy boob! A yap! A lame leprechaun! I don't leave my partner out in the heat. Capiche?"

"I figured you'd say that. Maybe not *that* exactly, but something along those lines. Well, preen your feathers then. We're going rogue."

Gwen had to get back to Avalon, and she could only think of one way to get Samson into her home unseen, and the kitchen chimneys were out. She raided a nearby campsite and returned with some cord —the kind you use to hang a hammock—and a wagon.

"Where did get that?" Samson asked when she returned. "Did you chisel it from some kid?"

"No, I traded for it."

"Baloney. You don't have anything to trade."

She didn't have time to justify her every move. Plus, the truth was she'd lifted it from a nearby family's campsite when they were off fishing or hiking or doing whatever it was that normal families did on vacation.

"Just sit in it."

Samson's eagle head cocked to the side. "You do realize I'm about three bucks fifty, right? I don't think a little Radio Flyer is going to cut it."

"It's all I could find. It will have to do. With any luck, we'll come across Unseelie guards quickly, and they can figure out how to get your big ass back to Avalon."

Samson's beak fell open. "What are you hatching, kid?"

"As far as they know, there's just you and Chessa. I'm certain they didn't see me back at the cemetery." She averted her eyes and shifted her weight. "The ones that did are dust. Right now, they're hunting a griffin. If Grimore is involved in whatever is happening here, I just need to talk to him, figure out if Liam's alive, and maybe find that friend of Chessa's. To do that, I need a way to get close. You're it. Now sit and let me tie up your talons."

"No way. You're not using me as bait. I'm no chump."

"You said you wanted to help. It's this, or head to London and get the fuck out of here. I'd prefer you took option B."

"Damn it, kid. Why is everything a damn drama with you?"

Gwen shook her head. They both knew this was a Hail Mary. She had to make this play because it was the only one that stood half a chance.

Samson's feathers puffed and his tail swished around. "I don't suppose you have a plan for busting out once we've got what we came for?"

"No. It will take me some time to get my bearings, and if I can convince Grimore that I'm on his side, that I'm against my family, then I may gain a bit of freedom. If not, we're both as good as dead."

"London isn't sounding so bad," he replied.

"Good. Go."

"Not a chance." The wagon creaked as Samson lowered his haunches down, but the tires held up. They were some kind of heavy-duty plastic. Gwen tied his talons and tried to pull, but she was too small to move the wagon.

"Wait here," she said. As she flew off, she heard him sigh and reply, "Where am I going to go? Hawaii? I could use a mai tai about now."

This is insane, she thought, but she flew up above the tree line and scoured the skies for the Unseelie. Not twenty feet away, a group of fairies was flying right toward her.

Please, Danu, let this work.

She waved them down. Thirty seconds later, they were upon her.

"You, there, halt!" barked one of the guards. Gwen didn't move beyond the wing fluttering it took to keep her aloft.

"My name is Gwendolyn Evenshine, and I am currently fifth in line for the Seelie throne. I have some business to discuss with Master Grimore," she said, injecting her tone with as much authority as she could. Her insides were jelly, but she fought to keep it from showing.

There were six guards in total, four fairies, a pixie, and a sprite mounted on a hummingbird, all armed with source sticks and who knew what else. Gwen wondered how the vest she was wearing would hold up against six source sticks at once. The thought sent a spike of terror through her. Of all the things she'd suffered, the source stick was in the top five worst feelings of her life. The fairy who had spoken fluttered within an arm's reach of her as the others surrounded her. There was no going back now.

"Is that so? He ain't said nothin' about expectin' no Seelie trash." He spat the word "Seelie," and the sprite laughed, her voice clashing with the tension of the situation.

Gwen looked the guard straight in his deep brown eyes. "He isn't expecting me. We have more in common than he knows. I'm afraid I'm a bit of a pariah in my family. As a gesture of good faith, I brought him a gift, but it's down below and it's too heavy for me to move alone." It was all true, except the part about good faith.

"This could be a trap," said the fairy to Gwen's left. Her hand was hovering over the source stick at her side.

"How do we know you don't have an ambush waitin' for us down there?"

"I suppose you don't," Gwen replied. "But if you don't come help me, I'm afraid my surprise may get away. You've been searching for a griffin if I'm not mistaken?"

"You're tellin' us you caught the griffin. And you did it alone?" Skepticism played on the guard's face, but Gwen could tell he was growing weary from hovering in place for so long. She was, too, truth be told.

"That I did."

"How?"

"That griffin is Sergeant Detective Samson Wayne. We've known each other a long time. He trusted me. Plus, he's nearly blind without his glasses. It really wasn't much to tie him up."

"She does know a lot about the escapee," said the same guard who'd spoken before.

"Would you shut up, Marla? Who's in charge here?"

"I'm just saying."

After a tense moment, the guard decided to leave the pixie behind to call for backup while he and the rest of the squadron followed Gwen down to the campsite where Samson sat torturing a Radio Flyer. He put up a good show of struggling against his bonds.

An hour later, Gwen was home. But the palace where she grew up, the building behind the glamour that made it look like the ruins of a tower, felt different somehow. Avalon had never been particularly welcoming, not to her, but it used to resonate with magic. She could still feel the power, but now it was a terrible, frightening sort—the kind of magic that could raise you up or devour you in a moment. She glanced over the southernmost edge of the palace to see if anything looked strange over the grove. For a moment, she thought she saw the gray clouds above the area flicker with light, and then it was gone. Gwen shuddered but kept her head high.

The wagon floated along, hoisted by fairies her escorts had summoned. It was an awkward sight, bobbing through the air, and it took a small legion. The guard who seemed to be in charge flew on Gwen's right, the mounted sprite on her left, and the pixie below her. The arrangement was no coincidence. The pixie could catch her in an instant and the sprite could gut her in less. Her escort served as a warning should she try any tricks.

Samson thrashed as larger Unseelie surrounded him once they were on hard ground. They dragged, pushed, and carried him through the broad palace doors.

Sorry, Sammy, thought Gwen as she watched them disappear

through the foyer. As she walked by the familiar statues, she brushed a hand along the door frame, dropped her inner defenses, focused on the warmth of the sunlight streaming in behind her, and gave in to the sensation of falling. Any information she could gather could help her put the pieces of the puzzle together.

Senses swirled around her, images and sounds. Smells and sensations. The foyer practically vibrated with energy, and it was impossible to focus. She saw goblins and sprites in Unseelie attire blurring into the familiar faces of smiling Seelie royals. The scent of lilac gave way to the metallic smell of blood. For a split second, she saw her brother how he once was, a young boy, chasing his best friend Corrin through the space. He almost seemed to see her before his face aged and his eyes became hard. She felt a spike of adrenaline that seemed to emanate from the statue of Joan of Arc. There was more, but she couldn't make sense of it without her equipment.

When the world came back into focus, Gwen was being thrust into the great hall. She stumbled, and her escort pulled her along. The hall seemed to have grown bigger, but it might just be that Gwen wasn't accustomed to seeing it barren of life and furniture. At the very back of the hall was a raised dais. The Council table had been removed, and the four thrones faced outward, and in one of the middle thrones sat Grimore. He smirked as Gwen was pushed forward. To his left was Queen Charis of Korranthia, her cold eyes boring into Gwen's, and to his right was a beautiful, golden-haired fairy Gwen recognized but couldn't quite place. The fourth throne was empty. Merely sitting on those thrones was treason. Gwen might not have wanted anything to do with power, but the sight of these imposters in her home, sitting on the thrones of power, really pissed her off.

"Gwendolyn Evenshine, we meet again," said Grimore in a flat, unreadable voice. Gwen ignored him and stared at the Korranthian queen.

"She was your daughter." Gwen's voice echoed off the stone floor and walls.

Queen Charis shook her head. "No. She was her father's daughter. She would have continued his work, pandering to humans, neglecting her own people in favor of the illusion of peace, all the while setting mortals above us."

The queen was humanoid herself, but sitting as she was atop a Seelie throne, her blue eyes blazed with magic, a magic the fae of Korranthia thought died in her bloodline long ago. Looking at her now, Gwen wondered how she'd ever seen her as anything but the fairy queen she was. Cold, terrifying, powerful—not much different than Gwen's own mother when it came down to it. Frankie deserved so much better.

Gwen clutched the locket hanging just below the amulet at her neck as she spoke as evenly as she could. "She was good. She wanted the best for everyone, fae and human alike. Had you given her the chance, talked with her, she would have been a better ruler than any of us. But you didn't. You sent a serial killer after your own daughter. You had her slaughtered. And for what? For power?"

"For freedom. Freedom for all fae. She never would have agreed to open the door, to allow Faerie to take back the earth."

Gwen struggled to get it together. She was quickly ruining her chances of convincing them she was an ally. She was sealing Samson's fate as well as her own. She swallowed the lump in her throat and worked to disguise her shock at Charis' words. Perhaps if she pretended she'd known the Unseelie goal all along, she could salvage her plan. "That's why I'm here," she said. "I will never forgive you for what you did to Frankie, but our people have been oppressed for too long, I agree with you on that." She was stalling and trying to get as much information as she could. Grimore must have seen through the ploy.

He stood, pulling Gwen's attention from the queen.

"You expect us to believe that you, a Seelie Royal yourself, have the first clue about what's going on here?"

"No. Because I don't. I do know that, even amongst the Seelie, there have been those who resent the relationships forged between the mortals and the fae. Those who resent hiding their true natures. We're not so different."

"Queen Charis has been Seelie her entire life. I have sworn no allegiance to any throne. All either side ever did was sit and wait. What are we waiting for? Humanity to die off? To kill the world? I will sit by no longer. The time of mortals is over."

Gwen had no idea how to stop this, but any hope she had depended on convincing those before her that she was on their side. "Is opening the fae realm even possible? It has been locked away for so long, most believe it mythical."

The beautiful young fairy on the third throne looked on with curiosity.

"You expect us to discuss such matters with you? You are amusing, I'll give you that." Grimore motioned for a guard. "Please do away with Miss Evenshine."

"Stop."

It was a simple command, but it stopped the guard in his tracks. He dropped into a bow before the young fairy. Grimore seethed but did not speak. Gwen swore she noticed his head drop a fraction in deference to the girl. Gwen realized her misstep. She'd assumed Grimore was in charge of this show, but she'd missed the true power.

"We will not make rash decisions. There is much to be gained by keeping Gwendolyn Evenshine alive."

Grimore lowered his head. "As you say, Your Highness."

Your Highness?

Between her upbringing as a Seelie royal and her education at the Fairy Godparent Academy, Gwen was familiar with all the monarchs across the globe, and this girl was a part of no Kingdom she'd ever studied. That must mean—

"You're Unseelie royalty?"

"I am the Unseelie Princess. I go by many names, but you may call me Moliana Eviscera. With my parents currently incapacitated, I speak for the Unseelie."

Everything clicked into place. Queen Charis, although powerful, only ruled Korranthia. She was out of her league here in Avalon. Grimore had used her to rise to power, and her place here was honorary at best.

Moliana…that name sounded familiar. As realization dawned on Gwen, the princess' face twisted into a cruel smile.

"Nice to see you again, Gwen."

It was at Corrin's funeral. Liam brought her as his guest. Gwen had barely given her the time of day. "Molly!" she gasped. "Is my brother alive? Where is Liam?"

The sound of a door opening reverberated through the great hall. A knot of Unseelie guards, mostly sprites and brownies, emerged from the door leading to the holding cells and marched to the center of the open space. They made a sharp turn to walk up the long runner leading from the entranceway to the four thrones. Gwen had to step aside to make way for them to approach.

They came to a halt next to her before the entire company took a step back in unison, leaving a fairy in chains where they had stood a moment before. Her wings were low. She seemed small, but there was no mistaking Indira Evenshine.

"Mother!"

Indira turned to look at Gwen, her eyes hollow. "Gwendolyn. You have to get out of here," she said, her voice raspy and dry as if she hadn't had a sip of water in days.

"How lovely of you to finally come home, Gwen." The voice coming from the center of the group of guards was clear, bright, and familiar. Liam.

"Liam! You're alive! I knew it!" said Gwen. Her brain swam. None of the scenarios she played out included so many people to rescue. How was she going to get them all out? That's when she noticed that Liam wasn't chained. The guards parted to allow him to saunter up to her.

"What, no hug from my dear sis? Don't you want to read me, Gwen? Figure out my motivations from snippets of my past?"

"Liam, I..." A realization hit her like the rubble of her life collapsing on her head. The fourth throne. This was why her family was being killed, to make Liam Seelie King. Indira's presence here could only mean one thing: she was the last obstacle to that goal—she and Gwen. Grimore already had the leader of the Unseelie. If he could get every faction of fae represented, he could wage open war on humanity. But Liam? Her sweet little Liam who played hide-and-seek with Corrin in the foyer? This couldn't be happening.

She abandoned her plan to convince them that she was switching sides. This was no longer a strategy game. She had to do something to stop this insanity, but she was just one fairy, stunted in magic, a screw-up by nature. She could think of nothing. "You don't know what you're doing," Gwen said. Her voice sounded foreign to her own ears, half pleading, half ordering.

"On the contrary. I know exactly what I'm doing. I'm not bumbling through life trying to prove myself to the world. Unlike you, I know who I am. I am Liam Evenshine, third in line to the Seelie throne, and I speak for the Seelie fae. For the forgotten. For the *abandoned*."

He closed the distance between them. As he hissed the last word, Gwen caught a glimpse of silver sparkling in his hand. A dagger. Before she could react, Indira screamed. She threw herself between them as Liam lunged at Gwen. The blade caught their mother between the ribs.

"No!" screamed Liam.

Gwen shot into the air while her mother crumpled to the ground. Below her, Liam dropped to his knees over Indira. She gasped for air, clutching her abdomen.

"Mother! Stay with me," he said. "This wasn't supposed to happen." Liam sobbed and murmured to their mother about how she was going to live out her life in comfort, locked up but taken care of. His voice reminded Gwen of the time he was sent to boarding school and begged to stay home. Here, in Avalon, not so long ago. But Liam wasn't a scared little boy anymore, and Gwen couldn't comfort him or even tell him how deluded he was. The vipers on the thrones behind him would have killed Indira as soon as her usefulness waned, just as they would kill Gwen. She had to get out of there.

"Guards!" called Moliana, rising from her throne. "Apprehend her."

Her voice was calm and hard, like molten steel. Gwen hovered for a moment as she shook off the shock of what transpired and looked around for a clear exit. Everywhere her eyes landed held memories. They weren't happy memories, but they were hers. In every one, her baby brother was her only ally. Now he'd just tried to kill her. Their mother was bleeding out on the stone floor. The great hall spun around her. Nothing made sense anymore. And there were guards everywhere. Where did they all come from? They hadn't been there a moment before.

A pixie slammed into Gwen. A jolt wracked her body, the hit from a source stick successfully deflected by her protective vest. She threw the pixie off her just to be pummeled by another guard and another. Gwen focused on her connection to the sun with every fiber of her being and reached down to brush her fingertips against the wand in her thigh-holster. She cast the best defensive magic spell she knew, one that made her appear to vanish, even to fae eyes. She'd only pulled it off once in practice, but there was no incentive like the threat of certain death. The effect only lasted a heartbeat, but it was all she needed. She dropped her altitude so she wouldn't reappear in the same spot and flew for the west hall. At the same time, she drew the gun. She'd come with two missions—break in and free her friends—and she accomplished the first. Now, she needed to get to Samson.

36

Chessa could tell the hive had been kicked. While Curtis worked to turn citizens into soldiers and Mrs. Walsh and the others developed a plan to invade, she and the pixie twins took on observation duty. Hobbes was stationed to the south, Marni to the north, and Chessa to the west. Getting close to the palace wasn't an option, but from the rooftop of a little B&B just outside Avalon, she could clearly see the tor and the tower atop it. Unseelie guards flocked from the grounds to the walls and into the fae structure beyond the glamour. It could mean many things, but Chessa knew the truth of it. Gwen had done something monumentally stupid.

She zipped from roof to roof until she made it back to the garage where their militia waited. "It's time!" she yelled before the door fully rolled open.

Curtis stood, feet on the ground, before rows of accountants, shopkeepers, IT professionals, teachers, and more. In the course of a day and a half, he organized the group into something resembling a real army. Every face turned toward him with fierce purpose, and he looked to Chessa. He might have been timid around Gwen, but here, he was in his element. "What is the situation out there?" he asked.

"Their forces have been pulled in. Something is happening inside."

"Gwen?"

"Who else?"

"This is what we've been waiting for. Mrs. Walsh, are you ready?" Curtis turned to the back of the garage, drawing Chessa's attention to Henrietta, who was now whining. The little dragon wouldn't calm down until Chessa greeted her. But it wasn't Henrietta that took Chessa's breath away.

Mrs. Walsh was sitting in a saddle on the dragon's back, her flowery gnome hat at odds with the crossbow strapped to her chest along with a quiver of iron-tipped arrows over a Kevlar vest. On her face was an expression of determination undercut with raw rage. "Let's take these bastards down," she growled. She flipped up a mask to cover her nose and mouth.

"Remind me never to fuck with a middle-aged gnome shopkeeper," said Chessa with a grin. Walsh gave her a nod and bent to pat Henrietta on the shoulder. Chessa walked over to the dragon and gave her a scratch under the chin while Curtis outfitted each of the crew leaders with a communications device. Once everything was set, he returned to the center of the garage.

"Crew A and B, you're a go!" he shouted.

A brownie stepped forward with his arm raised over his head. "For Avalon!" He took off at a run, followed by five or six others, all quick fae known for their mischievousness, though at the moment, there was nothing but resolve painted across their faces and purpose in their movements.

Once they were out of sight, a sprite stepped forward, mimicking the brownie's arm gesture. She gave a salute to Curtis and then led a group of sprites and goblins out of the garage.

"Mrs. Walsh, you're next. We await your signal."

The rest of the fae moved aside to let Henrietta through. Marni jumped up behind the gnome. She was the fastest pixie of the group and, despite having to recharge on rooftops, would be able to cover the distance between Avalon and the garage faster than anyone else. Mrs. Walsh gave Chessa a wave. "See you on the other side."

The baby dragon stepped into the sunlight, scales glinting and lavender eyes wide. She started clicking, but Mrs. Walsh spoke in low tones to her, quieting her nerves. When she spread her wings, they were wider than the garage. With a stretch and a whine, Henrietta pushed off from the cement and took to the skies.

Crew A would run distraction while Crew B took out as many guards as possible. Mrs. Walsh would watch from above, providing cover where necessary. When the Unseelie were fully engaged with the first wave, Marni would fly back within range of the comms devices and signal everyone else to move in. Their numbers didn't come close to matching the Unseelie's, but they hoped the element of surprise would be enough to overwhelm the enemy. It was all they had.

Chessa tried not to let the reality of their inevitable demise cloud her mind. These fae would go down as heroes. Whatever the Unseelie were planning, it didn't bode well for the world, that much was sure.

The signal came sooner than expected. Marni appeared at the horizon, her face pale. It was time. Chessa looked to Curtis.

"You find Gwen," he said. His voice sounded hoarse. "And get her out. She's more valuable than she knows. Do you understand?"

Chessa stared at him for a moment. If she didn't know better, she might think he had feelings for her best friend. Then she saw it in his eyes. He did. Chessa's heart hurt. Gwen hadn't made a real connection with anyone but her in the years they'd known each other, and here was this fairy, leading an army into certain death, begging her to save Gwen. Tears pricked at the corners of Chessa's eyes.

"Promise me?"

She had to reassure him, or his nerve might falter. "Of course, I'm going for Gwen. I'll get her out," she said. And she meant it.

Cutis gave her a tight smile then held his fist in the air. "For Avalon!"

The entire retinue screamed back. "For Avalon!"

A wave of fae took to the streets, alleyways, air, and rooftops. This was Glastonbury's last stand.

37

As much as she struggled, Gwen was no match for the sheer numbers of Unseelie guards that descended upon her. Her path to the western hall was cut off by an ogre. She had no choice but to bolt for the main entrance. She made it to the foyer where the fae statues looked down on her. She always thought they were as disapproving as her family. All except Robin Williams. The kindness in his eyes never made her feel like a failure. But now even he seemed to be laughing as a pair of trolls blocked the internal door behind her and a wall of armored fairies and pixies sealed the main entrance. She was trapped. More guards filtered in between the trolls. The odds were now what? Fifty to one?

She could just make out Liam bent over their mother through the crack in the double doors beyond the trolls. He seemed genuinely upset, which led Gwen to conclude that he truly never meant to kill Indira. He was a fool. Indira was always going to die here today one way or another, and if Gwen didn't get her ass in gear, so would she. She fluttered to the floor as grief washed over her. They'd called Indira queen, which meant her suspicion was correct. Azrah was dead and so were the others. Her entire family had been eradicated, and Liam was to blame. Sweet, stupid Liam played into the hands of an enemy they'd all been too caught up in their own affairs to notice. She remembered little Liam pulling pranks on the guards and laughing right here in this foyer, years ago. Tears welled in Gwen's eyes. She didn't know if she had it in her to fight anymore.

As if they sensed her weakness, the Unseelie descended upon her.

Whether her heart was in it or not, fighting was all Gwen knew.

She cracked a sprite across the nose with her elbow, kicked a goblin back into his colleagues with a boot to the chest, and flipped in the air, fluttering her wings, to land on the shoulder of a troll who advanced on her. She pulled the Glock and held it against the creature's huge, pale green ear. "Make a move, and I smoke Miss Carcass Breath here," she snarled.

Then, chaos erupted.

The front doors flew open, knocking pixies and fairies out of the air. They careened into the statues and walls like hail. A series of small fireballs lit up the entranceway. A moment later, a group of well-organized sprites filtered in, dispatching the usurpers before anyone had a moment to make sense of the attack. The troll beneath Gwen stiffened in the sunlight that streamed through the open door, turning to stone beneath her feet.

The sprite at the front of the rescue mission was a delicate thing that Gwen thought she recognized from the Glastonbury flower shop, but she moved through the Unseelie forces like a hot knife through butter. How was this possible? "Entryway secured," she said. "Asset number one retrieved. Sending her out now."

Gwen couldn't tell who she was talking to but assumed there was some kind of communication device on her somewhere. The sprite turned to Gwen, who descended from her stone perch to alight on the stone floor at the center of the room.

"Princess Evenshine, you are to go with Dawn for your own safety," ordered the sprite.

A young sprite with her white hair cut into a bob and sporting a Taylor Swift tee stepped forward and bowed as a group of goblins surrounded all three of them, weapons pointed outward.

"I have to get Samson out," Gwen mumbled numbly. She couldn't wrap her mind around what was happening here, but she wasn't about to leave Samson in the hands of the enemy.

"I beg your pardon, Your Highness, but we need to get you to safety. There's already a team going for the west wing, and if he's been taken, that's where he'll be. We don't have the numbers to take back all of Avalon, but we will save Detective Wayne if we can."

This wasn't right.

Gwen looked over the group, which had fallen into formation facing the internal door, flanked now by two stone troll statues. Despite their prowess, these weren't hardened soldiers. They wore leggings and cargo shorts and wielded as many garden tools as real weapons. And they didn't know Indira was dead.

"I am Gwendolyn Evenshine, and I hereby claim my birthright as Queen of the Seelie Court. You will not order me to leave. There is nobody alive who has that right."

Her words were met with stunned stares, and then every fae in the foyer bowed. She didn't want to endanger these people, but they had done that the minute they chose to take up arms against the occupiers of Avalon. There was only one thing to do now. "We press forward together."

The sprite in charge nodded, her eyes resolute, but then she turned away. "Boss G, it's like you said," the sprite said into her comms. "She's going back in with us. And she's claiming her place as queen."

Gwen could make out the sound of a voice coming through the sprite's earpiece. She was pretty sure it said "Fuck."

"Boss G?" That *couldn't* stand for Boss Glitter, Chessa's gaming handle in *Death Mob*, could it? "Chessa?"

"Boss Glitter said to relay a message, Your Grace. Please don't fault me for her words. She said that she's sorry about your mother." The sprite took a deep breath before continuing. "She also said that you're a pain in the ass and that you must listen to my directives during this mission or—or..."

"It's okay, you don't need to relay her threat. I accept your terms. You're in charge. Now, let's go save Sammy."

The exchange only lasted a few seconds, but it was enough for the Unseelie to regroup in the great hall. Their defenses were split a moment later when Seelie reinforcements filtered in through the front entrance and from the kitchens. So Chessa had implemented her plan after all. Gwen wondered how many fae were involved in this raid, but she put the thought out of her mind as she screamed and dove into the fray.

38

Chessa cussed. A part of her knew Gwen wouldn't be pulled away from the action. She might act as if she cared for nobody, but that was because she cared too much. There was no way she was going to run the other way while the fae of Glastonbury fought for her, *their*, home. From the sound of it, her entire family had been eradicated. Chessa couldn't imagine what Gwen was going through, and if they lived through the day, it was going to require helping put the pieces of her best friend back together. Knowing all this didn't make Chessa's current job any easier. At least they'd located Gwen, which was more than she could say for Samson, asset number two.

As much as Gwen had sworn she would keep him away from danger, he was as stubborn as she was. There was no doubt in Chessa's mind he was somewhere in the palace too. A fine pair they made. Chessa hoped he'd be back in a holding cell, and if the fates were on the Seelie side, that's where Norman would be too. If they could get in and bust everyone loose, she might be able to convince Gwen to retreat with the rest. It was the closest they would get to a victory by Chessa's calculations, at least today.

She wasn't fooling herself. This would not end when and if the assets were retrieved. There was something bigger going on here, and the fae of Glastonbury didn't have the numbers to win. Now that they located Gwen and the teams were searching for Samson, Chessa had another target in mind. When you come up short and can't back down, there's only one thing to do—find a way to stack the odds in your favor. Norman's weaponry might not be enough, but it certainly couldn't hurt. So, that's where Chessa set her sights.

She took Marni and Hobbes with her. Three pixies might just be fast and small enough to get through the chaos unnoticed. She planned to set Hobbes up with the surveillance equipment while she and Marni hauled weapons out of the hidden room as fast as possible.

Curtis was calling the shots on the raid, and that fairy didn't disappoint. Without his tactical brilliance and the comms devices from Mrs. Walsh's stash, one of which was currently in her right ear, they never would have made it this far. Chessa couldn't wait to introduce the collector gnome to Norman. Once this was all over, they could geek out over magical artifacts to their hearts' content. That was something Chessa would love to see.

Crew A secured the main entry as Crew B moved on to the western hall entry point near the holding cells. It was up to the main force to keep the Unseelie off-guard in the great hall long enough for Crew B to free the prisoners. The operation should keep the usurpers occupied long enough for Chessa's team to get in.

"Boss G, this is Crew B. We're taking hits, and we're outnumbered. We need reinforcements. We breached the entrance but are losing ground quickly."

"We got ya," replied Chessa. She gave the order for Mrs. Walsh and Henrietta to swoop in over the west wing and provide cover. Then, she motioned to the pixie siblings to follow and made her move.

One of the hidden passages Norman pointed out to Chessa ran from the back hall, near the grove, to a room not far from the hidden library. If she could only find one of the entry points, they'd be golden. Gwen originally wanted them to go in via the chimneys like fucking Santa Claus. It was a bad plan if they were heading for the holding cells in the western hall. The kitchens were located south of the great hall, off the same hallway as the secret passage, and they should be relatively quiet now that their small team had swept the area and joined Crew A. The biggest danger would be navigating the corridor near the grove. Chessa could only hope that the guards had been pulled into the skirmish.

It took three sprints to get to the chimneys, with rests on the palace eaves between. They could hear the distant sounds of the dual battles, and occasionally, Chessa could see Henrietta circling over the western gate. She touched the device by her ear and switched to the private frequency she and Curtis shared. "We're going in."

"Copy that. Come out alive," was the reply.

As expected, the kitchens were empty. Chessa peeked out the doorway into the south corridor and was relieved to find fewer guards stationed there than she previously saw on the surveillance feeds. Two fairies and a gnome stood at the door in the center of the hall. There was no way around them, so they'd have to go through.

"Marni, Hobbes, take out the fairies. You're faster than they are, and they won't be expecting you. Don't let them touch you with those source sticks. I'll take the gnome."

The pixies both nodded.

"Ready," said Chessa. "Now."

All three pixies zipped out the kitchen door. Marni, the fastest of the three, hit the closest fairy like a bullet, knocking him to the ground before he could make a sound. Hobbes struggled with the other fairy while Chessa pummeled the gnome.

It was over in a matter of seconds. The fairies were both unconscious, and the gnome groaned.

"Everyone ok?" asked Chessa.

"I think my nose is broken, but I'll live," replied Hobbes. Blood trickled from one nostril, and he wiped it with his sleeve with a wince. "He got me with a right hook."

"Better than a source stick," replied Chessa.

As they passed the door to the grove, the hair on the back of Chessa's neck stood on end. Her hand began to warm. The closer they got, the hotter it was until it felt like she was being branded all over again. "What the hell?" she groaned, dropping to her knees and cradling her burning hand.

Marni stooped down. "Are you ok? What's going on?"

"I don't know. It burns!" Tears welled up in Chessa's eyes. Footsteps thudded in the hall from somewhere nearby, growing louder.

Marni grabbed Chessa's arm and pulled her to her feet. "Sorry, Boss G, but we gotta get out of here."

The farther along the hall Marni dragged her, the more the pain subsided until Chessa could first walk on her own, then take to the air.

"Second to last room on the left," she panted. Both companions made the turn as a door by the kitchens flew open. Chessa caught sight of a group of four Unseelie as she flew into the room behind them.

Chessa ran her hands all over the far wall, where she remembered Norman pointing, looking for a loose stone or something that might open a secret door. There was nothing.

"Hurry, boss," said Marni. Hobbes moved furniture to block the door.

"I know it's here somewhere," Chessa said. The only adornment in the room was a portrait of some stuffy blueblood. Chessa moved it aside to expose a small lever that sat flush with the wall. She pulled it. With a satisfying click, a small secret door opened in the floor.

"Jackpot!" she exclaimed.

Hobbes lifted the hatch upward, exposing a tunnel barely large enough for a gnome to pass. Marni zipped into the space, and Hobbes followed as Chessa slid the portrait back into place on the wall. Once she stepped into the tunnel, she located an identical lever below the trap door and gave it a tug. The panel slid back into place, leaving them all in blackness. Thankfully, there was only one way to go.

"Just keep walking," whispered Chessa. "Follow the tunnel."

The passage led all the way to the hall outside the library, where they emerged from a hidden door in the base of a light fixture. From there, accessing Norman's hideout was a piece of cake. The hidden library was just as Chessa had left, only it felt empty without her mopey wizard friend.

"What is all this stuff?" asked Marni, gaping into the vault

"That's part of the problem," replied Chessa. "I don't know. Some of it is protective, some of it is offensive. It's all powerful."

"And old," replied Marni, picking up an antique bangle and turning it in her hands.

"Yes, and old. We don't have time to figure out what does what, but we need to get it away from those who would use its powers against us. It's only a matter of time before they find the secret passages. Maybe once we bust Norman out, he can help us figure out which pieces to use."

Chessa had just set Hobbes up with the laptop to run surveillance when her communication device kicked on. "Boss G, we're losing the western front." Curtis's voice sounded strained over the intercom as if he were entrenched in battle.

"Hold on, I'm coming," replied Chessa, severing the connection. "Damn it, Curtis, you were supposed to stay back and give orders."

Hobbes looked up from the computer. "Boss, you're going to want to see this," he said.

The feed from the western battle was bloody. The Glastonbury fae were outnumbered three-to-one in the hall, and there was no sign of the sprite and goblin forces. Chessa switched over to the feed from the great hall and saw why. They were fully entrenched in a battle of their own.

"Change of plans. Marni, empty the vault. I'll clear the balcony off the library outside this room. I need you to fly faster than you ever have before. Take as much contraband as you can out to the field. Leave a few fae to guard it and have others help you empty the place out. Guard your flanks. Give Hobbes your comms device so he can let me know what's happening. Hobbes, stay put. Watch the feeds and take command based on what you see."

"Aye," said both pixies in unison.

Chessa tapped her own communication device twice to join the main frequency. "Crew A, fall back from the great hall and reinforce the western gate from the inside. Crew B, keep fighting. Help is on the way."

"What are you going to do?" asked Marni as she followed Chessa out of the secret room.

"Probably die," replied Chessa. "Just get as much of this stuff into the right hands as you can. If neither Curtis nor I come back, get it far away from Avalon."

The west wing was chaos. Fae of all sorts flew and scurried, casting and deflecting attacks, both magical and tangible. There were swords and forcefields, explosions and fireworks, bodies cutting through clouds of dust and mist. Mrs. Walsh touched down in the space inside the wall with Henrietta moments ahead of Chessa, and the dragon's backside was sticking out of the large door. Unseelie slashed at her tail. Dragon blood spurted out, a dark red fountain spraying across the fae on the ground. The baby dragon screamed and backed out of the doorway, turning in a circle to try to lick her wounds, but the Unseelie were on her like flies.

Chessa darted in. She knocked three fairies back as Curtis engaged a brownie who was attempting to scale Henrietta to reach Mrs. Walsh. The gnome, for her part, picked off fae with her crossbow, expertly loading, aiming, and firing.

That's when Chessa saw the rifle aimed at Mrs. Walsh. She flew at the sniper perched on the roof, but the elf was too fast. The crack of the gun disappeared in the cacophony of battle. To Chessa, it sounded as if the earth split in two. Chessa couldn't tell where the bullet hit, but the gnome tumbled to the ground beside the dragon. Henrietta roared. It was the sound of a child watching their mother die before their very eyes.

"No!" screamed Chessa. She smacked into the sniper too late to alter what was already done, but she ripped the rifle out of his hands anyway and crashed the butt of it into the elf's flawless face. She heard the crunch of breaking bones and saw the shock register in his silver eyes before he plummeted off the roof.

Curtis was still battling the brownie, but they were no longer on the dragon's back. Henrietta was curled around Mrs. Walsh as no fewer than five Unseelie guards beat her with fists and source sticks. One moved in with a dagger. It was as if Chessa were outside her own body, watching in horror as she dove off the roof and tackled the pixie, a girl who might have been a friend under other circumstances.

A new sound vibrated the air around them. It was a low rumbling with what sounded like rain spattering intermittently. The Unseelie pixie rolled away from Chessa and clambered to her feet. She looked off into the distance, across the green of the tor, before her eyes went wide. She bolted without so much as a glance at Chessa. The other guards attacking Henrietta also scrambled away. What the hell?

Chessa turned her head to see an army approaching. The thundering was wings and feet moving across the tor toward the melee, and the spattering sound was slime creatures blinking into existence, each seeming to transport a pod of goo-covered fae. Curtis ran to Chessa's side. "It looks like we've got reinforcements," he panted, helping her to her feet.

"Are you sure they're on our side?"

Curtis pointed off into the distance. Chessa could just make out the green mohawk of a familiar half-ogre thundering toward them. Chessa had never been more excited to see Cross-Eyed Quincy in her life.

"Yeah, I'm sure," Curtis replied.

Chessa nearly grinned, but then she remembered Mrs. Walsh. Curtis was already approaching the whimpering dragon, but as soon as he got close, Henrietta raised her head, pure rage sparking in her violet eyes.

"Curtis, duck!" screamed Chessa. A fireball whizzed over his head.

"You alright?" called Chessa.

"Affirmative."

She breathed a sigh of relief. "I've got Henrietta. You focus on our troops."

Curtis nodded and backed slowly away from the dragon and downed gnome. When he was out of Henrietta's range, he raised his hand to his ear to activate his comms device. A moment later, Chessa heard his voice come through the general frequency, an order for Crew B to fall back and Crew A to hold the main entrance. It was the right call. With the added reinforcements, consolidating forces in the area where they'd gained the most ground would limit casualties.

A handful of fae emerged from the western entrance—what was left of Crew B. Two sprites stooped to pick up a wounded fairy on the way, their faces grim and bloodied. A lump formed in Chessa's throat.

She gave them a nod and advanced on Henrietta. "Hey, baby," she cooed. The dragon's eyes cast over her for a moment before returning to Mrs. Walsh, who was slumped on the ground, surrounded by gleaming black scales. Chessa carefully climbed over Henrietta's tail to look at the woman who rallied the fae of Glastonbury to battle. She was breathing, but shallowly, and there was blood. So much blood. Chessa stooped and touched her cheek.

Mrs. Walsh's eyes fluttered open. Chessa flipped her mask down to help her breathe a little better.

"Keep her safe," murmured the gnome, her voice a raspy whisper.

Tears welled up in Chessa's eyes, and she cradled Mrs. Walsh's head. "I will."

Curtis's voice cut through the comm in her ear. "Chessa, get out of there. They're rallying on the west side. They're forming up around you. Get out now!"

Chessa held Mrs. Walsh's hand as she watched her breathing slow and then come to a stop.

"Henrietta, baby, we have to leave," she said, her eyes fixed on the gnome's lifeless body.

The dragon roared. Not a wail of mourning, but one of agony. She jumped to her feet. Chessa ducked, using her body to shield Mrs. Walsh's lifeless form, as the dragon took to the skies. When Chessa raised her head, she saw that Curtis was right. Rows of Unseelie had formed around them. Henrietta circled overhead, arrows sticking out of her back as another volley flew at her.

"Henrietta!" screamed Chessa.

The baby dragon shot directly upward, and the arrows littered the ground all around Chessa and the dead gnome. Then, Henrietta fell.

Time seemed to stop. None of the Unseelie were focused on Chessa as a dragon plummeted from the sky. Chessa shook her head and mumbled the word "no" over and over. It felt like all the air in the courtyard had been sucked away. At the last minute, Henrietta's wings opened. Her violet eyes burned. She opened her mouth, and a stream of fire, blue and scalding, shot from her mouth. She spun in a circle, roasting the Unseelie alive.

The screams were terrible. All around them, fae burned, screaming and flailing. Armor melted into puddles on the grass, and the heat was nearly unbearable.

Henrietta lowered herself to the ground. She whined softly and put her head in Chessa's outstretched hand. Henrietta had just taken out an entire legion of Unseelie, but she was still just a terrified and traumatized baby looking to Chessa for safety.

Henrietta moved her head away to look around, but Chessa took control. She put a hand on the dragon's face, bringing Henrietta's attention back to her.

"No, don't look. It's okay, baby. We're going to get you out of here." She flew to take her seat on the dragon's back, and together, they rose into the air. When she looked down, Chessa saw the fire closing in on Mrs. Walsh, a pyre fit for a queen.

39

Gwen was in the thick of it when the sprite squadron pulled her back. She felt like her blood was on fire as she pulled magic through her celestial link and amplified it through the amulet. She was still limited by her spell knowledge, but with the augmentation, she was able to cast glamours that fooled even the fae in short bursts, making herself vanish or causing them to catch glimpses of things that weren't there, and generally sowing confusion so she could beat the crap out of anyone within reach. The Seelie sprites and goblins fighting alongside her seemed unphased by her glamours. They battled along the ground and walls, launching a few feet into the air with the aid of magical artifacts or stubby wings whenever it served their attacks. Gwen focused on the aerial assault. At some point, a pair of pixies joined her. The three zipped through the air, taking down enemies like dragonflies through a gnat swarm.

When the sprites moved forward, the one in charge barked orders with an authority that shocked Gwen considering how sheepish she seemed on first meeting. "Back, now!"

Gwen didn't owe anyone shit. She was the Seelie Queen, and these were invaders, occupiers in her home who threatened her power and her people. She blasted another fairy back then reached down and ripped the wings off a pixie whose attention had been drawn by the sprite's call. Pieces of tattered wing stuck out of her clenched fist, and the Unseelie pixie plummeted to the ground.

The sprite in command came out of nowhere to tackle her out of the air. "You said you'd obey my orders," she gasped as they fell. They hit the ground hard.

"What the fuck? We're winning!" shouted Gwen, rising to her feet.

The sprite tried to stand and went back down. She was injured. "I promised Boss G I'd keep you alive. We need to reinforce the western gate."

If they were needed in the western hall, the rescue hadn't gone as planned. And by the looks of it, their leader had a bum leg.

Gwen helped the sprite to her feet, stopping more than once to fend off an attack. She would go to the west wing, but not until she got this flower shop girl out of here. She dragged her back into the foyer.

"Roger that," said the sprite, answering some communication coming through the device in her ear. She yelled in that authoritative voice, "Team A, fall back. Now!"

"Change of plans?" asked Gwen.

"Yes, General Curtis says to hold the main gate."

"Curtis? By whose orders is Curtis a general?"

"Mine." Chessa, covered in blood, sweat, and Danu knew what else, stood beneath the buttress of the main door of the Palace of Avalon, sunlight pouring in around her. The statues of the immortalized fae in the entrance hall seemed to stand at attention. A moment later, everything went dark. Something large blocked the door. Was that a dragon? Gwen's mouth dropped open, but she couldn't find any words.

Chessa gave a little smile. "Good to see you too, Gwennie."

Gwen ran to her friend and wrapped her arms around her, all the adrenaline turning to grief. Something about Chessa disarmed her every damn time.

"Liam," she choked. "He killed Mother."

"Liam? No! Why? Oh, Gwen, I'm so sorry."

Wrapped in Chessa's arms, Gwen fought back the anguish. She remembered the look on her brother's face as he sauntered around the great hall. He slaughtered their entire family. Gammie. The babies. As much as she didn't want to believe it, her little brother was a monster. Perhaps she could have done something to stop him and prevent all this. She didn't deserve Chessa's comfort. She didn't want it. Once again, she embraced the anger. She let go of Chessa and backed up. When she spoke, her voice was grit and stone. "Did you get Samson?"

Chessa shook her head. "Not yet."

"Then why did we pull back? We were cutting through the bastards!"

"Because we've got backup and we didn't want to lose anyone we don't have to." Chessa motioned for the dragon to move out of the doorway. To Gwen's surprise, it did. She walked out the door as a flood of fae entered, reinforcements for the flower girl's forces.

Gwen pushed through them to follow Chessa, still trying to process the fact that there was a dragon that seemed to obey her best friend. A *dragon*. They'd been extinct for centuries. She had no idea what was happening, but if magical creatures were coming back from oblivion, it could be anything. "What is *that*?" she said, inclining her head to the beast.

"It's a *her*," Chessa corrected. Her voice held a note of sadness. "This is Henrietta. She just lost her mama too."

Chessa gave the dragon a scratch under the chin, eliciting a series of clicks. Gwen didn't know what to think. Now that she was outside, she could see that Henrietta wasn't as enormous as she first seemed. She was a baby, and by the looks of her hide, she could use a medic.

Once they passed through the gate, Gwen gasped. The largest gathering of fae she'd ever seen was amassed on the field of the tor of Avalon. They didn't look like warriors any more than the citizens of Glastonbury, but their sheer numbers were staggering. At the front, she caught sight of a familiar, mohawked half-ogre. Cross-Eyed Quincy. Unlike the others, he was ready for war, armed with an assault rifle and wearing belts of extra ammo strapped across his huge chest. Surrounding him were more of the Pub Nine barflies. Right off the bat, she recognized Jarvis, Dudlin, Thom, and a few others.

"What? How—"

Quincy met them halfway across the field, nodded at Chessa, then looked to Gwen. "What's doin', Wings? My supplies helping you out?" He flashed a lopsided grin, his gold tooth glinting in the sunlight.

Gwen struggled to catch up. She still hadn't processed losing her entire family and becoming Queen, and now there was an army gathered, ready for battle and led by the skeezy half-ogre from Boston who barely tolerated her. Maybe she hit her head harder than she thought during the skirmish.

Hobgoblins zapped into existence, depositing groups of slime-covered fae all over the field before melting into the ground, so the little army grew before her eyes. At least that explained how the reinforcements arrived, but it still didn't tell her why.

"What did you call me? Why are you here?"

"You showed up at my place talking some big shit. Every time you're involved in big shit, people die. I figure you earned the name Wings since you're always flying around, getting everyone into wicked trouble. But seeing as we're business partners now, I didn't want you to go flying into danger again. Or getting Chia killed. Bad business, you know? I figured some of my buddies might have something to say about the Unseelie taking over the world. See, we might not like the way things are run, but we do have lives carved out for ourselves. Word spread, and here we are, ready for some ass-kicking."

Now it was Chessa's turn to be surprised. "Excuse me. Did you say business partners?" she asked.

Gwen laughed. Openly, brightly, surrounded by fairies and ogres and sirens and gnomes. She laughed until her stomach hurt. Maybe it was the stress of the day or the grief of losing her family. Maybe it was relief.

Chessa and Quincy exchanged a concerned look.

With a loud zap, another hobgoblin appeared not ten feet away. He flashed a sickly smile before his body parted, revealing a handful of

KPD officers. At their helm was O'Toole, dripping hobgoblin goo and scowling. When he spotted her, he dropped into a bow.

"That's it. This is the apocalypse," said Gwen.

From behind O'Toole, a twitchy cop with sandy hair and big eyes emerged. Gwen recognized him as the rookie Pox. She'd had less than pleasant interactions with him in the past when she returned a bit of borrowed evidence. This kid worshipped Samson.

"Where's Sergeant Detective Wayne?" blurted the kid. O'Toole smacked his arm and he dropped into a quick bow before Gwen.

Chessa stepped forward to greet him. "He's been captured, but we're going to get him back. General Curtis is in charge, and he'll sort you out."

As if on cue, Curtis walked up, his frame stiff with purpose. "Hey, Q, can you get everyone's attention?" he asked, ignoring the new recruits who were being regarded skeptically by the half-ogre. When did Curtis have a chance to get so close to Quincy? The urge to laugh subsided, and Gwen stood still, listening, as Quincy used his big voice to get everyone to focus on the General.

Curtis, the mild-mannered fairy who reminded her of a lost puppy since the moment she took him on, was now a force to be reckoned with. He addressed the horde with authority, dividing them into factions, assigning a leader to each, and then calling a meeting of the leaders. Once that was done, he motioned for Gwen to join him. She stood next to him as he continued to speak, his voice augmented by a siren who stood nearby, using her magic to ensure all gathered on the tor could hear.

"Is our life perfect? No. What is a perfect life, anyway? We have struggles as we always have. Before the fae-mortal accords and the peace treaties, we were all as the Unseelie are now, wild and free. And before that? They say the realm of Faerie was brutal. It was a time when fae devoured other fae. But were we happy? Humanity feared and hunted us. What kind of freedom is that? Sure, we could fight back, but we were divided and spread thin, and no people, fae or human, want to raise their families with the fear of war looming over their heads. The Unseelie have been among us all this time, waiting for a moment when morale was low. Waiting for us to feel left behind.

They've been sowing the seeds of resentment for age upon age until they felt we were most vulnerable, most broken. As I look upon you all here, I don't see weakness. Tell me, fae of the Seelie Court, are we broken?"

A roar of "nay" answered him.

"Are we weak?"

This time the response was even louder. "*NAY!*"

Gwen tried not to gawk at the Seelie Guard. She'd badly underestimated him and felt like she was seeing his true nature for the first time.

"That's right! We are strong! They have attacked the very heart of the Seelie Court. They killed our leaders, they took our home, and they seek to lay claim to our lives. Will we allow it?"

The response was deafening. Gwen felt awkward standing next to this man, this hero who could rally everyday fae to war. All she ever wanted to do was save the people she loved, and here he was, a simple Seelie fairy, leading an army. He truly was a general. Leave it to Chessa to be the one to see it.

"I present to you your new Seelie Queen, Gwendolyn Evenshine!"

Was she supposed to say something? Her mind reeled. It was one thing to use the title to get her way, but here, with all these fae looking to her for leadership—here it was real. She never wanted to be a leader, to inherit systems she never helped to build. Curtis' words were strong, but there was more at work here than Unseelie corrupting society. Fae were angry. Seelie, Unseelie, Courtless. And they had the right to be. They wanted to call her queen. They expected her to lead them and protect them. Her. The failure who fought against the responsibilities of court her entire life.

Gwen looked around, expecting to see scorn or ridicule, but all saw she was expectation. She wanted to run. This had to be someone's idea of a sick joke. She stepped forward, trying to forget she was wearing a rank Metallica shirt and torn jeans. They cheered. She caught Chessa's eye, and the pixie nodded, a motion designed to be encouraging, but in actuality, it affirmed that this horror was real.

Once this was all over, she would have to set the record straight. She was no queen. But for now, there was only one thought eclipsing the self-doubt. She had to save her friends. She had to take back what was rightfully hers. The sunlight was warm on her face as she looked over the crowd, a ragged group of everyday fae and miscreants, standing before her, ready to go to war. Her people.

"Let's get these bastards out of my house!" she yelled.

Stomping and cheering rumbled over the tor.

40

Chessa felt like she was watching her best friend come into her own as she stood before an army of fae, accepting the role of Seelie Queen. Gwen never believed she was worthy of her place in her family or at the Academy, but Chessa always knew better. She wished she had time to celebrate, to give Gwen the coronation she deserved, but Norman and Samson were behind enemy lines, and the Unseelie weren't going to stay holed up in the palace forever. Besides, this was a much more appropriate coronation for Gwen. Traditional wasn't exactly her style.

After the address, Chessa fell in beside Gwen as they followed Curtis to a tent that had been set up some time during the battle. They passed the showers, where a group of naiads pulled water out of the ground, into the air, and let it rain down to hose the hobgoblin slime off new arrivals popping up all over the field.

"When did all this happen?" asked Chessa, motioning to the organized factions of fae. When she'd gone after the library vault, all forces were committed to the assault. There were no tents, showers, or legions of fae awaiting orders. Had they only arrived sooner, Mrs. Walsh might still be alive.

"They had already begun gathering when I returned to the field from the west wing," Curtis answered. "That half-ogre friend of yours was in a rage, but once I told him you were alive, he calmed down and got to work pushing the others around. I told him what needed to happen, and he got it done. He's really quite effective."

Gwen's mouth fell open, but Chessa grinned. "Yeah, Q is great."

"How do you do that?" asked Gwen.

"What?"

"See the best in everyone? Quincy has been nothing but a thorn in my side since you brought him into my life, but you don't seem surprised at all that he's a natural leader in the fae civil war. And Curtis? You made him a general, and he's fucking killing it!"

Curtis pushed a hand through his hair and chuckled.

"You've got to give people a chance, Gwen," replied Chessa. She didn't want to tell Gwen how many times she'd been disappointed by those undeserving of the faith she put in them over the years because she knew that was why Gwen was so closed off. She'd been hurt far more than she was ever validated. But now, she was slowly starting to allow people to surprise her, and Chessa wasn't about to say or do anything to get in the way of that. "And Norman deserves a chance too. He did horrible things, but nobody ever gave him a shot before. We've got to save him and Sammy."

"We will," said Curtis.

"What keeps the Unseelie from killing them both right now, as we waste time out here?" asked Gwen, her eyes growing dark.

"They could do that," said Curtis. "But they won't. Right now, they have no idea what our strength is. They've got scouts watching as our numbers grow, and the hostages are their only bargaining chips should they find themselves defeated."

"I know we've got numbers now, but we're untrained. The Unseelie have been preparing for this for Danu knows how long. They are warriors. We are grocers and bloggers and failed fairy godmothers and barflies..." Gwen trailed off.

"They may be warriors, but they're disorganized. They lived for themselves for so long, working together is a foreign concept. Besides, we have more to fight for," replied Curtis. "We will defeat them."

Something about Curtis' tone made Chessa believe him, but Gwen didn't look convinced.

Chessa scanned the gathering for any sign of Marni or Hobbes, but she saw none. She did, however, notice that many of the gathered fae were wearing antique-looking amulets, bracelets, and other paraphernalia. She couldn't help but smile. Talk about putting your faith in strangers.

Inside the tent, a group was waiting. Each of the leaders Curtis and Quincy had appointed stood with heads together, speaking in hushed tones. The artifacts from Norman's vault, the ones that hadn't been distributed, were stacked off to one side, and Quincy had a comms link in his ear. Gwen stood back, and Chessa didn't blame her. She had enough on her plate at the moment.

There were no furnishings in the tent. It was simply a shelter from the sun and prying eyes. As Chessa followed Curtis and Gwen toward the center of the tent, a commotion broke out behind her. The air seemed to sizzle, and fae yelled for everyone to clear the area. With a zap, a giant hobgoblin appeared in the space that had been occupied moments before, just beyond the tent's opening. He grinned yellow and wide, slime dripping down his rolls, before his center split open and a woman stepped out. Even covered in hobgoblin goo, Chessa recognized the witch and bolted to her side.

"Laural! What are you doing here?" she gasped before wrapping the new arrival in a hug, which caused hobgoblin slime to squelch between them. She saw Gwen shudder, but she didn't care. With the exception of Corrin's funeral, this was the first time she'd seen her cousin out in the world in years. If she was going to die today, at least she got to hug her again first.

"I'm a healer above all else," Laural replied. "I'm here to help. Unless someone has a problem with that." Her eyes cut over to Gwen, who was hovering just inside the tent.

Chessa held her breath. She doubted Gwen cared about Laural breaking her house arrest with all things considered, but she was queen now.

"I'm glad to see you, Laural. We can use all the help we can get," said Gwen, leaving the tent to stand before the witch.

Laural gave a barely perceptible smile before her eyes settled on Henrietta, lurking about fifty feet from Chessa, clicking and whining for attention.

"That poor baby is covered in arrows!" she gasped. "Do you have no healers at all? How do you expect to wage a war with nobody to tend to the injured?"

Gwen bristled, so Chessa jumped in. "There hasn't been time. Nobody was planning a war, but it seems that's what we've got." She cast a look at Gwen that was meant to remind her that she was queen and needed to keep her cool. It must have worked because Gwen bit her lip.

Instead of losing her temper or tossing out a quip, she took a deep breath. "Laural Moon, you are hereby in charge of all healing efforts. Take whoever you need from the field. There are many injuries, and there are sure to be many more before the day is over."

Laural didn't give any indication that she heard Gwen, but Curtis emerged from the tent with a uniformed Seelie guard, a brownie, and sent him to assist.

"They're waiting for you inside," he said to Gwen once the newly-formed healing squad began to walk toward Henrietta. Gwen didn't have a chance to respond before a voice in Chessa's earpiece made her jump.

"Fire, incoming! Take cover!"

"Get down!" She screamed.

Curtis grabbed Gwen around the waist and pulled her backward as the tent went up in flames.

41

Gwen heard screaming before she realized it was coming from her. Curtis' arms were wrapped around her waist, pulling her away from the inferno. Chessa dove for Henrietta and Laural. Fae darted off in various directions, the shower naiads running toward the blazing tent while everyone else fell back. Quincy took the field in strides, hesitating only a moment to allow the naiads to douse the flames at the front of the tent, before ducking inside. Most of the occupants had exited to watch Laural's arrival, but the few that remained zipped out, through heavy smoke and over the smoldering grass. The naiads encircled the tent and began to spin, palms to the sky, causing rain to fall over the conflagration.

A moment later, Quincy returned, soot smeared across his huge, scarred face, and a small form sheltered in his palm. He set the fairy down at Gwen's feet.

"Sorry, Wings. I done what I could," he said.

It was Aunt Ember. Gwen hadn't even realized she was here, yet there was no doubt it was her poor aunt lying in the grass at her feet. Ember didn't move. Singed shirt and blackened flesh were all that was left where Ember's wings once attached to her body, and she was barely breathing.

"Uncle Monty?" choked Gwen.

"There's nobody else inside," replied Quincy before shuffling off.

Curtis called for Laural, who came running, shouting orders at bystanders. Gwen couldn't make out words, just the buzz of activity. Curtis put a hand on her shoulder to lead her out of the way so Laural could get to work. In that moment, Gwen began to understand Azrah better. Her cousin had been no more prepared to become Seelie Queen than Gwen was, and Gwen felt utterly helpless. But as she looked out at the field, which moments before had been filled with determined fae about to face an enemy but which now was a sea of fear and chaos, she realized that someone needed to take charge. *She* needed to take charge. She caught sight of the siren standing next to a human boy. He shouldn't be there, but that was of little consequence at the moment.

"Hey, you," she called to the siren. "What's your name?"

"Maddy, Your Grace."

"Maddy, I need your help. Can you make sure everyone can hear me?"

The siren nodded, purpose replacing the fear that had haunted her eyes seconds before as she tapped into her magic and thrust out her hand. The air around Gwen rippled, so she began to speak.

"Seelie Fae! Our time for preparation has been cut short, but that doesn't mean we've lost. On the contrary, all they've done is piss us off. Pixies, take to the skies. Scout the airspace overhead for whoever started the fire and bring them to me. Sprites, create a perimeter. There will be more attacks. They won't give us time to organize. Naiads, spread out. You're our best defense against fire, and clumped together, you're an easy target. Be ready. Everyone else, form ranks and wait for General, um, Curtis' orders."

"Steele," said Curtis.

"What?"

"My surname. Curtis Steele."

"Oh." Gwen should have known that, but she was too preoccupied to be embarrassed. She made a motion for Maddy to cut the amplification and turned to Curtis. "Thank you, General Steele."

He gave a curt nod. "According to our pixie on the inside, there is a group of sorcerers standing between the palace and the western wall. They summoned the fire."

"Send a winged battalion to eliminate the threat. We've got to get on the offensive or they'll slaughter us right here in the open air."

"I couldn't agree more. I've got it from here. You go see to your family."

"Thank you, Curtis."

Laural was still fussing over Ember when Gwen approached, but her aunt was awake, even if she did look odd without her wings glittering in the sun. Unlike Gwen, most of her family kept their wings on full display at all times per Seelie royal custom. Gwen tore her eyes away from her aunt's bloody, singed back.

Monty sat on the ground next to Ember, his hand in hers. "Uncle Monty, I'm so glad to see you alive," said Gwen, fighting back tears that threatened to spill.

"I only left her side for a moment," he replied. He was openly weeping. They both lost so much already. Gwen couldn't begin to imagine what he was going through.

"It's not your fault," she replied, but she knew it wouldn't be enough.

"Gwendolyn, I know we don't have much time, but you need to know what you're up against," said Ember, her voice raspy as she struggled to sit up.

"Take it easy, my love," said Monty.

Ember gave him a look that he seemed to understand. He kissed her on the cheek and walked away.

"I already know. The Unseelie princess has worked some magic on Liam. She's behind all of this."

"Do not let love blind you. Liam is not innocent. He killed my children in cold blood. He stuck a knife in Arabella's back when she was fighting to keep the realm safe. She trusted him. And my Augie—"

"I know how much you must be hurting, but—"

"No! You don't!"

Gwen waited. Her aunt nearly died moments ago, and it would do no good to fight amongst themselves.

Ember took a deep breath. "Liam is not under a spell any more than you or I. He is not the boy you knew. He is a rabid animal, and he needs to be put down."

Ember lost both of her children in the course of a couple weeks. Gwen should have known better than to make excuses for their killer. She swallowed hard.

Ember looked to where Laural stood, and something sparked in her eye. It made Gwen uneasy.

"Laural Moon, I know you to be good and wise, despite the fate that's befallen you. Consider yourself royal confidante. What is said here stays here. Do you agree?"

"Of course, Lady Evenshine."

Ember smiled, a small, weak tightness of the mouth. She turned her attention back to Gwen. "Grace is alive."

Why in the name of Danu would she reveal that where Laural could hear? Gwen trusted the witch, but this wasn't information to gamble. Something else was going on here. Gwen was measured in her response. "Azrah told me as much."

"Yes, Azrah suspected your brother, and she gave the order to tell everyone, including your mother, that Gracie was dead. We believe that the Unseelie took the bait."

"So you're saying I'm not queen." Was that what this was about?

"As far as anyone knows, you are. Monty, myself, you, Gracie's mother, and now Laural are the only ones alive who know the truth, and it must remain that way. The Unseelie are not very organized, but they are powerful. Gracie must come of age in secret, and you must protect the Seelie throne until she does."

Gwen nodded. She wasn't sure exactly how she was supposed to do that, but she figured she'd start by getting the invaders out of Avalon.

"There's more. This battle you fight is bigger than an Unseelie uprising."

"What do you mean? This is a fringe group that has taken over Avalon, not even a full uprising. It's a group of fae discontents."

"Foolish child. It is far more than that. The uprising is worldwide and all-encompassing. Those 'discontents' as you call them infiltrated mortal politics to sow chaos so that the humans could be conquered with little resistance. They used spies and pawns in every kingdom to undermine alliances. They whisper in the ears of our Seelie brothers and sisters, taking advantage of the way they feel betrayed by their leadership. The regional royalty are all compromised. Every. Last. One. The Unseelie were patient. They gathered intel on every prominent figure, and they used it against us."

A lump formed in Gwen's throat as the weight of Ember's words settled in. "Matron Celeste."

"Yes. They used her and others to remove anyone they saw as a threat, and they did it all to set the stage for the battle you fight today. Liam did this. Do you understand?" Ember might be speaking to Gwen, but she was watching Laural like a hawk.

Gwen had deduced that Princess Francesca was killed for this, but there was another implication—they killed Corrin too. Oh shit. Ember was baiting Laural.

Gwen's attention snapped to Laural, but she was too late. The witch had gone bone still. Her eyes blazed red.

Gwen felt so stupid. Ember had played her. She should have seen it coming. Everyone in her family was always working multiple angles, even as they lay half-dead in the middle of a battlefield.

Shouting from the sprites at the perimeter told Gwen that something was happening on the field. Laural and her inner demon would have to wait. She ran to where Curtis stood, addressing the troops. A sea of fae emerged from Avalon in tight rows. There were hundreds upon hundreds, far more than Gwen initially took stock of. Perhaps numbers weren't in her favor after all. Winged battalions filled the air while ogres and gnomes fell into formation on the ground. But what concerned Gwen most was the fae she didn't see, sprites and brownies and smaller fae capable of going undetected for ambushes. She had to assume that for every insurgent standing before her, there were more in the wings. Gwen saw no sign of Grimore, Liam, or the Unseelie Princess, but that was unsurprising. A dark cloud formed over Avalon as winged fae polluted the air, the shining tower peeking through as the swarm prepared for battle.

That's when she heard it. The ominous rustling of vegetation. It was like the breeze through fall leaves, but there was no wind, and it grew ever louder. The vegetation came alive, grass bending and swaying as something moved across the field.

"Curtis." Gwen called out, but the general was already on the move with a small battalion of winged Seelie. They flew over the field to intercept whatever menace approached.

"Lutins!"

As the word reached her ears, the first wave of tiny, gnome-like creatures with sharp teeth and dead, black eyes leapt from the cover of the grass into the frontlines of her army. Screaming broke out as the little bastards fed.

42

Chessa hovered in the distance, giving Gwen time to speak privately with her aunt, but she saw it happening before anyone else—Laural losing control of the demon. A wave of lutins washed over the northern flanks of the Seelie, causing chaos and carnage, but Chessa had to leave that to Curtis and the others. She was the only one who stood half a chance against Gailan, the demon Laural fought to contain.

Gailan was the reason Corrin had been so protective over his hedge witch wife. Few understood the true nature of the possession. Laural was the most skilled healer of her time, called in years ago to perform an exorcism of a young boy who slaughtered his entire family in cold blood. Only it wasn't him. It was Gailan. Had Laural not been successful in extracting the demon from the boy, that entire town would have been razed, every creature, human or fae, massacred. Gailan knew nothing but righteous rage, responding to threats with merciless slaughter that extended well past the offending parties, and he knew no peace. Neither did the poor witch who became his vessel. Once he was freed from the prison of the boy's body, Laural tried to capture him in a box, a relic that was said to hold immense power, but Gailan tricked her. He shattered the box, unleashing everything it held, and searched for a new host. Laural found a way to take the demon into her own body. That was how she lived ever since, with a malicious monster lurking just under the surface. Chessa had no idea what made Laural lose control, but she did know that Gailan wouldn't limit his wrath to the Unseelie.

While Gwen crossed the field to Curtis, Chessa darted for Laurel. She was too late.

43

Captain O'Toole bathed the field in sorcerer's fire. He stood, surrounded by KPD officers, who defended him from the lutins already battling Seelie within their ranks, and emitted fire from both palms, creating twin columns that shot into the sky. They broke apart over the field and rained death from above. The smell of roasting flesh wafted over the tor.

Gwen was winded by the time she made it to the front lines. Curtis bellowed orders to gather all fire practitioners and have them join O'Toole's efforts. Gwen caught sight of Quincy's mohawk bobbing in the masses of embattled fae. Near him Jarvis thrashed, using his own dismembered limbs to beat down lutins as they launched at his face and torso. As she watched, Thom morphed into a horse and gave a great whinny before trampling the poor resurrected necromancer. Gwen dove in just in time to hear Jarvis scream out.

"Thom, why?"

"I've been Unseelie all along," yelled the kelpie. "You pathetic, little—

A throwing knife to the neck cut off his speech, which turned to a shrill horse scream before his body convulsed and morphed back into his kelpie state. Quincy rushed to Jarvis. It was too late. The barback frat boy necromancer was dead. Again. But so were the masses of lutins all around them. Without reinforcements, their attack was cut short. Gwen wondered how many other sleeper agents the Unseelie had behind her lines.

As fire practitioners laid waste to the tor, the Glastonbury locals gathered the wounded and dragged them to Laural's post at the bottom of the hill.

Gwen landed beside Curtis. Smoke filled the air, obscuring their view of Avalon.

"As much as I hate to say it, O'Toole saved a lot of lives just now," she said by way of greeting.

Curtis didn't pull his gaze from the field. "That was fast thinking. It could have been worse. We only suffered a dozen or so losses."

"Only," said Gwen, the word hanging in the air. It wasn't so long ago she put her entire life on hold for four years because of one life lost. Now a dozen were extinguished in the blink of an eye, and they counted themselves lucky.

Curtis's jaw clenched, and he bowed his head. "With your permission, Your Grace, I wish to move in. "We can't take the time to recover. Who knows what they will send next. We're sitting ducks out here."

Gwen's stomach roiled. Was she really about to send hundreds more fae to their death? This was so much bigger than she'd ever signed on for. She turned from Curtis to look over her army, mostly untrained with the exception of thirty or so Seelie Guard and a handful of cops. They were doing what they needed to, tending wounded, dispatching the few remaining lutins, and falling back into rank. Each face was drawn in grim resolution. Chessa was nowhere to be seen. Gwen needed the pixie to calm her nerves, but she was sure Chessa escaped the lutin assault. The little monsters were vicious, but they couldn't fly. Most of the casualties were sprites, brownies, and other smaller, grounded fae. Gwen turned back to Curtis, and he was staring straight into her eyes.

"They knew what they were coming here for," he said quietly. "Gwen, we can't let the Unseelie keep Avalon. This is our seat of power. It's our home."

"That's not why they took it," said Gwen quietly.

"What do you mean? It's a symbolic power move, right?"

"No. There's a portal to Faerie in the grove. They mean to open it if they haven't already."

Curtis looked like his brain wasn't connecting the pieces. "Faerie? You've got to be shitting me." Immediately, his cheeks flushed and he began to stammer. If the situation weren't so dire, Gwen might think it cute that he was so embarrassed by his own language.

"No, it's okay. You're right. We have to take a stand. I just hope we're not already too late. I can't imagine what will happen to the world if they succeed."

The Unseelie wouldn't stop until fae civilization as they knew it was ended and a new era dawned, a brutal era of force and domination. Everyone gathered on the field knew it, even if they didn't know the specifics about unleashing the legendary realm of Faerie upon the mortal world.

If everyone on the field lost their lives today, it would still be a small price to pay if they were able to stop the Unseelie. "Do what you have to do."

It was all Curtis needed. He shot into the air and began to shout directives. The tension broke as the airborne units rushed forward to meet the enemy, followed closely by Q's group of rowdy foot soldiers. Gwen watched in horror as the smoke cleared, revealing a scorched land, and, just beyond, the enemy.

Hundreds of Unseelie stood, larger fae at the front beneath a speckled sky, waiting for her army to come within reach. Dayglow led the Seelie air battalion, Quincy and the others following on foot over the charred and smoldering ground.

The front lines of the waiting Unseelie soldiers were armed. They took aim with guns, crossbows, and magical weaponry.

"We have to do something about the ranged weapons," Gwen said, but nobody was near enough to hear her. She doubted the Unseelie would use iron and risk killing their own with the air particles and stray projectiles, but simple bullets could take down plenty of fae. If she could think of a way to strip away the weapons, it might give her motley crew a fighting chance. Quincy had supplied as much contraband as he could, Kevlar vests, protection amulets, source-stick scramblers, but there wasn't nearly enough to go around, even with the influx of items from Norman's stash. The scene played out in slow motion before Gwen. Her troops rushed in, and when they were within twenty feet, the guns fired first.

Time caught up as soon as the sound reached Gwen's ears.

No Seelie fell. Instead, Unseelie fell in waves. Gwen blinked. What the fuck?

"Curtis!" she yelled, flying to where the general hovered. "What's happening?"

His words made Gwen's world swirl around her. "It's Laural."

The witch was halfway across the field, her hands held aloft.

Curtis yammered on. "The bullets. They stopped in the air and turned…" He trailed off, but Gwen could see the result with her own eyes. The rounds had hit between the eyes of every fae who fired. With horror and a wave of guilt, Gwen realized her mistake. While she was distracted by the lutin attack, Laural completed her transformation. This was the work of the demon Gailan.

"No!" Gwen choked on the word.

"She's on our side, right?" asked Curtis. Gwen could hear the uncertainty in his voice.

"You don't understand. Gailan is on no side. He is a demon of wrath, and he's going to kill everyone, Seelie included. We have to stop him."

Curtis seemed to get his wits about him. "No, *we* have to stop him. *You* have to stay here and stay safe. We need you alive by the end of this."

Gwen started to argue, but her general was already airborne.

From the safety of her place on the field beyond the reach of the enemy, she looked on as Laural floated barefoot across the tor, her hair levitating around huge horns, the air sizzling with power. A small form zipped around her, flying this way and that, and the demon swatted it away. Gwen watched powerlessly as Chessa was flung to the ground and Laural advanced on the enemy.

The Unseelie swarmed, their ranks broken by the death of their entire frontline. Laural reached them first, followed by the Seelie air reserves. Everything seemed to happen at once. Seelie fae engaged in the air, Q's unit thundered into the fray on foot, and Gailan began killing wave after wave of fae. They were gutted by the weapons of those around them, broken against the walls of Avalon, and smashed against the earth. Gailan was telekinetic death to all, Seelie and Unseelie alike. Gwen's forces were being slaughtered just as fast as the occupiers. Curtis shouted orders to the reserves, but Gwen couldn't make out his words. The sky was filled with explosions, and the ground was pure chaos. Despite Curtis' orders, Gwen couldn't just watch. She had to do something. With a backward glance to make sure nobody was around to stop her, Gwen hurtled toward certain death.

44

Chessa watched in horror as Gailan disappeared across the field. Her arm ached in a way that she knew was broken, but she didn't have time to sit around and nurse wounds. She was the only fae alive who stood half a chance of helping Laural regain control. And if she couldn't—well, that wasn't an option.

She was back in the air in moments, flying toward the battle that raged ahead.

"Chess! No!"

What the hell was Gwen doing flying into the open field in the middle of battle?

"Gwen, get back!" she screamed, but the fairy was speeding through the air. As soon as the Unseelie saw her, she would be toast. Fuck. Chessa changed direction to meet Gwen in the air. "You do realize you're target numero uno, right?"

"Yes, but I saw Gailan swat you. I had to make sure you were alright."

"Now you see, so get your ass back behind our lines. I've got to get to Laural."

Gwen's eyes were big, her cheeks flushed. "Only if you come with me."

"Gwen, I'm not the fucking Seelie Queen. *You* are. But I am Laural's only chance. I can't do this right now."

"Then we go together."

Chessa wished she had rope or duct tape to bind Gwen, but she didn't want to waste another second arguing with her pain-in-the-ass best friend. She darted toward Avalon. She didn't bother looking over her shoulder, but she knew what she'd see if she did—Gwen trailing behind. Pixies were faster, but their endurance was shit. She had to stop three times to catch her breath, so by the time she made it to the battle, Gwen was right by her side.

Chessa wove through fighting winged fae, searching for Laural amongst the carnage below. Blasts, energy pulses, bullets, and screams tore the very air around her, and she had to keep moving to avoid getting caught up. At last, she spotted her cousin. Laural levitated with arms outstretched, enormous burgundy and black wings sprouting from her back, twisted horns from her head. Words in a language unfamiliar to Chessa poured from her mouth in a voice far deeper than the witch's natural timbre. A circle of mutilated bodies created a wall around her. Some were still writhing.

"Danu help us all," muttered Gwen from where she hovered just below Chessa.

The thing that most unnerved the pixie, however, wasn't the carnage. It was the fae surrounding the scene. They were organizing on two fronts—Unseelie from one side, Seelie from the other, and their intent was as clear as a vision from the lake of the damned—they were going to take down the demon. And that meant killing the witch whose body it inhabited.

"Laural!" Chessa darted in to intervene, but Gwen cut her off. Gwen's arms wrapped around her waist and her head was pressed to Chessa's chest. Chessa's wings beat the air as she tried to tear free of Gwen with her one good arm, but the fairy was pushing her back, her own wings flapping at full speed.

Chessa screamed in frustration and pain.

"Chess, we're too late. You can't help her," gasped Gwen, her voice strained.

Below them, the demon's gaze turned upward. For a brief

moment, Chessa saw the red eyes disappear, replaced by Laural's soft golden ones. Chessa looked on helplessly over Gwen's shoulder as both sides of fae clambered over the wall of dead and dying. Then, they attacked. Magic and fury rained down in an explosion of light, rock, smoke, and blood. Chessa screamed again and thrashed against Gwen, but the fairy wasn't letting go. Gwen's small size had nothing on her grip, and her wings beat unrestricted, pulling Chessa away from the melee.

"Laural's gone, Chess. Do you hear me? There's nothing we could do. She's gone. But we can still save Norman. We can still save Sammy. Please, Chess, stop fighting me."

The smoke billowing upward from where her cousin once stood punctuated her point. Chessa cried out again, and Gwen squeezed harder, as Chessa realized she was right. There was nothing she could do for Laural now. Gwen lowered them to the ground a hundred feet away from the palace and the chaos. Chessa was so angry. She wanted to beat her with her bare fists. But in her heart, she knew the truth. Had Gwen let her go in, Laural would still be dead, and so would she. She sobbed as Gwen held her.

Not far from where they huddled, Quincy's forces roared and fought on, reminding Chessa that there were others here she cared about. They had to save Samson and Norman because, by the looks of the carnage around them, the Unseelie weren't pulling punches.

"You're right," she murmured.

Only then did Gwen let go and turn to look at her, the gold ring around her dark eyes flashing in the light. "We're going to make this right, Chess," she said.

Chessa pulled a hand across her face and swallowed hard. "No. We're not. Nothing could make this right. But we've got to win. Otherwise, it was all for nothing."

Gwen bit her bottom lip and nodded.

With Laural down, Gwen in front of her, Quincy beating the shit out of Unseelie forces, and Mrs. Walsh dead, the list of fae to keep tabs on was waning. But there was one creature who needed her most. "Where's Henrietta?"

Gwen looked back across the tor but didn't speak.

There in the sky, Chessa saw the baby dragon circling the palace. Unseelie archers atop the wall took aim, waiting for her to come within range.

"You save the dragon. I'm going for the griffin," said Gwen. Both fae kicked off the ground to launch into the air.

Chessa made a beeline for Henrietta, pushing her wings to keep going even as they ached from exertion. By the time she settled on the baby dragon's back, they were both too close to the tower for Chessa's comfort.

"Whoa, Henrietta," she gasped, pressing her palms against the larger creature's neck. A sharp pain tore through her arm and into her shoulder, causing a cry to escape her lips. The dragon clicked and snorted, but her eyes were still wild, and she wasn't stopping. Chessa zipped into the airspace in front of her and prayed to Danu the dragon wouldn't fly straight into her. Henrietta dropped elevation and resumed her trajectory toward the tower.

"Stop! You have to stop!" Chessa begged. She could hear shouting from behind her as the archers spotted them. "They're going to shoot you down!"

A whinny, the sound a colt might make when attempting to jump a fence to freedom, was the dragon's response. Smoke seeped from her nostrils. Henrietta's point was clear. She was going to war against the monsters who killed her mama.

Chessa never felt so helpless as in that moment. She looked back to Seelie command but everyone was too far away or occupied to help. Then, she spotted a shadow on the ground, heading their way, and fast.

"What the—"

The shadow stretched and shrank, taking the field as quickly as the descent of night. For a moment, it flickered into a familiar shape, pointed ears, a long, sleek tail. It was Sorcha, Gwen's pet shunni. As far as Chessa knew, the shadow creature was back in Korranthia, curled up on Gwen's bed or hunting rats down by Boston Harbor. How did she get here? And what the hell was he up to?

Sorcha's shape blurred back into murky shadow, and Chessa turned her attention back to Henrietta. She easily caught back up, but the dragon was still pressing on. "I know they killed Mrs. Walsh," said Chessa. "And they will pay, I promise. But we need you alive, baby. I promised your mama I'd keep you safe."

Henrietta roared. Not a click, not a whine, but a full dragon roar that reverberated off the halls of the palace of Avalon. It cut through the sounds of battle, sending a hush across the legions of fae. For a brief moment, weapons were lowered, spells were dropped, and the world stood still as all attention was on the creature of legend. The Seelie forces answered with a roar of their own. It held all the pain and desperation of a people fighting for their lives, land, and loved ones. The onslaught resumed.

Chessa flew after Henrietta. From here, she could see the archers taking aim. She even spotted two snipers, Unseelie who had eluded Laural, lining up shots from atop the tower. If she couldn't stop Henrietta, she had to do something to minimize the damage. Chessa peeled off and headed for the snipers. If she circled around behind them, she might be able to use her pixie speed to take them out before they knew she was there.

Nobody detected her. She leveled a flying kick to the wizard's arm, sending his weapon careening off the side of the tower. He fell backward into her second target. As they struggled to untangle themselves, Chessa went for the gnome's gun. Just as she was about to pluck it from his grasp, he jumped to his feet and swung it like a bat. She flapped her wings and was able to avoid contact, but the motion jarred her broken arm. She stifled a scream. Her break in focus slowed her down. The gnome advanced. He might be a great shot, but he was a terrible fighter. He muttered some insult and swung wide. Chessa easily flitted out of the way, and the gnome went over the edge of the wall. The wizard recovered, looked for his friend, then fled to the hatch leading down into the palace. In the time it took Chessa to neutralize the threat, Henrietta crossed into range of the archers. Chessa watched from the tower as a volley of arrows arched toward the dragon.

The shadow trailing Henrietta was now directly beneath her, darker than night despite sunset being hours away. Sorcha's feline form coalesced, running atop the smoke as if it were solid beneath her pounding paws. She leapt into the air and expanded, her inky darkness engulfing Henrietta before merging back into smoke and shadow. To onlookers, it seemed as if the dragon winked out of existence, but Chessa was close enough to know otherwise. The volley of arrows passed through the air, harmlessly littering the field below.

Chessa nearly fell off the tower. She'd never seen anything like it. A moment later, a line of fire erupted along the top of the wall. Archers screamed as they burnt alive or plummeted to their deaths.

"Holy shit," murmured Chessa. She spotted the shadow, barely visible against the blue sky through the smoky air. It was shaped like Henrietta, only somehow more sinister, with blurred edges as if it weren't entirely corporeal. It swept the space over Avalon, fire erupting in waves of death below. Chessa, having no desire to become barbecued pixie, flew down to meet Gwen at the western gate.

45

The western entrance to Avalon was now relatively unprotected as most of the Unseelie had amassed on the battlefield after the initial Seelie retreat. Gwen flew right through the gate, not bothering to stop to face the lone rock creature guarding the entrance. She zipped over his head, through the courtyard leading to the door, and into the hallway. Gwen was muttering a thank-you to Danu that the forces had been pulled to the northern front when the doors at the far end of the hall burst open. She ducked through the door closest to her. Voices floated down the hall, growing louder with every second. "You said there would be no resistance once we deposed the Evenshine matriarch!"

Gwen quickly recognized the assured voice of Princess Moliana.

Grimore answered. "My sources were wrong, it seems."

"Your sources? You're the most influential fairy in Korranthia! I thought you delivered me a kingdom, but instead you handed me a figurehead and an idiot Seelie prince. You watched as he gutted Indira on the floor of the great hall, her blood spilling uselessly on the floor."

"I didn't know that would happen."

"Your breadth of knowledge seems to be shrinking of late. The only royal blood I have left is my own and that simpering Liam's. You should have taken him to the grove so that we could use him to pass into Faerie at the very least."

"Your Grace, the fae realm is not hospitable to our kind just yet. None of our emissaries have returned, and those we've brought through have been less than amenable to the idea of serving us." That was interesting. As far as Gwen knew, Moliana Eviscera was the princess, not a queen, so the honorarium he used was telling. Grimore must know something the rest of the world did not.

"Then we make them," hissed Moliana.

"We don't have the time. These locals have proven to be a bigger pest than I predicted."

"Yet another failing in your judgement, Master Grimore. I should leave you here to die with the rest of them."

"I have served you faithfully since first we met, my Queen."

At his groveling, Moliana laughed. "You certainly tried, for what use your meager efforts have been. I will give you one more chance, but only if you offer yourself completely. When we get back to the Undying Forest, you will pledge Unseelie, and you will kill my father once and for all so we can end this tiresome charade."

Whoa. Gwen thought she had family issues.

"Yes, Your Grace."

Another voice broke in. "Gwen? Are you here?"

Shit. It was Chessa. Gwen peeked out of the cracked door and could just make out the pixie standing in the doorway, backlit by sun streaming in. She couldn't see Grimore or the Unseelie tyrant, but by the look on Chessa's face, they weren't far up the hall.

"Grimore, remove this obstacle," commanded Moliana.

The hairs on Gwen's arm stood on end, an early warning of the magic sparking in the hall. She threw open the door. "Chessa, get down," she screamed, but Chessa stood firm, her left arm raised, as she pointed down the hall. A pulse of energy ripped the door off its hinges and into the fairies.

"Not this time, motherfucker," said Chessa.

Gwen didn't know whether to laugh or scream at her friend. She didn't have time for either. In a matter of seconds, Chessa closed the gap and pulled her toward the guard's quarters. "Come on. We don't have long before they come to their senses, and I'm not sure how much more mojo these things are packing," she said, holding up her wrist and flashing the small, rune covered devices strapped to each. Her right arm hung limp at her side.

Together, they flew down the hall, passing over Grimore and the princess splayed across the floor. They didn't hesitate to determine whether the fairies were alive or dead. The room containing the holding cells was located in the middle of the long hall, and there were no sentries outside it. Gwen opened the door, and they flew in, finding Samson, Norman, and a handful of other Seelie prisoners waiting behind bars on the other side. For once, luck was on their side. One lone guard stood on the outside of the cells, a goblin with large eyes full of fear. Gwen moved to attack, but Chessa stepped between them.

"Hand over the keys, and you can walk out of here," she said.

The goblin stared, his eyes darting to the door and back.

"The Unseelie Princess is knocked out in the hall just beyond here, and she will have no knowledge of what you did in this moment. Your side is losing. They're dying. Don't you have someone you want to go home to?"

The goblin's orange eyes filled with tears, and he swallowed hard before nodding. "A little girl, Dinah. She calls me Diddy."

Chessa held out her hand. To Gwen's astonishment, he set the keys in her palm and walked out the door. Once he was gone, Chessa tossed the keys to Gwen, who set to unlocking the cells. From the first, an emaciated, scraggly wizard appeared.

"Norman!" said Chessa, flying up to wrap one arm around his neck.

The man staggered, and his voice sounded like rocks. "You came for me?"

"Of course we came for you! I would be dead if it weren't for you."

Norman narrowed his eyes at Chessa. "What's wrong with your arm, little miss?"

"I think it's broken. We can deal with that later. Right now, we need to get you all out of here."

Gwen's heart skipped a beat when Samson stepped out of the cell.

"Bind your bum arm with this," he said, ripping a piece of his shirt off with his beak. Norman took the cloth and set to work on Chessa while Gwen continued to open cells.

"Are you hurt, Sammy?" she asked.

"No, kid, my hide's tougher than a manticore's sting. Speaking of which, hey, Chessa, remember my friend?"

Gwen was trying to figure out if he was talking in detective mumbo jumbo again, but her question was answered when she unlocked the last cell. A manticore stepped, one paw at a time through the open door.

"What the fuck? I thought they were extinct," said Gwen.

"As extinct as dragons, it seems," said Chessa with a grin.

Gwen backed away to give the enormous creature space to get his body free of the cell. When he was out, he gave a roar that reverberated off the stone floor and walls and flashed a mouth full of pointed teeth. Chessa, her arm now tied to her torso, fluttered over to stand next to Gwen, who was trying to determine if she would need to take down a manticore before they could leave. The way this day was going, it would just be another on the list of impossible feats.

His mass barely fit inside the space between the cells and the wall, even with his tail laid straight behind him and wings tucked against his body. His mane brushed the ceiling. Gwen wondered how long he'd been crammed inside the cell.

"Hi, there," said Chessa as if she were crossing paths with an acquaintance in the grocery store line. "We didn't officially meet before. I'm Chessa, and I really hope you're on our side."

Gwen shook her head and took a step forward, putting herself between Chessa and the beast. Nothing could curb Chessa's spirit, it seemed. It was one of the greatest and most insufferable things about her.

Please don't eat her, she thought. She arched a brow as she took in the sight of the enormous lion-scorpion with dragon wings. He made Samson look like a kitten.

The manticore's thick white mustache twitched above his matching muzzle, but a flicker touched his golden eyes. Was that amusement? "Geoph."

"Jeff?" asked Gwen. This was a manticore! A real-life creature of legend and his name was Jeff? Unreal. "Short for Jeffrey the Eviscerator, Jefferson Death Plane or something?"

"No," roared the manticore.

"Just Jeff, then. Okay."

His scorpion tail swished back and forth, and his golden eyes seemed to flash. "It's Geoph," he growled.

Gwen swore they were saying the same thing. She looked to Chessa for support, but the pixie was giving her the kind of pointed glare that said "Shut up and go with it."

Gwen decided it was probably in her best interest to move on. "I can only hope you're Seelie."

"I don't do charity. I'm on my own side."

Could this be what Grimore meant when he said that fae pulled through the portal were unwilling to serve? Dragons. Manticores. The implications of the Unseelie pulling creatures from the Faerie Realm were too vast to deal with right now. "That's reassuring."

Gwen didn't have the luxury of time to convince Geoph that he should join the Seelie cause, and she felt like she'd already started off on the wrong paw with him. She turned, hoping the manticore wouldn't put an end to her on the spot. Though, it would make things easier.

Samson gave a nod in Geoph's direction. "He's alright, kid. We had time to get acquainted, and his whiskers are in the wind."

Whatever that meant.

Samson leaned in. "What's the plan?"

Gwen shook her head, desperate for some inner voice to tell her what to say. She looked over her small legion of questionable loyalties. One manticore. One griffin. One disgraced wizard. Two humanoids. And three pixies. "The plan is to stay alive. Outside this door, there are two dangerous fairies and who knows how many of their minions. Make a right, and you can get out the way we came in. The door at the end of the hall."

Chessa narrowed her eyes at Gwen. "What are you going to do?"

"I'm going after Liam."

"The hell you are! You're the Seelie Queen, for fuck's sake. People need you."

At that, the air seemed to be sucked from the room. Some of the fae gasped, a few even bowed. Samson smiled, but his eyes were full of sorrow. Norman's head fell and his expression was unreadable.

Gwen stiffened. "My brother is my responsibility."

Chessa wasn't backing down. "As queen, you are more than Gwen. Family is important, but all those fae out there? The ones dying for something bigger than themselves? They are your people. They are *your* responsibility."

"And as queen, I need to protect my people."

"As your best friend, I need to protect you. I couldn't protect Laural, I'm sure as hell not losing you too. Where you go, so do I."

Endangering Chessa was the last thing Gwen ever wanted to do, yet it seemed to be the only thing she was good at. "Chessa, I love you. I just want you to be safe."

"Of course you do. I'm awesome. But so are you, and you're not going anywhere without me."

Gwen sighed. "Do whatever you have to, but please, stay alive. The rest of you, head for the door at the end of the hall. There's a battle waging outside. The Unseelie have staged a hostile takeover of Avalon, and they will not stop there. If you care for an orderly life harmonious with humanity, report to General Curtis Steele, and he'll assign you to a battalion. Otherwise, kiss life as you know it goodbye."

Gwen couldn't tell if any of them would do as she said, and at this point, it didn't matter. She'd done what she'd set out to do, finding Samson. The rest was up to fate. "Alright then, let's move out!"

46

June 20
The Summer Solstice

Chessa was torn between following Gwen into the thick of battle and throttling the pain-in-the-ass fairy with her bare hands. If they made it through this alive, she planned to drill Gwen's importance into her thick skull. She opted for option A, but only by a narrow margin. Samson followed too. Gwen always dove headfirst into danger without a thought for those affected by her rash actions.

But it was Liam. Gwen always had a soft spot for him, and Chessa couldn't blame her. She'd never leave her own sister to die, even if Corra betrayed everyone they both loved the way Liam had. She followed Gwen to the left, casting a backward glance just long enough to notice that neither Grimore nor Moliana Eviscera were anywhere in sight. Had they gone back into the heart of Avalon, or had they fled, leaving Liam and the rest to face the mob of enraged Seelie fae desperate to take back their home? At this point, nothing would surprise her.

As she zipped down the hall, Chessa could hear Samson at her back. Only the manticore had turned right. The rest of the small legion followed behind their queen, ready to fight and die at her word. Gwen really did underestimate her own power.

"Gwen," called Chessa, making the fairy slow her pace. "What are you going to do when we find Liam?"

Gwen faltered. "I don't know."

"You'd better come up with a plan. I know he's your baby brother, but he murdered your entire family. He's overthrowing the Seelie Court. You can't set him free."

"Don't you think I know that?" Gwen stopped flying so abruptly, Samson nearly steamrolled them both. Her Docs thudded on the floor as she landed. Chessa couldn't read her expression, but it reminded her of the early days when the fairy had been mourning the death of Princess Francesca. It was equal parts pain and rage. It scared the shit out of Chessa.

"I will make him pay for his crimes."

"And what will that do to you?"

Gwen ignored the question and turned away. She strode the rest of the way down the hall on foot, Chessa nearly jogging to keep up despite being slightly larger. The slapping of Samson's back paws on stone and the footsteps of the rest of the party provided a beat, turning this into a kind of death march. When Gwen flung open the wooden door, the space beyond was in chaos. Unseelie bled and died on the floor, some ran, some engaged with Seelie forces in the air, and some stood motionless, their faces drawn in shock as Quincy's forces made them fight for their lives. This was not the way their plan was supposed to play out.

Chessa's palm warmed as they entered the great hall. *No, not again,* she thought, determined to ignore the mounting pain.

"Oy, it's the Seelie Queen!" The voice sounded like it emanated from a large troll. Chessa briefly wondered if it might be the same one Norman saved her from what felt like years ago. It couldn't be, not unless Unseelie necromancers far outpaced the ones she knew. She didn't have time to ponder mortality at the moment, though. Fae large and small skirmished throughout the great hall. Gwen moved quickly up the right side of the room, dodging fighting fae by weaving through the crowd or flying over those who attempted to engage her. She didn't slow, even when first Samson, then the rest of their posse, were dragged into the fight. Chessa ducked blows and darted between figures, attempting to stick with Gwen while also surveying the space for danger. When her gaze swept by the center of the hall, her blood went cold.

An enormous dragon sat in the middle of the melee, black scales gleaming in the fae lighting. Its eyes burned red, pure rage emanating from the creature in curling wisps of white smoke escaping from its mouth. Queen Charis Gaviton sat atop the dragon, stiff and regal, holding two lengths of barbed chain.

The great hall was enormous, but the beast made it look like Laural's living room. Chessa wondered how the Unseelie managed to find a full-sized dragon and fit it through the palace doors when Charis cracked the chain over the dragon's head before bringing it down. The barbs smacked into the dragon's scales, and it launched for Gwen.

47

Gwen was focused on only one thing—her brother. She made her way along the wall where Quincy's forces kept the invaders occupied, determined to reach the thrones on the other side and end this as quickly as possible. She wasn't sure Liam would still be there, but that's where Indira's body had fallen. Since he hadn't been with Princess Moliana in the west hall, it was the only place she knew to look.

She'd just taken down a sprite when she heard Samson's roar, but she couldn't make out his form in the fighting. She hoped he lived through this day. She hoped they all did.

Suddenly, her entire periphery was cast into shadow. Gwen turned just in time to see a dragon bearing down on her. She raised her hands and braced for impact.

A whip cracked over her head, and the dragon crashed to the ground. For a moment, a hush fell over the room. Quincy pushed through the crowd, yelling for his soldiers to guard the queen. All eyes focused on the stiff, cold form of the beast and on the woman who was flung from its back. Gwen tried not to think about the fae who hadn't been fast enough to avoid being flattened by the dragon. There was nothing to be done for them now. Queen Charis sprawled on the ground, unconscious or dead, Gwen couldn't tell which. It was an unceremonious end to the woman who had her own daughter slaughtered. And for what? For this? Gwen bit her lip and turned her attention back to the beast.

"Is that a fucking dragon?" she said, rising from her crouch and turning to see what horror could possibly take down a creature that size so immediately.

Behind her stood Geoph the manticore, his scorpion tail swishing overhead.

"What did you do?" Chessa murmured as she flew up and landed on the manticore's back.

Geoph gave a great shake that made her take to the air again. "Repaid my debt," he said.

As he spoke, Unseelie rebels pressed in. A fairy lunged for Chessa, but Quincy jumped and knocked it out of the air with a source stick. Samson was back near the doorway, surrounded by a horde of goblins, all with spears they jabbed as he danced out of the way.

"Thanks for the assist, Jeff," said Gwen.

"It's Geoph," rumbled the manticore. Without another word, he flapped his wings and got just enough air to stomp the usurpers in front of Gwen. Another few hops, and he'd cleared a path straight up to the dais.

Gwen stood, stunned. She could now see all the way to Liam, sitting on his stolen throne. The look of terror on his face reflected her own sense of awe at the might of the manticore.

"I believe this makes us even, *Your Grace*," Geoph said before turning tail and heading out the main doors.

"Did he say his name was Jeff?" asked Quincy. "The way he flattened them Unseelie, I think I'll call him Hopper."

At that moment, Gwen decided two things. One, she'd make a point out of never crossing a manticore, and two, she'd better haul ass before the corridor he created filled with Unseelie again.

Gwen ignored Q's characteristically inappropriate timing. "Quincy, I need to take the front of the room. Do you think you can hold them off?"

"We got this far," replied Quincy. He pushed back into the crowd, yelling orders, and a group of Seelie ran up the corridor, trampling any Unseelie who got in their way.

Gwen beat her wings faster than she knew she could, flying low in their wake. When she reached the dais, she was surprised to discover that Norman, Samson, and Chessa had all fallen in behind her. A moment later, there was a rumble of noise as Korranthian Seelie clashed with Unseelie forces behind her, pushing and maneuvering to construct a living barricade between the dais and the fighting throngs. With a force at her back, Gwen faced the thrones.

Only one was occupied. Liam sat, a glittering silver crown of vines and thorns on his head. He might think he looked regal, but to Gwen, he was a petulant child playing make-believe.

"It's over, Liam. The Unseelie are using you. Come down and kneel before your queen," she said, ignoring the little voice inside telling her she was as much of an imposter as he was.

"You will never be my queen. And it is I who used them."

The last glimmering hope Gwen held for the redemption of her brother extinguished in an instant. She'd hoped he would show some remorse for all that he wrought, but he sat there claiming power while their mother lay not twenty feet away in a pool of blood.

"How could you? Corrin and Laural and everyone? You killed them all."

The words bubbled out of her, but she didn't care. Everything they'd faced, all they lost, all Gwen lost, was because of Liam.

"So the witch is dead too?" He had the audacity to smirk at her. "Pity. She had a great rack."

Gwen heard the commotion of Chessa being held back, but she didn't break eye contact. Her voice was low and lethal. "I said kneel before your queen."

"And I said fuck you. You are not the fae queen. Our people have been oppressed for far too long, and you have done nothing but serve yourself since the moment you were born. I'm trying to do something here, to build something better for our people. For *my* people. Either you are with me, or you are against me."

"Building something? By slaughtering citizens? By unleashing Faerie on the world?"

"The before-times were brutal, but they were ours. No fae will ever have cause to hide again."

Gwen's face softened. "Liam, I know that life hasn't been perfect for the fae. I know it hasn't even been close to perfect for you. But you've lost. You will not be opening the Faerie realm. That crown doesn't make you a king. Grimore and Moliana left you here to die."

"Then kill me."

"I don't want to kill you."

"You don't want the crown bad enough. I've killed and I would die for this cause. So do it. Kill me. You have no other choice." Liam stood, brandishing his blade. He moved toward Gwen.

Chessa squeezed free from Samson's hold and lunged. In that moment, a series of observations bled one into another. The crown upon Liam's head flashed. Norman stiffened. And Liam's lips curled into a smile.

Chessa hit the ground.

She didn't fall per se. Her wings still flapped, but the air below her was simply gone. She cracked her head on the hard stone floor. Norman dropped to his knees over her.

"It's the crown of Oberon," he murmured just loud enough for Gwen to hear. "It protects him from all attacks."

Gwen turned her attention back to Liam. When she looked at him, she didn't see a tyrannical fairy driven to madness with a yearning for power. She saw the little boy from her vision running the halls with Corrin. She stepped toward him.

"Make your move, sis. The crown will break you," he hissed.

She took another step. Then another. Liam stared defiantly.

"Liam, I don't want to hurt you. I never wanted to hurt you." Her voice cracked, and she took another step.

Liam held out his dagger as if to ward her off. His eyes began to dart around. "How are you doing this? You can't attack me."

Gwen kept coming. "I'm not attacking you, baby brother. I love you." Tears were running down her face now.

Liam charged.

Gwen's magic ignited in her blood. She felt the warmth of the sun giving her power, and she channeled it all into her arms as Liam closed in. Instead of blocking him or fighting back, she embraced him. The touch broke down the barrier between them, and she saw him, all of him, for the first time.

She saw fragments of his life, of her leaving, of Corrin's wedding, of him weeping in the woods not far from where they stood now. She saw their mother slap him across the face when he cried. She saw empty halls and felt the profound loneliness of one who had been left behind. The face of the Unseelie Princess appeared. She felt the warmth of her touch, the feeling of belonging. She felt all that anger being channeled into the world at large, the way things were. The way they could be. She felt it all. All except the blade sliding in between her ribs.

She cradled her little brother, now bigger than she, and cried. She moved her hand up and knocked the crown off his head.

Norman rushed the dais and smacked a thick palm into the much smaller fairy. Liam was ripped away from Gwen and hurled backward. She crumpled to the ground. Liam hit the wall with a sickening smack and slumped to the floor, mouthing something she couldn't hear. Gwen reached her hand out toward him, but he was out of reach. As the world darkened around her, she watched as blood pooled beneath Liam's head and the light in his eyes was extinguished.

48

When the crown fell from Liam's head, the world snapped into focus around Chessa. Unseelie fled the hall, chased by what remained of the Seelie forces. Her hand burned like it was thrust into molten steel. She barely noticed the pain of her broken arm pinned beneath her. She rolled onto her side and raised the branded palm to her face. Morgan's sigil glowed white hot on her skin. Terrified, Chessa tore her gaze away from her hand to look for help.

Gwen was down, and so was Liam. Norman stood over the Seelie Queen, the look on his face gutting Chessa. She forgot her own pain as adrenaline took over. She had to get to Gwen. Chessa pushed herself up with her uninjured elbow then let her wings do the rest. As she lowered herself onto the dais next to Norman, he seemed to snap out of it. He looked at her, horror haunting his empty gaze.

"Why is your hand glowing?" he asked.

"No idea," she replied through gritted teeth, the reminder causing her brain to process pain once again. She looked down at Gwen. "What happened?"

"He stabbed her, but she managed to get the crown off his head. I think I killed him." The words sounded hollow.

"You did what you had to do, Norman." She reached for the dagger in Gwen's side.

The wizard flinched. "Don't pull it out. She'll bleed to death."

"If I don't, she's going to bleed to death anyway," Chessa replied. Blood soaked through Gwen's shirt and vest. "Get me something to wrap around her. We'll put pressure on it." With one fluid motion, Chessa pulled the dagger from Gwen's side and let it clatter to the ground. She used her unbound, glowing hand to press against the wound.

The burning somehow intensified, but she didn't let up. She couldn't let Gwen die.

Suddenly, Chessa was walking outside in the sunlight on the tor. There was no battle, no fae slaughtering each other for power. There was merely blue sky, clean air, green grass, and Gwen. Gwen was smiling in a way Chessa rarely saw. The sun was high and huge, and Chessa could barely see for the power of its light. For a moment, it was in the sky, then the light radiated from Gwen's skin in all directions.

Someone was yelling in the distance.

"Let go, little miss!"

She thought she heard Norman, but he was nowhere in sight. Nobody was.

"You have to let go! Please!" He was begging.

Chessa let go.

She was back on the cold floor, blood covering her hand, which was no longer glowing. Gwen lay in front of her, light emanating from her skin the way it had in the field moments before. Her eyes fluttered open.

"What did you do?" sputtered Gwen.

"I don't know. What did you do?" The room was spinning, but the pain in Chessa's hand was fading. None of this made any sense to Chessa, but Norman was nodding like an idiot. "Norman, do you know something?"

"I only suspected until now. But I don't know how you unlocked it."

Both women stared at him and said, "Unlocked what?" in unison.

"Do you know how Morgan le Fay rose to power?"

"Yeah," replied Gwen, pushing herself up from the floor. Of course Gwen knew about Morgan le Fay. She was raised in Avalon.

Gwen was talking clearly now, with no hint of pain. "She founded the Unseelie when the world turned against her. They accused her of witchcraft, sedition, and worse, and she withdrew from humanity, taking refuge in Avalon. That about sums it up, right?"

"Wrong. What she did in that cave with Arthur changed the course of history."

"Well, yeah. She seduced him and their bastard son went on to kill him, bringing about an end to Camelot."

Norman didn't seem to notice. "Wrong again! They say she seduced Arthur in order to overthrow him, but those were the lies of a reckless king and his power-hungry wizard. She did no such thing. She healed him."

"That's part of the history books too," said Chessa. She put a hand on Gwen's arm, and Gwen shot her a comforting look. It didn't feel like the time for a history lesson, but Norman seemed intent on finishing his story.

"She healed him from something that shouldn't be healed. She healed him from death itself."

"Necromancy?" asked Chessa.

"No. Necromancy is a flawed art. It requires enormous sources of energy and the dead are never quite right after. Necromancy is unnatural. What Morgan did was something more."

Chessa struggled to understand. "And you think I somehow got her power?"

"I don't know. But you just did something, and the queen is alive. She was dead moments before. You pressed your glowing palm bearing the mark of Morgan le Fay to her wound, and here she is breathing and staring at me like she's going to kick me arse. That can't be a coincidence."

"How?" Chessa asked. A million questions swirled in her mind, the implications of this power just beginning to occur to her.

Gwen was looking down at her own hands. "All day, I've felt magic coursing through me, and when I felt you here with me, all my walls came down. I touched my magic."

Chessa felt her eyes go wide as the pieces fit into place. "The summer solstice. Your empathic touch. The connection between us. You used your power to unlock the magic bestowed upon me by Morgan le Fay, and I used that magic, and yours too somehow, to bring you home."

"I've seen magical artifacts, and I've seen the sloppy work of necromancers, but this? This is something different," Norman said.

"The pain in my hand subsided after Gwen woke. But I've felt it before. I think it happens when I'm in close proximity to death."

Chessa looked at Gwen, who was now standing in the great hall, the bodies of her mother and brother not far from where her boots were planted on the dais. The pain hadn't flared back up again, and Chessa had no idea if she could use the magic again. But she had to try.

She looked at the crumpled body of Liam Evenshine. "Do you think—"

Gwen snapped to attention. "No."

"But Gwen, if it works—"

"If it works, we will be right back where we were. I may not have been able to bring myself to kill him, but Liam is gone." Her voice lowered, and Chessa could hear the pain. "Let him rest."

Norman turned away, and Chessa could feel his grief. He'd been trying to redeem himself by serving the people he betrayed, and in doing so, he killed another Seelie royal. If they were right about the power of the brand on her hand, Chessa had the power to bring him back, but Gwen seemed certain.

"Indira?"

Gwen closed her eyes. "Chessa, we don't know what this magic does to you. My family has failed the fae. I don't want to risk you to undo what has already been done. And there are so many others who died today. Fae who should have never been here."

Suddenly, Chessa knew exactly what she had to do. "I have to try it one more time, no matter what it does to me," she said. "I hope you understand."

As she darted over the mangled bodies of the injured and dead, her palm began to warm again. It began as an itch and increased in intensity until it burned, but this time, she was glad for the pain. Gwen had been right. The magic drained her. Even now, filled with adrenaline, exhaustion weighed heavy on her body. She zipped through crowds of fae outside the tower, many still locked in a battle they didn't know was over, fueled by sheer willpower. The dead were all around, and the pain was nearly unbearable by the time she found who she was looking for.

Laural lay motionless, bloodied, and broken on the pavement near the southernmost end of the building. Chessa fought the urge to try Morgan's power on anyone else. She didn't know how to wield it, and if she only had one shot, she had to use it to bring back the one witch who could save many others.

By the time Norman caught up with her, Chessa was perched on Laural's shoulder, holding her palm to the witch's pale forehead. With her eyes clutched shut, she trailed her hand downward, over the witch's eyes, lips, and chest, before pressing her palm to the center of her being, just over the solar plexus. Light blazed around the spot, blinding her. Morgan's power funneled through Chessa, the vessel used to focus and direct it. The light erupted, the blast sending Chessa careening backward. She slammed into a pile of dead fae and blacked out.

WHEN SHE CAME TO, everything was quiet. She was in a lush bedroom, tucked into a bed that could hold a pair of trolls. The walls were painted lilac, the floor covered with a fluffy white rug, and the matching furniture was high-end. There were no signs of battle. Something about this space made Chessa feel warm and safe. Until she moved and was hit by a wave of vertigo.

Afraid she might hurl on the luxurious duvet, Chessa climbed out from beneath it. Her arm was no longer bound to her side, and when she moved it, there was no pain. She stretched before giving her wings a flutter. Everything seemed to work. Fighting another wave of nausea, Chessa flitted to the end of the bed to steady herself. The only decoration in the room was a framed photo sitting atop the white bureau. A young Gwen smiled back at her, the fairy's arm thrown over the shoulders of a surly-looking fairy boy. Liam. This was Gwen's room. Tears filled Chessa's eyes as she remembered that Liam was gone and her best friend had lost her entire family. She needed to find Gwen.

A door leading to a balcony was slightly ajar. Chessa zipped outside to find Laural sitting in a rocking chair overlooking the ravaged Glastonbury Tor. Chessa sunk to her feet in shock.

"It worked," she whispered.

Laural's face morphed from surprise at the pixie's sudden appearance to concern. "You shouldn't be up. Get back to bed!"

As if on cue, Chessa's stomach rebelled. She just made it to the edge of the balcony before losing control. Laural was at her side in a beat, stroking her back with one shaky hand. A tingling sensation overcame Chessa and filled her with strength. "I can't believe you're alive."

"It's more than that, little cousin," the witch replied. "He's gone."

Chessa's breath caught. "Corrin has been gone for over a year."

"No, not Corrin. Gailan. When you brought me back, the demon was no longer held captive inside of me. I don't know if he fled when I died or if you pushed him out with whatever magic you used to resurrect me." Tears welled in Laural's eyes. "I'm free."

Laural wept openly, the most emotional Chessa had seen her since she and Corrin were first dating. She'd not been allowed her feelings for fear of losing control, but now that she was free, she cried like a baby. Chessa settled on her shoulder and wrapped one arm around the back of her neck. She never expected Laural to live, let alone be rid of the demon who kept her captive for most of her life. At least *something* good came of all they'd been through.

After a few tense moments, Laural settled, sniffed, and stood. "There are so many injured to look after."

"Yes, you're needed now more than ever."

The tears in Laural's eyes dried, and she stood up straight. She was no longer the unreadable, distant fortress Chessa had come to know, but she also wasn't the wide-eyed girl she once was. She was strong, she was warm, and she was ready to take on the world.

"I've set up a healing station and I'm using the communication device you had in your ear to direct a veritable army of makeshift nurses, but yes, I could do even more down on the field. But first, we need to get you back to bed."

Chessa flew to the railing and smiled at her cousin. Corrin would be so happy to see his love like this, the force of nature she was always meant to be, standing firm to help others. She grinned. "Bed? Fuck that!"

She flew off the balcony to go find Gwen.

49

Gwen stood amidst the carnage littering Glastonbury Tor. The fields she frolicked in as a young fairy were now a wasteland. The Unseelie laid down their weapons once word got out that their leaders abandoned them or died attempting to hold the throne. Some disappeared into the setting sun, some bent the knee, and a few others were captured by Quincy's battalion of enforcers. Gwen tasked Curtis with gathering the wounded, Seelie and Unseelie alike, into the main library where they could be seen to by the fae working under Laural, who was issuing orders from Chessa's bedside. Gwen still couldn't believe the witch was back. Chessa was somehow the smartest and the stupidest pixie on earth. She could have died bringing back the one witch who could help the most.

Everywhere Gwen walked, fae bowed. It was unnerving. With orders given, fae scurried this way and that, locking up prisoners, seeing to the wounded, and moving supplies. There was nothing for Gwen to do but witness the suffering of her people. She had no idea what she was doing, and she was a fairy of action. Without a goal, it was hard to keep her mind from venturing into dark places.

Uncle Monty appeared before her. "Your Grace," he said with a deep bow.

"Please don't," said Gwen. "How's Ember?"

"She's doing as well as can be expected. She's working with the injured in the library. Staying busy helps keep her from dwelling on all we've lost. She is an Evenshine, after all."

Gwen nodded. "And how are you?"

"Broken."

Gwen left the word hanging in the air. They were all broken. They lost children, brothers, sisters, cousins. They lost the very things that were supposed to usher them into the future, and the way ahead was murky.

Monty reached out and took Gwen's hand. "Thank you," he said.

"For what?"

"For justice."

Gwen sighed. "Justice alone isn't enough to live for. I learned that the hard way. I hope that you and Ember can find peace someday."

"So do I." Monty turned and walked back toward the palace.

Gwen wished she could do something more, but there was nothing that would bring back Arabella or Augustus. Nothing to bring back Indira or Liam. Memories of young Liam running from her on these very grounds, a broad smile plastered on his little face, flashed across her mind. She fought back emotions. She couldn't feel them. Not now. If she did, they would destroy her.

Something crossed the sun, casting a shadow all around her. A ubiquitous, amorphous darkness settled next to her and seemed to bleed into the ground at her feet, coalescing into a tiny animal and leaving a baby dragon on the grass. Sorcha, her shunni, wrapped around her legs, making a quick figure eight before disappearing back into the darkness from which she came. She must have sensed Gwen's sorrow. She rarely approached while Gwen was awake.

Turning to the baby dragon, Gwen bit her bottom lip to keep it from quivering. When she met Henrietta's eyes, she saw her pain mirrored back.

A familiar voice startled Gwen. "You tried to keep me confined to bed, you bitch!"

Gwen heard Chessa before she saw her, and her grief was washed away by relief. Laural told her the pixie would pull through, but with everything that happened, she couldn't let herself believe it until this very moment.

Chessa tackled her from behind, and the dragon gave a low whinny like a unicorn might make upon seeing its favorite nymph approach.

"Get off! I'm your queen for Danu's sake!" Gwen laughed as Chessa released her and flitted over to Henrietta, whose wings were fluttering with joy.

"Be careful, baby, or you'll hover away," said Chessa. She gave the dragon scratches under the chin as Maddy, the siren girl from Long Wharf approached with a bucket of salt water to cleanse the dragon's wounds.

Emotions swirled around Gwen. Exhaustion, sorrow, regret, fear. For someone with empathic magic, she sure was a mess when it came to her own feelings.

"Chess, I'm sorry," she said.

"You have nothing to apologize for. I'm just glad we both lived through this," replied Chessa, hugging Gwen again. "Have you gone to the grove yet?"

"Curtis sent a scouting party about an hour ago. Do you know anything about the Faerie realm?"

"Only what I've deduced from Liam's little villain monologue," replied Chessa. "But there's something I need to tell you. When I was near the door leading out there, Morgan's brand, it reacted."

Gwen wasn't sure what Chessa was trying to say. "What do you mean it reacted?"

"It hurt. It hurt the way it hurts when I'm near death. I don't know what they were doing to open the portal, but I think it involved blood magic."

Gwen's heart fell into her stomach. They'd never found some of her family members. A cold uncertainty swept through her, and when Curtis approached a moment later, she knew exactly what he was going to say.

"Your Grace, can we go somewhere private to talk?"

50

Chessa!" exclaimed Maddy with a grin after Gwen had left with Curtis. Chessa knew whatever he had to say must be pretty bad if he wanted privacy. Today would take a heavy toll on everyone. She turned her attention to the young siren. It was surreal seeing the girl here.

"Hey, mer-girl. Did I hear you brought that human boy to Avalon?"

Maddy blushed. "Dalton overheard Mother and me as we were leaving. He didn't want me to go anywhere dangerous without him. He's been seeing everything happening, but to him, it looks like a mortal affair. He knows better, though. I, well, um, I told him."

The boy stepped from behind the dragon. "Hello," he said awkwardly.

"What you must think of all of this," said Chessa with as neutral a smile as she could manage. Human minds are fragile things. The haunted look in the boy's eyes revealed that the glamour might have concealed the nature of the fae, but it didn't protect him from the brutality of war.

"He needs to go home, Maddy," she said. "You both do."

"We're booked on the first flight we could get to Boston," said Maddy.

"I'm glad to hear it."

Henrietta pressed her nose into Chessa's palm, and she gave her a reassuring pat.

"Cute dog," said Dalton. "Can I pet him?"

As the mortal unknowingly cooed to a dragon as if it were a Saint Bernard, the earth began to shake. A moment later, a pulse blasted through the air, pushing them all to the ground.

"What the hell was that?" gasped Chessa.

Instead of an answer, she heard Dalton screaming. Henrietta was sniffing him as if trying to help, but he held his hands up between them.

Chessa flitted over to pull Henrietta back, and Maddy scampered over to him. Dalton rolled into a fetal position, his head tucked in his arms and his body convulsing.

"A dragon! And you! You're some kind of a bat or something." He raved but kept his head covered.

"I told you about my world, baby. I told you," cooed Maddy, using her siren song to calm his shaking while she stroked his head. "It's okay. I'm here."

Chessa looked into Maddy's eyes. "I'm sorry, but I have to leave you to take care of this. I have to warn Gwen. Something's wrong with the glamour."

A month ago, she thought dragons and manticores were extinct. Her worldview expanded over the past few days, but not nearly as drastically as the view of the poor boy from the streets of Boston. This must have been what Moliana and Grimore were up to, shutting down the glamour that protected the fae realm from humanity in the UK. Judging by Dalton's reaction, there would be humans all over the realm losing their shit. Just when she thought they'd won, she was reminded how insignificant they all were in the grand scheme of kingdoms and realms.

51

As soon as he understood the situation, Curtis made sure Gwen was guarded and took off in search of Herbert Dayglow. As a Seelie Ambassador, he'd have more knowledge about the cloaking mechanisms in place in the UK, and right now, that was more pressing than Gwen's dead relatives rotting in the grove. At this point, she was numb to everything.

Twenty minutes later, Chessa came to tell her they found Herbert in the great hall using his advanced perceptive magic to attempt to fit a full-grown dragon out a door sized for ogres and trolls. Even that not-so-little dilemma would have to wait. Gwen met Curtis and Herbert on the quiet side of the tor.

Old Herb refused to discuss matters of Seelie security in the presence of anyone outside the Council, such as it was. Only once Gwen had a sound barrier placed by the sirens and Curtis had created a fifty-foot barrier from any living creatures did he confide to Gwen that the UK fairies held stations at Stonehenge, the Hill of Tara, and Edinburgh Castle. Each station utilized a team of fairies to cast cloaking glamours that were broadcast by sirens specially trained to work with magic waves rather than sound waves. The system was far more efficient than the Glamour Squadron back home but also far more fallible.

At Gwen's order, Curtis dispatched battalions to each of the locations.

As she awaited news, Gwen asked Quincy to organize a clean-up, gathering the dead on the south side of the tor so the bodies could be identified and families notified. It was a great job for the remaining KPD forces onsite. Meanwhile, Herbert returned to the dragon problem.

He'd successfully removed the creature from the great hall and relocated it to an undisturbed part of the grove when Curtis returned with news.

"All glamour facilities are intact but one. Only Stonehenge is compromised. The staff onsite has been slaughtered. There are no witnesses, but we have to assume this was carried out by Grimore or Princess Moliana," he told her before bringing in one of the guards to offer a detailed description of the scene. One thing was certain— Moliana had earned the surname Eviscera.

"We should have ended them when we could have," she said quietly.

"From what I understand, things could have easily gone the other direction had you tried. Don't worry, I've got security details in place at all glamour hubs. If they make a move, there's a kill order in place," replied Curtis.

Gwen nodded. She never realized just how ruthless a ruler needed to be, but letting Moliana and Grimore go free simply wasn't an option, not if the alternative was possible.

"Do you think this was part of their original plan?" she asked. "They were going to unleash Faerie and destroy the glamours. What would that gain them?"

Curtis shook his head. "Pure chaos."

After a long, tense moment, she asked "Do we know what damage was done?"

"There's no telling. The glamour was down for fifty-three minutes by my calculations. Most of the fae in the region were here, fighting on one side or another, but we don't have the census reports for the big cities yet."

"I need you to get that information for me quickly."

Curtis nodded. They had to run damage assessments in order to mitigate stories spreading. Humans were too social. There were always tales circulating about the fae, and most of them had roots in truth, but a mass exposure like this would be harder for their logical minds to explain away.

"Can we kill their communications?" she asked.

"The exposure is limited to portions of England and Wales. We can't take it all down, but I could arrange for a 'natural' event to blast through London and a few of the suburbs. That should keep much of the populace from spreading rumors too quickly. Country folk are known for their tales, and there wouldn't have been as many sightings outside the metro areas anyways."

"Do it. We need to contain this." Gwen shook her head. "What a shitshow."

52

Gwen sat on the back of the baby dragon, clinging to Chessa for dear life. Of course, if she did fall off, it would only take her a moment or two to get her bearings and use her own wings, but that did little to break the fearful awe of soaring over the Glastonbury Tor atop Henrietta. Gwen had done everything in her power to take control of the situation with the glamour, and she trusted Curtis to do whatever was needed. There wasn't a creature on the tor who didn't respect his authority now. They landed on the east field, which was filled with more fae than she'd ever seen in one place.

Doing her best to appear regal, she flew down from Henrietta's back and stood in front of the wall surrounding her childhood home. Chessa stood to her right. Quincy took the place next to Chessa, declining his head ever so slightly as he passed Gwen and earning a scowl in return. Curtis arrived moments later and stood to Gwen's left. A quick motion with his hand, and a line of sirens shuffled the center of the crowd, standing ready to amplify the words that would formally end the battle for the heart of Avalon.

Gwen stepped forward. "Fae of the world, I speak to you all, not only to the Seelie but also to those we fought against. I may be Seelie Queen, but my duty is to all fae. For too long we have only looked out for ourselves, and today, we paid for that." The faces Gwen could make out in the crowd looked confused, skeptical, and some even angry.

"Everyone here stood for something greater than themselves. The reason the Unseelie Princess was able to raise such a formidable army was because of resentments boiling beneath the surface of our society. Justified resentments. She took advantage of our wounds to make a play for power. Historically, the Unseelie wanted nothing to do with humanity, but the wilds have been decimated as humanity grows, and there are very few places on earth for fae to retreat to. The Unseelie way of life is not sustainable in modern times. The only way forward is coexistence."

At that, the prisoners began to push and holler insults. Still, Gwen continued. "That said, your leadership has failed you all."

Now, it wasn't only the Unseelie beginning to revolt.

"You can argue all you want, but that doesn't change the facts. The Seelie way is also not sustainable. For decades, we have pressed on, pretending that our Council and our regional royals knew best, but we were wrong. We were all wrong. And now, we may be exposed to humanity."

It seemed as if the entire field took a collective gasp. Until this moment, nobody knew the glamour had failed, that the fae way of life had been compromised, but Gwen didn't see where hiding it changed a thing.

"The glamour that protected this region was broken. Moliana Eviscera and Grimore sought to unleash the Faerie realm, and when that failed, they tried to expose us. For centuries, our existence has been nothing more than children's stories, fairy tales, they call them. We've kept it that way for the sake of our own preservation. We have no idea what the ramifications of this exposure will be, but I'm here to help find a way forward for Seelie, Unseelie, Courtless, and any others threatened by today's happenings."

"There will be changes. Regional royals haven't represented fae interests for far too long, and my family hasn't represented fae interests for even longer. In an effort to coexist with humanity, we've placed them above our own people. It has to end. Something has to give. The bloodshed here today proves this."

A hush fell over the crowd as Gwen's words sunk in. Gwen didn't know what she was going to say next. The words just fell out of her mouth, taking on a life of their own. Who was she to question the fae way of life? For a moment, she nearly faltered. She looked back to Chessa. Tears were streaming down the pixie's face, and she nodded encouragement. It was the sign Gwen needed to press on.

"I can't pretend I know how to heal us. I don't know what the future holds. But I do know that things can't continue as they have. So, please, go home to your families. All of you, Seelie and Unseelie alike. Bury your dead. Grieve your losses. And know that I will be here, working to find a new way, a better way, for us all."

Quincy stepped forward.

Damn it, Q, now's not the time, thought Gwen. When she leveled a gaze in his direction, he dropped to his knee. Curtis, Samson, and Chessa followed suit. O'Toole and the KPD legion did the same. Gwen watched in awe as a wave formed in the crowd as the Seelie all bowed to their new queen. It was as if she were out of her body watching someone else stand before the fae as their leader. This couldn't be her life.

Some of the Unseelie took to the skies and some slinked away, nearby Seelie rustling and calling out but not moving to stop them. More miraculously, some of the Unseelie stayed put, eyes wide as if seeing a new future dawn. Gwen hoped she could deliver.

When she returned to the great hall, she found that it had been cleared, the injured carried off to Laural and the dead taken away. She walked with Curtis a step behind, to the place where Indira had fallen. The stone was a little darker where her blood had soaked in. Gwen bent down to touch the spot, dropped her defenses, and felt the power of the summer solstice ignite the magic in her veins. Senses washed over her.

Images of Gwen and Liam as young fairies, flitting through the halls, the warmth of a mother's love followed by the sound of Indira's own voice scolding them, a flash of her father's kind eyes, the sharp pain of grief, more images, sounds, and smells than Gwen could ever hope to catch swirling by in a chaotic tangle, Gammie shaking her head in disapproval. The world pressing in from all sides. The smell of burning wood. Herbert Dayglow stroking her hair, warmth in his eyes.

It all faded into blackness.

When Gwen snapped back into the present and shakily rose, processing the last bits of data from her mother's life, she felt the presence of someone before the tears cleared from her blurry eyes. Curtis was standing defensively over her, his back to Gwen and a source stick in his hand raised and pointed at the face of a man that made him look like a fruit fly.

The size of a rock giant, the man looked very old but moved with the nimbleness of youth. He wore a wolfskin cloak over his shoulders, and his warm brown skin was wrinkled around dark eyes that drew her in. She didn't know who or what the man was, but she sensed a power in him.

"Name yourself," commanded Curtis, his voice dripping with unspoken threat, though Gwen doubted the source stick would do much to stop this visitor should he move against her.

"I am Moshup, and I travelled far to appear before the one they are now calling queen."

"Stand down, Curtis," said Gwen.

Curtis hesitated a moment then did as she commanded. As he shuffled to the side, he kept the source stick in hand.

"You made the trip quickly. I've only been queen for a few hours."

"I have my ways."

From the knowing look on his face, Gwen did not doubt he did.

"You look familiar, but I can't say I've heard your name before. Are you Seelie?" she asked.

"I am only myself."

"Courtless, then?"

"That is your word, not mine. If my face is familiar, perhaps you have seen my visage depicted around Korranthia. That is what you call my ancestral land, is it not?"

"You're from Korranthia? No offense, but I think I would have noticed you walking down the streets of Boston."

"You would be surprised what your kind has missed. I am not the only being that has eluded your notice, and that is what I am here to remind you."

Gwen looked to Curtis to see if he knew anything more than she did, but he was staring down Moshup, probably waiting for him to make a move.

"Dragons, manticores, and now you. It seems I have a lot to learn."

"Then you are not a lost cause, it would seem. I am no dragon or manticore, though I respect those creatures. They've been around longer than your kind. I am a teacher. I cared for the people of my land long before colonizers brought you to our shores."

"Then you are fae also, and the Seelie Court will welcome you."

"I am not here for welcome. Your Seelie Council has never stood for my people. We have always been and always will be, and your Council is but the glint of sun off the scales of a trout. I come before you because I sense the winds of change. Change is inevitable as seasons come and go, and the season of the Seelie Court has come to an end. I'm here to deliver the message of my people. We accept no rule but our own."

With that, the giant lifted a foot and stomped. The stone cracked beneath him, and his footprint was left in the floor of the great hall of Avalon. Before Gwen could wrap her mind around any of it, Moshup turned and walked away. Curtis moved to stop him, but Gwen held up a hand. She'd had enough conflict for the day, and Moshup didn't seem to be looking for a fight.

53

So that's it. You're staying in Avalon?" Chessa's voice was muffled by her mouthful of potatoes. The small room off the kitchens held a dining table for twelve and nothing else. It was where Gwen's family would eat when they didn't want to be observed by the masses.

"The way I see it, I don't have much of a choice. As I was reminded, the season of the Seelie Court is at an end. I need to find a way forward for us all."

"I still don't know what you mean by all that," replied Chessa. "Shit's broken, sure, but how are you even going to begin by fixing it?"

"My family has always worked to fix things. I think right now, it's time to listen. We can't rebuild a fae government without understanding the fae. And if I've learned anything over the past week, it's that I don't know anything."

Chessa nodded. "Damn, Gwen, you've sure come a long way."

"I didn't have much of a choice. You and Sammy made sure of that when you went and got yourself captured."

"Change was coming one way or another, kid. Can't bury your head in the sand forever," said Samson.

"What about our PI business, then?" asked Quincy, gulping wine from a giant tumbler Norman dug out of the kitchens. After making a wisecrack about being poisoned by the turn cloak, he'd pulled the wizard into a headlock and mussed up his scraggly white hair. There were no angels here, or demons either. Just a fucked up fae family.

"Yeah, about that," said Chessa. She never thought she'd see the day when Gwen and Q would become friends, let alone partners. It seems that some fae could still surprise her on occasion. "Want to clue me in?"

"About what, partner?" Quincy's grin was contagious, and Chessa couldn't help but smile back.

"I just want to know how you ended up becoming a partner in *my* firm."

"He's only a quarter partner," explained Gwen.

"Same as our esteemed queen."

Samson shook his head and pecked at a chicken leg.

"Oy, ain't that cannibalism?" asked Quincy.

"I'm half eagle, not half chicken." Samson made the motion to push his glasses up his beak before poking himself in the face and lowering his talon.

Chessa laughed. "We'll get you to the optometrist for a new pair once we get stateside."

At that, Gwen's face fell.

"Don't worry, Gwennie. You're queen now. You can keep a couple hobgoblins on retainer for when you need an emergency Branagh night."

"I'm not sure they're planning on sticking around. They never helped the Seelie before."

"You can't be too sure. I'd imagine a few of them would rather help build a new world than smuggle pixie dust and weapons. You should give them the choice." Chessa took another big bite of loaded potatoes.

Gwen just smiled and looked at her with some expression she couldn't quite place. Chessa wasn't really upset about Q joining C&F Investigations. Without Gwen to run intimidation, she could use some loyal muscle. Besides, his connections were invaluable.

She swallowed a mouthful then noticed that Norman was sitting away from everyone else. "How about you, Norm? Are you ready for a fresh start in the good old US of A?" asked Chessa.

The wizard cast a sheepish look at Gwen before meeting Chessa's gaze. He nodded and ducked his head.

Gwen must have noticed too. "You don't need to slink around. I know what you did. And I also know what Chessa says about you. She always sees the best in everyone, and I'm trying to as well," she said.

Chessa placed a hand on Gwen's shoulder. She might not have been close to her family, but offering forgiveness for his part in the assassination of her great aunt must be difficult, especially on the heels of losing her entire family.

"Thank you, Your Grace," replied Norman. Tears flowed freely down his face. "I'm so sorry for everything."

"Me too," said Gwen before standing abruptly and retreating from the room.

Chessa gave herself an internal kick. She should have realized that Gwen was about to bolt. She followed her out the door, catching up in the stairwell leading to the tower.

"Gwen, wait."

"Chess, I just need a minute. This is all so much."

Chessa understood. Gwen had no time to grieve before the weight of the world was thrust upon her shoulders. She went from surly, purposeless fairy to Seelie queen in a blink, watching half her family die and losing the rest, having unfamiliar deities popping up with cryptic messages, and working toward rebuilding an entire form of government all over the course of a week give or take a few days.

"I know. I just wanted to ask you if you're sure you're okay with us leaving next week. I could stay, you know. Help you get reaccustomed to Avalon."

To Chessa's surprise, Gwen broke out in laughter. "There is no getting accustomed to this. Some fae might find stability in life, but it's not in the cards for me. This isn't a hot bath that takes soaking in before you're comfortable. I was born into this, but I will never get accustomed to it."

"Oh, Gwen. Then let me stay with you."

Gwen shook her head and flapped her wings, slowly rising up the stairwell. "You misunderstand. It will never be comfortable because it shouldn't be. You see what happens when rulers become comfortable. But it is my lot, not yours. You have a life back in Korranthia. One thing, though?"

"Anything."

"Look out for Sorcha for me."

Chessa kept pace as they reached the top of the stairs and stepped out onto the tower balcony. The fields of the tor stretched out around them, and beyond that, trees and buildings. Gwen perched on the railing, and Chessa settled in next to her. They sat like that until the sun went down and lightning bugs began to flicker in the grass below.

54

C&F Investigations wasn't the same without a surly fairy with her feet on the desk, but it was a good deal busier. Over the past few months, the Seelie Council disbanded, replaced with a representative government tasked with enacting a series of fae protection protocols, and the ripples of change could be felt all the way down to the dark alleyways of Korranthia. Gwen kept the title of queen, though, which Chessa found puzzling.

The changes she was making were undeniable. Fae who never had a voice began to reach out, seeking help on cases that would have been swept under the rug in the before times. It didn't hurt that C&F hired an Unseelie receptionist—a wizard looking to start a new life after he'd gotten caught up with the wrong crowd. Between Norman and the half-ogre hero of the Battle of Avalon with ties to the Korranthian underworld, Chessa had more hopeless cases cross her desk than she was able to take on. Gwen offered to send help, but Chessa knew it would undermine the trust of those in need to see Seelie royal representatives in the office, even if the new queen was making good on her promises.

Chessa was down at the docks visiting Maddy, Dalton, and Mora —once the boy had time to adjust to the existence of the fae world, he'd taken on the task of becoming a dragon expert, even helping Henrietta settle into her new home at the Graves—when her cell buzzed in her back pocket. The screen showed Norman's impassive face and scraggly beard. She stepped out of the little whale-topped ticket booth to answer.

"What's up Norm? We got another case?"

"You could say that."

Norman held his phone out to pan to the makeshift lobby, really just a ratty couch set up in an apartment living room. Standing near the door, dripping hobgoblin goo was the Seelie Queen, a smirk on her face and a bottle of Jack in her hand.

"Get over here, I want to watch *Gremlins* again," said Gwen before Norman panned the camera back to himself.

"Shall I cancel your appointments for the evening?"

Chessa grinned. "You better believe it."

THE END

ACKNOWLEDGMENTS

I sure do have a lot of people supporting me. This book is dedicated to my parents, Colleen and Paul Caron, who helped make me the whack-job I am today. My love affair with fiction started when I'd read chapters of The Secret Garden with my mom after school in the 3rd grade. She always taught me to embrace the magic in life. And my dad has been a steadfast force both in my life and in his pursuit of a career doing what he loves. I couldn't ask for a better role model.

Thank you to my husband Alex, who is always along for the ride, helping me work through plot holes, chilling with the kids when I go to conventions, and disarming the device in my brain that sometimes starts making a beeping noise. He always knows which wire to cut and which to leave intact. And thanks to my girls, my little forces of nature, who provide constant inspiration.

Thank you to my amazing beta readers, both those who read with a fine-tooth comb and those who hang on for dear life while I drag them through a maze of interconnected revelations via chat. This book wouldn't be the same without Nicole Bross, Matt Harshaw, Sara Bond, and John Hermsen.

Thank you to John Hartness, my editor and publisher, for believing in me. Thanks for all that other stuff too, but without your faith, none of it would exist. Thank you to Misty Massey for being a fabulous editor who sees my blind spots, to Kristen Gould for the polish, and to Susan Roddey for nailing the amazing cover!

As always, thank you to Dr. Hew Joiner and the Georgia Southern Bell Honors Program faculty of 2000-2004 for supporting and nurturing my worldview. I would not be the same me without you. And thanks to the other teachers who believed in me from early on:

Mr. Clark, who hammered grammar through my thick skull, Dr. Tilley, who was as much friend as teacher, Mrs. Beals, who never let me call it in, and Mr. Friedman who somehow knew I'd go the science route six years before I did! I don't know where all of you are at this point, but if you ever end up with one of my books in your hands, I want you to know what an impact you had.

I also want to thank the convention runners who do so much to validate me as both a writer and a person: Jennifer and James Liang, Darin Bush, Allie Charlesworth, and Jesse Adams, and all the other people involved with the many conventions that have added immeasurable value to my life. Also, thanks to all the amazing convention attendees who do so much to support my work. Thanks to Tonya and Rick Dorsey and Dino Hicks for making me feel like this little dream of mine might actually be worth it.

Thank you to all the Falstaff Misfits, my publishing siblings, for always hyping me up and having my back in so many ways. From the wisdom imparted by Patrick Dugan and Stuart Jaffe to the impromptu check-ins and hang-outs with Darin Kennedy, Jessica Nettles, and Sarah Madsen and the ConTinual fun with Jim Nettles and Gail Martin, the Misfits truly are my second family.

Finally, I want to thank my official bookstore, Read It Again Books in Suwanee, GA for their support and for keeping signed copies of all my books on the shelves. Kim McNamara always helps uplift indie press authors, and Nicole Yackley ensures people know about the stories I write. I love Read It Again!

ABOUT THE AUTHOR

Sarah J. Sover writes fantasy crossover stories. *Fairy GodMurder*, starring a fairy godmother with a vendetta and a killer pair of Doc Martens, is the first in her noir Fractured Fae Series from Falstaff Books. Sarah's debut novel, *Double-Crossing the Bridge*, released from The Parliament House in 2019, hitting the Amazon bestseller list in humorous fantasy. Additionally, Sarah writes short fiction about bumbling knights and impossible baby krakens.

Don't ask Sarah where she's from if you're looking for a straightforward answer. In any given conversation, you may pick up a midwestern accent with random English pronunciations offset with a y'all or two. Despite all the places she's lived, Sarah feels most like she's come home when she visits family in Michigan.

A degree in Biology from Georgia Southern University and a background in animal care help Sarah craft worlds capable of turning the strongest stomachs. In addition to fiction, she's written for Dan Koboldt's *Putting the Fact in Fantasy* and for Writer's Digest Magazine.

When she's not writing, Sarah spends her days with her brilliant daughters and husband Alex in John's Creek, Ga. Rescue pup Gandalf the Grey and danger noodle Santana are freeloaders in their house. Sarah enjoys listening to groove metal, dancing to blues, creating art, binging superhero shows, battling through Hyrule, and sipping a good IPA. Having mostly conquered her fear of public speaking, she's been found geeking out on panels for conventions such as Writer's Digest, JordanCon, Multiverse, AtomaCon, and Monsterama. For appearance information, social media links, and pictures of Gandalf, check out www.SarahJSover.com.

ALSO BY SARAH J. SOVER

Double-Crossing the Bridge

Fairy Godmurder

FRIENDS OF FALSTAFF

Thank You to All our Falstaff Books Patrons, who get extra digital content each month! To be featured here and see what other great rewards we offer, go to www.patreon.com/falstaffbooks.

PATRONS

Dino Hicks
John Hooks
John Kilgallon
Larissa Lichty
Travis & Casey Schilling
Staci-Leigh Santore
Sheryl R. Hayes
Scott Norris
Samuel Montgomery-Blinn
Junkle

www.ingramcontent.com/pod-product-compliance
Lightning Source LLC
Chambersburg PA
CBHW050023120726
47903CB00006B/1882